THE TERRAN
PRIVATEER

BOOK ONE
OF THE DUCHY OF TERRA

THE TERRAN PRIVATEER

BOOK ONE
OF THE DUCHY OF TERRA

GLYNN STEWART

FAOLAN'S PEN
PUBLISHING
faolanspen.com

This edition published in 2018 by:

Faolan's Pen Publishing Inc.

22 King St. S, Suite 300

Waterloo, Ontario

N2J 1N8 Canada

ISBN-13: 978-1-988035-45-1 (print)

A record of this book is available from Library and Archives Canada.

Printed in the United States of America

1 2 3 4 5 6 7 8 9 10

First edition

First printing: July 2016

Illustration © 2016 Tom Edwards

TomEdwardsDesign.com

Faolan's Pen Publishing logo is a trademark of Faolan's Pen Publishing Inc.

Read more books from Glynn Stewart at faolanspen.com

CHAPTER ONE

ADMIRAL JEAN VILLENEUVE OF THE UNITED EARTH SPACE Force charged off of his shuttle like an aggravated bull. He hated the Belt Squadrons inspection tours: days crammed into a tiny ship flying out from Earth, followed by weeks of squeezing through obsolete ships, many lacking even artificial gravity, to make a show of the UESF caring about its back-of-beyond postings—and their role in dealing with the increasing level of outer system piracy.

Now the Space Force's chief supplier of warships had decided to demand a detour at the end of his trip, bringing him to this strange space station even *he*, the Chief of Operations for Earth's spaceborne military cum police force, hadn't been aware existed.

Villeneuve was a tall man, with the distinctive pale skin of someone who'd spent their entire adult life in space. His once-black hair was almost pure white now, still cropped close to his scalp to allow for the spacesuit helmets of his youth.

Today he *stalked* into the Nova Industries Belt Research Station in his full white dress uniform, with its gold braid, its silly little half-cape, and the four gold stars of the only full Admiral Earth's Space Force *had*.

The station looked older than he'd anticipated when he got the "request" to meet someone from Nova Industries here. Most new stations were built as rough spheres, maximizing interior volume now that Earth had artificial gravity. The research station had clearly started as the massive ring of a centripetal gravity facility—and Villeneuve was *sure* Nova Industries had never reported this station to him!

As he reached the edge of the shuttle bay, a trio of white uniformed aides trailing in his wake, the blast-shielded doors retracted to reveal a single man in a crisp black business suit. The man was young—*far* too young to be Villeneuve's contact....

And then Jean Villeneuve's brain caught up to his eyes and he stopped hard, staring at the frustratingly young features of Elon Casimir, chief executive officer of Nova Industries—and a man who had *no* business being a week's flight from Earth!

"Welcome to BugWorks, Admiral Villeneuve," Casimir told him cheerfully. "I think you'll be very pleased with the little demonstration we've pulled together for you today."

"You little *connard*," Villeneuve snapped at Earth's youngest multibillionaire. "If you've delayed my trip home for some stupid stunt..."

Casimir held up his hands defensively.

"Please, Admiral, I am many things—but I am never a waste of your time."

"BUGWORKS? SERIOUSLY?" Villeneuve asked the CEO half an hour later. Casimir had taken him to a surprisingly well-appointed private office and served up small glasses of the Admiral's favorite French brandy. He could tell he was being played, but the man whose company manufactured the hulls, engines, and missiles that made up the UESF's spaceships was usually worth his time.

"In the grand tradition of SkunkWorks and EagleWorks,"

Casimir confirmed. "They wanted to use Bug-Eyed monster, but it took too long to say."

"'They,' Elon?" the Admiral demanded, eyeing the younger man. Casimir did not look the part of a multibillionaire CEO. His suit was the latest style, but his brown hair was long in a way that was currently out of fashion and his face was chubby, his eyes a warm blue. He looked like everyone's favorite cousin.

"BugWorks has been Nova Industries' main research facility for about fifty years, Admiral," Casimir told him. "She was the first of the big ring stations built outside Earth orbit, arguably *before* we really had the capability to do so."

"Why wasn't I aware this station existed?" Villeneuve demanded. "*Mon dieu*, Elon—if something had happened out here..."

"We...may have allowed the UESF to think the station was decommissioned," Casimir admitted. "We've never really hidden it— the Facility is on all of the lists—but when we switched her to artificial gravity, we let your people think we'd scaled it back."

"All right," the Admiral allowed slowly. "Why? That was a dangerously stupid thing to do—even underestimating the population out here could have caused problems!"

"We had our own resources here if needed," Casimir said calmly. "And...well, your people have been anything *but* supportive of research the last few years."

Villeneuve winced. There was a strong feeling amongst the Captains and Admirals of the Space Force that the weapons and systems available to them were good enough. Combined with a worry that major advancements would invalidate their own skills, they'd stubbornly resisted supporting research.

The Chief of Operations disagreed, but he was just one voice. Even with the increasingly disturbing pace of losses to piracy outside the belt, the Chief couldn't convince the Governing Council to fund research when all of his subordinates didn't think it was needed.

"Bluntly, the only research that the UESF has funded for the last ten years has been the hyperspatial portal system. We had a *lot* more that was really promising," Casimir noted. "This facility was where we developed the artificial gravity tech, so we had a giant pile of engineers and scientists out here *anyway*, most of whom had been working on various Space Force or privately-funded research anyway."

"*Qu'est-ce que tu as fait,* Elon?" Villeneuve asked slowly. Even at seventy years old—a hale late middle age in 2185—he still slipped into his native French when aggravated and speaking to people he *knew* understood him. Elon Casimir spoke twelve languages fluently. *Another* thing to be jealous of the man for.

"Ten years ago, my father sold our board on BugWorks," Casimir said quietly. "He had the opportunity to fully explain it to *me* before he had his stroke."

Even twenty-second-century medical technology couldn't save someone dead on arrival with a thumbnail-sized blood clot in their brain. The elder Casimir had been brilliant, eccentric, and rich beyond belief—none of which had saved him when his body had betrayed him.

"Since we believed the technologies we were working on had major military and civilian applications, and since the United Earth Space Force was refusing to fund the research, Nova Industries— aided by a significant application of the Casimir family's personal fortune—completed the research ourselves," Casimir continued, his voice still calm and quiet. "You're lucky we did, too," he continued. "You know we've been testing hyperships. Without some of the tech that came out of BugWorks, those ships would be impossible."

"You...completed an entire new generation of military technology with *private* funding?" Villeneuve asked, making sure he was understanding Casimir correctly. Nova Industries was a *huge* corporation, and Casimir was unbelievably wealthy, but he was talking a multi-*trillion*-dollar investment at least.

"Enough civilian and secondary applications have already arisen from BugWorks to cover a third or so of the costs," Casimir pointed out. "Even if the military applications fall through, we will earn back our costs eventually just from those.

"But the military possibilities are...transformative," he continued. "Including the hyperdrive, we have developed four systems we believe that the UESF will want on *every* ship. I brought you here today so we could demonstrate them for you."

"If you want me to sell them to *my* Captains, the people who are the reason you didn't get funding for this, they'd better be *fantastique* —impressive," Villeneuve warned.

Elon Casimir grinned, managing to look even younger than his thirty-odd years.

"Oh, believe me, Admiral Villeneuve, you are going to be impressed."

CASIMIR PROCEEDED to drag Villeneuve out onto an observation shuttle—a luxuriously appointed craft over three times the size of the UESF standardized shuttle the Admiral had arrived on. Every part of the passenger compartment except the floor was covered in high-quality monitors, allowing the two men to watch the big space station drop away beneath their feet.

"Over to your left, you can see the yard where we've been building the XC ships," the CEO told Villeneuve. "They're our 'Experimental Cruiser' hulls, a modular design with a frankly *ridiculous* power-generation capacity that we've used as a platform for all of our tests.

"Ahead of us you'll see XC-Zero One," he continued. With a brush of fingers through the haptic interface suspended above the screen, Casimir adjusted the view to zoom in on the ship.

Villeneuve studied it with a practiced eye. There was little to compare its size to as they approached, but the ship seemed large for an experiment. It followed similar lines to the UESF's current battleships, a squished cigar-shape tapering to a flat prow at the front from the engines at the back, except...

Unlike a UESF ship, the cigar tapered *both* ways.

"Where are the engines?" he asked.

"That's the first tech we're going to demonstrate," Casimir told him. "Since I know you're wondering," he continued, "XC-Zero One, also known as *Raptor*, is five hundred and eighty-six meters long with an average beam of one hundred meters. She masses just over two million tons—though that's due to reasons we'll discuss in a few minutes."

"That's a cruiser," Villeneuve observed dryly. "Right. A cruiser that's a third longer than my battleships and masses almost three times as much. How much of that is fuel? Which also brings me back to my original point: where are her *engines*?"

Casimir held up one finger in a "hold on a minute" gesture and took a small microphone from a concealed holder on the bar.

"Captain Anderson," he said into it. "Begin the demonstration."

There was no audible response, but *Raptor* started moving... accelerating *impossibly* as the big ship turned into a blur that rapidly receded into a barely visible dot. Villeneuve stared in shock as Casimir used the display interface to zoom in on the ship, blurring along at an impossible velocity—only to make a physically impossible turn and blaze back to the observation shuttle at the same impossible speed.

"*Raptor* and the other XC ships are equipped with what the scientists and engineers at BugWorks call a 'gravitational-hyperspatial interface momentum engine,' he said calmly. "The crews working with them just call it the interface drive. It's capable of accelerating from zero to forty percent of lightspeed in just over six seconds with no inertial effects."

Villeneuve stared at the ship as it came to a halt in front of them again.

"Elon," he said slowly, "that's *impossible*. That *violates the laws of physics.*"

"So does the hyperdrive," Casimir pointed out dryly. "BugWorks has spent the last ten years playing with the consequences of hyperspatial anomalies on our understanding of physics. The interface drive is, so far as our experiments can prove, almost one hundred percent inertialess. The drive pushes anything smaller than about a tenth the size of the effect field to the side and...well, you'll see what happens when it hits something larger than that shortly."

The Admiral stared at the strange ship, considering the potential. His current generation of warships was built around heavy lasers and lots of massive missiles. Those missiles couldn't even *catch* Casimir's XC ship.

"You said you had more technologies to show me," he said levelly, trying to control the urge to hyperventilate.

"Of course," Casimir confirmed. The shuttle—still, thankfully, using what looked like normal fusion thrusters—continued on its course. They orbited over the big asteroid that the Research Station orbited beside, and a second of the impossible ships appeared on the screens. The CEO gestured and zoomed the display in on it.

"XC-Zero Two, *Hammer*, is also equipped with the interface drive," he noted. "She won't be maneuvering much herself, though. She has a different system to demonstrate."

Once again, Casimir grabbed the microphone and ordered the Captain to begin the demonstration.

Hammer moved smoothly, with a grace to the cruiser's motions that just looked wrong to a man who'd grown used to the fusion torch battleships and cruisers of Earth's Space Force. The experimental cruiser angled away from the asteroid, aiming herself at another, smaller, rock that Casimir promptly highlighted in the display.

"That is asteroid five-two-zero-zero-nine-five," the CEO told Villeneuve. "Ninety percent nickel-iron by mass, roughly eight hundred thousand tons."

The mass and nickel-iron percentage lined up very neatly with the UESF's current battleships. Somehow, the Admiral doubted that was an accident.

"Watch," Casimir instructed, zooming the screen in further.

As *Hammer* passed the big rock, moving at a speed Villeneuve recognized as a crawl for the strange ships, there were six bright flashes of light. That was it, all that could be seen with the naked eye, even at this zoom.

Villeneuve blinked and looked to the asteroid, only to swallow hard. The asteroid was *gone*.

"Can you rewind that?" he asked.

"Of course."

The image went backward in slow motion, the vaporized metal of the asteroid recombining into the chunk of iron and rock. The impact points appeared, then turned into streaks of white light that connected with *Hammer*.

"What were those?" Villeneuve finally asked.

"A logical development of what you saw with *Raptor*," Casimir told him brightly. "Point four cee was the best we could achieve for anything we wanted *humans* to survive on, but by pushing a smaller craft and being willing to accept levels of radiation instantly lethal to humans, we could build a smaller device capable of sustaining sixty percent of the speed of light for roughly sixty seconds."

"A missile," Villeneuve breathed.

"Exactly. We didn't bother with a warhead," the CEO continued. "It hits at point six cee, Admiral. Despite the drive shunting anything much *smaller* than its effect field aside, impact with something *larger* results in a catastrophic collapse—one that releases the full kinetic energy of the drive's contents and velocity. Any warhead we've developed would be redundant. It's a smart inertialess weapon. If you don't shoot an interface missile down, it *will* hit."

And hit with *gigatons* of force, Villeneuve noted. He could do that math, at least to an order of magnitude. If even *one* of these XC ships fell into the wrong hands, the Space Force was *dead*.

"What have you *created*, Elon?" he breathed. "This is a *monster*."

"It is necessary to sometimes look beyond the immediate," Casimir said very quietly. "You know as well as I do that Dark Eye is starting to intercept some *really* odd modulated-energy patterns as we scan the nearby stars. I agree with the conspiracy nuts on this one, Admiral—they're alien comms. Someone has moved into the neighborhood and we don't know what they're here for. If they're moving around faster than light, they have hyperdrives—which means they have the interface drive, Jean. It's a logical progression."

"You built these to keep humanity safe from bug-eyed monsters?" Villeneuve asked. He wanted to disbelieve, but the man was very earnest...and the Admiral had no hesitation admitting that Elon Casimir was *smarter* than him.

"Hence BugWorks," the CEO continued. "Any alien with a hyperdrive will have these weapons, Admiral. Some kind of defense was needed."

"You mean you have a plan to give me something *other* than nightmares?" the older man asked dryly.

"All of these systems are for sale, Admiral," Casimir returned. "But yes. If you look over *here*"—he highlighted and zoomed in on a different spot in the screen to reveal a third of the XC ships—"you will see XC-Zero Three: *Scapegoat*.

"For reasons that will shortly become obvious, *Scapegoat* is a drone," he noted. "We have four systems to demonstrate, Admiral. You're aware of the hyperdrive, and you've now seen the interface drive and the interface missiles in action.

"If you wait a few minutes, you'll see *everything*."

CHAPTER TWO

ANNETTE BOND WATCHED THE COUNTDOWN ON THE BIG SCREEN at the front of her bridge. *Tornado*'s bridge was a two-tiered affair, with a horseshoe-shaped balcony above the main command deck providing space for another dozen consoles and attendant techs.

Right now, the bridge crew was a fifty-fifty split between ex-UESF personnel and Nova Industries technicians reviewing the function of the various consoles. Unlike the other XC series ships, XC-04 was complete in every way that mattered—she had the interface drive, the interface missiles, the hyperdrive, and the special armor her part of Elon Casimir's demonstration was meant to prove out.

Unlike XC-02, she'd even been equipped with a beam armament, a new generation of heavy lasers notably more efficient than—though otherwise identical to—the current armament of the UESF's battleships.

Tornado was also the only one of the four cruisers equipped with a hyperdrive, which was how the big ship was currently in orbit around Jupiter. She could, quite handily, have made the trip on her interface drive—but Nova Industries had believed that she'd have been picked up by the sensor arrays the United Earth Space Force had assembled in Earth orbit.

"I can't believe we're going to shoot up our own ship," her executive officer, Pat Kurzman, said calmly. Technically, his station was in a secondary control center—but *Tornado*'s combat information center was theoretical only, an empty void on deck fifteen.

"That's why we named her *Scapegoat*," Annette told him calmly, her eyes on the countdown as it hit sixty seconds. *Tornado*'s Captain looked like a rogue high school cheerleader, a curvedly athletic blue-eyed blonde woman one hundred and seventy centimeters tall. She *had* been a cheerleader in an Idaho high school—twenty-five years before. The long, braided pigtails had been cut off when she joined the United Earth Space Force at twenty and replaced later on with a single, shorter, golden braid nestled against her neck.

"I ran the numbers," Kurzman admitted. "She *should* be able to take a full salvo, but we've only ever used single missiles in the tests so far."

"If we blow her up," Annette shrugged with a cold smile, "it will still be an effective demonstration, if not necessarily the one the boss wants. We're out of time," she finished, cutting off her XO. "Hyper portal in ten seconds."

"Emitters are charged. Programmed for the ten-second hop," the oddly tall and gaunt form of her navigator, Cole Amandine, reported. Amandine was one of the still very few humans born and raised in space, with much of his life before artificial gravity had been invented. Only intense physiotherapy allowed him to walk in full gravity, and he still wore a concealed powered exoskeleton for long periods of walking or standing.

Annette Bond took a deep breath and focused her eyes on the unimaginably impressive size of Jupiter's Great Red Spot beneath them. There were other humans this far out—a few research stations, the beginnings of a colony scooping hydrogen from the gas giant—but none had arrived as quickly as they had, and none would return as quickly as they would.

The timer hit zero.

A dozen emitters that Annette didn't even *pretend* to understand the science behind flared with energy, invisible beams of force that lashed out into empty space and *tore* a hole in reality.

The hole burst into existence with a brilliant flash of blue light, and *Tornado* slipped into it with surprisingly practiced ease—more practiced than Annette would have expected from the exactly nine times the crew had done it before.

A new timer flashed up on the screen, counting down the ten seconds they were scheduled to be in hyperspace. The screens didn't show anything else—hyperspace was a literal void to the human eye, so Nova Industries had set the screens to automatically turn off after entering the portal.

Hopefully, the BugWorks people had lined up their part of this demonstration. The time lag prevented them from communicating reliably with the rest of the demo, so all Annette could do was hope no adjustment to the original schedule had been sent in the last few minutes.

"Opening the exit portal," Amandine told her.

"Stand by maneuvering and weapons," Annette ordered "You know the plan."

A new portal opened in the void of hyperspace and *Tornado* flashed through at one hundred and twenty thousand kilometers a second. They were *exactly* on target, three light-seconds away from the Belt Research Station and their target: poor XC-03.

"Maneuvering, take us past *Scapegoat* at a point one cee firing pass," she snapped. "Weapons, give me a broadside into her as we pass."

Broadside was a relative term as *Tornado*'s missile launchers were arranged in six sets of four all along her hull. Given the maneuverability of her inertialess weapons systems, there was no angle at which she couldn't fire all twenty-four weapons at a target. By only firing the weapons on one side of the ship, however, they would deliver a blow they were sure that *Scapegoat* could survive.

Twelve streaks of light blasted away from the big cruiser as they swung by, crossing the hundreds of thousands of kilometers still between them in two seconds. Annette nodded in relief as all twelve weapons slammed home into the other XC ship—and *Scapegoat* survived.

"Assess the target," she snapped.

"Banged her around a bit," Harold Rolfson, her weapons officer, reported. "Systems are reporting some internal damage and a few of the laced plates have shifted around. Computers estimate a ten percent reduction in combat capability were she fully equipped."

"All right, let's give the good Admiral a show," Annette ordered. "Maneuvering, bring us in to ten thousand kilometers and hold the range. Weapons, hit her with the beams. Cycle them across the hull— we want to light her up, not slice up anything we damaged with the birds."

"Yes, ma'am!"

Liking a stooping falcon, *Tornado* turned on her heel and charged back at her prey, beams of coherent light leading the way.

VILLENEUVE STEPPED past Casimir silently and pressed his hands into the haptic feedback field, zooming in on XC-03. Haloed in the light from beams he judged close in power to those mounted on his battleships, the ship seemed unharmed.

"I saw what those weapons did to a rock," he finally said. "How did she survive *that?*"

"'That, so we're on the same page, was twelve interface drive missiles impacting at sixty percent of lightspeed," Casimir confirmed. "The ID missiles mass roughly one metric ton each, providing a kinetic energy at impact of just over two and a half gigatons. While the lasers are a different type of energy, with the difference in scale... it's not entirely surprising the lasers don't do much, is it?" the CEO concluded, gesturing at the screen where *Tornado* continued to bathe *Scapegoat* in coherent light for a few more seconds.

Finally, *Tornado* ceased her attack run, turning to drop herself into a high escort position over the observation shuttle.

"While working on manufacturing the exotic matter for the hyperdrive emitters, one of the technicians missed a decimal point and a negative sign," Casimir explained with a sigh. "I'm pretty sure she was hungover, and her boss wanted to fire her—but, fortunately for everyone, one of the scientists on the site took a look at what had been created.

"We were aiming for matter with negative mass, which is a stone-cold bitch to manufacture and store," he continued. "What that slip of the numbers gave us was *compressed* matter. Density is practically off the scale, and the stuff is functionally immune to kinetic force—it has *no* give to it whatsoever."

"Neutronium," Villeneuve noted aloud. He wanted to say it was impossible, but Casimir had been proving him wrong on that point a lot today.

"Not...quite," Casimir concluded. "I'm led to understand that the process *could* create something that was functionally neutronium, but that it would require exponentially more power than the compressed matter we currently manufacture."

"So, your XCs are...armored in compressed matter?"

"Their armor plates are about sixty percent of the thickness of those used on our current battleships," the shipbuilder replied. "If that was all compressed matter, I'm not sure even the interface drive could move the ship. We've used a sandwiched design with impact-absorbing gels, nickel-iron, and a layer of compressed matter."

He gestured to the ship that had survived a salvo fit to wipe entire squadrons of the UESF out of space. "There are weaknesses where we combine the plates," he admitted. "But as you can see, it's very effective."

"*Tornado* is complete, then?" Villeneuve asked. "All four of your monster techs?"

"Indeed," Casimir confirmed. "Some of her internal systems are incomplete and she'd need a larger crew to actually be combat-effective, but Captain Bond has been very pleased with her ship."

"Bond," the admiral repeated. "That's right, Bloody Annie is one of your test captains, isn't she?"

"She was *supposed* to command *Of Course We're Coming Back*," Casimir reminded her. "*Your* people raised a stink about that."

Of Course We're Coming Back had been Earth's first hyperdrive-capable ship, sent on a scouting mission to Alpha Centauri a year before. Villeneuve's Captains had *exploded* at the thought of Bloody Annie commanding the mission—and insisted that a *real* UESF officer command the operation.

Bond had only been a year from her not-so-genteel forced resignation from the UESF at the time, an incident that still made Villeneuve furious. He'd known his Captains were an old-boys and -girls club, but he hadn't expected *that* level of trouble from them.

"When I got up this morning, I thought Earth had over ninety capital ships," Villeneuve told Casimir. "Now you have shown me that we have one: *Tornado*. That ship needs to be under UESF command, Elon. How much?"

Casimir quoted a number. Villeneuve winced—*Tornado* was going to run the cost of *two* battleships.

"I'll sort it out," he promised. "And I want the other three XC hulls brought up to the same spec and ready to deploy."

"It will happen. You'll need to deal with *Tornado*'s crew yourself," Casimir warned him. "About a third of the people aboard are yours, seconded United Earth spacers. The rest are mine. I won't sell their contracts, and they'll follow Bond when she tells you to go to hell."

Admiral Jean Villeneuve winced again. Bloody Annie was going to do just that.

"I will deal with Annette," he said quietly. "*I* was, after all, the one who got her what she wanted."

"She's been the best captain I could hope for," Casimir told him. "I'll miss her, but *goddamn*, does that woman need to be a soldier."

CHAPTER THREE

Annette waited for the shuttle to settle down in *Tornado*'s landing bay with far more trepidation than she allowed herself to show. Her back was rigid, her posture perfect, years of training as a United Earth Space Force officer still showing as she waited for her boss and the UESF's commander to arrive.

Kurzman stood next to her, and if her executive officer wondered what his Captain was thinking, he said nothing. Annette Bond didn't believe in stupid questions, but she did believe in *inappropriate* ones —and Kurzman knew anything about his Captain's past or personal life qualified.

The sensors reported that the landing bay was safe and the blast shield retracted. Two men had exited the shuttle and were walking toward her, and she knew both of them.

She'd worked for Elon Casimir for three years now, ever since it had been made *very* clear to Commander Annette Bond that even though she had been entirely *correct* to push for the prosecution of Captain John Bowman for his crimes, doing so had ended her UESF career.

Admiral Jean Villeneuve had already been Chief of Operations there. He'd sat as the judge at the trial that had condemned Captain Bowman to death for no less than *fifteen* counts of aggravated rape of enlisted spacers under his command.

Charges that, if the Captains under Villeneuve had had their way, would never have been laid. Annette Bond had pushed, argued, presented evidence, and sworn affidavits for *six months* to force the trial, and then cajoled, supported, and *mothered* the young women in question to get them to actually testify.

Bowman had been convicted and sent to the needle for destroying *their* lives.

In exchange, Annette had been quietly informed that no Captain in the Force would take her as their executive officer again, and that there were no open staff slots. The Captains wouldn't work with her, wouldn't talk to her. She had no future in the Force, so when she was offered early retirement, she took it.

Villeneuve hadn't been involved in that—but he also hadn't stepped in to *stop* it. It took every ounce of her self-control not to glare at the old man as he calmly walked across the deck to meet her.

"Boss," she greeted Casimir, then gave the other man a sharp glance. "Admiral."

"Captain Bond," Casimir replied, taking her hand warmly and smiling. She gave him a fractional crack of a smile, and the young executive shook his head at her in a familiar amusement.

Villeneuve offered his hand.

"Captain," he said softly.

She looked back at him and didn't take his hand, leaving him hanging in the chilled air of the landing bay until Casimir cleared his throat sharply. With a glare at her boss, Annette finally shook the Admiral's hand.

"Do you have a meeting room set up?" Casimir asked. "The Admiral and I have come to an agreement in principle, and I'd like to fill you in."

"Of course," she confirmed crisply. "Follow me."

Like the rest of her nonessential features, *Tornado*'s conference facilities were lacking much of anything. They *existed*, which put them ahead of many items that remained empty voids in the hull. The table was the exact same cheap folding plastic as currently filled the cruiser's single mess, with chairs from the matching set.

It was hardly what Casimir was used to, but she'd made sure he knew what he was getting into when they'd discussed it the previous day. His response had been to note that he'd held board meetings on asteroid mining stations.

"Captain, Admiral, please sit," he told them as he stepped up to the head of the cheap table. He took a seat himself, laced his hands together and faced the two officers.

"Captain Bond, you should be aware that as of midnight tonight, *Tornado* will become a United Earth Space Force vessel," Casimir said bluntly. "All of the personnel seconded from the UESF will revert to active duty at that time."

"I see, sir," Annette said coldly, suddenly feeling as if the ground had been yanked out from underneath her. She'd had a month aboard *Tornado*, getting her out of construction, all of the gear loaded into her modular construction, and ready for this demonstration. She should have known she'd be working herself out of a job. "I'll inform the rest of the crew to start packing their things."

"We want to keep the crew, Captain Bond," Villeneuve interjected. "I have the authority in my own right to close the purchase agreement and offer provisional contracts to the Nova Industries personnel aboard. My aides have been drafting our offers on the way over."

The admiral pulled a flimsy—a thin, flexible display that could link into a portable computer or hold a small bit of information itself —from his uniform jacket and laid it on the table.

"This is the offer we put together for you," he said quietly.

Annette didn't even look at it. She glared at Villeneuve. Part of her *wanted* it—wanted to walk back into the United Earth Space Force and *grind* the Captains' faces in what their attempt to suppress research had created, along with their rejection of her. The rest of her had *no* interest in going back to the people who'd betrayed her people's trust and cast her out for seeing justice done.

"My contract with Nova Industries is more than sufficiently remunerative for me," she replied, her voice very cold and precise. "It also contains penalty clauses for early termination."

"I will waive those clauses," Casimir said instantly. "Hell, you've got six months left on your contract, Annette—I'll pay it all out."

"And if I want to stay with NI?" she asked, suddenly afraid.

"We're building an entire *flotilla* of survey ships—ones that the UESF will *not* be commanding," Casimir noted with a glance at the Admiral. "They *could* use a Commodore. But...Annette, please. At least hear the Admiral out."

Villeneuve glanced at Kurzman and then at Casimir.

"Elon, Mister Kurzman, can I speak to Captain Bond in private, please?" he finally asked.

Annette had a momentary urge to refuse, to kick the man out of the room and off of her ship—for about another eight hours, she *had* that authority.

"Of course," Casimir replied before she could give in to that impulse. "Pat, with me, please."

Before the Captain could object, her XO followed their boss out of the room, leaving Annette Bond alone in the room with the man who'd done nothing to save her career—and the piece of electronic paper bringing her back to the Space Force that had betrayed her.

———

ADMIRAL JEAN VILLENEUVE waited calmly for the two Nova Industries people to leave the room, taking advantage of the moment to study the woman across the table in the dark blue merchant uniform. Her wearing that uniform instead of his own dress whites represented one of his greatest failures as the head of the UESF.

"Are you at least going to look at the offer?" he asked softly. He knew he'd failed Annette Bond once. This was his chance to make it right and do right by the Space Force at the same time. If he played his cards right, the coterie of Captains who'd driven her out, undermined the Force's research and development, and almost covered up John Bowman's crimes wouldn't survive the game.

"Why?" she replied flatly. "I'm *not* coming back, Admiral. You don't have enough money."

"Commodore of a survey flotilla?" Jean observed. "Yeah, I wouldn't want to miss that either. Elon is supposed to be *helping* me, the little brat."

Bond glared at him in silence. Jean had been glared at by *heads of state* who had less weight behind their anger than she did, and he sighed.

"You *are*, I should point, a Reserve Space Force officer," he pointed out gently. "You've taken the deposit every month for five years; we pay that so we can recall when we need you."

"That's meant for war," she told him. "Peacetime is just a financial penalty."

"And one Casimir would probably pay for you," he agreed. "Hear me out at least, Captain Bond? I'm *asking*. You don't owe me anything."

"No," she confirmed. "I don't. But Casimir clearly wants me to listen, so talk."

She obviously had no intention of even looking at the flimsy, so Jean drew it back to himself and glanced down the text, making sure he remembered the offer correctly.

"We both know you'd have made Captain at least a couple of years ago if Bowman hadn't been an epic piece of scum," he noted. "So, the offer is to bring you back at full Captain, with seniority based on your years wearing the title for Nova Industries. Much the same for your people: everyone comes across at an equivalent rank to what they've been doing and with appropriate seniority.

"You keep *Tornado*," he pointed out. "You get the full privileges and authority of her Captain, *including* veto right on the officers and crew we'll need to fill in around the cadre you already have."

"And the rest of the Captains will treat me like something they'd scrape off their boot," Bond replied. "You tried, Admiral, and it's not a bad offer—but no, thanks."

"They won't *be able* to," Jean told her with an exasperated sigh. "You will command the *single most powerful ship* in the Space Force. A ship that could single-handedly destroy the *entirety* of the Space Force in an afternoon.

"A ship we will be acquiring more of as fast as possible," he continued. "Commands for *those* ships will be assigned based on experience with a brand-new class of vessels with completely different performance parameters.

"Damn it, Bond, I'm handing you a chance to make those idiots *obsolete* and *choose* our next generation of Captains. I need to break that club as badly as you *want* to," he pointed out, "or I'll just leave this problem to the next Chief of Operations. I can't micromanage who ends up on *Tornado*—but I trust you to pick men and women I'd be proud to pin oak leaves on.

"What else *can* I offer you?" he asked.

Finally, *finally*, he got a crack of a smile.

"John Bowman's head," she noted. "But you gave me that already." She shook her head. "All right, Admiral. I want your promise that you'll back me to the hilt—I *don't* trust your Captains."

"Some of them are actually decent people," he pointed out. "But I promise. I'm not going to bring you back in and cut you off. If you take the eagle I'm promising, I'm behind you all the way."

"This ship will still need work," she pointed out. "I don't know how much of our...shortfalls Casimir has told you about."

"He basically told me you could fly and shoot," the Admiral replied. "I was honestly surprised you had a conference room."

CHAPTER FOUR

"I'm sorry, Captain, but it will simply not be possible to meet your requests."

Annette leaned back in her chair and eyed the man sitting across from her with a self-satisfied smirk on his face. Commodore Joseph Anderson was a heavyset man with tanned skin, and the current head of logistics for the United Earth Space Force.

They both wore the dark blue service dress uniform of the United Earth Space Force, a general requirement aboard Earth's military orbitals, but where Annette Bond now wore the silver eagle of a Space Force Captain, Anderson wore a single silver star of his senior rank.

They'd last met when *Captain* Joseph Anderson had stood as Captain Bowman's defensive character witness during Bowman's trial. He'd made it very clear that day that he regarded Annette's pursuit of her Captain as a betrayal of the Force.

"Which part of my requests is a problem, sir?" she asked, keeping her voice level and cold. "Was it the supply of interface drive missiles that were specifically manufactured and delivered for *Tornado*'s use? The seventh fusion power generator core that was *also* specifically built for *Tornado*, and whose absence means I have an open core installation in my engineering section?

"Or was it the food and other logistical supplies standard for the commissioning loadout of any United Earth capital ship? Supplies you have known would be required since *Tornado* was brought into United Earth service a month ago?"

The smirk remained constant.

"All of these pose issues," Anderson noted. "IDMs are a scarce resource in the Space Force right now. Other ships have needs as well, Captain. Yours has no special priority. The core has not been delivered, and we are having issues with the supplies. Your requests will take several weeks to complete."

Several weeks that Annette would have to delay the formal commissioning of *Tornado* in Earth service. She smiled coldly and pulled her official communicator out of the jacket of her undress blues. It slid apart with ease, the two scroll-like ends separating and providing the data feed to the e-paper screen between them.

"I'm sorry, Captain, but making calls in your superior's office is rude," Anderson snapped. "You may have been able to get away with that in civilian service, but you are back in the Space Force now!"

"You have a choice, Commodore," Annette told him flatly. "In about a minute, I am going to call Elon Casimir, and you can explain to him where the missiles and fusion core his people delivered thirty-six hours ago have gone astray to. I'll note, for your benefit, that the interface drive missiles used by *Tornado* are a completely different design from the stopgap design used to provide *some* usable firepower to the rest of the Space Force. No other ship currently in commission can *fire* a properly sized IDM.

"Once we're done explaining your misplacement—or potentially *grand larceny*," she observed, "to Mister Casimir, I will call Admiral Villeneuve, and you can explain to *him* why you are intentionally stonewalling the commissioning of the only warship worth the name in the UESF."

"I will *not* be threatened," Anderson snapped, lunging to his feet.

Annette remained sitting, looking up at him as she tapped a button on the communicator.

"Hi, Michelle," she said brightly to the middle-aged woman who appeared on the screen shortly. "Can you get Elon for me? It's a bit of an emergency; logistics is telling me that we have a foul-up here."

"Of course, Annette," Elon Casimir's personal assistant replied. "He's in a meeting with the Russian President; it will take him a minute or two to get free. What can I tell the President Sokolov is going on?"

"You wouldn't *dare*," Anderson hissed.

"Let me conference in Admiral Villeneuve," Annette told Michelle. "I'd like him to at least know what I'm doing if I have to inform a member nation's head of state that the UESF is being obstructive."

"Shut that *off*," the Commodore ordered. "Fine. I'll make it happen."

"Do you still need me?" Michelle asked, with an arched brow.

"Let Elon know I called," Annette said calmly. "Play him the recording; he needs to know what's going on."

"Of course. Luck."

Annette slid the communicator closed and looked back at Anderson.

"So, I will have my missiles, my power core, and consumables aboard by twenty hundred hours?" she asked calmly.

"I can't make that happen in twelve hours!"

"Those deliveries were scheduled for twelve hundred hours," Annette pointed out. "I'm giving you eight hours of grace, Commodore. Anything beyond that, and the *Governing Council* will know you're impeding Earth having a real defense."

She smiled coldly.

"I'm sure you've seen the recent reports from Dark Eye?"

A MONTH'S worth of work by Nova Industries main shipyard plat-form had filled in many of the voids inside *Tornado*'s hull, but there would always be certain oddities of her layout that grew from her being an experimental ship.

The interior of the ship was still very modular, and while the combat information center and many other sections had been filled in, other parts were still empty. *Tornado* didn't have the external hull space for, say, more weaponry—but she had internal modules and power generation capacity to spare. The cruiser really didn't *need* the seventh fusion core she'd forced Anderson to turn over—she only operated on three. Annette had insisted on it because the design called for it and Anderson had pissed her off.

The entire crew quarters had been built into one module, inside a second layer of armor and buried at the core of the ship, which led to some oddities in the layout. One of them was that Annette Bond's executive officer's quarters were directly opposite hers.

Since Anderson had managed to come through only twenty-two minutes after her deadline, she'd been able to inform Admiral Villeneuve that *Tornado* would commission on schedule, which meant that she and her XO were due on the main deck in full dress whites in just under an hour.

Annette took a moment to be sure her own long tunic, with its high collar and stiff shoulder boards, was straight and properly buttoned, then rapped sharply on Kurzman's door.

"Commander? Is there a problem?" she asked through the hatch.

"Give me a moment," the newly commissioned officer replied. A few seconds later, he opened the door and looked up at his taller captain helplessly. Kurzman was a short man, stocky and well-muscled but without the height needed to carry off the tunic.

Worse, he clearly had *no* idea how to wear the tunic, the shoulder boards, or the associated cobalt-blue tie. He'd misbuttoned the tunic, only one of the two shoulder boards was properly fastened, and he'd used a type of tie knot that just did *not* work with the cut of the Space Force tie.

"*How?*" he demanded as he saw her perfectly turned-out uniform.

"Maxwell Base OTS," Annette told him crisply. "Plus two years of Space Force Academy."

"They covered the tie?"

"They covered the uniform," she replied crossly. "Now hold still."

Obedient to a fault sometimes, Kurzman complied.

It had been *years* since she'd helped fellow cadets put the uniform on at the Academy, but she wasn't surprised to find she still remembered it. In under a minute, she'd rebuttoned and straightened her executive officer's tunic, reattached his shoulder boards, and tied his tie.

"There," she concluded. "You'll embarrass me less now."

Kurzman relaxed slightly and nodded his thanks. She'd half-expected the problem—Kurzman was a merchant spacer who had spent his career as an officer aboard the big transfer ships running between Earth and Mars. Merchant spacer uniforms were much less demanding than the Space Force's.

"I checked in with everybody before I started dressing," he told her after a moment. "We are fully stocked on munitions, fuel, food, and all other consumables. Core Seven is online and has been tested up to one hundred and ten percent capacity."

"I assume we're not running at that now?" she asked.

"No," he confirmed. "We're running all seven cores at less than fifty percent capacity. All systems are showing green, *Tornado* is ready in all aspects to be commissioned, ma'am."

"Thank you, Pat," she told him quietly. "It's been one hell of a month. Glad to have you with me."

Kurzman appeared unsure how to respond to that—and settled for a safe silence as Annette led the way toward *Tornado*'s outer hull.

TO A FANFARE OF TRUMPETS, Morgan Casimir—a golden-haired cherub of three years old held in her father's arms—pushed the button that fired a bottle of champagne into *Tornado*'s prow. Cameras zoomed in on it, showing it as it shattered and sprayed broken glass and golden bubbles across the armored prow of Earth's newest warship.

Everyone applauded the little girl, who turned a beaming bright smile on the crowd, and the commissioning ceremony itself was over. Annette remained standing next to the platform, allowing herself a rare full smile at Morgan—the little girl, for whatever reason, seemed to *adore* her. She *heard* her XO sigh in relief and saw him visibly sag from the unfamiliar parade rest.

"We still have to circulate," she murmured to him. "Separately, at that."

"I can glad-hand, boss," Kurzman whispered back. "I just can't do this god-awful uniform."

"Get used to it," Annette ordered. "If I'm reading the cards right, we're going to be doing a lot of full-dress affairs. *Tornado* is the Force's newest and shiniest toy."

"Wonderful. I'll go say hello to the natives, then," the man replied in an exaggeration of his natural British accent.

Kurzman glanced around, set his eyes on a cluster of civilians, and sauntered away from Annette. She, despite what she'd told him, remained standing next to the dais where she'd read her commissioning papers, formally taking command of *Tornado* as a United Earth Space Force officer.

"Auntie Annie!" Morgan squealed, providing Annette about half a second's warning before the girl torpedoed her way into the Captain's midsection.

Annette gently and awkwardly patted the child on the head, looking around half-desperately for Elon Casimir. She *liked* Morgan, inasmuch as she liked any child, but this was *not* the place for it.

"Come here, Morgan, or you'll muss Captain Bond's uniform." The older Casimir thankfully arrived to her rescue. The blonde child detached herself from Annette—only to attach herself to her father like a limpet.

Casimir simply smiled and ruffled his only child's hair as he met Annette's eyes.

"The uniform looks good on you," he said quietly. "Better on you than a lot of these twits." He gestured to the gathering with his head. Roughly a third of the UESF's ninety-four Captains were in the room, at least *pretending* to like their newest compatriot.

"To be fair, most of *these* ones are decent," she admitted. "I had a veto on the guest list—not a perfect one"—her gaze touched on Commodore Joseph Anderson and she barely concealed a snarl—"but enough to weed out the true scum."

"Villeneuve needed you for this more than I did," Casimir told her. "You were never comfortable commanding anything without guns, either. Made you feel vulnerable."

He met her responding glare with a disarming smile and shrug.

"You belong here," he finished. "And you are the woman of the hour. It's your ship, which makes all of these people your guests."

"And I should be talking to them and not my old boss?"

"Pretty much," Casimir agreed with a wink, reminding her of *other* things he'd been at one point. "I'll always back you, Annette. You may not work for me anymore, but that ship is still my baby and I trusted you with her from the beginning."

"I appreciate it," she told him. "But I believe I see an Admiral approaching, and in this new job, stars trump even you."

Casimir gave her a wave that vaguely approximated a salute and swept Morgan away into the crowd. Annette took a moment to relax from what had been a friendly chat, and then turned to face an older woman she didn't know with the tripled stars of a Space Force Vice Admiral.

"Vice Admiral Katherine Harrison," the tall white-haired woman introduced herself, offering her hand. "We've never actually met, though I spent several days reviewing your reports on Captain Bowman prior to the Admirals' Board a few years back."

Annette felt the cold mask settle over her face. While the Admirals' Board *had* voted to prosecute Bowman in the end, she hadn't been privy to their discussions and doubted the margin had been broad—the *Captains'* Board had voted 'lack of evidence to charge,' after all.

"Bad memories, I apologize," Harrison said after a moment of awkward silence. "Between you and me," she murmured, glancing around to make sure no one overheard her, "let's just say that I think it's about damned *time* we found a way to put you back in uniform. Whole thing was a mess and you deserved better."

"If you say so, ma'am," Annette said flatly, and the older woman laughed.

"I *do* say so, Captain Bond," she replied. "Someday, you'll believe me. Until then, just do the job."

"That's what I do," she said. "That's what I did that cost me the job."

"Yes," Harrison agreed flatly. "And that's why you had your pick of enlisted spacers for *Tornado*. Some Captains tried to hold their people back, but there wasn't a Chief in the Force who wasn't going to back the woman who saved Bowman's people from that sick bastard."

"I don't know if you've been advised, but my Alpha Squadron's battlewagons have picked up the first wave of stopgap upgrades," the Admiral told Annette. "I'm going to need to pick your brain on interface missiles and compressed-matter armor when you have a free hour later. I'll even buy the beer."

"I don't drink beer," Annette pointed out. Certainly, after everything that had happened, she wasn't going to drink with *Space Force* officers.

"Then I'll buy tea," Harrison said calmly. "We'll talk later, Captain. I hear a buffet table calling my name."

With a firm nod, Alpha Squadron's Admiral moved on, leaving Annette Bond gazing after her in confusion. She didn't know any of the Force's Admirals except Villeneuve by anything more than reputation, but Harrison was not what she'd expected of the Canadian contribution to the UESF Admiralty.

If she hadn't been distracted by Harrison's surprising charm, she'd probably have been able to dodge the reporter. As it was, she turned around and found herself facing down the stereotypically perfect, immaculately coiffed features of a tall black-haired woman in a long black dress and a media headset.

The headset faked being a decorative headband well, but not perfectly enough to fool a practiced eye that could identify the "stones" that were actually cameras. Everything the woman saw and heard was recorded, though *probably* not transmitted live.

If it was being transmitted live, Annette would make sure heads rolled.

"Captain Bond, the people of Earth need to hear from the woman of the hour," the reporter said fiercely, her eyes flashing conviction. "Many have questions as to how a woman who hasn't been a Space Force officer in over four years now holds what we are told is suddenly the premier command in the Force!"

"Technically, I have always been a reserve officer," Annette pointed out, swallowing her anger. Recorded or live, punching out a news reporter on camera was a *bad* idea. "Who are you?" she demanded.

"Jess Robin, Global News Network," the woman replied crisply. "Reserve or not, you haven't been an active duty officer in years, and have suddenly leapt past officers with years of experience to command this unique vessel. Many of our viewers wonder just *how* a woman such as yourself got the role."

Annette stepped forward into Robin's space, pushing the taller and more conventionally attractive woman back a step.

"Are you really going there, Miss Robin?" she asked. "Last time I checked, this was the twenty-second century. Isn't it a little out of date to imply I'm sleeping with someone to get my job?"

The reporter, to her credit, actually looked embarrassed. *That* stinker had to have been fed to her in advance, and she'd managed it with aplomb.

"Then explain to our viewers why you were selected for this command over so many experienced officers?" she finally managed to recover and ask.

Annette sighed. Her options had narrowed down to punching the woman or answering her question. Annoying as the affair was, she couldn't gracefully extract herself now.

"As you said, *Tornado* is unique," she said quietly, forcing Robin to give up some of the personal space she'd defensively reclaimed to guarantee her recording. "Many details of her specifications are classified, but the key point is one that isn't: *Tornado* possesses an interface drive.

"Interface drives are reactionless and inertialess—they're giving physicists a headache across the entire star system. The skills necessary to handle one are entirely different from a fusion torch ship—the 'experience' you speak of has now become obsolete.

"No one else in this system has as much experience with the interface drive as my crew does, so the Space Force brought us in to man the first true starship of the United Earth Space Force," she concluded. "My understanding is that Nova Industries intends to start delivering civilian interface drive ships inside the next four months—before the end of the year.

"It is *necessary* for the Space Force to have ships capable of matching the performance of those civilian vessels to maintain our role as the arbiter of peace in the system.

"That requires a crew and captain experienced with this type of ship. I was not selected over more experienced officers, Miss Robin," she said flatly. "I was selected because I was the *only* experienced officer."

Robin made an odd glance aside, and Annette realized she was wearing video contacts linked to the headset. *Someone* was getting a live feed and sending the reporter questions. From the way her face momentarily twisted in disgust, the suggestions they were providing weren't to her taste.

"Is it true, Captain, that Dark Eye is suggesting we're going to see alien contact in the next few years?" she finally asked, and Annette stared at her for a long moment. The reporter had acquired a mischievous grin that made her all-too-perfect face suddenly far more human —and *much* more attractive.

"I have no idea what you're talking about," she said slowly while reminding herself the reporter was at least ten years her junior.

"Please, Captain, the Dark Eye Interstellar Surveillance System is an open secret now," Robin insisted. "You'd have been briefed on it as a senior Nova Industries employee, let alone as a Space Force Captain!"

"Miss Robin," Annette said flatly. "*If* some sort of sensor net like you discussed existed, I would not be allowed to talk about it, regardless of whether or not the secret had been compromised."

Dark Eye was a network of small and mid-sized satellites spread throughout the inner system, a joint Nova–Space Force project. She'd seen the results and agreed with Casimir—*somebody* was out there. She was also bound not to talk about it by both her Nova Industries' nondisclosure agreement *and* the United Earth Space Force Code of Justice.

"But if aliens *were* coming, they'd have ships like *Tornado*?" Robin asked.

That was a sensible question. From the way the reporter's eyes were flickering to read whatever feed was coming to her contacts, it was probably less sensationalized than her bosses liked.

"Most likely," Annette allowed. "That is why Admiral Villeneuve is seeking funding to upgrade the Space Force as quickly as we can. Our fusion-torch warships are obsolete; they would stand no chance against a fleet of ships similar to *Tornado*."

Out of view of her headset's cameras, Robin made a clear "touché" gesture. Whether she'd meant to or not, she'd allowed

Annette to bring the conversation around to convincing people to support the Admiral's expansion plan.

The reporter opened her mouth to ask another question, but she was cut off as *every* Space Force communicator in the room went off with an emergency alert.

Annette pulled hers out and opened the scroll-like device, skimming the text. Dark Eye had detected multiple hyperspace portals forming just inside the asteroid belt. Current estimate was twenty ships had emerged from hyperspace fifteen minutes previously.

Even if all four XC hulls and the new survey flotilla were complete and online—which they *weren't*—Earth didn't have twenty hyper-capable starships.

CHAPTER FIVE

THE ROOM EXPLODED INTO CHAOS. ANNETTE WAVED THE reporter back and charged into the crowd, forcing her way through to Admiral Villeneuve. The UESF Chief of Operations was surrounded by shouting, swearing, panicking officers

"Admiral!" She tried to get his attention, shoving through the crowd somewhat gently. Villeneuve didn't seem to hear her, and then someone shoved her back.

She recognized Commodore Anderson about half a second *after* twenty-five years of martial arts training kicked in and dropped the big logistics officer to the ground with a resounding thud.

That got everyone's attention, a circle of space appearing around her and allowing Admiral Villeneuve to turn his gaze on her.

"Captain Bond?" he asked slowly.

"Sir, *Tornado* has eight interface drive shuttles aboard," she told him crisply. "If everyone can *calm down*, we can send the civilians to Orbit One on the torch shuttles and have all of the Space Force officers back to their ships in under ten minutes."

Villeneuve's gaze flickered to where Anderson was groaning to his feet, but even the man Annette had just floored was looking at her with a degree of surprised respect—and hope.

"Make it happen," the Admiral ordered. "I'll stay aboard *Tornado*."

"With respect, sir, your place is on Orbit One," Annette told him quietly, stepping closer to the Admiral as she gestured to Kurzman to start corralling people. "Someone has to take overall command of Earth's defense. You can't be at the tip of the spear—and we both know *Tornado* has to be the tip of the spear."

For a moment, the senior uniformed officer of Earth's defenses looked rebellious, but then Villeneuve sighed and nodded.

"You're right, of course," he confessed. "I'll coordinate the civilians and be available by communicator until I'm in Command." Villeneuve glanced around. "I'm placing you under Harrison's command, with Alpha Squadron. She'll have her orders by the time she's aboard *Challenger*."

"Yes, sir," Annette told him. "We won't fail you."

"I'm not worried about you failing me," Villeneuve said quietly. "I'm worried that we've already failed Earth."

ANNETTE REACHED her bridge as the last of the interface drive shuttles exited the launch bay. That part was done on *chemical* rockets, not even fusion thrusters, to keep the mothership safe. Once the shuttle was a kilometer or so clear of *Tornado*, their smaller drives turned on and they whisked away at forty percent of the speed of light.

Their courses amidst the cluster of warships in high earth orbit were *very* carefully calculated. Each flight between ships lasted seconds at most. They were spending more time docking and offloading passengers than they were flying at full speed.

Beneath the fleet, rapidly dropping away toward Earth and the geostationary orbit of Orbit One, Earth's largest space station and the

Space Force's command center, were the old-style shuttles that had originally brought the Captains. It would have taken forty-five minutes or more for those ships to get their passengers home.

Ahead of the rest of the shuttles was the one carrying Admiral Villeneuve, pushing the limits of what its artificial gravity could handle to get the Admiral to the command center before everything came apart.

"What are our visitors doing?" Annette asked as she dropped into the command chair at the center of the horseshoe-shaped bridge and put on her command headset.

"They spent five minutes sorting out their formation and started heading our way," Harold Rolfson, now *Lieutenant Commander* Rolfson and her tactical officer, reported. "Definitely interface drive ships, but either their tech is *behind* ours or they're taking it slow. Inbound at point one cee."

"Any idea on the size?"

"Dark Eye is trying to resolve, but the sensors weren't built for that," Rolfson told her. The new rank had put the man in Space Force blue working fatigues, but so far they hadn't managed to convince him to trim his shaggy red hair or beard. Annette had quietly squished one complaint from a regular Force officer already.

"They were built to sweep everything within a hundred light-years, not give us shiny pictures of ships inside the Belt," Annette agreed. "Check with Solar Traffic Control—*their* sensors should be able to give us a better idea."

"Yes, ma'am!" Rolfson replied. "I didn't think of that."

"We're all trying not to panic, Harold," she reminded him. "It's going to be a rough day."

"Ma'am, we have a signal from *Challenger,*" said Annette's new com officer, a Space Force regular named Yahui Chan. She was a tiny Chinese woman, delicate-boned and dark-haired, and seemed to know her job inside and out. "Admiral Harrison sends her compliments and says that Alpha Squadron and escorts are moving out to intercept the unknowns. She requests that we accompany her."

Annette nodded. She guessed that Harrison wasn't sure whether Villeneuve had had a chance to tell Annette she was under the Admiral's command.

"Inform Admiral Harrison we will take up high escort position above *Challenger* and that *Tornado* has been placed under her command," she ordered Chan. "Lieutenant Commander Amandine" —she turned to the pale-skinned navigator—"please drop us into that position. We'll stay in formation with the torch ships until ordered otherwise."

"That's going to be a bit of a headache, ma'am," Amandine told her. "Our engines just don't...*work* like that."

"I know. Do your best," she ordered.

"Ma'am." Chan called for her attention again. "We're receiving a transmission—it's on the Space Force emergency frequency, using our encryption and file format, but the feed is just...weird."

"Who's transmitting?" Annette demanded. This was a bad time for *anyone* to be playing games with the emergency frequencies.

"I think...the aliens, ma'am."

THE IMAGE CHAN put on the bridge's main viewscreen sent shivers of atavistic fear down Annette's spine. Without anything familiar to compare the creature to, there was no certainty to its size, but her hindbrain insisted that it was some giant monster from the deep, here to overturn fishing boats and eat primitive fishermen.

The alien was an immense, multi-armed, squid-like being. As Annette forced down her fear, she identified the four largest tentacles acting as legs, supporting the soft-skinned mass of the creature's main body. Easily over a dozen smaller tentacles waved around the being, manipulating controls and moving screens. Strips of cloth wrapped around the body contained pockets and what she guessed to be insignia.

Four jet-black, unblinking, eyes were focused on the camera, and as the creature shifted, a hard black beak came into view. The beak opened and a series of sibilant hisses with an occasional beak snap came out.

It went untranslated long enough for Annette to think they were truly doomed, and then a voice overlay came onto the video—along with a scrolling text translation at the bottom of the screen.

"I am Tan!Shallegh, Fleet Lord for the A!Tol Imperium," the alien commander told them. The voice it had presumably chosen was a soft male baritone with a crisp British Received Pronunciation accent. Both its name and the name of its empire included a strange beak-snapping sound that came surprisingly close to the clicks Annette had once heard a Xhosa junior officer use when calling home.

"Your system has fallen into my region of authority for some time. While my preference was to allow you to develop naturally, emissions from your new hyperdrives have drawn the attention of our enemies. It would be a failure in my responsibility to my Empress to allow your world to fall into the hands of those enemies."

The creature paused, the hisses fading to silence. All of its tentacles twitched in the same direction in a gesture reminiscent of a shrug. Annette wondered if that was intentional—and if so, how long *had* this Tan!Shallegh been studying Earth?

"It is my responsibility to inform you that your system has now been annexed as a Class Four Dependent World of the Imperium," the translation continued a moment after it started speaking again. "A planetary administration will be assembled over the next few five-cycles under an Imperial Governor. If you cooperate, elements of your existing government structures will be incorporated and a swift and peaceful transition will be achieved."

The tentacles shivered again, in a gesture that did *nothing* for Annette's calm.

"Resistance will be met with overwhelming force," Tan!Shallegh told them flatly. "Your fate is decided. Yield and you will benefit.

Fight and you will be crushed. I expect the full stand-down of your fleet within one twentieth-cycle of your receipt of this message."

The image froze, though not before the text translation helpfully converted "one twentieth-cycle" into "seventy minutes".

Silence reigned on *Tornado*'s bridge. An alert buzzed in Annette's ear, and she tapped a command that linked Kurzman into her headset.

"What do we do, Captain?" her executive officer asked.

The same question was on all of her people's faces as she glanced around her bridge, and she pitched her voice loud enough that everyone could hear.

"For now, we proceed on plan," she told them. "Fall into formation on Alpha Squadron and move out to meet our tentacled friends. Responding to that *bullshit* is the Governing Council's job."

The Governing Council might not rule Earth—but its members commanded the Space Force. If they told Annette and her fellows to fight, they'd fight. If they told the United Earth Space Force to surrender...the Force would surrender.

CHAPTER SIX

"Can you tell me what we're looking at yet?" Villeneuve demanded as he stepped into the massive central command center on Orbit One. The room resembled nothing so much as an amphitheater, a central display tank showing the entire star system at a massive scale surrounded by ascending circles of monitors and workstations.

There were eighteen battleships and seventy-four cruisers in the United Earth Space Force. Somewhere in this room, there were at least five screens displaying data from each of those ships. *Tornado*'s section wasn't fully online yet, but he'd passed a few techs improvising with screens stolen from the Belt Squadron.

"Yeah, but you're not going to like it," the commander center's Shift Chief, a Rear Admiral James Mandela. He was a big black man who resembled the historical images of his famous ancestor more and more as he grew older.

"Captain Bond had the idea of using STC's systems to get a clearer look," Mandela continued. "That worked like a charm, enough to make the rest of us feel like idiots, but this is what we got."

He gestured, and one of the techs flipped a feed up into the central display. Twenty silhouettes, with numbers and scales giving

Villeneuve an idea of the size of what he was looking at—and how doomed Earth was.

"Twenty ships, exactly what Dark Eye estimated," Mandela noted. "Eight big bastards just over two kilometers long, six mid-sized cruisers about on par with the new XCs, and six guys on par with our old battleships. The last six are hanging back," he pointed out. "I'm guessing them as landing transports, an invasion force for if we refuse to comply."

Admiral Jean Villeneuve looked at those twenty ships and felt the world fall out from underneath him. If those ships were remotely comparable to *Tornado* and the other XCs, one of the big ones outmassed his entire fleet. Most likely, they were even *more* advanced than *Tornado* and a single one of the cruisers could take on his entire fleet and win handily.

"Rear Admiral Mandela," he said quietly, his words ashes in his mouth. "Issue the order to activate the Weber Protocols and go straight to Phase Two. My authority."

The Weber Protocols were the policies and strategies designed for alien conquest of Earth, born at the same time as the Dark Eye program and the United Earth Space Force. At Phase Two, scientists and designers around the star system were going to be hustled into secret hiding places. Caches would be pre-placed, buried, and forgotten.

Even Villeneuve didn't know most of the details of the Weber Protocols. Even at Phase Two, the preparations were organized on a cell basis. The Protocols were a precursor to defeat or surrender—but Phase Two, at least, was reversible.

At Phase Three, those cells started pulling holes closed behind themselves and the scientists they'd taken with them—often with explosions. He and Casimir had discussed it over the last month as well—at Phase Three, all records that BugWorks had ever existed would be wiped—and the station itself would be abandoned and destroyed.

Once Phase Three was done, the United Earth Space Force

would have destroyed *itself*. Phase Two was bad enough, but in this situation it could only be the first step.

Mandela swallowed but nodded firmly. "It will be done."

"I'll go talk to the Council," Villeneuve told the younger man. "I can activate Phase Two, but everything after that is up to them."

THE CHIEF of Operations of the United Earth Space Force entered his office next to the command center and threw up the video conference onto the walls around him. The argument he expected was already ongoing.

"We cannot blithely surrender Earth to invading monsters!" the American Councilor was bellowing. "My president will *not* permit this council to so blatantly betray its purpose."

"And what will you do when the rest of the world kneels to reality?" the Chinese Councilor replied. "Rely on farmers with guns to stop orbital bombardments?"

"Perhaps we should ask Admiral Villeneuve his opinion," the English Councilor interjected, quelling her compatriots.

There were twelve members on the Governing Council. Like the UN Security Council it had grown out of, there were permanent seats for China, Russia, England and the US. Franco-Germany and South Africa had claimed permanent seats on the *new* body—in exchange for vast quantities of money and manpower for the initial Space Force. The other six rotated through the other nations, all of whom supplied at least *some* of the resources for Sol's defense.

Resources they were now learning were vastly insufficient.

"I have no desire to add my name to Marshal Pétain's on the list of French commanders to resign in the face of overwhelming force," Villeneuve said quietly. "But you pay me for honest advice. The United Earth Space Force lacks the resources to withstand this enemy. The lightest of the warships we face, assuming any rational balance of technology versus a *galactic empire*, can likely destroy our entire fleet.

"We cannot hold. I have already ordered the initiation of the first phases of the Weber Protocols."

"We just signed off on a *ten-trillion-dollar* modernization program," the American Councilor snapped. "I expect better than 'we lack the resources,' Admiral!"

"*Tornado* is the only truly modern ship in the Space Force," the Admiral replied. "Alpha Squadron and her escorts have been updated with interface missile launchers, and the battleships have been fitted with compressed matter–laced armor plating over critical components.

"The rest of the UESF...is worse than useless," Villeneuve said quietly. "If you order it, Alpha Squadron and *Tornado* will engage these A-tuck-Tol." He did his best to imitate the clicking sound used by the alien. "I will resign my commission before I will order the other squadrons into battle. Without interface drives, interface missiles or compressed-matter armor, it would be murder."

The Council was silent. Finally, the Franco-German Councilor leaned forward into his camera.

"*N'abandonne pas*," he said finally. "This Council, the Space Force—we were created to guard the peace of Terra in the face of threats both internal and external. We cannot, Admiral, throw down our swords without at least *trying*."

"We will fail," Villeneuve told him. His words fell like anvils into the silence, and he knew the Councilors already knew. "Our men will die for nothing. For that matter, Councilors, you *all* stand to benefit if these A-tuck-Tol incorporate our current structures into their colonial government."

The Councilors were silent again, glancing at each other, until the South African Councilor sighed and shrugged. She was an attractive black woman that Villeneuve had known for years.

"Many of our countries have suffered under human colonial regimes," she said flatly. "We would betray our people, our oaths, our nations to kneel before an *alien* conqueror. Fight, Admiral. We understand the likelihood of victory, but we must stand regardless."

Villeneuve bowed his head. He'd worried they hadn't understood. They had. They just didn't see a choice. And unless he was willing to *mutiny* to surrender, that meant he would send his people to a war they couldn't win.

"In that case, Councilors, I request authorization to fully activate the Weber Protocols."

CHAPTER SEVEN

KEEPING PACE WITH THE FUSION TORCH BATTLESHIPS OF ALPHA Squadron was painful. Left to her own devices, *Tornado* could have intercepted the A!Tol ships dozens of millions of kilometers away from Earth. Forced to stay with ships still operating under Newton's laws—ships now burdened with tens of thousands of tons of armor they had never been designed to carry—meant they were going to cross paths with the aliens barely ten million kilometers from Earth.

The experimental cruiser's bridge was silent. Annette had nothing to say, and her people went about their business in silence. More than anyone else in the system, this crew knew how hopeless the battle they were about to enter was.

"Ma'am," Rolfson said quietly through her headset. "*Raptor* is moving. But she's..."

Annette looked at what the tactical officer was seeing and sighed.

"Unmanned and unarmed," she confirmed. "She's operating under computer control—they're going to drop her into the sun. We're scuttling her, Harold."

"Are we surrendering, then?" he asked.

"I don't know. The deadline isn't quite up yet."

The aliens had slowed down as their deadline approached, staying outside the range at which they would be able to fire on Earth...assuming their missiles were comparable, at least. Alpha Squadron was cutting that distance, millions of kilometers now behind them as they closed on the aliens.

If even Vice Admiral Harrison knew what the plan was once they reached their own missile range—roughly ten million kilometers—she hadn't shared it with anyone.

"Ma'am, we're being looped in on a transmission from the Governing Council to the aliens," Chan told her.

"Show it," Annette ordered. Everyone knew they were at most ten minutes from a suicide charge. There was no point keeping secrets.

The main screen settled into an image, mostly likely computer assembled from multiple feeds, of all twelve members of the Governing Council sitting around a conference table facing a central camera.

"Tan!Shallegh," the black woman in the center opened, nailing a guttural stop that almost perfectly matched the beak snap the alien had used. "We are the Governing Council of the United Earth Space Force, tasked by the people of this world to secure their peace and liberty against all threats."

It seemed somehow right and perfect that a woman from a culture that had suffered from Earth's own colonialism delivered the planet's response to being asked to surrender to a *new* colonialism.

"You have asked us to kneel. You say it is for our own good," she said flatly. "We have heard these words before, from the worst of our own. We have believed them in our own past, and millions have suffered for it.

"This world is ours. We will not kneel. Leave or be driven from this place."

The screen cut to darkness and Annette swallowed hard.

"That's it, then," she told her people. "Stand by all weapons systems. Prepare to bring the drive to full power—I don't know what the plan is yet, but we sacrifice our greatest strength if we stick to a ballistic course."

A moment later, a note dropped onto Annette's console telling her she had a direct link from the flagship—and Orbit One.

The command headset came with a fold-down screen that fitted over her eyes, providing a mostly private method of conversation if the Captain was quiet. It wasn't perfect—for real privacy, she would have to leave the bridge—but it was the best she was going to get in a battle.

The link resolved into two images, one of Admiral Villeneuve in an office above the main command center—behind him she could see the big amphitheater through the glass—and the other of Vice Admiral Harrison on her flag bridge, wearing an identical headset to the one Annette wore.

"Admiral, Captain," Villeneuve greeted them. "Your orders, as approved by the Governing Council, are to make a high-speed pass of the A-tuck-Tol," the Admiral had a lot more trouble pronouncing the click than the South African Councilor had, "force and hit them with as many missiles as you can deploy. Admiral Harrison"—he sighed—"you are to close and attempt to force a point-blank engagement with your heavy lasers as well. With their likely maneuverability, that will be difficult, but your lasers are the second most powerful weapons we have available."

"I understand, Admiral," Harrison replied, her voice surprisingly level for a woman who *had* to know she'd just been condemned to death. "We will do you proud."

"So you both know, and you are authorized to share this with your crews if you choose, we have activated the full Weber Protocols," Villeneuve said quietly. "Research facilities are being evacuated and set for demolition across the star system. Even *I* don't know where any of the backup facilities are. We are preparing for a resistance—but we need to know as much about our conquerors as we can learn."

"That seems doomed to failure, sir," Annette told him, her voice even quieter than needed to keep the conversation private. "Without a space force, without ships, what can that resistance accomplish?"

"Which brings me to *your* mission, Captain Bond," the Admiral replied. "You're familiar with the concept of a letter of marque?"

"Authorizing a privateer, yes," she confirmed, wondering where he was going.

"You possess the only armed hyperspace-capable ship in this star system," he explained. "While you will join Alpha Squadron in the initial missile engagement, you will *not* close to laser range. You will *pass* the A-tuck-Tol force and enter hyperspace. From there..." He sighed again. "From there, I must leave what to do to your discretion, Captain, but we will shortly be tightbeaming you *everything* Dark Eye has picked up in the last twenty years. Hopefully, you'll find something of use.

"Attack their shipping. Steal their technology. Learn their weaknesses—find a way to *free our world*."

Annette stared at him in silence for a long moment. The mission sounded like a nightmare—operating with no logistics, no support, in the service of a fallen world. She saw no end to it but her death and the death of her crew—but her gaze was drawn to Admiral Harrison.

Alpha Squadron was being asked to die to cover her escape. Harrison hadn't hesitated for a second to accept that fate.

Could she do any less?

"I'll make it happen," she promised. "Somehow."

"Good luck, Captain, Admiral," Villeneuve said softly. "May God go with you."

———

THE GOVERNING COUNCIL may have rejected the A!Tol ultimatum, but the alien fleet seemed entirely unbothered by the approach of the Terran battleships and their escorts. They moved back up to ten percent of lightspeed, closing the distance between themselves and Alpha Squadron at a mind-boggling rate.

The six fusion torch battleships had pushed their rockets and artificial gravity as hard as they could but still had built up barely a twentieth of the velocity of the alien force. The accompanying dozen fusion cruisers could have pushed a bit harder, but unlike the battleships, they had *no* compressed-matter armor. Just interface missiles.

Tornado followed the older ships, fifty thousand kilometers above them and struggling to stay *slow* enough to match their speed. The moment would come for Annette to fully unleash her ship's capabilities, but that time would be after the fight was joined.

Every one of the "stopgap" interface drive missiles—built into chassis far larger than needed to allow the older ships to launch them —had been loaded onto Alpha Squadron. The nineteen ships under Admiral Harrison's command were the only vessels with even the slightest chance of standing up to the aliens.

"They're not breaking off," someone reported on the command channel linking all nineteen ships. "Do we order them away or..."

"No," Harrison said firmly. "We fire at eight million kilometers or when they do. No more warnings."

Rolfson was paying attention, as a timer and distance counter to that line in the sand appeared on the main viewscreen. Not even two minutes.

"Amandine," Annette called. "I want a two-light-year hyperspace run plotted before we even open fire."

"Already done, ma'am," he replied instantly. "I have courses for one through twelve light-years, opening the portal one million kilometers past the A-tuck-Tol."

"Well done," she told him. In other circumstances, his prompt competence would have earned an attempt at a smile. Not today. Not when everything was coming apart.

"Chan, have we received a data dump from Command?"

"We've got *six*," the comms officer replied. "One from Orbit One, four from different Dark Eye platforms. Sixth looks to be from BugWorks. All are finished downloading but are encrypted and require your code for access."

"Good. Rolfson." Annette turned to her tactical officer. "No pussyfooting around with these bastards, but I don't want to use more than ten percent of our ammo."

"That won't go far," he warned. "Ten salvos, that's it."

"I know." She shrugged. "I have no idea when we'll be able to rearm, though. Pick one of the cruisers and dump full salvos into it until we have an idea of just how much compressed-matter armor the assholes have."

"Yes, ma'am."

Annette glanced at the timer. The A!Tol were maneuvering to open up their formation. The smallest ships were dropping back—definitely transports of some kind—while the cruisers and battlewagons were clearing their lines of fire. Even the *Terrans* had been in range for a while now, so she was sure the tentacle freaks had ranged on them a while back.

"Specified engagement range in ten seconds," Rolfson reported. "Bogey C-Five is dialed in."

Annette leaned back in her command chair and rotated her own personal screen to show her Earth. As the last few seconds ticked away, she took a last long look at her homeworld.

THE TERRAN BATTLESHIPS FIRED FIRST. Despite being built for a combat environment where weapons that weren't facing the enemy was useless, the ships were smaller than *Tornado* and only carried four launchers in each broadside.

Of course, they had four of those side-mounted weapons batteries —and interface missiles didn't need the extra velocity the launchers provided. Each of the six battleships launched sixteen missiles, followed by eight from each of the old cruisers. *Tornado* added her own twenty-four missiles, and a torrent of unspeakably fast weapons streamed toward the invaders.

Those invaders seemed remarkably unperturbed. Long seconds

passed as missiles flashed across space at sixty percent of lightspeed—and then, finally, as if sighing in disgust at the foolish barbarians, the A!Tol responded.

Tornado's sensors proved unable to resolve individual missiles in the swarm that emerged from the alien ships. *Hundreds* of weapons came swarming out—moving at *seventy-five* percent of lightspeed.

"Take us to maximum velocity and start evasive maneuvers," Annette ordered, her voice cold. Alpha Squadron was doomed. Even *Tornado* might not survive what was coming—and the alien missiles would hit *before* the Terran weapons.

"Rolfson, engage incoming missiles with the lasers," she continued. *Tornado*'s lasers, big and small, had been explicitly designed with the sensors and mobility to target weapons significantly faster than her own. Thankfully, Alpha Squadron had received many of those same upgrades.

"Amandine..." Annette paused and swallowed hard. "Set course for your hyperspace entry point."

There were no acknowledgements, but she saw her people set to their tasks. The fusion torch ships couldn't match *Tornado*'s maneuvers. All she could do for Alpha Squadron was pray.

Lasers flashed in space, vast amounts of energy lashing out at the inbound missiles. Some died. Most didn't.

Tornado lurched as missiles struck home. Her artificial gravity hadn't needed the overpowered generators the other warships used to avoid their acceleration—which meant *far* too much of the impact made it through.

Annette was hammered into her safety straps, cursing as the tight fabric cut into her.

"Status report!" she snapped.

"We're still here," Kurzman said in her ear. "Minor fractures along the plate lines; damage control is on it." He paused. "Ma'am, we took six point-seven-five-cee kinetic hits. That's incredible."

"Not enough," she said quietly. "What's Alpha Squadron's status?"

"The cruisers are gone," he replied sadly. "So are two of the battleships. *Challenger* survived; they continue to fire."

Annette blinked. She'd expected to hear that Admiral Harrison's force was *gone*. The armor plating had done even better than they'd dare hope. Despite the hammering, *four* battleships had survived and continued to spit fire at the aliens.

Now it was Earth's turn and she focused her attention back on the screens, focusing on *Tornado*'s salvo as it crashed down on one of the mid-sized vessels the UESF had labeled cruisers.

Even with compressed-matter armor, *that* salvo had to hurt. All twenty-four weapons were still on their way...the A!Tol hadn't even been *trying* to shoot down her weapons. That made no sense...

Still kilometers short of their target, *Tornado*'s missile salvo ran into some kind of invisible barrier in the void, exploding in shockingly bright releases of kinetic energy as the impossibly fast weapons ran into some kind of equally impossible barrier.

"They have some kind of energy shield," Rolfson exclaimed. "That's not *possible*."

"So were our missiles ten years ago," Annette said grimly. "Did anything get through?"

"Negative, ma'am. Hard to say if we even made them *twitch*."

She studied the salvos in view with hard eyes. There had to be *something* they could do. All of the salvos so far had been launched widely, set up to have dozens of missiles converge on a target at once to give active defenses the biggest possible headache. It might not help, but they could at least do something different.

"Rolfson, retask any of our missiles you can still adjust to try and hit the same spot on C-Five's shields," she ordered. "Then sequence our launchers to send a steady stream at that point until either we hit that ten percent of our magazines or *something* gives."

The alien ships continued forward, as if the weapons Earth had thought were unimaginably powerful were useless toys. Further salvos focused their fire as the remaining four Terran battleships burned hard to close the range.

For several moments, the aliens simply took the fire, but as Alpha Squadron and *Tornado* continued to pour it on, they clearly passed some previously decided point. A second swarm of missiles blasted out, bearing down once more.

"We can portal out before they hit," Amandine said quietly. "I don't know if our missiles are doing anything."

A stream of over sixty missiles was now lunging straight at the enemy cruiser designated C-5. Annette had no idea if it would work —but she also had no idea if *Tornado* could survive the salvo now heading her way.

"Do it."

Moments later, the emitters flared to life and tore open a bright blue hole in reality. In a flash of impossible energy, *Tornado* vanished from the Sol system.

CHAPTER EIGHT

Jean watched Alpha Squadron desperately try to close the range with the alien ships, their engines flaring to levels he *knew* were dangerous to the crews, and wished he could call them off.

It was too late now. Everything he saw was a minute or more out of date, and any orders he sent would take as long to arrive.

"*Mon Dieu,*" he whispered as the second swarm of missiles blazed out, so much faster than anything Earth could muster in her own defense. "*Pardonne-moi. J'avais tort.*"

Forgive me. I was wrong.

He forced himself to watch. He'd sent Admiral Harrison and ten thousand men and women to their deaths—whether or not they could forgive him, *he* had to watch their fates.

As Alpha Squadron's survivors charged for the center of the A!Tol formation, the alien ships simply...moved out of the way. Accelerating to forty percent of lightspeed, there was no way the invaders would be brought to a point where the battleships' lasers could *hit* them.

Lines of light appeared on the main displays, the computers marking where Admiral Harrison's people tried anyway. Lasers flashed in the void, missiles slammed into alien energy shields—and then the alien missiles reached their own targets.

Two more battleships died, even the compressed-matter plating over their vitals not enough to shrug aside the incoming fire, but *Challenger* and *Enterprise* had somehow survived, their armor shrugging aside multi-gigaton blows.

"Look!" someone exclaimed, and Jean's gaze was drawn to one of the techs at the hastily assembled station for *Tornado*. "Bond got one!"

On main display at the center of the room, one of the red icons was breaking up—a cruiser, destroyed by the focused stream of fire *Tornado* had launched before she fled.

"Show me the replay," the Admiral ordered. He needed to know how it would work. "And please tell me that Harrison is doing the same thing."

A technician sitting near Jean gestured him over as he focused his screen on C-5 and set his screen back in time.

With every sensor in the Sol system trained on the alien fleet, they had a surprising level of detail on even the individual ships. The Admiral saw each missile coming crashing in as a bolt of light, and could *see* the shield react.

Coruscating patterns of light lit up part of an invisible sphere with each hit—and as the missiles struck home again and again in rapid sequence, the pattern spread larger each time. Then, suddenly, there was a *hole* in the center of the pattern, a black splotch with no light at the center of the glittering pattern.

Two missiles shot through the hole in the shields before it closed. They crossed the gap between the shields and the ship faster than Jean could comprehend and ripped through the half-kilometer-long cruiser like it was made of tissue paper.

"They have no armor," he breathed. "Get through those shields..."

"*Challenger* is down," someone announced. "*Enterprise* has lost engines; they are disabled."

Remembering he was watching a recording, Jean turned his attention back to the main display.

Apparently, Harrison *had* been following Bond's strategy. Another cruiser was missing—but the Terran force was down to a single battleship on a ballistic course.

"Order them to surrender," he barked. "It's over."

There was a two-minute delay between what he saw and when they would receive his message. He hoped—he *prayed*—that they got it in time.

Ninety-six seconds after they lost their engines, *Enterprise* exploded. Four distinct fireballs emerged from her hull, vaporizing her hull plating and scattering the compressed-matter lacing into space as her reactors all went critical simultaneously.

Captain Montoya had self-destructed to prevent the A!Tol from going over his ship's files.

"It's over," Admiral Jean Villeneuve, Chief of Operations for the United Earth Space Force, repeated heavily. "People!" he bellowed, attracting the attention of the command center crew. "It's time," he told them. "Go to Final Phase Weber Protocols. Wipe your computers and proceed to the civilian portion of the station.

"Disappear," he ordered.

Around him, screens started to flicker and shut down as the final system wipes took place.

"There'll still be comms from your office," the tech who'd shown him *Tornado*'s kill said quietly. "What do we *do*, sir?"

"If you don't have an assignment under the Protocols, go home," he told the young man. "Go home, and pray the conqueror's boot is gentle. We're done."

JEAN VILLENEUVE FELT VERY old as he leaned against the window in his office, looking out over the now-dark screens and terminals of the UESF command center. The security system told him everyone was gone. He was alone now.

There wasn't even much of a sensor feed anymore. At this phase of the Weber Protocols, the Dark Eye platforms had self-destructed and the UESF's computer network was *gone*. He was still linked in to the Solar Traffic Control network, though, and it showed the cascades of escape pods and small craft from the ships still in Earth orbit—and the flash as the first self-destruct went off an abandoned ship.

He adjusted his sensor view to show him what they could see of the aliens. He was already sick to his stomach. He didn't need to watch his fleet scuttle itself.

Jean intentionally knew *nothing* about the details of the Weber Protocols. If there was anyone the aliens were sure to interrogate about the resistance, it would be him. With a sigh, he returned to his computer and fired off a data packet containing everything they'd recorded of the final battle to the BugWorks station.

Hopefully, Elon Casimir could do *something* with it before he scuttled the secret research station.

The A!Tol continued their inexorable approach at a speed he *knew* was crawling for them. He wished they'd just get it over with, charge into Earth orbit and force the situation. Even if they did, though, he still had to do what came next.

With the UESF computer network wiped—and, in some cases, physically destroyed—he didn't have a lot of tools still available to him. Communications was really all he had left.

A few keystrokes brought up the same channel the A!Tol had used to communicate with Earth's defenders. He checked the camera was working and checked his uniform was presentable. He might have to surrender to an alien conqueror, but that didn't mean he shouldn't put on the best face possible.

"Fleet Lord Tan-tuck-Shallegh," he greeted the alien, the words ashes in his mouth. "I am Admiral Jean Villeneuve, the commander of the United Earth Space Force. It is my charge to defend this world against any and all threats—of exactly the type you represent.

"Despite my oaths and my own desires, you have demonstrated that it is not possible for our forces to resist you. I am left with no choice but to offer the unconditional surrender of Earth's defenders."

He sighed. "I must warn you that while my surrender is *technically* binding on the national militaries on the surface, it is possible—indeed, likely—that it will not be honored by everyone. My surrender functionally dissolves my organization and removes my authority."

The transmission left, carrying with it any hope of a free Earth. All he could do now was wait.

The response came surprisingly quickly—the strange alien must have responded as soon as he received the message. It seemed there was *some* urgency on the other side.

"Admiral Villeneuve," Tan!Shallegh greeted him. "I accept your surrender with your noted codicils. I would have preferred to have reached this point without loss of life, but I understand the weight of oaths.

"My soldiers will be arriving to secure your station in a few minutes. I look forward to meeting you in person."

CHAPTER NINE

TORNADO EMERGED INTO AN EMPTY VOID, ROUGHLY HALFWAY between Sol and Alpha Centauri. With no stars within light-years, the light from the dissipating hyperspace portal was the only source of color.

When it faded, only the cruiser's running lights picked out anything around them—but there wasn't much to pick out. A scattering of loose dust, as lost between the stars as they were.

Annette grimaced. If even *she* was mentally devolving into goth poetry, her crew was probably worse. They'd just cut and run from the fight for their home, abandoning their world in the face of an apparently unstoppable enemy.

She needed them sharp and thinking.

"Rolfson," she snapped. "I want your department on the Dark Eye data and whatever that dump from BugWorks was. I'll unlock it for you as soon as I get a chance, but *also* make sure your people get a meal into them first.

"There's no point in rushing anything." She sighed and shook her head. "No point at all, really. Unless something comes up, I won't expect a briefing until tomorrow evening."

"Understood, ma'am," the bearded officer said slowly. "Anything in particular we should look for?"

"Think like a pirate, Harold," Annette said dryly. "Mainly? As much detail on where we're likely to find *anything* out here as you can pull together."

"Arrr, ma'am," he replied. It was a sad, pathetic, thing—but it was an attempt at humor that got a few weak smiles from the bridge crew.

"Chan, I'm going to need an all-hands announcement," she told her com officer. "Our people need to know what's going on."

The tiny Chinese woman tapped a few commands on her screen then looked up at Annette and nodded silently.

"People, this is Captain Bond," Annette said into her headset microphone. "I know not to underestimate the rumor mill. I should have told you before, but I think we're all still in a bit of shock."

They had been in hyperspace for hours, but she didn't think anyone had done anything but stare at their screens in that time. *She* certainly hadn't.

"As the rumor mill has had plenty of time to spread, we have left the Sol system. While the battle was ongoing when we left, I have no reason to believe we were victorious. It is almost certain that the full Weber Protocols have been activated and we are now the last remaining capital ship of the United Earth Space Force."

She paused, letting that sink in.

"While I'm sure there are doubters among you, I can't imagine most of you think I made this choice on my own. We received orders prior to the engagement with the A-tuck-Tol to do just this. Admiral Villeneuve has provided an authorization and mission once known as a letter of marque and reprisal.

"We have been charged to become privateers, seeking out and capturing A-tuck-Tol shipping and technology. My orders are to raid military shipping, steal technology and learn about our enemy.

"Our final objective is to gather enough knowledge and technology to be able to return to Earth and drive the A-tuck-Tol from our world. This will take time. This will take effort, blood, sweat and tears from us all.

"Our mission may well end in our deaths, far from home and forgotten," she warned her people. "But we are also Earth's *only* remaining hope."

She paused, wondering if there was more she should say, then shook her head.

"Thank you," she told them. "We *will* go home. We *will* save Earth. I promise you."

———

THE FILES from Dark Eye and Orbit One opened instantly to Annette's codes. They were little more than direct data dumps, sensor data organized by date. There was some analysis in the Orbit One file, but nothing that leapt out as "the captain must read this now."

She forwarded those files to Rolfson for his team to review. *Tornado* had some truly amazing computer support, which, combined with the team her tactical officer had combed from the best of the UESF, should allow him to pull *something* useful from the data.

Annette intentionally left the data dump from Nova Industries for last. If anyone was going to include any surprises for her, it would be Elon Casimir. She wasn't surprised in the slightest that the moment she typed in her old Nova Industries security code, her screen promptly faded into a video.

The long-haired chubby face of her former employer faced the screen from a room she recognized as his office in the BugWorks facility.

"As I record this message, the A!Tol fleet has just sent their ultimatum," he began. Unlike any of Annette's crew, he nailed the tongue click that was the closest any human could come to the beak snap in the middle of the word.

"You are receiving this message because Villeneuve has ordered you to flee the system and raid enemy shipping. The order hasn't been given as I sit here, but these are the circumstances that call for that option.

"I must apologize, Annette. While Admiral Villeneuve and I had discussed Case Privateer, we never raised it with you. We hoped to have more time. Hoped that we'd have all four XC ships fully equipped and deployed at least, and that you wouldn't be the only Captain we'd be sending off into the deep void."

Casimir stood, the camera following him as he crossed the unappointed office to a window looking out over the ring of the station. His office was in one of several "towers" originally built to expand working space on the spinning station. The station no longer rotated, but the towers made for a useful separation from the main ring.

"I know...I knew more than I told even you, let alone Villeneuve," he confessed. "*Of Course We're Coming Back* was only one of three survey ships. *Hidden Eyes of Terra* was...lost. Captured by the A!Tol, I believe. *Oaths of Secrecy* and *Of Course We're Coming Back* scouted over a dozen systems and placed scanners in all of them.

"*Oaths of Secrecy* completed a sweep to pick up all of the data they'd acquired. Both the raw data and my people's assessment are included. There are several systems and apparent trade routes that will be of value to your mission.

"*Of Course We're Coming Back* will be leaving shortly after you do, with whatever she can record of the final battle. *Oaths of Secrecy* is better able to hide herself. She's going to hide in-system and try and learn what she can of how these A!Tol implement their conquest."

He shook his head.

"Both of their Captains have been advised to place themselves at your disposal," he told her. "They're not warships, barely even useful as transports, but that's two hulls you won't have any other way. *Of Course* now has an interface drive. *Oaths* has the parts aboard to *install* one but is currently using ion thrusters for stealth.

"If we'd had more time, you'd have been pulled into the Case Privateer preparations inevitably just by having a hyperspace-capable ship. We've been using the two we have to place caches of supplies—munitions, fuel, food—in several systems. The largest is in Alpha Centauri and is where the survey ships are expected to meet you."

Casimir stepped back to his desk, looking at the camera and appearing far older than his limited years as he appeared to consider saying something.

"I've known about the A!Tol Imperium for sixteen months," he finally confessed. "I know...almost nothing about them except that they exist and that Earth was in their territory. We're a very distant frontier at best, though, Annette. A privateering campaign may make it far too expensive for them to operate this far away from the core of their power.

"But"—he raised a finger—"there may also be some truth to the claim that their enemies would have come for us if they hadn't. I know even less about them—only a name: the Kanzi. Your mission is to drive the A!Tol from our world, but you *need* to learn more about their enemies.

"I will back you against any enemy Earth faces, but I'd prefer we didn't leap from the frying pan into the fire.

"We need data, Annette. Everything I know is included in the attachment to this message. Anything we learn later will be sent along with *Of Course We're Coming Back* and *Oaths of Secrecy*. But... it's all so little. We're a tiny fish in a giant galaxy, and we don't even know which way the current is going.

"Find out for us.

"God speed you, Annette Bond. If this task must fall to someone, I'm glad it fell to you."

The recording ended, and Annette found herself looking at the now-unencrypted directories. The organization was of an entirely different magnitude than the UESF data. There were directories for analysis, star data, hyperspatial spectrographic spikes, alien races, known worlds....

She doubted there was a lot of *depth* to anything even Nova Industries had. They may have known things the Space Force didn't, but if they'd known enough to make a difference, Elon Casimir wouldn't have concealed it.

"Rolfson," Annette opened an intercom to her tactical officer. "I hate to hand you a task and tell you to drop it, but I'm forwarding you the data that Nova sent us. I think we'll want to go through that first."

CHAPTER TEN

FOR THE SECOND TIME IN TWO DAYS, *TORNADO* ERUPTED OUT OF a hyperspace portal. This time, they weren't emerging into empty space, and sensors sang into space: radar, lidar, and more exotic techniques sampling the space around Alpha Centauri as the cruiser emerged into potentially hostile space.

Thanks to *Of Course We're Coming Back*'s survey mission, Annette and her people knew the exact layout of the Alpha Centauri system. Both components of the binary system had two close-in planets orbiting their individual stars, while three more planets followed long, oddly shaped orbits around both stars.

All were rocky worlds, only one even of Earth's size. Alpha Centauri A2 fell, just barely, into the habitable zone of its parent star. *Of Course*'s survey mission had named the frigid world "Hope" when they'd first located it.

Further investigation had shown the naming to be apt: Hope was a life-bearing world, with shaggy animals and wide-leaved plants well adapted to its low temperatures and long winters. It wouldn't be a *comfortable* place for humans to live, but humans could live there.

Which meant, of course, that the supply cache Nova Industries had been assembling was on Alpha Centauri AB2, the outermost rock of the system. AB2 had absolutely nothing going for it—no valuable minerals that weren't more easily extracted from asteroids, no life, not even enough sunlight to run a solar panel.

It was perfect for hiding.

"Are we seeing anything?" Annette asked.

"Negative," Rolfson replied. "Alpha Centauri looks as dead as it did when *Of Course We're Coming Back* came through. No emissions signatures of any kind."

"Is *Of Course* herself in system?"

"I don't see her," he said. "We don't know when she left, though."

"Amandine, take us to the coordinates of the depot," Annette ordered. "Rolfson, keep an eye out. We're *supposed* to be seeing the survey ships showing up, but that doesn't mean that the A-tuck-Tol won't be showing up themselves."

Tornado started to move, slipping closer to the rock at a speed her crew would have thought impossible a year before—and that was still slow compared to their enemy's warships. They were still grinding through their analysis, but Annette was sure she'd seen at least one A!Tol ship reach at least forty-five percent of lightspeed to dodge Terran missiles.

All evidence suggested that Annette's single ship was outclassed by her enemies in far too many ways. The first task of their new mission would be to start finding ways to fix that.

THE PROBLEM with coordinates on a planet is that the starting point for longitude, especially, was completely arbitrary. Anyone giving you a position on a planet also had to give you their reference point, turning even the most detailed of coordinates into, effectively, "ten thousand kilometers west of the big mountain range."

Fortunately, *Tornado*'s computer contained the entirety of both the abbreviated official survey of AB2 and the later, secret survey done to locate a good spot for the cache Nova Industries had located. They had more than enough data to reliably identify the dormant volcano Casimir's people had picked and settle into orbit above it.

"Are we picking up anything from the caldera?" Annette asked. Surely, there had to be a beacon or *something*.

"I've got nothing, ma'am," Rolfson told her. "The entire mountain is something like fifty percent iron and titanium *and* notably warmer than the rest of the planet. Outside of some kind of transmission, we're not picking up anything from here."

"Sounds like a fantastic place to hide a weapons cache," Kurzman noted. In the absence of an immediate threat, he was back on the bridge with Annette. The bridge even *had* a seat for him; it was a cramped thing, without much in terms of screens or controls, but it provided a place for a senior observer to be present.

"Agreed," Annette said. "Kurzman, go get suited up. You're leading the Service detachment."

"Don't we have a Service officer for that?" her XO said dryly.

"We do. And right now, until I'm a *hell* of a lot more comfortable with what's going on, I want you or me on every off-ship op. Everything we say, everything we do, reflects on Earth now. We can't afford to screw this up."

"You realize that even the most junior Special Space Service grunt can snap me in half with one hand, right?" Kurzman pointed out. "What happens if they don't *want* a babysitter?"

"Oh, make no mistake, Commander," Annette told him with a tiny crack of a smile. "You're not *their* babysitter."

MAJOR JAMES ARTHUR VALERIAN WELLESLEY, second son of the fourteenth Duke of Wellington, commanding officer of the Fifty-Second Company of the Special Space Service, managed to not even sigh when the executive officer arrived with their briefing—such as it was!—and told the Major he'd be accompanying whatever troop was sent down to the surface.

"You'll need to suit up up here" was his only reply, a level of control he felt was solely possible due to generations of stiff-upper-lipped ancestors *glaring* at him from the beyond over even the *thought* of snarking off to his superior.

Wordless, James gestured for two of his Service people to help the XO while he and his Alpha Troop Captain stepped into his office.

While the United Earth Space Force had drawn its structures and traditions from the US, French, and Chinese air forces and navies, with an inevitable leavening of British naval sensibilities, no one had put much thought in the early days to providing boarding contingents.

Faced with a need to recapture ships seized by pirates, the UESF had ended up turning to the world's special forces—and discovered that the British Special Air Service were the only people with an actual training scenario on the topic.

Fifty-two percent of James's people were Chinese at this point, but the traditions that shaped the elite boarding troops of the UESF were British, a Special Space Service that recruited from the world's best.

And spent much of its time babysitting.

"I'm bringing the headquarters section down with Alpha Troop," the tall, dark-haired aristocrat told his senior troop leader. "I'll want your team sweeping for the cache, the section and I will stay with the XO."

"Any idea how large the zone will be?"

"No. Nova Industries didn't give us that much data," James replied. "But then, we weren't expecting extra supply, so I think we'll take whatever we get."

"Amen, Major."

"Get your boys and girls on the shuttle," James told him. "I'll go make sure the Commander hasn't accidentally hooked up the wrong tubes."

THE SHUTTLE DROPPED from orbit like a rock, fast enough to make the Major nervous. He knew, intellectually, that the interface drive meant the landing craft could stop anywhere the pilot chose—but all of his experience in landing drops was on more conventional spaceplane-style shuttles.

"Miss, you have done this before, right?" he asked the shuttle's pilot quietly.

The redheaded young woman made a shushing gesture.

"It's Lieutenant," she pointed out. "Lieutenant Mary McPhail."

"Leftenant McPhail," James allowed. "You *have* done this before, right?" he repeated.

"Yep. Twice."

"Twice?"

"Which is once more than any other pilot aboard *Tornado,* which is why you got me. Now, unless you want to be a high-velocity *smear,* shut up and let me do my job."

The Special Space Service Major shut up.

Alpha Centauri AB2 was an airless rock, but the volcano was approached far too quickly for James Wellesley's peace of mind. He was about to say something when suddenly they were *inside the caldera,* rock walls screaming past at hundreds of kilometers an hour.

McPhail finally hit the controls, slamming the forty-meter-long shuttle into an instant hover with no warning—and no inertia. The sight alone sent James's stomach reeling, and only ironclad self-control kept him from visibly reacting.

From the way the pilot glanced back at him and grinned, she had been expecting *some* reaction. He met her gaze levelly for a long stiff-upper-lipped moment, and then winked at her.

"What are we seeing on the scanners?" he asked.

The younger woman turned back, running through the results of the shuttle's sensors.

"We're in the middle of the caldera, about two hundred meters beneath the rim," she told him. "But...I'm not picking up *anything*. As far as hiding things goes, I don't know if they could have picked anything better—but I'm wishing someone had given us a *key*."

James considered for a moment, glancing at the sensor data being fed to his spacesuit helmet.

"How narrow were the coordinates they gave us?" he said. "As I recall, they were long."

"Yeah, but that's almost garbage data when you're talking about coordinates on an inhabited planet," she pointed out.

"Except we have the *exact* mapping they used," he said. "Those coordinates should get us within a hundred meters or so, right?"

"Moving us to the exact coordinates," McPhail allowed after a moment. "Let's see what we find."

ANNETTE WATCHED the relayed data from the shuttle's sensors on her command displays. The main video feed was up on the bridge's main display, but she was digging into the more-detailed sensor reports, looking for the clue they were all missing.

She doubted Casimir had given them inaccurate coordinates, but it appeared that the Nova Industries crews had hidden the cache extremely well. It would take time to find it, which also raised questions about just how accessible it was going to be.

"Hyper portal!" Rolfson suddenly snapped. "I have a hyper portal forming at three million kilometers."

"Dammit," Annette swore. "McPhail—get back up here."

"Ma'am—I think we found it!" the pilot replied. "Not sure; we're going to pulse the IFF."

"Negative, pull back up to orbit," Annette ordered. "We may need to run."

"It could be *Of Course We're Coming Back*," Rolfson reminded her. "The portal itself is interfering with our scanners; we can't resolve the newcomer."

He was right. The odds were that the arrival was one of their expected visitors—but they couldn't be sure.

"We're Earth's only hope," she told him. "No chances. McPhail, you have thirty seconds to make orbit; we're going to round the planet and pick you up. Rolfson, get the launchers up. Amandine, set a course to pick up the shuttle and have us ready to flee if we're facing more metal than I want to tangle with."

A chorus of confirmations echoed back and Annette leaned back as her cruiser leapt into motion. With the interface drive, the trip *back* up to the ship was a matter of moments, McPhail rocketing the shuttle out of the airless volcano caldera at twenty percent of the speed of light.

Amandine dove the cruiser down closer to the planet at an only slightly more sedate pace. The shuttle cut its interface drive a few kilometers short of the bigger ship, and the navigator nailed the pickup *perfectly*, matching velocities for a fraction of a second and scooping the shuttle into the landing bay.

The dive took the hyper portal out of view behind AB2, and Annette examined what data they had as closely as she could. All she could tell for the moment was that a ship had exited hyperspace. The A!Tol presumably had *some* kind of better detector for this, one less blinded by the strange radiation that came out of the portal.

"All launchers primed, all lasers charged," Rolfson noted.

"Coming around the planet, you'll have a clear line of fire in... three, two, one...now!"

"Gotcha!" the tactical officer announced. "We have a line of fire, lighting up the target with radar and lidar."

"If there's a threat, return fire immediately," Annette ordered, mirroring Rolfson's consoles to her screen. Passive scanners weren't giving them much—their current array of sensors could only tell her that the ship was *probably* smaller than *Tornado* and wasn't using a reaction engine.

They didn't have a way of detecting the presence of a gravitational-hyperspatial interface. Like the ability to see into hyper-portal, she suspected the A!Tol had a solution for that—one of many pieces of technology they were going to need to steal.

As it was, an interface drive could be identified only by speed and the way it maneuvered, and detailed identification was going to have to wait for the radar pulses to return from their ten-second-each-way journey.

"Target is moving at point two cee," Rolfson announced. "Definitely an interface drive. No confirmation on size yet...radar pulses returning...now."

"Ma'am, we're receiving an IFF code!" Chan reported loudly a moment later. "It's *Of Course We're Coming Back!*"

"Rolfson?" Annette asked. "IFF doesn't guarantee truth," she pointed out when her com officer looked at her questioningly. It was *unlikely* the A!Tol had already stolen and duplicated Terran Identify Friend or Foe transponders, but they *had* opened their communications through an encrypted, UESF-only channel.

The tactical officer was running through something on his screen, but finally looked back up at her and nodded.

"Active scanners confirm," he said aloud. "I can't read the name on her hull from here, but she's definitely a Nova Industries survey ship."

CHAPTER ELEVEN

With *Of Course We're Coming Back* in orbit to help guide the shuttle to *exactly* the right spot, James watched McPhail tuck the shuttle deeper into the empty mouth of the volcano. They'd managed to pick out a clear shot of artificial metal before being recalled, and *Of Course*'s crew had confirmed they were in the right spot.

Following the instructions, they pulsed the shuttle's UESF IFF code and waited. Nothing happened for a few moments, and then what had *looked* like an entire chunk of rock wall smoothly pushed outward and slid down, revealing an entrance just large enough for the shuttle to land in.

"I didn't think the survey crew had interface drive shuttles," McPhail said aloud. "But there is *no* way anyone landed one of the spaceplanes in *that*."

"Looks like you were wrong about being the most experienced pilot on these toys," James replied with a smile as he studied the cave. It had clearly been a natural formation originally, probably an old lava tube. A prefabricated door had been brought down and installed over the entrance and then covered in local rock.

The inside still had no atmosphere but looked to have been

smoothed with mining lasers. Standard-sized UESF shipping containers had been neatly lined up along one side, taking up less than a quarter of the available space—but still representing two entire loads for the small survey ships.

"Set us down," he ordered. "We're going to go take a look."

"Can do, sir," she replied. "Be careful," she continued after a momentary pause as the shuttle vibrated to touch down. "I get the feeling you and I will see a lot of each other, and I'd hate to be proven wrong."

With a small shake of his head, James Wellesley gave her an affirmative salute to the top of his helmet visor and stepped out of the cockpit to collect his men and their senior officer cargo.

"WE NEED to check each container individually for its manifest," Kurzman told the SSS troopers as they stepped out of the shuttle, carefully adjusting to AB2's lower gravity. The spacer missed that step, but James grabbed him before he face-planted on the smooth volcanic rock.

The Nova team had done a good job of making the cache safe, but smashing into the floor could still crack the Commander's faceplate, and there was no more air here than anywhere else on the desolate worldlet.

"Didn't we get a manifest from *Of Course?*" the Major asked as he carefully settled his nominal superior on the ground.

"Casimir didn't give them one," Kurzman replied. "He was playing this whole thing way too close to his chest—*two* survey ships he didn't tell anyone about?" The short officer shook his head. "I'm downloading an access code to your tacnet. *Of Course We're Coming Back*'s crew didn't have it, so even the manifests we're pulling weren't available."

"Wonderful," James said calmly. "All right, people—take it in patrols; that's ten for each of you."

The four four-person patrols from Alpha Troop, plus the one from the Major's company headquarters section, moved out. He designated sections of ten containers for each patrol, making sure all fifty were going to be checked out.

"This doesn't seem like a lot," he said on a private channel to Kurzman.

"About a hundred thousand cubic meters of supplies," the executive officer pointed out. "But...yeah. If it's half-and-half food and missiles, it's about six months' worth of food and a single reload for *Tornado*'s magazines."

"We had supplies aboard already, right?"

"We had full magazines and we only shot off ten percent of them," Kurzman confirmed. "We were...lighter on food and water. We can *carry* a six-month supply, but we weren't expecting to need it. *Tornado*'s only loaded for two months."

James grunted. Eight months' food and water and a single set of missile reloads didn't sound like much to take on an interstellar empire.

"Sir, I think we need the XO," one of his troopers reported.

"Oh?" the Major replied. He was already gesturing for Kurzman to start moving toward Delta Patrol. His people had all been five-year-veteran noncommissioned officers of their national militaries before even being *considered* for the Special Space Service. He trusted their judgment.

"We've been briefed on every piece of tech we crammed into *Tornado*," the soldier replied in a Texan drawl, "but ain't *nobody* mentioned something called an 'intra-hyperspatial anomaly scanner' to me."

The XO suddenly accelerated, almost leaving James behind as the stocky officer charged toward the container.

"Commander?"

"I thought that was just a theory," Kurzman replied.

"Theory's fine, Commander, but what *is* it?" James asked.

"It's eyes that can see in hyperspace."

"YOU FOUND *WHAT*?" Annette asked her XO and ground forces commander.

"The manifest for one of the containers says its holding an 'intra-hyperspatial anomaly scanner,'" Kurzman told her. "I've never heard of it, but given what the hyperspatial anomaly scanner the survey ships have can do..."

Annette nodded slowly. A large portion of the data Casimir had given her was hyperspatial anomaly scans of the stars surrounding Sol. With those scanners, you could detect a ship in hyperspace from regular space—but the signature propagated at lightspeed. Its only use was to map where people had been, which was helping Rolfson's team map out potential targets.

Tornado remained blind in hyperspace, though. The blank void they saw defeated any sensor they had beyond about a light-second—but if Casimir's people had found a way to detect other ships in hyperspace...

"That could be handy. Well done, Commander. Anything else unexpected in Casimir's presents?"

"Nothing yet," Kurzman told her. "About what we expected—food, water, missiles."

"Have McPhail bring a container of missiles back up when you return," she ordered. "We need to fully restock our magazines as we plan our next move."

"Any ideas on that?"

"A few," Annette admitted. "I gave Rolfson until morning to pull together a briefing, though. If you can find a manual for that intra-hyperspatial scanner, that could help our plans too."

"We'll crack her open and see what she looks like," her XO promised. "We'll be back aboard before the briefing. Don't wait up for us."

CHAPTER TWELVE

Captain Andrew Lougheed of *Of Course We're Coming Back* had come aboard *Tornado*, joining Annette's senior officers in the still-rough conference room. A series of petty officers had swarmed over the room over the last few days, setting up a proper briefing display so that Rolfson could give the summary he'd now had days to prepare.

Annette noted that the bearded tactical officer did *not* look happy. She wasn't surprised—she hadn't expected him to come up with anything particularly *positive* out of the data from Casimir and Dark Eye.

"Any concerns with *Of Course We're Coming Back*, Captain Lougheed?" she asked the survey ship's commander. Lougheed was the man that the UESF had insisted hold that command instead of her, a bulky Chinese Canadian.

"We're not used to having the interface drive yet," he admitted. "We've had a shuttle with it for a while, but the one on the ship itself is new. I wouldn't object to borrowing some of your engineering team's time—we have a grand total of twenty-four people aboard, and we're seeing some odd glitches."

"Kulap?" Annette glanced over at her engineer.

Kulap Metharom was a tiny Thai woman who'd been the lead engineer on Nova Industries' gravitational-hyperspatial interface momentum engine project. She'd been the one to coin the "interface drive" shorthand, and had decided to baby the first fully equipped experimental cruiser—a process that had led her into a uniform and command of *Tornado*'s two hundred–strong engineering department.

"We can spare," she said quickly. "Will sort after."

Lougheed nodded slowly, clearly taking a moment to process Metharom's not-entirely-standard English.

Taking that matter as settled, Annette stood and faced her staff from the front of the room. Along with Lougheed and Metharom, she had Rolfson, Amandine, Kurzman and Wellesley gathered. Between the seven of them, they now represented every O-4 and above left of the United Earth Space Force.

Though, for that matter, if the full Weber Protocols had been activated, the United Earth Space Force didn't *exist* anymore, though that was a rabbit hole Captain Annette Bond had no interest in diving down.

"All right, people," she said. "We've got a lot to cover today. Lieutenant Commander Rolfson has been digging through everything we were given by the folks back home of what we know of the galaxy. Captain Lougheed was the source of some of that data, so I'd ask you to chime in if we're off base.

"Kurzman and Metharom have been going over the handful of extra toys Nova Industries snuck in with the supply cache, and Captain Lougheed...well, you saw the end at Sol. We're probably best off starting with you."

She met the dark-skinned Captain and smiled sadly. She'd insisted on seeing the sensor data herself, and they'd pass at least a report on to the crew, but her senior officers needed to hear the truth.

"I think we all need to know where we stand."

Lougheed nodded and sighed, replacing her at the front of the room and pulling out his com unit. A quick tap of the scroll-like device against the wallscreen linked the two, and he easily threw up a tactical plot showing the battle for Earth as *Tornado* had left it.

"Your trick with streaming missiles at a single point proved effective," he noted first, the plot behind him moving in recorded real time as he spoke. "Your salvo took out one of their cruisers, and Admiral Harrison repeated the trick before *Challenger* was destroyed.

"There were no survivors from Alpha Squadron, and the rest of the Space Force was scuttled as per the Weber Protocols," Lougheed said grimly. "I think...we expected less of the Force to *survive* that far."

"We did," Annette confirmed. "But...there was no point in having the remainder of the Force fight. Alpha Squadron were the only ones with compressed-matter armor and modern missiles."

"Speaking of compressed-matter armor, watch this." Lougheed brought up a video, overlapping the tactical plot with a video. "This was assembled by the Orbit One command center after the first cruiser went down, using footage relayed from Alpha Squadron's ships and the missiles themselves."

The room was silent as they watched the stream of missiles slam into the invisible energy shield, and the expanding pattern of light as the shield was slowly overwhelmed—and then the missiles snuck through.

"Two hits?" Annette asked questioningly. "We took out one of the A-tuck-Tol's cruisers with *two hits*?"

"The one Alpha Squadron took down shortly afterwards came apart after *one*," Lougheed added. "What little analysis was done before they shut down under the Weber Protocols suggests that their cruisers, at least, not only don't have compressed-matter armor—they don't have *any* armor."

"I guess if you have an energy shield that can *eat* forty or fifty cee-fractional missiles, you don't need it," Kurzman noted dryly. "Still...

the shield clearly has vulnerabilities we can exploit. Vulnerabilities that backing it with our armor would help reduce."

"Indeed," Annette agreed. Acquiring an energy shield for *Tornado* was high on her priority list, even if she wasn't yet sure *how* they would do so.

"What happened after the UESF surrendered?" she asked Lougheed.

"The A-tuck-Tol boarded Orbit One and the other major orbitals immediately upon arriving in orbit," he told her. "I didn't get a lot more detail after that, but I can tell you one thing: the boarding troops? They weren't A-tuck-Tol."

"They weren't?"

Lougheed tapped on his com unit and another video replaced the one of the cruiser's destruction. The screen showed one of the landing bays on Orbit One, with half a dozen of the space station's police force standing a stiff-backed but unarmed escort around the station administrator and Admiral Villeneuve.

An airlock door slammed aside, and strange forms in black armor started to emerge. Annette half-expected something out of a nightmare, but the first wave of a dozen troopers were humanoids. Squat, wide, creatures with disproportionately large heads, but bipedal humanoids.

The second set of aliens were...more what she'd expected. The A!Tol were *significantly* larger than she'd gathered from the video of Fleet Lord Tan!Shallegh. The armored, tentacled creatures stepping into the bay were over two meters tall, carrying themselves on their center tentacles with the manipulators waving all around as they approached Orbit One's authorities.

There was no sound, but the initial meeting seemed to pass without violence before the footage cut off.

"That was as much as we got before we left the system," Lougheed told them. "At that point, the surrender of the orbitals had gone peacefully and the groundside militaries had been summoned by the A-tuck-Tol to honor the UESF's surrender."

"Facing an enemy with possession of the orbitals, the official policy of the British military is to surrender immediately," Major Wellesley told them in his irritatingly precise accent. "I believe that is also the Franco-German plan."

"The Americans won't," Annette said with a sigh. "They'll fight. They can't *win*, but they'll fight. And the Weber Protocols will set up a resistance movement as well. The A-tuck-Tol won't find Earth easy to hold.

"However, there is no point in us returning without some kind of advantage or plan to turn 'difficult to hold' into 'liberated,'" she noted. "Rolfson, you've been going over everything that Dark Eye and Nova sent us. What have you found?"

"Nothing good, though a lot that may prove useful," her tactical officer replied. "May I, Captain Lougheed?" He gestured to the wallscreen.

"Of course."

With everyone seated again, Harold Rolfson stepped up to the wallscreen and tapped it with his com unit, taking over control of the screen and bringing up a pseudo-three-dimensional display of the stars around Sol.

"The farther we go from Sol, the older our data is," he warned. "Dark Eye has been sweeping systems out to sixty light-years, and Nova Industries scouts ran a loop about ten light-years out covering the same stars. Inside that ten-light-year loop, our data is relatively current. Outside it..." The bearded officer shrugged.

"The good news, such as it is, is that we appear to be on the ass end of nowhere," he noted. "Further out along our arm of the spiral, we found almost nothing. There's probably at least a few survey ships or similar out there now, but if there was nothing there fifty years ago, there probably isn't anything significant now. Except...here."

A pair of stars, both ten light-years farther along the rim, flashed red.

"This is where *Hidden Eyes of Terra* was supposed to scout on the mission she didn't come back from," Rolfson noted. "We presume one or both of these systems contains an A-tuck-Tol base of some kind. Could be as simple as *Hidden Eyes* ran into a patrol ship, or we could easily be looking at a relatively new fleet base.

"Hyperspatial anomaly scans suggest that hyperdrive traffic to this system"—he tapped one of the two—"started picking up about twelve to thirteen years ago. That would be consistent with assembling a fleet or logistics base to support expansion in this area."

That was promising. While a fleet base was almost certainly beyond their ability to assault, they could probably pick off ships going to and from it.

"When we look toward the galactic core, though, we see a *lot* more traffic," Rolfson told them, rotating the view to focus on those stars. "Our ten-light-year sweep was empty, but we did pick up activity starting at the thirty-light-year mark, and it was *busy* fifty years ago around the sixty-light-year line."

A number of systems highlighted in orange, some with thick circles around them and some with thin.

"Based on Dark Eye's scans of electronic emissions and the scout ships' scans of hyperspatial anomalies, we believe these systems to be inhabited. Thicker bands represent higher likely populations."

The orange systems formed the edge of a creeping sphere, the edge of an expanding Imperium.

"What I found interesting was *these* systems," the tactical officer pointed out. A small number of systems shaded purple. "They're about equally far away toward the core, though slightly farther from Earth on a direct line, and show similar traffic patterns—except they share *no* traffic we detected with the orange systems."

"I was warned the A-tuck-Tol had enemies," Annette told the others. "Kanzi or something like that. Any idea which of these is which?"

"The orange systems are definitely A-tuck-Tol," Rolfson said firmly. "Backtracking Tan-tuck-Shallegh's fleet leads us to this system." One of the more lightly banded orange systems flashed with a red caret. "Our guess is that system *definitely* hosts a significant A-tuck-Tol military base, supported logistically by the larger colonies around it.

"We're looking at the edge of their Imperium," he admitted. "Wideband scans from beyond the sixty-light-year mark are picking up signals suggesting dozens, if not *hundreds*, of inhabited systems. But what we're picking up there is so diffuse, we can't give any details. Only an impression of sheer size."

"We're minnows facing a great blue whale," Annette agreed, looking around the table. "I suggest we all get that into our heads now. We need to dance and pirouette, play the game better than they can. Right now, we can potentially take on a single A-tuck-Tol cruiser —but if we get caught by a squadron or one of the bigger ships they brought to Sol, we're dead.

"So, we need to be smarter. We need to learn to do things we didn't think were possible. And first on that list, gentlemen, ladies, is that we need to learn how to intercept and board ships in hyperspace."

"But that *isn't* possible!" Rolfson objected.

"Nova Industries disagreed with assessment," Metharom told the tactical officer. "Major Wellesley, Commander Kurzman, brought back sensor. Nova design. Scans for anomalies *inside* hyperspace."

"The manuals say they tested it, but I'm not sure how," Kurzman noted. "I want to experiment with using it to track *Of Course We're Coming Back* through hyperspace. It may well allow us to track ships but not give us enough detail to be able to engage with missiles."

"In theory, once in hyperspace, missiles and shuttles can move around exactly as they do in normal space," Amandine pointed out. "It's just that our normal sensors and navigation systems don't work."

"We'll be dumb-firing missiles and navigating shuttles by dead reckoning," Annette agreed. "Until, at least, Metharom can build a version of the hyperscanner we can mount on shuttles and missiles. Boarding flights are going to be especially risky."

"We took the job," Wellesley replied calmly.

"Indeed." She looked around. "We are privateers now. We *need* to capture ships—for technology, for information, for *supplies*. Without these things, we are doomed to fail and Earth remains a conquered world."

She met Rolfson's eyes.

"You've been studying this more than the rest of us," she noted. "Do you have a suggested place to start?"

He nodded and tapped one of the systems banded in light orange.

"Here. Yellow dwarf star, only has a catalog number on Earth, but looks to have had a small colony founded fifty-three years ago. My understanding is that we don't want to attack civilian targets, but there is probably a military defense of some kind. We can engage under our own terms and extract local knowledge from the defenders.

"It's also a logical stopover point for ships headed to Sol," he noted. "We can raid supplies being sent to Tan-tuck-Shallegh and benefit both ourselves and the resistance."

"Captain Lougheed." She turned to *Of Course*'s commander. "Feel up to a scouting run ahead of us?"

"I'll note, ma'am, that *Of Course* has no weapons."

"Metharom—can we fix that?" Annette asked.

"We can't fit her with launchers, but interface missiles don't really need them," the engineer pointed out. "I can rig up a remote initiator and then she should be able to use her probe racks to carry, say, eight or nine missiles?"

Lougheed sighed.

"Better than nothing," he admitted. "What about *Oaths of Secrecy*?"

"She's not due here for another week. We can hit this system and be back in ten days—we'll leave an IFF-triggered beacon for *Oaths*, telling her to hide out and install her interface drive. We'll be back before too long—and as much as in some ways we have all the time in the world, I'd rather free our home sooner than later!"

CHAPTER THIRTEEN

"Hyperspace emergence in thirty seconds."

Captain Andrew Lougheed nodded his acknowledgement silently. *Of Course We're Coming Back* had been the first hyperspace-capable survey ship launched, and the only one anyone had admitted to until everything had come apart at the seams. His twenty-four-strong crew knew each other—and their captain—well by then.

He was the only UESF officer aboard, a command dropped on him by the maneuvers of the Space Force's Captains who had point-blank *refused* to see "Bloody Annie" command something so prestigious.

Lougheed had *taken* the command—he'd have been a damn fool not to—but that didn't mean he liked how he'd got it. That the woman the UESF had tried to exclude was now humanity's only hope was an irony he hoped those captains were still alive to appreciate.

"Status report?" he asked.

"*Tornado*'s people got the interface drive purring like a kitten," Mandy Tall, his engineer, reported. "Missile initiators are giving me green signals; everything is showing at hundred percent and green."

"All right, people. Let's see what we find."

"Emergence...*now*," his navigator reported. The void of hyperspace on their sensors suddenly lit up with the bright blue flare of the hyperportal and his little ship shot through it.

The G-KCL-79D system was a complete blank on their charts. They knew it was an G3-class yellow dwarf star forty-three light-years from Sol and had had hyperspace trails leading to it on a regular basis starting over fifty years before. They assumed it had a habitable planet, but as *Of Course We're Coming Back*'s sensors drank up the light from the system, Andrew Lougheed became one of the first humans to see the star's planets.

"Throw everything up on the main screen," he ordered.

Like the later XC ships, *Of Course* had been based on UESF designs. While the much-smaller survey ship's bridge didn't have the upper balcony for support staff, it followed the same horseshoe-with-a-wall-at-the-front basic design.

As the sensors absorbed light and radiation and assembled a picture of the star system, his survey officer—now also in control of the ship's handful of missiles—Sarah Laurent threw the information on the big screen.

A single gas giant marked the outer edge of the system, with an utterly massive asteroid belt that put even Sol's Kuiper Belt to shame splitting it off from the four rocky inner worlds. More data came trickling in and confirmed that the third planet was roughly equivalent to Earth, a blue-and-green marble almost three-quarters water.

"Almost makes you homesick," Laurent observed. "Gravity's a little lower than Earth, average temperature a little higher, lower axial tilt means calmer seasons. Nice world."

"I'm guessing somebody else thought so too?"

"Oh, yeah," she replied. "Artificial emissions like *whoa*. Orbitals aren't nearly as intense as Earth but...damn, that's a *space elevator*."

Even in the late twenty-second century, a space elevator was still a concept that was occasionally dusted off, compared to modern technology, and regarded as impractical with an atrocious cost-benefit ratio. But...

"That would make setting up the colony easier if they dropped one down from orbit, wouldn't it?" he noted.

"Assuming they can make the cable cheaper than we could," Laurent pointed out. "Sir, I'm not picking up anything definitively military."

"Not surprised," he told her. "I'm guessing we're looking at a handful of sublight patrol ships and defensive platforms in orbit, and they're not exactly going to stick out to this kind of high-level view. Karl—take us in. I want us to swing past the planet at ten million klicks as fast as the interface can carry us."

"Can do," Karl Strobel replied. "Bringing up the drive; we'll make the pass at point four cee."

"Record everything, Sarah," Lougheed ordered Laurent. "Set up transmission pulses so that *Tornado* will get everything we've got when they emerge."

He leaned back in his chair and eyed the planet, the closest confirmed bastion of the Imperium that had conquered his world.

"Let's see what our tentacled friends do."

OF COURSE We're Coming Back was a small ship even by the standards of the pre-*Tornado* United Earth Space Force, a twenty-two-meter cylinder a hundred and fifteen meters from bow to stern. With only twenty-four crew aboard and no weapons except those bolted to her outer hull, she had spacious working areas and powerful sensors but not much else.

As originally designed, she'd sacrificed a fifth of her length and a quarter of her volume to fusion rockets and reaction mass for them. With the rockets themselves ripped out and the reaction mass cut by three-quarters, that had left plenty of space to install the interface drive and a few other toys once Lougheed thought of something to put in there.

Unfortunately, Nova Industries designers had only really established one possible speed for the interface drive that humans could survive. While *Of Course* was a fraction of *Tornado*'s size, her speed was the same.

Lougheed's major concern was that A!Tol ships were demonstrably faster than his vessel. Playing bait for them was a risk only ameliorated by his ability to *probably* jump into hyperspace when threatened.

"Let me know the instant you see anything move," he told Laurent as they dove toward the planet.

"Dialed in a few," she noted. "So far, pretty sure they're all civvies—the ones that are moving are running away from us at a quarter-light."

"Interesting," he said aloud. "We didn't see any benefit to building lower-speed drives, but if they're *running* at that speed..."

"They probably can't go faster," Laurent agreed. "They're all smallish, too. Biggest is four hundred meters long, maybe two million tons. Hard to say for an interface drive ship."

"Tag that big ship," Lougheed ordered. "Our job isn't to chase civilians, but if nothing else in this system looks of value, Bond will probably go after that one."

"Marked in the data upload, but I think she might want to look at *that*."

"That" was a ship that had just started moving from orbit. She was big—six hundred meters long, hundred meters around—and moving *fast*. She went from at rest in orbit to point four cee in seconds, charging in the opposite direction from *Of Course*.

"I'd call her a cruiser, but she's running and we're tiny," his science officer told him. "I'm guessing military transport."

"Damn." Andrew watched the transport run. "She's going to make it into hyper before anything we send *Tornado* reaches them, but that's *exactly* what Bond wanted. Damned odd reaction, though."

"Why? It's the right one—she's cutting the chance *Tornado* will grab her by a lot."

"Because *those* are defense boats," Lougheed replied, tapping on three more moving icons—ships not much bigger than his own survey ship, though almost certainly more heavily armed. "And we're not tangling with them—get us away from them, Karl; I don't want to find out they're faster than us the hard way."

He watched the screen shift as *Of Course* reversed her vector in a matter of seconds, suddenly careening away from the planet as fast she'd been heading toward it. But the military transport kept running.

"You're right in that her stunt will *probably* save her from *Tornado*," he continued. "But it wasn't necessary to save her from us. We're bird-dogging for a privateer—but how did our tentacled friend *know* that?"

Laurent looked back at the screen, where the freighter continued to flee. It would be a few minutes until the ship knew for sure that *Of Course* was breaking off, but she looked likely to enter hyperspace before that.

"Because they've seen it done before," she said quietly. "And it wasn't us."

"No. It appears our A-tuck-Tol 'friends' *already* have a pirate problem."

CHAPTER FOURTEEN

ANNETTE WAS *ALMOST* STARTING TO GET USED TO THE STRANGE appearance of a hyperspace portal appearing out of the disturbing gray void of hyperspace, bright blue light flaring into existence from nothingness, then the starry black of the real universe emerging from the center of the portal.

Then *Tornado* flashed into the "real world" and the portal collapsed behind them, light and nothingness alike fading away into prosaic stars and blackness.

"We're receiving a data dump from *Of Course We're Coming Back*," Yahui Chan reported. "Transferring last update to tactical—timeline is minus three hundred twelve seconds."

"What have we got?" she asked Rolfson.

"*Of Course* aborted their scouting run at a full light-minute as local patrol craft started to pursue them," Rolfson noted as he skimmed the highlights Lougheed had sent them. "There is one large sublight civilian craft hiding in the asteroid belt—we have enough data to locate her—and what appeared to be a military transport was running for hyperspace."

"Military transport?" Annette asked. "When will they make the portal?"

"Roughly twenty-five seconds ago," Rolfson replied. "From our tests on the anomaly sensor, we *should* be able to ping her. We might not be able to catch up, though."

"Well, the colony and their sublight ships aren't going anywhere," *Tornado*'s Captain replied with a cold smile. "Amandine—take us back into hyperspace. Rolfson—have the anomaly scanner ready to go."

"What about Lougheed?" Kurzman asked over the link from CIC.

"We'll want him to jump and head for Rendezvous Point...Charlie, I think," Annette concluded. "Chan—let him know."

"On it." Charlie was an arbitrary point one point nine light-years away from this system. It was the farthest rendezvous point they'd set up short of Alpha Centauri. If those patrol craft proved to be hyper-capable, even that could be dangerous.

"Hyperspace reentry in ten seconds," Amandine reported.

"Missiles standing by; Major Wellesley reports his people ready to go," Rolfson said. "Scanner is coming online now."

"Hyperspace reentry...now."

A new portal flashed into existence and *Tornado* disappeared into it. The cruiser had been in the G-KCL-79D system for less than two minutes.

Nothingness enveloped the screens again, a disturbing gray *lack* of anything resembling regular light or vision. They had visibility of about a light-second. Beyond that, until very recently, Terran starships had been blind.

"What do we have, Harold?"

"I've got a ping," he announced. "Giving you a tac-plot."

The diagram that appeared on the main screen resembled nothing so much as an old-fashioned radar screen. *Tornado* sat at the center, with a large mark near her showing where the computers figured the star system was.

A third dot, roughly a light-month away in real space, showed the other ship. She was moving away from *Tornado*—fast.

"What's her speed looking like?" Annette asked.

"I'm making it point four cee on the interface, just over two thousand cee in real space," Rolfson reported.

"Amandine—can we catch her?" she demanded.

"Depends on her course," the navigator replied. "Taking us after her; let's see how the angles play out."

Tornado leapt through the nothingness toward an anomaly their eyes couldn't process.

"Can she see us?" Rolfson asked Kurzman over the link to CIC.

"Depends if she has something like the anomaly scanner," he replied. "I wouldn't bet against it."

"If she's as fast as we are and can see us coming, I'm not sure we'll catch her," Annette said aloud. "But we can use the practice. Give it your best shot, Cole. Rolfson—think we can land a hit from here?"

"Maybe, but we can't *talk* to her, so I don't know what good it would do. Probably bounce right off her shields, too."

Annette nodded. She'd reached much the same conclusion herself, but she wanted that ship. It was exactly what she was after...

"Ma'am, we have another ping!" Rolfson noted. "Behind us, other side of G-KCL. Looks like point four five cee, twenty-two fifty cee in real space."

A new dot appeared on the scanner, marked with a flashing red to designate an unknown contact.

"That's warship speed, I'm guessing," the Captain said quietly. "Any idea of her course?"

"Intercept, ma'am," Rolfson replied. "She's coming in hard and fast and she's aiming to cut us off."

"Project her vector for me," Annette ordered.

"On the plot," her tactical officer confirmed. "Remember he can change at any time, though..."

"I wrote our book on interface-drive tactics, Rolfson," she reminded him. "And we're going to need it. Forget the transport—we can't catch her, and this bastard is going to catch us unless we do something tricky."

She studied the plot and what little data they could see of the pursuing ship.

"Do we know *anything* about our friend?" she asked.

"Only that she can pull point four five cee," Rolfson admitted. "All the anomaly scanner tells us is where she is."

"Let's see what she's thinking," Annette said. "Amandine, let's pull a ninety-degree shift—*away* from Point Charlie. I don't want our friend looking for *Of Course*."

"Adjusting," the navigator responded.

"Let's see what our friend does," the Captain said slowly. If they were after *Tornado*—and she was reasonably sure they were, they would change course about...now.

"There he goes," Rolfson announced. "Wait—I have a new anomaly. Closing at point seven cee!"

"Just one?" Annette snapped. "Could we be seeing multiples together?"

Seventy percent of lightspeed had to be a missile, but the A!Tol would know one missile was no danger to *Tornado*.

"Just one," her tactical officer confirmed. "Probability is over ninety percent. That's...weird."

"And the bird's too slow," Kurzman interrupted. "A-tuck-Tol missiles were moving at point seven *five* back in Sol. Something's not adding up."

"Stand by the lasers; see if you can dial the missile in for a clear shot."

"We've only got a light-second or so before the laser disappears with the rest of the EM radiation," Rolfson admitted. "I don't think we can hit in that time."

"Then we'll take it on the armor," Annette said grimly. She had a suspicion about that missile—just one, and clearly an inferior weapon to the A!Tol navy's missiles? If she was *wrong*, however, *Tornado*'s armor could demonstrably take the hit.

The missile blasted into the tiny bubble around *Tornado* where her regular sensors could see things, screamed in to barely ten kilometers away, and promptly ripped itself apart as its interface drive self-destructed, destroying the missile in a sharp blast of light.

"What was the purpose of *that*?" Rolfson asked.

"Amandine, cut us to zero velocity," Annette snapped. "Keep us in hyperspace. Rolfson—charge the laser capacitors and make sure all launchers are loaded."

"Ma'am?" the tactical officer asked—Amandine was too busy bringing the ship to something approaching a halt relative to the system they'd left behind.

"That was a warning shot," she told them. "That's not an A-tuck-Tol ship, people. That's a *pirate* who was after the same prey we were —prey that we closely match the size and speed profile for. So, we're going to haul over like a terrified transport, let them close until we can *see* them...

"Then we're going to take down their shields with missiles and shoot to disable with lasers. Right now, we need an intact ship to study. If our friend over there wants to play pirate, I'm perfectly willing to call him competition and gut his ship for parts."

THE BOGEY'S reaction lined up disturbingly perfectly with Annette's predictions. As soon as *Tornado* slowed to a stop, the strange ship made a beeline straight for her. With the variable compression of hyperspace, the apparent pirate crossed something like a light-year of real space to reach the Terran ship, and even the light-second or so that both ships' sensors could actually *see* at represented several light-days.

"Stand by," Annette said quietly as the dot drifted closer and closer to that line. "Be *very* careful, Rolfson," she warned the bearded tactical officer. "I want to live through this—but I also want that ship intact enough to board."

Harold Rolfson confirmed her general opinion of his intelligence by ignoring her unnecessary last-minute reminders and focusing on his sensors, trying to get a clear image of their target a few fractions of a second before their target saw them. To disable the ship, he needed to know where her reactors were—and they had no idea what the other ship even *looked* like.

His captain had the same data on the screens of her own chair, and the main viewscreen was showing the zoomed-in section of the void where they expected the ship to appear. Once the two ships were within visual range of each other, the fight would likely be over in moments.

The entire bridge seemed to be holding their breaths—and then the enemy was *there*.

One moment it was simply a darker patch of void, and the next the pirate was emerging from the gray nothingness into the fuzzily delineated zone where electromagnetic radiation could still travel inside hyperspace. It was an odd-looking ship to eyes used to the squashed cigars of United Earth Space Force ships, different again from the smooth lines of the A!Tol warships that had attacked Sol.

It looked like a horseshoe made of boxes, two long rectangular chunks of hull meeting a third block at the back. Nothing about it was elegant or smooth, a rough assembly of components and dirty hull, protected by an energy screen from any threat.

"Firing," Rolfson announced. Bright streaks flashed across the empty space, interface drive missiles crossing the gap faster than the mind could process. Light flashed across the force field, rippling patterns of energy marking the futile attempts of the defense to stay together.

Twenty-four missiles hammered into the screen—none of them on a course that would hit the actual *ship*, but all on courses that would miss it by half a kilometer or less. The force field bubble lit up all around the pirate—and then collapsed.

The lasers that followed were truly invisible to the human eye, high-powered ultraviolet beams as powerful as those mounted on the

Terran battleships. Four beams pinned the ship in perfect synchronicity, punching holes through her hull and punching out every fusion reactor Rolfson had detected.

Even as *Tornado*'s tactical officer fulfilled his orders with relish, the Terran cruiser rang like a bell, the massive ship *lurching* as enemy fire struck home.

"Damage report!" Annette snapped.

"Three hits; armor is holding," Kurzman replied from CIC. "DC teams heading out to check the connections, but we seem to be okay."

"Our friend?" the Captain asked Rolfson.

"Power is down; she is...gently spinning, ma'am. One disabled pirate ship, delivered as requested."

"Good." Annette smiled, considering the ship on her screen. "Order Wellesley to launch his assault but hold his own shuttle."

"Ma'am?" Kurzman asked.

"I'll be joining him," she told her XO flatly. "I need to see what this galaxy we've wandered into looks like. You have command, Commander Kurzman."

CHAPTER FIFTEEN

Major James Arthur Valerian Wellesley was the direct descendant of the Iron Duke, the man who had crushed Napoleon at Waterloo and half a dozen other battles. The blood of over a dozen generations of soldiers and British nobility ran in his veins, honed by ten years of service in the Royal Marines before he'd been recruited by the Special Space Service.

It took every ounce of his cultural and military training to *not* call his Captain a blithering idiot to her face.

"Ma'am, this is unwise," he told Captain Bond as the blonde woman finished strapping on her suit with expert skill.

"Yes," she agreed calmly, pulling a recoilless submachine gun from the rack and loading it with rocket rounds. "But necessary. We have no idea what we're going to find, Major, and some of the decisions we'll need to make aboard that ship will be...political. Which makes them mine."

"Transmissions delays aren't that high," he pointed out. "And my people will need to keep you safe."

"Focus your people on their jobs," she snapped. "I'm perfectly capable of defending myself." She tapped the SMG. "Check my qualification scores when I re-upped, Major. But do it in the shuttle. We need to move."

Three of James' troops had already crossed to the alien ship and he was receiving reports of heavy fighting. His people *needed* Alpha Troop and the headquarters section, even if bringing his last twenty people into the fight meant he was bringing the *Captain*.

"If we still had higher authority, I would be registering a complaint," he warned Bond. "But fine, let's go."

"At this point, Major, I *am* higher authority," she replied. "That's why I need to be there."

"That's why you need to not be *shot at*," James snapped back— but he snapped back while shepherding his men onto the shuttle.

He also looked up Bond's qualification on the gun she'd grabbed, hoping for some measure of peace of mind. As the data scrolled onto his screen, he chuckled quietly to himself inside his helmet.

She wasn't lying about taking care of herself. All UESF officers were required to qualify on both rocket and slug rounds for the Force's standard twelve-millimeter automatic pistol and encouraged to qualify on the twelve-millimeter submachine-gun. Annette Bond had qualified Expert on both when she'd returned to uniform.

With a perfect score.

JAMES WATCHED CAREFULLY as McPhail slotted her shuttle neatly into the ugly hole through the pirate ship that *had* been one of the reactors. The powerful laser beam had created a perfectly circular hole one meter in diameter.

The explosive vaporization of metal and components in that circular hole, plus the escaping superheated plasma from the holed fusion reactor, had turned the wound into an irregular void over fifty meters wide clear through the ship.

The interface drive shuttle wasn't a lot *smaller* than the hole, but the pilot made flying a spacecraft into a jagged metal cave only slightly bigger than her ship look like a normal part of the job.

"We're as far in as we're getting, and I've lined up the exit hatch with what I *think* was a corridor," she told him. "Good luck, Major."

With a nod to the pilot, he rejoined his men and the Captain, gesturing for someone to open the shuttle hatch.

"Listen up, people," he said briskly. "We don't know the interior layout of this ship, but we're coming in just above where the reactor was. Everyone *else* is looking for shield generators and tech to haul out, but we're hunting for the bridge. Best guess is that it's in the connector of the horseshoe, so that's where we're headed.

"You've got a waypoint, but it won't line up with the corridors or decks. Keep moving in that direction, keep your eyes open, and stay in your teams."

"What about the locals?"

"If anyone looks like they're trying to surrender, bind them and we'll pick them up later," James ordered. Given that his people had no way to *communicate* with the pirate crew at all, that was... unlikely. "Let anyone run that tries to run. If you're facing weapons—take them down. No chances, people; I can't get replacements if you get yourselves killed!"

He checked the radar-pulse maps that the other three sixteen-soldier troops had been making as they pushed into the ship. They were nowhere near Alpha Troop and had been focused on sweeping Engineering, but the general layout of the ship was likely to be similar.

"Keep your pulse-mappers running and uploading," he ordered. "Stay in touch, watch each others' back, and MOVE OUT!"

His headquarters section moved last, with Captain Bond in the center of the patrol of four troopers accompanying the two officers. She'd taken her placement with reasonable grace, too.

James wasn't enough of a fool to go first—he was second, about a second and a half behind the SSS trooper who touched down. They already knew from the other troops that the ship still had artificial gravity and light.

It didn't seem to have much else, though, James noted. They landed in what appeared to have been a control center for the fusion reactor. The consoles were all dark, and half a dozen bodies lay where they'd been blown across the room. The aliens were wearing vac-suits designed to withstand vacuum, not the force of the probably still-fusing plasma that had ripped the wall away.

He focused on the bodies for a few moments, letting his helmet camera record them. Six individuals of what he guessed to be four separate species. Without time to open the armor, he could only classify them as A!Tol, tall bipedal, small bipedal, and what appeared to be a hexapod the size of a horse. Three of the six were the hexapods, but the only one he recognized was the distinct many-tentacled form of Earth's conquerors.

"No wounded, sir," one of his troopers noted. "These guys died instantly."

"They have vac-suits, same as our people," Bond interjected. "Anyone who survived would have retreated past emergency airlocks. You'll start hitting resistance when you hit air, Major."

"Same as training back home," he replied. "Let's move, people."

THE EMERGENCY AIRLOCK was about ten meters farther into the wrecked ship, a somewhat featureless slab of metal that would have slammed down as soon as atmosphere started to be lost. A control panel had swung open when the airlock door had closed off the section, but was flashing a white screen with strange characters on it.

"I can't *read* this, but I'd say they locked it out after they used it," James' electronics specialist said after looking at it for less than a second. "Give me thirty seconds—I don't care what language they speak; the rest of the troops report they use wires same as we do."

The woman was good to her word, and the lock slid partially open under her ministrations. James led the team into the lock and glanced back at the specialist.

"How long to open the other side?"

"On your order," she replied.

"Everyone expect trouble," he ordered, pulling a grenade from his webbing and standing to the side. The gap between the two emergency bulkheads was big enough for all six of them with room to spare—but not enough room to allow for cover. "Open it."

Two wires James could barely see crossed and the inner door started sliding upwards. As soon as the gap was large enough, he rolled the grenade under it.

The metal floor vibrated under his feet as the weapon went off, a ricocheting shard of metal bouncing under the door and pinging off his leg armor.

"Go!"

Two of his troopers ducked under the rising door, covering the hallway with their weapons—opening fire almost immediately at targets only they could see. One slammed back into the door, grunting over the network as *something* hit him.

"Cover him!" James was through the door a moment later, realizing too late that Captain Bond was right beside him.

The hall was filled with smoke and shadows, several bodies stacked up where his grenade had shocked a hastily prepared defense. A trio of vac-suited aliens were firing at his people, and even as James opened fire, one of them went down.

Seconds later, it was over. Seven aliens lay dead in the hallway of their ship and James turned to check on his trooper.

"I'm fine," Karimi snapped. "Didn't penetrate the vac-suit armor."

"Everybody still up?" James asked. A chorus of affirmatives answered him. "All right, folks—watch for bad guys and follow the bouncing ball."

ANNETTE FOLLOWED the Service troopers carefully. She needed to be here—seeing the inside of what a reasonably "modern" ship in the A!Tol Imperium looked like had value all of its own—but she also knew they were trained and prepared for this situation and she was not.

As they pushed deeper into the ship, though, she was linked into their tactical net, collating information from the four troops and thirteen four- and five-trooper patrols sweeping through the enemy ship. Their micro-pulse maps were giving her a surprisingly solid idea of what the ship looked like overall, as did their encounters with the enemy.

The ship was *big*. Bigger than *Tornado* by a significant margin—two hundred meters long, three times as wide, a far boxier structure. But despite its size, they'd run into a limited number of crew—alive or dead. The mapping was starting to suggest that a chunk of the ship was blocked off, probably cargo space.

Whatever she was *now*, the big boxy ship had clearly been built as a cargo hauler—on a *massive* scale. *Tornado* wouldn't fit in the pirate's cargo compartments—but one of the older UESF battleships that had fought alongside her might have.

Even so, they were running into far fewer people than she would have expected. *Tornado* had a crew of nine hundred. She would have expected about the same aboard the pirate ship, but the SSS teams had run into barely two hundred aliens so far.

"Major, either this ship is *extremely* automated, or they've pulled their crew back to protect something," she warned Wellesley. "*I* would be arming crewmembers to protect the bridge in their place."

They were drawing close to where she figured the bridge was as well. If there were a few hundred aliens taking up defensive positions somewhere, they were going to run into them here.

"We could hold up, bring in the rest of the company," he suggested. He didn't sound enthused.

"No—I'm worried what they might still be able to do," Annette replied. Even without main power, it was possible the crew might manage to fire off a missile salvo and damage, if not destroy, *Tornado.* "Just be ready for trouble."

"Sir, ma'am," the point trooper suddenly said over the tactical net. "I think you need to see this."

She let Wellesley lead the way, her own weapon covering the Major as they rounded the corner to see what the patrol had found.

Annette stopped dead when she saw it, looking at the scene in surprise. So far, they'd run into a handful of defenders and seen bodies in the areas of the initial hits. Now, the corridor in front of them looked like a slaughterhouse.

The corridor widened out into a gallery linking several levels, with a clear set of paths leading up toward where she guessed the bridge was. The open space served a double purpose of easing access while allowing clear lines of fire to help protect that access if attacked.

The pirates *had* been prepared to do so, in a fashion that *would* have required Wellesley to bring up the rest of his company—except everyone left in the gallery was dead. At least thirty or forty vac-suits were scattered through the space, representing at least eight different species.

The hexapods they'd seen in the first room were the single largest group, though outnumbered by the rest of the dead. Studying the bodies, she realized that about half of the centaur-like creatures seemed to be wearing heavier armor—and the ones wearing heavier armor seemed to have been defending the bridge.

"Wellesley, you see the ones in heavier armor?" she asked

"Yeah. Looks like those were the actual boarding troops," the Major observed. "And it looks like a good chunk of the *rest* of the crew turned on them."

"I think we need to get to the bridge, Major," Annette told him. "Something *really* weird is going on here."

"They're aliens, ma'am. How do we judge what's weird?"

She shook her head at Wellesley and gestured for him to lead the way.

"I speak fluent starship, Major—which also tells me the bridge is that way."

———

EXITING the gallery left them in a corridor leading toward a set of heavy security doors. Someone had set up a crude barricade of metal tables and other objects. More bodies were stacked up in front of the barricade, and the point man dodged back around a wall as gunfire greeted him.

"What have we got?" Major Wellesley asked immediately.

"Looks like six of the centaur types and a lot of dead friends," the point man replied, running the few seconds of footage backward on the tacnet. "Machine guns—*big* ones—and probably got grenades and such on the webbing. Bit of a headache."

"Got a suggestion, Corporal?"

Annette was studying the footage herself as the discussion went on. Unless she was severely mistaken, they were looking at the end result of a failed mutiny—one that had almost certainly occurred *after* she'd disabled the ship.

"Use the Kay-Forties to bounce grenades down on them," the point man said instantly.

Annette had no idea what a "K-40" was—beyond a vague memory of it being an attachment to the SSS's standard assault rifle—but Wellesley was nodding his agreement.

"Captain, would you think there was anything in that corridor us blasting to hell is going to cause issues?"

Apparently, since he had her, the Major was willing to use her knowledge. She checked over the footage again.

"I doubt it," she replied. "Doesn't look like they're any more inclined to put volatile lines near the bridge than we are. Blow it up all you want, Major."

"Good. Corporal Danzig has a great idea," Wellesley told his men. "Load your Kay-Forties, high vee frag grenades."

Each of the Special Space Service Troopers pulled a round cylinder off of their webbing and slid it home in the smooth-barrelled launcher attached to the bottom of their rifles—the K-40 under-barrel grenade launcher, Annette finally remembered.

"Let the guns call the angle," the Major ordered. "Fire on the ricochet...NOW!"

Five weapons coughed, firing grenades into the far wall. The explosives bounced around the corner, hopefully ricocheting into the barricade, and then detonated.

"Go!" Wellesley bellowed. He grabbed Annette's shoulder before she could obey, though, physically yanking her back from the line of fire.

"*Not* you," he said flatly.

A moment later, the gunfire ended and the two officers went around the corner. The guards were dead, mostly down to the grenades and the survivors finished off by gunfire.

"Nice work," Wellesley complimented his men. "Danzig—prep a charge. *Carefully.* We're almost certainly going to want *something* from the bridge."

The trooper nodded, his grin visible even through his helmet, and started patting his webbing, pulling out a detonator and other bits from the pockets and holders on his armor. For a few seconds, most of the SSS team was looking at him, not at the bridge door.

Annette was more concerned about the bridge—and was the first to spot it opening. Someone had spent a *lot* of money on that door: it was huge, made of heavily reinforced metal, and went from fully closed to wide open in fractions of a second.

There wasn't even time to shout a warning. *Tornado*'s Captain simply opened fire as more of the centaurs charged out. Four more of the centaur-like aliens, one of them the biggest she'd seen yet, charged out with machine guns in their hands.

The Special Space Service trained *extremely* competent troops.

Distracted by the prospect of explosives or not, one of the team had been standing watch with her eyes on the door. Her assault rifle fire joined the spray from Annette's gun, putting the lead two hexapodal centaurs down in the first few seconds.

Machine gun fire slammed into the trooper, sending her flying as heavy bullets hit her armor. Annette focused her fire on the big ones, walking explosive rocket rounds up the first creature's torso and knocking them back into the bridge.

The last hexapod was still moving, though, the big machine gun lining up with Annette. Time seemed to slow as the captain stared down the barrel of the weapon—and then the barrel lurched sideways with its owner.

What looked like nothing so much as a *chair* had slammed into the alien's rear flank. She wasn't sure if the cracking sound was the furniture or the centaur-like alien's legs, but before the creature could do more than turn, a *massive* form slammed into it.

Thick armored tentacles wrapped around the hexapod's throat and a metallic box on the big A!Tol's central torso spat a series of sibilant hisses Annette couldn't understand. The suddenly pinned alien went limp, clearly dropping the gun, and submitted.

The armored A!Tol, the biggest of the small number of the immense tentacled creatures Annette had seen to date, released the hexapodal centaur and slowly, keeping all of its tentacles where the Terrans could see them, tapped a command on the box.

"We surrender," the voice said in flat, mechanical English. "I will order the remaining crew to surrender to your troops. There should be no more death."

"You're the Captain?" Annette managed to force out, stunned that this alien could communicate with her.

The A!Tol's tentacles shivered in a way that sent shivers down the Terran Captain's back.

"No." A tentacle pointed at the biggest of the hexapodal centaur corpses. "*She* was the Captain. She refused to surrender when I said I had a translation program for your species. The...crew objected."

"Will they all obey you?"

"I am Ki!Tana," the creature said in that flat tone. "I was First Sword. They will obey."

The translation program was clearly being a bit *too* literal there, but Annette got the gist. This creature was the XO. With the Captain dead—at Annette's hands, no less!—the crew would obey it.

"Order them to stand down," she commanded. "Then we'll talk."

CHAPTER SIXTEEN

It became rapidly apparent that most of the crew had been avoiding Major Wellesley's soldiers. Once Ki!Tana sent out her unintelligible orders, aliens of all shapes and sizes started to materialize out of dark corners and side corridors the Special Space Service troopers had missed. They appeared with their hands or other manipulators raised, clearly a relatively universal gesture for "I am unarmed."

There were...a lot fewer than Annette would have expected. She doubted her ability to read Ki!Tana's body language, but the drooping of the alien's tentacles suggested that it had been expecting more as well.

"No one else seems to be showing up," Wellesley finally told Annette. "I make it one hundred eighty-six prisoners, including Ki-tuck-Tana here."

"Are you certain?" the alien asked, the computer-generated voice creepily monotone.

"It's possible that some of your crew aren't coming out of hiding," the SSS Major said calmly, his tone suggesting more sympathy than

Annette would have expected the man to feel for a big tentacled alien. "That's everyone who's surrendered."

"This ship had a crew of six hundred and fifty," Ki!Tana said. The voice was still monotone, but it seemed to be learning. There was a *hint* of emotion to it, which was more than it had started with. "Between the strikes on the power centers, your soldiers, and Kiki-theth's madness, we have lost so many."

"You attacked *us*," Annette pointed out.

"We did," Ki!Tana agreed. "And many may have deserved worse fates. But they were my friends. As are those who live." The big tentacled creature shook, its manipulator tendrils shivering in a way that was only slightly less creepy on multiple exposures.

"But I must speak to your leader about the future now," it continued.

"I *am* our leader," Annette told the alien. "I command the United Earth Space Force's Operation Privateer, our countermeasure against your species' conquest of my world."

No point mentioning that Operation Privateer was three ships, two of which were effectively unarmed. The A!Tol pirate didn't need to know that.

"Ah. You are here. And you killed Kikitheth yourself. That does make this easier." Several manipulator tendrils waved toward a door leading off from the bridge. "Shall we use the captain's office? We have mutual value to discuss."

Even through the armored vac-suit, Annette could see Wellesley tighten. He might actually let her walk into a closed room with an alien roughly three times her size, but she was going to have to explicitly order it—and even without saying a word, he was *right*.

"Of course," Annette agreed cheerfully. "Major Wellesley? If you and one of your troopers would accompany us."

A *horrible* clacking sound emerged from the big A!Tol, and Annette realize the creature was snapping its beak together repeatedly—something the translator wasn't translating and yet...it was laughing. The alien was *laughing* at her.

"I am no threat now," Ki!Tana told her. "But bring your soldiers."

―――――

THE PIRATE CAPTAIN'S office was centered around a long couch, clearly designed for the big, hexapodal centaur who'd commanded the ship. The other seats were closer to stools, simple arrangements that worked for most species. Both Annette and Ki!Tana were able to sit with ease.

The rest of the room looked like a junker's paradise. The walls were filled with displays of choice bits of machinery and other trophies pulled from victims across the years. A banner of some kind covered the back wall, its sigils and heraldry entirely unfamiliar to Annette. Pride of place amongst the trophies was a gold circle containing what Annette realized, after a moment's inspection, was a tentacle holding a sword.

"Kikitheth was so proud of that one," Ki!Tana said, gesturing at the circle. "The commissioning seal of an Imperial Navy destroyer. Poor ship wandered into a pirate muster. They took the destroyer, but Kikitheth commanded the only ship to survive—of *twelve*."

"This ship is no equal to your military," Annette noted carefully. "They are faster, with superior weapons."

"Indeed," the A!Tol confirmed. "*Your* ship, however, was slow enough that we mistook her for a transport. Your weapons, inferior, your armor...impossible. Interesting combination."

"I am Captain Annette Bond, privateer for Terra. This is Major James Wellesley, my boarding team commander. You wanted to talk. Talk," Annette ordered.

"Your ship, Captain Bond, has no shields. Low-efficiency, brute-force engines. Slow missiles. Lasers instead of proton beams. You boarded my ship to steal our tech."

She winced. The A!Tol was dangerously perceptive.

"Perhaps," she allowed. Everyone was still in vac-suits, which helped conceal her reaction from the alien who *probably* wouldn't identify it. "Do you have a point, Ki!Tana?"

She *tried* to imitate the mouth-click the translator was using as a substitute for the A!Tol's beak snap. She was somewhat pleased with the result, though it was going to take a lot more practice until she was *comfortable* with the sound.

The alien responded with the same beak-clacking as before. Ki!Tana, it appeared, found many things funny.

"While my function was as First Sword, my relationship with Kikitheth was...one of ownership," the alien told her. "In exchange for settling my debts—which were large—Kikitheth owned my time, skill, and mind for twenty long-cycles. As you have defeated Kikitheth in reasonably fair combat, under the same pirate code that deal was concluded under, that contract now passes to you."

"Didn't you instigate a mutiny against your previous contract-holder?" Wellesley interjected. "This sounds like something of a poisoned fruit, ma'am."

"I am afraid the translator does not handle metaphor well without practice," Ki!Tana replied. "But I must note that I did not intend to start a mutiny. I advised my captain and owner that I possessed a translation program that would allow us to surrender. Since I assumed she was not *mad*, I did so on an open channel so our crew would not needlessly sacrifice themselves."

"And instead, this Kikitheth chose to fight," Annette said. "Exactly what does this 'contract' entail, Ki!Tana?"

"You are obliged to provide food and board for myself and to pay a stipend to fund my hobbies—some of which, such as collecting odd translation programs, have proven to be of surprising value! In exchange, as I said, you own my time, skill and mind for the fourteen long-cycles remaining in my contract."

"Why are you telling me this?" Annette asked. "If you had said nothing, I would have had no reason to believe this existed."

"It is a duty under the contract and the code," Ki!Tana replied.

"Also, you intrigue me, and there is little left in this galaxy I find truly intriguing."

"So, if we wanted you to help gut this ship for parts to upgrade ours, you'd do that under your contract?" Annette asked slowly.

"This ship is now useless," the A!Tol told her, and the translator's tone seemed even flatter than usual. "With the destruction of the power cores, we lack the ability to generate a hyperspace portal—so we are trapped. We must either be rescued or taken prisoner. Gutting this ship for parts does not hurt *me*, provides value to my new owner, and allows me to argue for the sake of my former crew."

"And what argument would you make for them?"

"On my own, I have the knowledge to identify parts that should improve your own systems, transport the shield generator, and similarly provide value to you," Ki!Tana said. "With the surviving crew of *this* ship, I could do so much more efficiently and leverage their knowledge to aid your upgrades."

"Even assuming I am willing to trust *you*, how could I trust them?"

"You intend to be a privateer," the A!Tol replied. "Pay them. A crewman's share of the value of any loot—you may find it wise to provide such to your existing crew as well. Loyalty to the uniform of a conquered world only goes so far."

Annette sighed. She *wished* she could argue.

"You could upgrade our ship and install the shield generator on your own?" she asked. She wasn't sure she believed that.

"Captain Bond, I was working on starships when your race was just realizing that they *could* reach orbit," Ki!Tana said. "Allow me to bring my old crew with me, and I will have this ship's finest gear installed in your ship in a few cycles. If you leave us, we will die regardless. Let us be your guide to this great galaxy."

"We need it," Wellesley murmured over a private radio link. "If it'll help us...we need its knowledge. Ma'am, its translation program alone could save lives."

Annette sighed again.

"Very well, Ki!Tana," she said softly. "I accept your contract and your service. I suspect feeding you and my soon-to-be crewmembers is going to be a headache, but we need you."

Unspoken, though she suspected the alien understood perfectly, was that she was also unwilling to leave the survivors to die in hyperspace. Her mission might require her to do things over the next few years she would regret—but she saw no reason to start just yet.

THE PIRATE SHIP—ANNETTE hadn't bothered to learn its name and didn't see any reason to do so—might have been crippled, but it still managed to maintain gravity and light from her auxiliary power. The Terran captain wondered just what that auxiliary power was—her own ship had massive arrays of batteries that would run emergency systems for about twenty-four hours. If the pirate ship's reserve power was equally limited, it could eventually be a problem.

For now, there were air, gravity, and light in the eating area that Wellesley's men had escorted their prisoners to. Everyone was still in their vac-suits, which limited Annette's ability to distinguish species, but it looked like the survivors were from seven separate species.

Ki!Tana, interestingly, was the only A!Tol among the prisoners. She made a mental note to check in on that later, but she was starting to suspect that Ki!Tana was of very few A!Tol aboard—and a very strange A!Tol at that.

"How do you *feed* this kind of variety?" she asked the tentacled alien,

"UP," her new companion answered. "Universal Protein. Plus species-specific vitamin powders. We'll want to bring those stores with us, but it's all artificial and relatively easily manufactured, given access to carbon."

Annette's understanding was that proteins from completely

different biospheres would likely be toxic to each other. Apparently, the A!Tol had fixed that problem, along with allowing those species to talk to each other.

"Here," Ki!Tana said abruptly, opening a cupboard and pulled out several boxes and sets of earbuds. "These are for Indiri, but I think they will fit your ears." Manipulator tentacles flowed over the translator device for a moment and lights flashed on both Ki!Tana's own translator and the new one.

"I've downloaded your language and set it as the user language," it continued. "It won't translate emotion initially. The software is smart, but it can only do so much without live experience."

"So, the more we humans use it, the better the software will get?" Annette asked.

"Yes," the alien agreed. "Once we have the crew in service, we can reconfigure these for all of your personnel. Any being you encounter will have one. The A!Tol Imperium has twenty-nine member species. Few can learn that many languages."

"Major, is the air safe?" Annette asked.

"I'm not sure I trust the emergency air to last for long, but yes."

"All right. Let's show our potential new crew who they're going to be working for."

Facing the collected prisoners, she removed the helmet from her vac-suit to place the earbuds in her ears. For the first time, she breathed the air that the pirates had used on their ship, and it was surprisingly bearable. She was half-expecting to smell filth and debris and for the ship to be half-maintained.

Instead, the air was crisp, fresh—with a hint of something that smelled vaguely like lemon. It was better than the air on *Tornado*.

Shaking her head slightly, she attached the box of the translator to her chest and joined Ki!Tana facing the alien prisoners. She was vaguely aware of Wellesley doing the same thing but replacing his helmet once he had the translator buds in.

Two of the Major's troops—over thirty soldiers—guarded the

walls and exits from the big room. The others were sweeping the ship for any more survivors and checking on specific concerns that Ki!Tana had told them could risk the ship's integrity *before* they were done looting her.

"Crew," Ki!Tana said loudly, the big A!Tol's voice echoing its sibilants and clicks through the room. The translator picked up the word easily, and Annette figured the rest of the crew was wearing the same devices. "We've been defeated. Kikitheth is dead, slain by the leader of these humans. You are all aware of my contract with Kikitheth. It now passes to Captain Annette Bond, who leads these humans.

"She has been given a mission familiar to us all: to act as a pirate acquiring resources and tech to aid her homeworld. Since we now lack an employer, I have suggested that she hire us to assist in upgrading her vessel and completing our mission. Captain?"

Tentacles flicked in Annette's direction and she stepped up, hoping that the translator would render her speech into something the aliens could understand. She barely trusted the device still, so simple was better.

"You will die if you stay here," she told them. "In trade for helping us strip this ship of parts of value and tracking new targets, you will receive the same share of the loot as my own crew."

Which was, admittedly, a ratio they were going to have to quietly work out—probably with Ki!Tana's help.

"We will also feed you and, if we end up somewhere it is safe for you to do so, drop you off and allow you to make your own way from there. My ship has enough space to provide you decent quarters, and you may bring personal items with you.

"Ki!Tana has convinced me you will be of value. Prove her right."

She stepped back, gesturing for the big alien to handle the rest.

"Anyone who wants to stick with me, come forward," the tentacled creature told her crewmates. "You know *my* honor if nothing else."

That seemed a winning argument. All of the surviving pirates stepped forward, forming a surprisingly orderly line to meet with Ki!Tana and Annette.

"James, touch base with Kurzman and Metharom," she told the Major quietly over their private link—turning the translator off first. "Let them know we just picked up two hundred more crew who we're going to need to keep a *very* sharp eye on."

CHAPTER SEVENTEEN

"I THINK WE'RE DONE HERE," METHAROM TOLD ANNETTE, THE engineer reviewing a set of specifications of the pirate cruiser *Rekiki's Fang*. The captain and her enforcers' hexapodal, centaur-like species were apparently Rekiki. "From what Ki-tuck-Tana tells me and the data she's provided, we've removed the shield generator, significant components of their interface drive—components that should enable us to improve the efficiency of our drive—and emptied their magazines."

"Do we trust that...thing's information?" Kurzman asked. "These missiles are impressive, but I'm worried to fire them!"

Annette met her XO's gaze levelly, then glanced around the rest of the officers in the plain conference room. If matters continued to progress to her satisfaction, they'd probably move one of the broad stools the A!Tol had brought with her—and, apparently, Ki!Tana *was* a her—in there so the alien could join the staff briefings.

Things were still too unsure with their new friends and crew to do that just yet, as Kurzman's comment proved out.

"While I'm not entirely sure that this 'contract' Ki!Tana has is nearly as 'you kill it, you bought it' as she says it is, she does appear to be honestly giving her loyalty to me," she pointed out. "Without her help, we probably wouldn't have been able to identify the *shield generator*, let alone the components we've pulled to upgrade the rest of our systems. I'm not going to, say, cancel the program in the AI that's monitoring every move of our new alien crewmembers," she noted, "but so far, they've played fair with us."

"I'm left with the conclusion that Kikitheth *really* pissed off her crew at some point, and not just by refusing to surrender," Wellesley said. "They turned on her and the other members of her species far too quickly and violently for there not to have been underlying issues."

"Agreed," Annette replied. "For now, we watch Ki!Tana and the rest of the aliens, but otherwise, we treat them like what they have asked to become: members of a privateer crew."

"Paid in shares," Kurzman noted. "Do we even *have* a structure for shares for privateer loot?"

"To my surprise when I looked it up, yes," *Tornado*'s Captain told him. "Of course, it's for *reclaimed* pirate loot and assumes that a significant chunk goes back to the original owners. I've run it by Ki!Tana, though, and if we designate that equivalent chunk for 'ship operations and upgrades,' it's an acceptable set of rules."

It also put ten percent of everything in *her* pocket, which she had every intent of also funneling back into the ship. A tap on her com unit flipped it to her senior officers.

"Unless someone has a major complaint, I plan on using this structure," she continued. "I'll be including Ki!Tana in the senior officer share, which will reduce your shares, sorry."

Given that the scheme, as modified, put forty percent into the ship, ten percent to the captain, five to the XO and split *fifteen* amidst the remaining senior officers, even Ki!Tana's inclusion meant each of them would get three percent of any loot they took.

"This is academic until we actually *take* a prize," Rolfson pointed out. Her tactical officer had apparently decided to braid his hair and beard while she'd been aboard *Rekiki's Fang*, and now looked even more like a Viking than he normally did. It seemed appropriate.

"Our first step is to pick up *Of Course We're Coming Back* and return to Alpha Centauri to meet *Oaths of Secrecy*," she reminded them. "We'll finish our upgrades while we do that, and we'll digest what *Oaths'* data shows us about the occupation of Earth.

"After that, Ki!Tana and *Rekiki's Fang*'s computers have given us a number of possibilities. I am confident that the share of booty will not stay an academic issue for long," she promised them.

DESPITE ITS RELATIVELY SMALL SIZE, *Of Course*'s small crew meant the living space provided to her Captain was, in Andrew Lougheed's opinion, excessive. He had a three-room suite—living room, office, bedroom—almost as large as the rooms would be in an apartment on Earth.

Excessive for a ship or not, he could pace from one end of his office, through his living room, to the other end of his bedroom in forty-six steps. In the two *days* since *Of Course* had arrived at the rendezvous point, he'd paced it often enough that the count was burned into his mind.

Small as his crew was, he still couldn't allow his crew to see how agitated he was. *Tornado* had gone after what appeared to be a freighter, but it hadn't looked likely that she'd catch the ship. In that case, he would have expected Captain Bond to return to Rendezvous Point Charlie to make a plan of attack to raid the system itself.

Instead, his ship had sat in deep space, waiting for her return. There hadn't been an agreed-upon wait time, but at some point he'd have to give up. Without *Tornado*...all the two scout ships could really do was go home and surrender. *Oaths of Secrecy*, built in secret as a spy ship, might be deadlier than his own vessel, but it was unlikely she could be deadly enough to act as a privateer against the magnitude of enemy they faced.

His com buzzed. Andrew stopped pacing, glancing over the mirror to make sure he didn't look too disheveled, and then stepped up to the intercom in his office.

"Lougheed."

"Sir, *Tornado* has arrived," his watch officer told him hurriedly. "Captain Bond wants to speak with you immediately."

"Relay her to here," he ordered. "Move us into formation with *Tornado*; we'll move on Bond's command."

"Aye, aye, sir."

A moment later, the image of his bridge faded into the image of a similar office aboard *Tornado* and the blond hair and worn face of Captain Annette Bond.

"Captain Lougheed, it's good to see you."

"Good to see you too, Captain Bond," he replied. "I was starting to worry."

"I apologize for the delay; we had an unexpected encounter," she told him. "Someone else was pursuing the same ship and mistook us for them. We were, Captain, in a case of delicious irony, attacked by pirates."

"Is everyone all right?" he asked. He presumed if there was notable damage, his people would have told him, but that didn't mean there hadn't been casualties.

"We have a number of wounded SSS troopers but no fatalities," Bond said. "We suckered them and took their ship partially intact. Pirates having all the loyalty of mercenaries, it seems, we now have almost two hundred new crew and a pile of *very* interesting parts and components in my cargo hold."

"I didn't know *Tornado* had a cargo hold."

"We do," the cruiser's captain replied. "Storage for consumables, if nothing else. We also have several very large voids in our hull to allow for upgrades, which were readily converted into storage space."

"Alien crew? How are we even talking to them?"

"We also acquired translator tech. I'll have Metharom forward the design and software over—we can build the hardware surprisingly easily, but the software is...not very compatible with ours." Bond shook her head. "We have yet to manage to interface the translation software with our own main systems, so we're running on personal translators for now."

"Are we talking universal translators here, ma'am?" Andrew asked carefully. *That* he knew was impossible, but other things he knew to be impossible hadn't been...

"No, just *very* smart learning software loaded with a number of languages. If I'm following what I've been told correctly, the software we have has the most and second-most common languages for each species in the A!Tol Imperium."

She nailed the click perfectly, to Andrew's surprise. Apparently, *Tornado*'s captain had been practicing.

"We're going to need some time to sort out building this hardware into *Tornado*," Bond continued. "We picked up a number of engineers, but the biggest value is an A!Tol named Ki!Tana. She's...apparently sworn herself directly to my service—it's complicated," Bond said in response to Andrew's surprised eyebrow.

"We're watching all of the aliens carefully, but we're going to need their technical skills to get everything working. At a minimum, I want the damn shield generator online before we go hunting again."

"So, Centauri then, ma'am?" Lougheed asked.

"Indeed. Rest, hardware upgrades, check in with *Oath of Silence*. Then we see how complicated we can make the A!Tol's life around Sol."

CHAPTER EIGHTEEN

Tornado and *Of Course We're Coming Back* had been in Alpha Centauri for almost half an hour before they saw any sign of *Oaths of Secrecy*. Despite being even more delayed than planned, Annette was starting to worry that the second scout ship had failed to escape Sol—a situation that would require them to abandon the caches *Oaths* had placed.

"Any sign?" she asked softly as the big cruiser slid into orbit of AB2, directly above the volcano holding the cache of missiles and supplies. "I know she's supposed to be sneaky, but..."

"Nothing," Rolfson replied. "The entire system is dead, no starship signatures. Feeling real lonely, boss."

"Keep sweeping," Annette ordered. "If she isn't here, we're going to have to do a fast pickup and find somewhere else to do Ki!Tana's upgrades."

The big A!Tol was on the bridge now, listening in through her translator. Annette had noticed the alien's skin changed colors with her moods, and was starting to even pick up some of the more common ones. Somehow, the fact that her planet's conquerors *literally* wore their feelings on their skin amused her.

"Wait...ma'am, we're receiving a transmission from the surface," Chan reported.

"The surface?"

Rolfson answered his Captain's question by zooming in on the caldera holding the Nova Industries cache to show the black-painted hull of *Oaths of Secrecy* tucked into the side of the crater above the cache entrance. From the angle, Annette judged that anyone who wasn't directly above the volcano would have no chance of detecting the ship.

"I have Captain Sade for you on the radio," Chan said after a moment.

"Put her on," Annette ordered with a small shake of her head.

Captain Elizabeth Sade, Nova Industries, was the type of woman who made Annette feel like an over-aged battle-ax. Sade was space-born, which gave an ethereal grace to her hundred and eighty–centimeter height and carefully braided crown of golden hair. Annette had seen Sade emerge from hard engineering work still looking completely put together except for a few smudges that managed to make her look *better*.

She'd wondered just what had happened to Sade when the woman hadn't ended up as an XC test captain. Now she knew—Sade had been pulled into an even blacker corner of Elon Casimir's operations than Annette had.

"Elizabeth Sade," she greeted the other woman. "Were you trying to give me a heart attack and force me to abandon my supply caches?"

"It was easier to install an entire new engine without relying on artificial gravity," Sade replied, her eyes then widening in shock as she spotted Ki!Tana. "Wait, why do you have one of those *tentacled fucks* aboard your ship?"

"Control yourself," Annette snapped. Sade was...almost a friend, but that was still a line she was unwilling to see crossed. "You'll be briefed, but for now, Ki!Tana is part of my crew and works directly for me.

"We needed data on the A!Tol. She's also an engineer, which is going to keep us all busy here for a few days. She's on our side."

"'She'," the younger Captain repeated slowly, looking like the word tasted disgusting to her. "I don't know what side 'she' is on, but I know what her people have been doing back home."

"I'll need a briefing," Annette told her. "Report aboard *Tornado* at eighteen hundred hours. I'll have my staff ready." She grimaced. "I can't imagine I'm going to like it."

"It could be worse," Sade admitted. "But…it's not pretty."

ANNETTE LED Captain Sade into the conference room that had become their de facto staff briefing space, making sure that all of her human officers were present. Ki!Tana might be required later, but Annette hadn't even had to *ask* the alien not to be present for this part of the meeting—she'd volunteered to miss it. The A!Tol seemed to understand that this had to be a meeting for the humans.

"It's good to see you, Elizabeth," Lougheed greeted his fellow scout captain. "Did you get your upgrades complete?"

"We have an interface drive same as everyone else now," Sade confirmed. "Not quite sure what I'm going to do with it without a missile or laser to my name, but I've got it."

"We'll get there," Annette told her. "For now, well, you were in Sol later than any of us. What happened?"

Sade sighed, nodding slowly.

"We left a week after the invasion," she said quietly. "A positive sign, I guess, is that the news was still broadcasting at that point without much interference."

"Useful as propaganda, I suppose," Kurzman said.

"They were being sufficiently uncomplimentary to the conquerors that I'm not sure that's the case," Sade admitted. "It appeared, from what we were receiving anyway, that the A-tuck-Tol had every intention of maintaining at least some free press." She shook her head. "I wouldn't have expected it, but they left the press mostly alone. We had other sources as well, relaying through UESF Intelligence, to confirm the news reports as well. The full files are being transferred to *Tornado* and *Of Course* as we speak, but we are talking a week's worth of news reports."

"You were there, Captain. Summarize," Annette ordered.

Sade swallowed and nodded, almost shivering as she considered how to present her thoughts.

"The world changed in a week," she finally said. "Hell, the *universe* changed in a week. I don't know how to summarize that, but I'll try.

"First, it's important to know there was no...indiscriminate bombardment. The aliens seem to regard civilian locations as safe zones, even when it puts them in danger."

"That sounds like there *has* been bombardment?" Rolfson asked.

Sade nodded sharply, taking a deep breath before she continued.

"They demanded the surrenders of the national militaries as soon as they reached orbit," she continued slowly. "Most complied. The United States and the Russians didn't. They'd both apparently been stockpiling surface-to-space missiles—hundreds of them.

"It...didn't end well," she told them all. "After the first launches, the aliens hit the launch sites with kinetic strikes from orbit. The American sites were far away from civilians—they leveled them all. Some of the Russian sites...weren't.

"The aliens didn't bombard those. They landed troops and tanks and took them out on the ground. No civilian casualties that I know of—I don't even know how they can be that careful."

"You can't pull off that kind of response without deaths," Chan objected. "People died."

"Yes," Sade said sharply. "A lot of people. Soldiers, only doing their jobs, only following orders—trying to protect people. But...very few civilians."

"They don't want martyrs," Annette noted grimly.

"After that, they dissolved everything above the city level for government," Sade continued. "With power-armored troops—not even the tentacled bastards themselves, a couple of other species—to enforce the order. They ordered all the military people to go home. Said there'll be pensions for all soldiers, but...how much paperwork can you get done in a week?" She shrugged. "They might keep their word on that, they might not.

"There were riots," she said in a disturbingly level voice. "*Everywhere*. They told local law enforcement to get the situations under control—or they would."

"What happened?"

"Some places...overreacted. Others...did nothing. Both had the same result—power-armored troops, low-level fly-bys. They have some sort of mass stunning weapon, knocked out entire crowds with a single pulse. Fewer people died where the bastards did intervene than where they didn't.

"Five days in, they introduced a new planetary governor. Some mess of syllables I can't pronounce; it's in the news feeds. One of the big tentacled bastards. She's apparently appointing continental sub-governors to which the existing municipal governments will report."

Sade shook her head.

"So far, the reports I had suggested they were at least *talking* to the mayors and city governments they've left in place, but everyone higher has just been sent home. There was some organized resistance when they landed in the US, but..."

"How bad?" Annette asked. No one *else* in the room was from the United States, but she knew her countrymen. She doubted they'd rolled over for any invader, even an alien one.

"I don't know how they did it, but they got ten goddamn divisions into the field against the landings in Washington DC. Tanks, helicopters; it looked for a few hours that they'd make a real fight of it. Then Tan-tuck-Shallegh told them to surrender or be forced to."

The ethereal blonde captain shivered.

"No offense, ma'am, but they were *Americans*. Their response was...pithy. It turned out no armor, tank, or defense system we have can protect against their stunners. They knocked out over *a hundred thousand soldiers* in a single pass. Their biggest difficulty was finding a way to keep the fucking *chopper pilots* alive.

"They took out the American military resistance in under fifteen minutes with no fatalities," Sade concluded. "Civilian resistance continues, but their patrols are in armor that can stand up to anything we've got short of anti-armor rockets, and their vehicles carry energy shields that can stand up to those. Neither the news nor Intelligence has *any* reports of successful attacks on their ground troops."

"The Weber Protocols call for a wait period before initiating real counterattacks," Rolfson noted. "The resistance so far is...well, civilians with guns. It'll be a different story once the Weber teams start moving."

"Hopefully," Sade said quietly. "The fuckers don't seem to be engaging in retaliations... Hell, in a lot of cases, they don't even bother to *shoot back*. That's how *fucking helpless* Earth is."

"Thank you, Elizabeth," Annette told her. "That's what we needed to know—Earth is fucked unless we can do something to change the odds."

She laid a flimsy on the table in front of her. "I suggest you all look at this," she told her staff. "I'll distribute copies to everyone, but this is our Letter of Marque.

"It officially states that we are neither Nova Industries nor United Earth Space Force ships anymore," she continued. "The UESF, especially, is functionally dissolved. We are charged, however, and authorized under this document to act as 'agents of the Earth government,' with the right to wear uniforms and be treated as soldiers.

"We are charged to capture any enemy shipping we encounter, to steal or trade for any technology we believe can help Earth, and acquire ships and allies if possible. I am authorized to act as ambassador plenipotentiary with the full authority of the Governing Council of Earth when dealing with such allies.

"As Captain Sade has told us, our home has been conquered. No resources they have can turn that tide. It falls to us"—she tapped the flimsy—"to find those resources. We are officially charged and authorized as Privateers of Terra—and we, my friends, are Earth's only hope."

IT TOOK time for the shock to fade. For all that they had all known Earth had fallen, it was something entirely different to hear the realities of that fall laid out by Captain Sade. To *see* how the woman who'd had to watch it happen felt about it.

There would come a time to review news and intelligence reports, to go through *Oaths of Secrecy*'s own sensor records for corroborating evidence, but for now, Annette kept her senior officers locked in the conference room while they worked through it. It would never do for these men and women to look distressed or upset in front of the crew.

Annette was surprised by how much the news affected her. She really had nothing back on Earth to tie her down—an ex-husband currently leading a research drilling operation in Antarctica and her...complex friendship with Elon Casimir, but that was it. No children, and her parents had passed on years ago. Most of her Nova Industries coworkers were now part of her little fleet.

And yet.

Her world had been conquered. Entirely apart from her oaths as a UESF officer and her promises to Jean Villeneuve, that simple fact raised her hackles and awoke her anger. She didn't grieve for Earth— Earth wasn't lost yet—but she was angry. The A!Tol were going to regret coming to her planet. And speaking of the A!Tol...

"This is not news that's easy for us to handle," she said aloud. "But we also have work to do. Metharom and Ki!Tana have details to go over for us." Annette nodded to the engineer, who swallowed and returned the gesture firmly. "Given the news, if anyone *isn't* willing to be in the same room as an A!Tol, I'll understand—but we need her."

Annette glanced around the room again, meeting the gaze of each of her officers in turn. Each of them nodded in turn, some more slowly than others. Finally, she met Major Wellesley's gaze. The Special Space Service Officer sighed and nodded.

"A lot of people in our uniform died because her species came to Earth," he said quietly. "It wasn't her, and I'll deal. But..."

"I know, James," Annette replied. "For that matter, I think Ki!Tana knows."

With her officers in agreement, she sent a ping from her com unit to Ki!Tana's. The big alien found the scroll-like human devices *adorable*, but she was perfectly able to use one. The A!Tol equivalent, apparently, was very similar to the translator—basically a subvocal microphone and earbuds linked wirelessly to a computer box concealed somewhere on the being, though she also used a flimsy-like screen for visual display.

The A!Tol had been close by and arrived less than a minute later —trailed by one of Wellesley's men. The trooper saluted the officers and stepped back out of the room.

"I didn't think you were under guard," Annette asked.

"I requested that Major Wellesley provide a guard once I learned that you had news from your homeworld," Ki!Tana told her. "My appearing as a prisoner may help settle tempers that will be heated."

That was clever. She glanced at Wellesley, who made a small gesture toward the alien, clearly implying that it had definitely been Ki!Tana's idea. For being completely alien to Annette's crew, the big creature seemed to understand them disturbingly well.

"You and Metharom told me you had an update on the upgrade plans?" Annette asked, waving for the engineer and the alien to take over the front of the room.

Ki!Tana filled the space next to the wallscreen and *still* sent atavistic shivers down Annette's spine. Out of her armor, the A!Tol's tentacles were a dull gray color and her main torso was multicolored, almost chameleon-like in its shifting hues, and bullet-shaped. She utterly dwarfed the tiny Thai engineer, easily twice the height of *Tornado*'s Chief Engineer.

"In terms of full components we pulled from *Rekiki's Fang*," Metharom noted first, "we have two proton beams, a shield generator, and one hundred twenty interface drive missiles rated for point seven cee."

"Kikitheth bought the best missiles she could afford," Ki!Tana's artificially flat voice explained, her skin fading to a dull purple color. "This meant we had very few missiles for our launchers."

"These missiles are actually *smaller* than our own," the human engineer continued. "With some rearranging, we can store them in the magazine space required for ninety-eight of our old missiles. This gives us five salvos of faster missiles, and then the remainder of our magazines of the point six cee birds."

"That's a nice opening punch," Rolfson said. The tactical officer sounded pleased—as he should be. Another ten percent of lightspeed on their first few salvos would be *very* valuable.

"You are unlikely to acquire comparable missiles in future," Ki!Tana warned. "Navy missiles are superior but also have superior encryption and protection I would not have codes for. Dan! force missiles will be similar to the Navy."

"What are...Dan-tuck forces?" Kurzman asked.

"The Dan! are...semi-autonomous sub-regions of the Imperium," the big alien said. "They owe allegiance to the Empress and provide ships and men for the Imperium but have broad control of their own affairs."

"Like a feudal duchy," Annette noted. The big alien's skin flashed bright blue, a pattern she'd already recognized was equivalent to a human nod.

"Yes. The translator has updated to use that word," Ki!Tana replied. "Most of the species homeworlds are now duchies. Their fleets are built to the same standards as imperial ships. You are unlikely to capture imperial or ducal missiles in a state where we can override their controls.

"Pirates are less careful, but most will have inferior weaponry to those we took from Kikitheth. To acquire comparable missiles, you will need to purchase them—and currently, to be blunt, you have no trade goods of value."

"There were goods we *could* have taken from *Fang*," Annette told her staff. "But we were focused on acquiring useful tech. Speaking of which—the shield generator?"

"We have already begun installation," Metharom said quickly. "With aid of our new alien crew, it progresses faster than hoped. Installing the relay transmitters will take time. A week, maybe two, still."

"*Fang*'s shields didn't stand up to a single volley from our launchers," Rolfson noted. "Can we upgrade the shield at all?"

"You have a lot of power available," Ki!Tana told the tactical officer. "That helps. Your reactors, are however, disturbingly inefficient —*Fang*'s reactors produced twice as much power in two thirds the space. They, of course, were not available for transfer."

Annette's staff's response to that could *politely* have been called a chuckle.

"Can you do anything with our existing plants?" Kurzman asked slowly. "My understanding is that we did rip out a bunch of components at your direction."

"I will need to examine the fusion cores in detail," Ki!Tana said. "If they are comparable to A!Tol plants of a similar technology level, I should be able to increase your power output by fifty percent without changing their fuel consumption. We will need much of that to power the upgrade I intend to install on the momentum drive.

"I cannot bring your ship up to even *Rekiki's Fang*'s speeds without a yard, but I believe I can add roughly two percent of light-speed to your velocity. Enough to catch even military freighters, given time."

"You see, people, why I wanted Ki!Tana to be here," Annette told them. "She has been working on starships longer than any of us have been alive."

"How can we trust you?" Captain Sade demanded of the big alien. "You're a member of the race that conquered our world *and* a pirate. You turned on your last captain. You could betray us in a moment!"

"I am bound by contract to Captain Bond," Ki!Tana answered. Her skin was purple again. "You neither know nor understand my people, but realize this: we do not lie. We cannot conceal our emotions, which makes it a useless endeavor among our people. We may break our promises, even our sacred oaths—we are sapients and sapients change—but we do not make them falsely."

"We also have no choice," Annette told Sade calmly. "Without Ki!Tana and the other alien crew, we'd have no chance of being able to stand up to even the heavy pirate ships, let alone the A!Tol themselves."

"So, we upgrade *Tornado*, strap proton beams to her, and go hunting?" Kurzman asked. "Not much of a plan."

"*Tornado* has few holes in her armor and we don't have the means to make more," Metharom replied. "We're going to have to take out two of her lasers to mount the proton beams. Not sure what to do with the lasers, but we need them out of *Tornado*."

"Strap them to the scout ships," Lougheed suggested with a laugh. "We don't *have* armor," he continued, "and if we do a similar upgrade to our fusion plants, we'll have the power for them. I wouldn't mind having a weapon after I fire off my one missile salvo."

"That sounds reasonable to me," Annette agreed. "Metharom, Ki!Tana?"

"Doable," Metharom agreed as Ki!Tana's skin flashed to a soft red color.

"Once we've upgraded the ships, we will need to go hunting," the blonde captain told her people. "We'll have done everything we can do without a yard, and we'll still need a lot more to take back to Earth."

"Your best option is to buy upgrades and better technology at A!Ko!La!Ma!," Ki!Tana told them. "It is a pirate station, where many things are available for sale. If you have prizes and bring them there, you can acquire even higher-quality upgrades and have access to a yard to upgrade your vessels.

"You could also acquire schematics and tech to help your world," she continued. "All things are for sale at A!Ko!La!Ma!."

"I can't pronounce that," Kurzman said quietly. "Not without throwing up, anyway."

"A pirate haven?" Annette replied. "Where everything is for sale? Let's just call it Tortuga."

"Very well," Ki!Tana accepted. "Take prizes, Captain. Bring them to Tortuga. There you can buy all that you seek—and your ship is already powerful. There will be those at Tortuga with intelligence and targets they may be willing to share to bring an extra heavy into the fight."

CHAPTER NINETEEN

In Major James Wellesley's experience, it was inevitable that once soldiers settled in anywhere for any significant length of time, there would rapidly appear first a still, second a bar, and third a place for officers to hang out and pretend the first two things didn't exist. Often while indulging in the fruits of the still.

Most of the people on the surface of Alpha Centauri AB2 were his Special Space Service troopers, but there was also a continuous stream of engineers and logistics teams. They'd set up scheduled flights, and that meant the occasional overnighter. A slew of prefabricated structures from *Tornado*'s stores had been set up on the slopes around the cache to provide *somewhere* on the planet to be without a spacesuit.

At one end, a second lava tube cave had been sealed off with the prefab structures and pumped full of air. Since it wasn't a prefab structure, James officially "did not know" about it or the bar and still that had sprung up in it.

He was at the other end of the linked-together structures, where a carefully balanced and supported platform hung out over the caldera, with a transparent wall providing one *hell* of a view.

Currently, the little observation room was empty, leaving the Major alone with his thoughts as he looked out over the empty heart of a volcano that had last erupted while the dinosaurs walked Earth. His thoughts were bleak.

His older siblings were in the UK military. His father served in the House of Lords. From the news they'd received, both of those entities had been dissolved. His family was *probably* safe, but he didn't know. He couldn't know—and neither could any of his soldiers.

The Special Space Service's Fifty-Second Company consisted of exactly seventy men and women, including James himself. They'd taken *Rekiki's Fang*'s crew by surprise and faced only the low velocity slugthrowers the aliens regarded as 'safe' aboard ship.

Further digging into the pirate ship's armory had left him feeling physically ill. The pirates' weapons were clearly second-grade, obsolete, poorly maintained crap, but if Kikitheth's people had actually managed to break out the plasma rifles and power armor stored in the armory, the Terran boarding action would have been over.

Some of the weapons had been designed for bipeds with manipulators similar to human hands. He had twenty plasma rifles they'd refitted for his people, and thirty-two of the aliens who'd joined up had power armor and weapons they could use.

Twelve of those aliens were Rekiki, and the big hexapod reminded James of nothing so much as crocodile centaurs. They were ugly, they made him uncomfortable, and since their gear had been meant for Kikitheth's personal guard, they were the most heavily equipped troops he had.

That still left forty-five of his Terrans with assault rifles and none of his SSS troops with power armor. Boarding actions were going to be dangerous, and their entire *mission* was going to be a series of boarding actions.

"The volcano is already dead, Major," a voice observed from behind him. "You can't kill it by glaring at it."

James spun in place, his hand going to his pistol, then flushed as he recognized the stocky form of Commander Kurzman.

"I didn't expect anyone in here," he confessed. The XO, he noted in a corner of his mind he kept carefully turned off when actually on duty, was surprisingly muscled for a Space Force officer.

"It's all right, Major," Kurzman replied, stepping up to join him in looking out over the crater. "I didn't mean to surprise you."

"It's quite a view, sir," James said slowly, eyeing the other man carefully.

"It is," Kurzman agreed. "You don't need to call me sir," he continued. "You report to Bloody Annie, not me. Call me Pat."

Wellesley realized he'd outright *flushed* at that. What was he, a giddy schoolboy?

"All right...Pat," he told the other man. "We are, after all, a long way from anyone to call us out on it. Call me James."

"Oh, the Captain would call us out on anything that caused trouble," Kurzman said cheerfully. "She didn't get a nickname worthy of her new pirate queen status by being *nice*."

James laughed, glancing at the door to make sure no one *else* wandered in on them. Glancing back, he saw the other officer had produced a bottle of wine and a pair of glasses from inside his jacket.

"It's quite a view and I'm not flying back up for a few hours," Kurzman said slowly, almost shyly. "Share a drink?"

HOURS TURNED to days turned into a week and then two weeks orbiting AB2, every minute hanging over Annette's head. There was no point rushing. It would take time and money and effort to retake Earth—but every minute, every hour they spent upgrading the ship was time the A!Tol ruled her world.

"Are we ready for the tests?" she asked the big A!Tol who currently seemed to be her best hope of liberating her world. The irony was not lost on her.

"Chief Metharom?" Ki!Tana asked in turn, her beak and eyes turning to look at the screen linked to engineering. "All of the parameters for both systems appear clean up here, if we have the power to feed them."

"All reactor cores are one hundred and fifty-two percent of design capacity," *Tornado*'s engineer replied. "Stress levels low, comparable to running ninety-five percent of design. I'm impressed, Ki!Tana."

Many of the crew still stumbled over A!Tol, but everybody who worked directly with the one tentacled alien they had aboard had mastered *her* name.

Ki!Tana's skin flashed a pale red—pleased acceptance, apparently —and she turned back to Annette.

"We should be able to energize both the shields and the proton beams without issue," she noted. "I believe we are ready for the tests."

"Thank you," Annette told the alien, whose skin flashed an even deeper red. It might *look* like she was blushing, but the tone was, so far as Annette could tell, simple happiness. Ki!Tana was surprisingly appreciative of how well most of the crew treated her—and the fact that her happiness was *so* obvious was helping create that kindness.

There were exceptions, of course, but the big alien was probably still the most accepted of their new nonhuman crew.

"Charge the shields," Annette ordered Rolfson.

There was no visible change. Nothing on the screens feeding from the exterior of the ship was altered—but the tactical display now showed a two-kilometer-wide sphere around *Tornado*.

"Shield is active and...holding," Ki!Tana announced after studying her panel. "We are sustaining approximately twice the strength *Fang* was achieving with this generator. This should be sustainable long-term, but I would not suggest running more power through it. This is as much as this generator can safely produce."

"All right. Run it for a few minutes while Lougheed sets up his run," Annette ordered, then flipped up a screen connecting her to *Of Course We're Coming Back*. "Everything looks green on this end, Captain Lougheed," she told the scout ship's commander. "Set up for one run with a missile—*please* make sure it will miss us if the shield fails—and then for a laser sweep."

"Moving in, holding position at one million kilometers," Lougheed replied several moments later. "We will fire on your command."

Annette let several minutes pass in relative quiet, then turned to Rolfson and Ki!Tana.

"Any concerns?"

"Nothing on my screens," the red-bearded tactical officer reply. "Ki!Tana?"

"Everything is clear," she replied. "I am certain as I can be without testing."

"All right," Annette turned back to her junior captain. "Lougheed —fire at will, wait sixty seconds, then try the laser."

There was no response—and then the bright white streak of a point six cee missile flashed across space and vanished in a flash of white light as it impacted the shield and released its kinetic energy.

"Shields holding," Rolfson announced. "Minor blip, nothing severe."

"Results appear as expected," Ki!Tana agreed.

The blond Captain leaned back in her chair and waited for the laser test. She didn't even *pretend* to understand how the shield worked—it was a development from the same gravitational-hyperspatial interface that propelled her ship, but that was as far as she got.

"Laser firing," Rolfson reported. "*Of Course* is holding the beam, shield is holding up but weakening rapidly on that point." Seconds past. Ten, fifteen, twenty. "Shield has *failed*," the tactical officer reported. "*Of Course* is ceasing beam."

"Sustained beam fire is a weakness of the energy shield," Ki!Tana explained as the data came in from the test. "Normally, evasive maneuvers would prevent such a long stream on a single portion of the shield."

"Twenty-two seconds from that laser would drill a hole a kilometer or two deep into a planet," Rolfson said dryly. "I can live with that being the *weakness*."

"It would take less time, of course, versus an Imperial ship of the line's proton beams," the big alien replied. "Even feeding the extra power through it, realize this shield is not equivalent to an Imperial cruiser's defense."

"I know," Annette said quietly. "We hit the same spot with over sixty missiles to break an Imperial ship's shields. Even double the *Fang*'s survivability is a pale shadow of that."

She smiled coldly. "However, speaking of proton beams, I believe Captain Sade has delivered us an asteroid?"

Like for the weapons test back at BugWorks, they'd brought up an asteroid roughly the same mass and composition as one of the old UESF battleships. It was smaller and lighter than *Tornado* itself, but it gave them a solid baseline for what the weapons could achieve.

"Lining the ship up and charging the beams," Rolfson reported. "We have the target in our sights."

"Fire," Annette ordered.

Like the lasers they'd replaced, the proton beams were invisible. The asteroid simply...disintegrated. The beams ripped through the full half-kilometer length of the nickel-iron rock in less than a second, forcing Rolfson to hastily cut the beam off.

"Damn," someone murmured and Annette very specifically did *not* look to see who said it.

"Rolfson?" she asked.

"The good news is that'll punch through shields in seconds," he replied very slowly. "The *bad* news is that they're lightspeed and so useless past four, five hundred thousand kilometers most of the time.

"The *really* bad news is that the proton beams would do a number on even *our* armor," Rolfson concluded, "and Ki!Tana says these are *popguns* compared to the Navy's beams."

CHAPTER TWENTY

Andrew Lougheed smiled to himself as *Of Course We're Coming Back* erupted through the hyperspace portal into a brand-new system. Unlike the last time, he even knew what this one was called—Messeth, according to the charts from *Rekiki's Fang*.

They'd matched up the results from Nova Industries surveys and Dark Eye's scans against the charts as well. The guesses and analysis that had been pulled together were surprisingly close, though A!Tol charts showed their active colonies all well coreward of Earth. It didn't look like they were to blame for *Hidden Eyes of Terra*'s loss, since the survey ship had been nowhere *near* their space.

"What are we seeing, people?" he asked aloud. The scout ship's main screen was showing the system according to the charts: six planets, the fifth a super-Jovian gas giant they'd picked up from Earth years back, the rest rocks of various sizes. The real point of interest was planet two, Ikiseth, the only world in the system with its own name in *Fang*'s databases.

Ikiseth was a comfortably habitable world with a climate Andrew would love to visit—low axial inclination, slightly farther out than Earth from a much warmer star. A large portion of the planet had similar average temperatures to Earth's tropics and little extreme weather.

It was an A!Tol Imperial colony and the charts listed its population as including *nine* separate species—but the largest population was the semi-amphibian Indiri. Andrew understood there had been a few of them aboard *Rekiki's Fang*, but none had survived the mutiny to join the Terran privateer fleet.

The planetary population was only a passing concern for him today, except in that the eighty million sapients on the planet made it one of the largest colonies within sixty light-years of Earth. That meant the planet had a major trans-shipment station in orbit—and was a logical stopping-off point for ships heading to Earth.

"Planets are lining up with what we expected," Laurent reported. "I'm picking up a space elevator, half a dozen big stations—wait! I've got four patrol boats, look to be the same design as in G-KCL-79D. And...the queen in the deck. Will you take a look at her?!"

The screen zoomed in Ikiseth, Laurent highlighting several features. The biggest station was linked to the surface by a massive tether, the space elevator that apparently was a default feature of A!Tol colony expeditions. Five smaller stations were scattered in geostationary orbit along with an entire constellation of civilian satellites.

The four patrol boats were less of a concern this time—*Of Course* was still an eggshell, but with *Tornado*'s old laser now mounted to the "top" of the scout ship, she had real teeth.

Laurent's "queen in the deck," however, was a quarter-kilometer-long, elegant-looking hypership that matched their new databanks listing for an A!Tol destroyer. Smaller than any of the vessels the aliens had brought to Earth, the ships spent most of their time running convoy escort and courier missions through the Imperium.

The lightest ship the A!Tol Navy deployed, the ship could also eat *Of Course* for lunch without even noticing.

"Well, let's see if we can get her attention," Andrew said with a grin. "Take us in at point four cee, but keep your options open and assume that destroyer has a tenth of lightspeed on us. We want to see what's in the system, not get vaporized."

"Yes, sir," Strobel chirped in response. "I like not being vaporized."

Moments later, *Of Course* blazed across the system like a rogue meteor, drawing every eye around.

Behind her, having exited hyperspace through the same portal, *Oaths of Secrecy* drifted forward on cold gas thrusters, quietly studying the system for prey.

THE HYPERSPATIAL ANOMALY sensor didn't provide a great deal of detail. Sitting on *Tornado*'s bridge, Annette could see where *Of Course* opened the portal back into hyperspace—that was hard to miss; portals were *big* anomalies—but the scout ship itself was only visible for a few seconds.

"That's odd," Rolfson said softly. "They must have dropped their interface drive."

"And there's why," Annette told him as a second portal opened ten seconds later. The pursuing ship would have been *well* out of range of *Of Course* in regular space, but the compressed nature of hyperspace meant they'd have been able to bring the scout ship to bay there.

Except that, according to Ki!Tana, the A!Tol didn't have any better tools for scanning hyperspace than *Tornado* did. Their anomaly scanners were significantly longer-ranged than *Tornado*'s, but the limitations within that range were much the same.

Having cut their interface drive, *Of Course* was now effectively invisible to the A!Tol ship.

Tornado's interface drive was already off, the privateer cruiser floating in hyperspace outside the Messeth system, waiting for information from its two scouts. The plan had been for *Of Course* to draw the patrol boats out of position—a plan Lougheed had clearly decided to upgrade.

"The destroyer is entering a search pattern," Rolfson noted. "But if I'm reading their vector correctly, those last few seconds under drive before *Of Course* went silent were enough to completely mess up the A!Tol."

"Ki!Tana, how far away can they pick up us opening a portal?" Annette asked the big alien.

"It depends," she answered. The A!Tol now had an almost-permanent position at the back of the bridge where she could see the screen and provide feedback on the strange and wonderful galaxy she knew better than anyone else aboard *Tornado*. "If we open the normal way, full power and straight ahead, she can pick us up from a light-year of real space distance. If do it slowly, low power, and only big enough for *Tornado* to fit through...fifty-fifty chance she won't pick us up from here."

"Amandine, can we *do* that?"

Annette's navigator shrugged, then checked his screens.

"I *think* so," he finally admitted. "We didn't design the emitters for that kind of fine tuning, but we *can* control the power feed. It won't be perfect and it'll be slower, but I think we can do it."

"It's always slower," Ki!Tana told him. "A *lot* slower—and more vulnerable, too. The people *in* Messeth will still see you."

"So long as we leave that destroyer searching a needle in a hyper-spatial haystack, I don't care," Annette told them both. "Make it happen, Amandine. Ki!Tana—help him if you can."

It was a sign of the big alien's growing acceptance aboard *Tornado* that Amandine didn't even complain at being told to work with a member of the species that conquered Earth. He just gestured the big alien over and got to work.

Annette leaned back in her command chair, watching the destroyer carefully. With the upgrades they'd ripped from *Rekiki's Fang*, she could take the destroyer. With an energy shield extended around *Tornado*'s compressed-matter armor, they were unlikely to even be damaged.

She'd rather avoid that. Little as it appealed to her, she had to think like a *pirate* now—and that meant going after lightly armed ships with valuable cargo. It was highly likely that destroyer had been guarding a freighter of some kind. *That* was her target.

———

ANNETTE BOND HAD at this point gone into and out of hyperspace over a dozen times. Unless she'd had a reason to think about it, she would have said the transition had no sensation at all. If forced to stop and recall, she might have remembered a momentary sense of discomfort.

Creeping through a hyperspace portal barely larger than her ship, taking over ten full seconds to make the transition, was a *very* different story. That slight discomfort she'd barely noticed before was now a seconds-long sensation of dizziness and nausea, building on itself until the cruiser *finally* exited the portal.

From the echoing sigh of relief around her bridge and Ki!Tana's pitch-black skin, she was hardly the only one impacted.

"Is everyone all right?" she demanded. A chorus of "I think so," "Yes," and "Maybe?" answered her, her bridge crew rapidly recovering from the impact.

"Check throughout the ship," she ordered. "Let sickbay know to expect casualties." She glanced at Ki!Tana. "You didn't mention that part."

The alien's black skin rippled, slowly fading toward the rainbow ripples of calm.

"I perhaps should have mentioned that I have never *done* that before," Ki!Tana replied. "And I would not care to do so again."

Annette chuckled. "So, you *don't* know everything," she observed.

Ki!Tana's knowledge and skill had been intimidating. Annette wasn't entirely sure how old the A!Tol was, but she knew her way around the Imperium and its technology better than anyone else aboard—including the other alien recruits.

"Ma'am, datapulse received from *Oaths of Secrecy*," Chan announced. "Captain Sade specifically notes what appears to be a hyper-capable military freighter like the one we missed at G-KCL-79D."

"Well, that's promising," Annette agreed. "And this time, they're not outrunning us. Lieutenant Commander Amandine—take us after that ship. Maximum interface drive."

She smiled coldly as her ship leapt from a standstill to forty-three percent of lightspeed. Still slower than the destroyer Captain Lougheed had lured out of the system, but hopefully faster than the freighter.

"How long until they see us?" she asked.

"We emerged eight light-minutes away," Rolfson told her briskly. "She'll see us in a little under seven minutes, by which point we'll be almost halfway to her."

"Prep a missile warning shot for if she tries to run," Annette ordered. "If she *keeps* running after that, try and disable her with lasers. Whatever happens, I do *not* want that ship escaping into hyperspace."

"Yes, ma'am," her tactical officer replied crisply.

"Amandine—whatever course she tries, see if we can cut her off," *Tornado*'s Captain continued. "We don't have *that* much of a speed edge; every bit of angle you can give me makes Harold's job easier."

"What about *Oaths*?" her XO asked. "Or the patrol ships, for that matter?"

"I'll talk to Captain Sade," Annette replied. "You keep an eye on the locals—if they're threatening us or *Oaths*, put a missile spread into them."

At a hundred meters and *maybe* a quarter-million tons, the patrol boats had neither the shields nor the active defenses to stand off *Tornado*'s missiles. She *probably* couldn't kill all four with a single salvo, but the boats' commanders had to know they were out of their weight class.

"Get me Sade," she told Chan. A moment later, the image of the wispy blonde captain appeared on her command chair screen. "Captain, what's your status?"

"Drifting toward the planet under cold jets and keeping our eyes peeled," *Oaths of Secrecy*'s Captain replied. "I'm guessing you want me to start being less quiet?"

"Not yet," Annette told her. "I want you to stay nice and quiet while we make a lot of noise chasing that freighter. I'm hoping to take her down with *Tornado*, but we're also going to herd her in your direction. If you get a shot, take it. Aim to disable. I want her cargo."

"We don't even know what her cargo *is*," Sade pointed out.

"If we can't use it, we can sell it through Ki!Tana's contacts," Annette replied. "We'll make it work."

"Your call either way," the junior Captain acknowledged. "Good hunting."

THE FREIGHTER'S crew was slow off the mark. Annette wasn't sure if they hadn't been paying attention or hadn't had the right crew on duty, but they didn't bring up their drive until over five minutes after they would have picked up the closing privateer.

But the ship was still capable of forty percent of lightspeed, and *Tornado* was now overhauling her at a little more than three percent of light. It was a mind-bogglingly fast speed in many circumstances, but in this case, it might not be enough.

"Fire the warning shot," Annette ordered.

A moment later, a single missile blazed across the void. The missiles they'd stolen from *Rekiki's Fang* could hit easily the freighter at this point—but destroying the freighter was pointless.

The missile slammed into the freighter's shield on a vector that would never have hit the ship, sending light flaring out across the energy screen.

There was no change to the freighter's course.

"Will we intercept her before she can open a hyper portal?" Annette asked.

There was a limit to how close to a planet or star a portal could be opened, but at almost half the speed of light, those distances could be crossed with ease.

"Probably, unless we're delayed," Amandine told her. "And there's the delay they're hoping for."

The four patrol boats that the scout ships had picked up earlier were now charging out from the planet. The angle was in their favor: unless *Tornado* changed course directly away from them, they *would* catch the cruiser.

Annette wondered if the quartet of tiny ships would actually be worth anything against a pirate. From what she'd seen of *Rekiki's Fang*, the pirate ship could have taken all four boats—though it would have been more of a fight than it was going to be for *Tornado*.

"Let's see if we can head them off," she said calmly. "Rolfson—target the closest and feed her a dozen missiles."

"Yes, ma'am."

Twelve bright sparks flashed to light, closing the distance to the patrol boats in a blur. The small defending ships maneuvered and launched their own missiles in response.

The boats had shields, but they were designed to stand against pirates with half a dozen missile launchers instead of a true warship. The shields flared with light as the missiles struck home, then collapsed in a bright flash as they were overwhelmed—the ship they were supposed to protect vanishing similarly the next moment.

"We have twenty-four missiles inbound, and the other three boats are running for their lives," Rolfson reported in satisfaction. It took an interface drive barely ten seconds to completely reverse velocity—and the patrol boats had done just that.

"Let's not test the shields with those missiles," Annette ordered. "We have missile defenses. Use them."

Given the ubiquity of energy screens and high maneuverability of interface drive ships, the A!Tol apparently didn't bother with active defenses against missiles. Annette suspected they were right and that the mass and energy required by *Tornado*'s suite of antimissile lasers had better uses.

Since she *had* them, however, she was going to use them.

A single missile made it past the suite, slamming into *Tornado*'s new shield and vanishing in a blast of fire.

"Shield status?"

"Overflow buffer at point six percent," Kurzman reported from the CIC. "We can take a lot more hits like that before we need to worry."

"That's what I like to hear," Annette replied, allowing herself a small smile. "And our freighter friend?"

"She changed course while we were shooting at her, but we've adjusted to follow," Amandine replied. "No material change to *our* intercept time, but she's now entering Captain Sade's intercept envelope."

"Is she?" *Tornado*'s Captain murmured, studying the screen. "Well then, it seems *Oaths of Secrecy* will have the honor today." She leaned back in her chair. "Inform Captain Sade to engage at her discretion—but I want the ship intact."

The end of the chase was surprisingly sudden. *Tornado* was six million kilometers behind the freighter, closing the range at roughly nine thousand kilometers a second. They were nearing the point where *Tornado* would have to make a dangerous attempt to disable the A!Tol transport with missiles or pursue her into hyperspace.

Then *Oaths of Secrecy* brought up her interface drive. She was two million kilometers away from the fleeing transport—but *ahead* of her. Five seconds after the scout ship started her lunge, the big laser they'd mounted along her keel fired.

The freighter's shield held for less than two seconds, and the laser washed over the ship—intentionally cutting power to only fry sensors and controls, not gut the ship.

"They've cut their interface drive and are transmitting their surrender," Chan told the bridge.

"Inform Major Wellesley he has work to do," Annette said as she let herself relax slightly. "Everyone else, keep a sharp eye out for that destroyer. After all this, I don't want to be chased off at the last minute."

CHAPTER TWENTY-ONE

JAMES'S COMPANY WAS NOTABLY BIGGER NOW, WITH AN ENTIRE troop's worth of power-armored Rekiki providing a new heavy support section. They were the only pure alien troop, though, as he'd expanded his four existing troops to six, slotting three power armored aliens and three human-carried plasma weapons into each sixteen-sapient troop.

His headquarters section was now seven people. He'd taken one of the plasma rifles for himself and incorporated the last two aliens—a squat, trilaterally symmetrical mobile fungus named Pophe, whose real name was apparently unpronounceable and whose species were called the Frole, and a tall blue-skinned biped named Ral.

With the deaths of many of the Rekiki aboard *Fang*, Ral's species —the Yin—were the single largest group of aliens aboard *Tornado*. Despite being, on average, thirty centimeters taller than humans and having faces closer to a bird's than a human's, the blue-skinned aliens seemed to get along well with their new crew.

Ral himself had demonstrated an ability to go poop joke for poop joke with James's headquarters section, which the Special Space Service Major took as a positive sign.

His headquarters section and the Rekiki troop—his new Golf Troop—were the second wave. The first was, once again, his Alpha Troop. By the time McPhail docked the shuttle with the transport and he made his way aboard, they'd already taken control of the landing bay.

The human SSS troopers were mostly dwarfed by their alien comrades in their power armor, but they were also clearly in charge. The pirates weren't bad as inexperienced troops went, but the Special Space Service was Earth's *best*.

Three A!Tol stood in the middle of the bay under the watchful eye of James's people. He approached them directly, allowing the Rekiki to spread out behind him.

"I am Major James Wellesley," he said flatly. "Your ship is now a prize of the UESF. You will bring your crew to this landing bay and await further instruction. Resistance will be met with lethal force. Do you understand me?"

The translator mounted in his armor repeated his words in a series of sibilants and clicks. All three A!Tol's skin was a burnt orange hue he hadn't seen on Ki!Tana yet—he was *guessing* anger or possibly embarrassment.

"You're nothing but pirates," the Captain replied, his beak snapping sharply as his beady eyes bore down on James, who ground his own anger under its heel.

"And my opinion of your species is worse," he snapped back. "Do you understand my orders?"

The burnt orange color went even darker.

"Yes. We will comply."

"Good."

James turned his back on the aliens, trusting his troopers to keep them under control.

"Sweep the ship," he ordered his Troop Captains as the remaining shuttles continued to disgorge his troopers. "Alpha Troop, Golf Troop, maintain security here and act as a reserve. Bravo Troop, get me an ID on the cargo. Everyone else, round up the crew and bring them here.

"We're on the clock. Go!"

"MA'AM." The voice of Bravo Troop's commander dropped onto Annette's private link. "You need to see this."

Tornado's Captain quickly checked the connection—the young woman commanding Wellesley's Bravo Troop had linked the Major in as well as the XO, but it was only the four of them. Whatever she'd seen, she thought it needed to be kept very quiet.

"Show me," she ordered, linking one of her command chair screens to the channel.

A moment later, the screen flickered into the view from Mumina Bousaid's helmet. The Libyan soldier was looking over a vast open void, presumably one of the cargo holds aboard the freighter they'd captured. A power-armored Yin, even taller than Bousaid's impressive height, was running a bright arc light along the hold, showing dozens of identical honeycomb shapes.

Each cell of the honeycomb held a cylindrical object, about a meter and a half across and ten meters long.

"My God," Annette whispered. "Are those *missiles?*"

"Translator says the labels call them Mark One Hundred Five Momentum Drive Missiles for the Imperial Navy," Bousaid said quietly. "This hold contains about two *thousand* of them—and this ship has eight holds."

"Well done, Troop Captain," Annette told her. "*Well* done."

She leaned back in her command chair, studying the frozen image of the dozens of honeycombs full of supremely lethal weapons for a long moment. Finally, she gestured Ki!Tana over to her.

"You implied there was a state we could acquire Imperial missiles in where we'd be able to use them," she reminded the alien. She pointed to the tiny screen. "Is 'still in the packaging' that state?"

Ki!Tana stared at the image for easily ten seconds, her skin color rippling through large chunks of the rainbow.

"Yes," she finally said. "We should be able to load the software we do have onto those weapons. They will be less effective, but not by much. That is a lot of missiles, Captain. The Imperium will not let the theft of this many weapons go unnoticed."

The alien shivered all of her tentacles in what Annette was starting to suspect was an A!Tol shrug, and her skin settled into an unfamiliar dark blue tone.

"May we speak in private, Captain?" Ki!Tana asked.

Annette glanced around the bridge. Everything was in order for the moment, and she could keep her headset with her and be alerted to anything.

"My office," she agreed.

THE DAY OFFICE attached to *Tornado*'s bridge was sparse, designed as a space for the Captain to work without leaving the bridge unattended, as opposed to the office in her quarters intended to be her main workspace.

It held a desk, a computer, and just *barely* enough space for the big tentacled alien to squeeze in across the desk from Annette.

"The Navy will pursue you," the alien told her. "You have captured a military freighter and one full of munitions they clearly plan to use. They keep close control of those missiles."

"Let them," Annette replied. "I'll outrun and outmaneuver anything I can't fight."

"Your ship is not that powerful, Captain," Ki!Tana told her. "You are now easily a pirate heavy, though there are more powerful pirate ships, but you still are barely a match for an Imperial cruiser—a squadron of which could easily bring you to bay and crush you."

"You were already operating as pirates when we met you," she countered. "The game isn't that impossible."

"No," the alien agreed. "But there are choices you must now make, Captain. That ship will be crewed by just over one hundred and fifty Navy personnel—most likely primarily A!Tol, if the Captain is. They prefer only semi-mixed crews.

"You do not have the cargo capacity or the time to transship those missiles," Ki!Tana continued. "You must take the ship itself if you want its cargo. What happens to the crew?"

That stopped Annette's thoughts in their track. She hadn't even thought of the crew of the ship—her plan had been to take the most valuable parts of the cargo and flee, but Ki!Tana was right. She wanted *all* of those missiles.

"The ship has shuttles and lifepods, yes?" she asked, buying herself time to think.

"She was designed by my people," the alien replied. "She has far more of them than she needs. You *could* eject the entire crew and still have life pods for your prize crew. They would then tell your enemies who you were. They would tell the Navy that a rogue human ship is out here causing havoc."

"They saw us run," Annette pointed out. "They know that."

"And if the crew of this ship reports, they will know you now have alien crewmembers and translators," Ki!Tana said. "Your threat level will increase. They will have more information with which to pursue you, and you will be in greater danger."

"And you would suggest, what, killing them all?" *Tornado's* Captain snapped. She should have considered that as being a necessity. Was it a line she would cross?

"I suggest nothing in this case," the big alien replied, her voice annoyingly flat through the translator. The devices had improved their ability to relay emotion into English, but they were still imperfect at best.

"If you kill them all, you will be harder to trace," she continued. "The Navy will know less about you and will have no basis on which to start hunting for you. But."

"But?" Annette demanded.

"But they will hunt you harder. There are two types of pirates to the A!Tol: thieves and murderers. Thieves are punished when caught —but murderers are *sought*. Thieves will be hunted in the course of duty. Murderers will have special task forces devoted to them.

"But without witnesses, you are far harder to track," Ki!Tana noted. "Many darker pirates have hunted for years and retired successfully. As a rogue warship, you may see a special task force regardless."

"'May'," the Captain repeated. "In my world's past, pirates had a tradition: when they intended to take no prisoners, they flew a black flag. It is, my alien friend, far easier to *stop* killing than to start, isn't it?"

"Yes," the A!Tol agreed. The blue hue of her skin was fading suddenly, easing into a lighter color.

"I think today we reward surrender with life," Annette said quietly.

"You are the Captain," Ki!Tana replied. "And the holder of my contract. The decision is always yours."

CHAPTER TWENTY-TWO

MISSILES.

No *wonder* the freighter Captain looked like a grouchy snake pit. James's people had just taken an entire *squadron's* worth of missile reloads.

"Is that the last of the crew?" James asked his Troop Captains.

"Scans aren't showing anyone else, but there are probably corners we wouldn't see them in," his Charlie Troop Captain replied. "Are we taking over?"

"Force prize crew is on their way over now," he confirmed. "Captain wants this hunk of metal moving *before* the squids' destroyer comes back to check on her."

"Watch it, sir—you have incoming," one of his troopers cut in on another channel.

James looked up to see what the trooper was warning him about. The smallish A!Tol commanding the ship was moving toward him, two battle rifle-armed Terrans escorting the—male, James understood from the size—alien back to him.

At some point between their first conversation and now, the orange had faded from the Captain's skin, leaving only an inky, purplish black tone to the alien's torso as he reached the Terran Major.

"Is this all of your crew?" James demanded, gesturing at the collection of A!Tol his people had corralled into the center of the landing bay. He'd been trained at rapidly assessing the numbers of a crowd of humans, but those skills were only so applicable to a distressed mob of tentacled aliens ranging from one and a half meters to well over two meters tall.

"Yes," the Captain replied. "What will happen to them?"

James hadn't received orders yet—and until he got orders, he was going to act on his own discretion.

"Those shuttles." He gestured at a set of cargo spacecraft along one wall of the bay. "How many would be required to hold your crew?"

The A!Tol looked at his ship's parasite craft, his manipulator tentacles fluttering in the equivalent of a human shrug.

"They are not designed for sapients," he told James. "All of them."

As he spoke, however, the dark, fear-laced tone of his skin began to flash with elements of yellow—a color James had never seen on an A!Tol below. Given that the shuttles were *huge* and they only needed to get the aliens to the planet they'd left behind them...

"You lie poorly," James told the alien bluntly. "And so I am forced to guess. You will get two shuttles. Start loading your people onto them."

He pinged his Alpha and Golf Troop leaders—the latter was his only alien Troop Captain.

"Move the squids onto two of their cargo shuttles," he ordered. "Keep an eye on them and don't let them in the cockpits till I give the word—we'll dump them on our way out-system."

"You are letting us go?" the A!Tol asked, his skin now a very dark blue.

James looked the strange creature in the eye.

"I may be the last officer of my service after your race ripped my home apart, but I remain a soldier," he told the transport captain. "I still have my honor."

WHATEVER GAME KI!TANA was playing—and as they reentered the bridge, Annette was more and more certain that the big A!Tol was playing some kind of game—it had been made irrelevant while they were off the bridge.

She received Wellesley's report with relief she didn't allow herself to show. Ki!Tana, however, slowly faded to a calm red color. Despite what she'd been telling Annette, the alien was clearly pleased with the result.

"Where's our prize crew at?" Annette asked Rolfson.

"Lieutenant Mosi is boarding now," he confirmed. "She has twenty Space Force personnel and ten of our alien crew, which we think should be enough to run the ship at least temporarily."

"She has the same code-hacking tools we used aboard *Fang*," Ki!Tana noted. "They may take longer, as this is a military ship."

"Any sign of our destroyer friend?" the Captain asked. "She's what's going to set Mosi's time limit."

"Nothing yet," her tactical officer replied. "The patrol boats are hiding in orbit. They're scared shitless—but they'll probably fight if we move against the planet."

"I have *no* intention of trying to raid a planet with a hundred ground troops," Annette told him. "That would be stupid."

"Not arguing, ma'am," he agreed. "Looking forward to have those missiles in my magazines, though. I'll feel a lot happier about going up against a Navy ship if we have the same birds."

"Agreed. Keep an eye out for her," she ordered. "The *instant* you have a sniff of a hyperspace portal; I want to know."

"Mosi will hurry, ma'am," Rolfson said quietly. "Twenty minutes, maybe thirty. We should be good to go then."

"Be ready to move as soon as the freighter is ready." Annette glanced at the screen, checking on *Oaths of Secrecy*. Her second ship was floating on the other side of the freighter, all three ships within a few thousand kilometers of each other.

"IT LOOKS like they're giving up, sir," Laurent announced, highlighting the A!Tol destroyer on *Of Course We're Coming Back*'s main screen.

"Any sign from the system?" Andrew asked. If *Tornado* and *Oaths of Secrecy* had achieved anything since *Of Course* had lured the destroyer out, they should have *left*.

"Nothing," she replied. "Both *Tornado* and *Oaths* are still in-system. I make it ten minutes or less before the destroyer drops back out of hyperspace."

"Damn," he murmured. "Can we do anything?"

"If we brought up the drive, we'd lure her away again, but then we won't be able to hide," Laurent told him. "Our missiles won't get through her shields, and she's got nastier beams than us if we get close enough to use the laser."

"And if she sees us, she'll catch us," *Of Course*'s Captain agreed. His ship's upgrades were lacking compared to *Tornado*. She was still only capable of point four cee, still limited to a handful of externally mounted missiles and a laser, still fragile as cheap paper.

"Show me her likely portal points," he ordered.

A shaded area appeared on the screen. The map was still sparse, the lack of features in hyperspace still something Andrew was getting used to. The destroyer was a single dot, their only real information on her coming from their encounter in the Messeth system. The Messeth system itself was simply a set of circles marking the danger zones around each planet and the star itself.

"Unless she changes course, she'll be over half a million kilometers away in hyperspace when she passes us," Laurent reported. "We could close to laser range in moments, but..."

"She has proton beams and an energy shield. We don't," Andrew noted. "She'll portal what, a million klicks from us?"

"Bit over, yeah," Laurent confirmed. "What are you thinking, boss?"

"*Tornado* can take her," *Of Course*'s Captain said confidently. "But I don't think Captain Bond would object to an ace up her sleeve. Tall." He opened a channel to his engineer. "Start warming up the interface drive. *Don't* bring it online, but when I give the order, I want full speed on the bounce."

"I'll make it happen."

"All right," Andrew Lougheed said calmly, studying the dot on his screen and wishing he could see more of what they were doing. "Let's see what our tentacled friends do next."

"HYPER PORTAL!" Rolfson snapped. "Emergence at ten million kilometers. Looks like our friend the destroyer."

"Mosi, what's your status?" Annette demanded of the young officer leading the prize crew.

"We're into the command interface, but we're unlocking systems one by one," the black-skinned Zimbabwean replied breathlessly. "We'll have interface drive in a minute or two, but we're at least ten minutes from having the hyperdrive."

"You're out of time," Annette told her flatly. "Sade!" She pulled *Oaths of Secrecy*'s Captain into the channel. "Mosi's team will have interface drive momentarily. As soon as she does, you *both* take off for Rendezvous Alpha. Mosi—you'll ride through on *Oath*'s hyper portal. It'll be tricky flying, but you can do it."

"We can miss the portal ourselves after generating it; give her a clear path," Sade suggested. "Shouldn't even be tricky. We'll need time and a safe space to do it."

"I know. I'm going to go buy that for you," *Tornado*'s Captain replied. "Seconds are about to get expensive, ladies. Spend as few of them as you can."

"Yes, ma'am," Mosi acknowledged.

"Already underway, ma'am," Amandine told her as she turned to her navigator. "They'll range on us first. There's nothing we can do about that."

"Keep the laser suite up," she ordered Rolfson. "Prep our own missiles. I'd rather not have this fight, but it looks like I lost that argument."

"All tubes are loaded with point sevens," he replied. "Proton capacitors charging—we'll have a full charge by the time we're in beam range. Lasers the same."

"Estimate we'll be in range of their point seven fives in one minute," Amandine reported.

"Ki!Tana. Anything specific we should be expecting?" Annette asked their resident alien.

"Her first goal is going to be to secure the freighter," the old pirate told her. "She'll expect you to be similarly armed to most pirate heavies—better than her but not by much, as they need a lot of cargo space. She'll try and hammer down your shields with missiles while closing to retake the transport."

"And when that fails?"

"She'll turn and try to close to proton beam range," Ki!Tana said. "I am guessing, Captain," she warned. "But that Captain will have two priorities: recapture the freighter and protect the planet. Capturing or destroying *Tornado* will not register except to help with one or both of those."

"She can keep the damn planet, but I'm taking that ship."

"Incoming!" Rolfson announced. "Fourteen missiles coming our way."

"Please return the favor, Commander," Annette told him. "All launchers."

"Yes, ma'am. Five seconds to range."

The seconds blinked past and *Tornado*'s response flared into space. Twenty-four missiles blazed toward the destroyer, passing its own salvo as they went.

"Engaging with antimissile lasers."

Annette gripped the armrest of her command chair. They'd upgraded *Tornado* a lot, but last time they'd faced A!Tol Imperial Navy ships, she'd watched the UESF die around her.

Rolfson was getting better with the lasers, the last of the missiles dying well clear of the privateer's shields. *That* appeared to get the destroyer's attention and the smaller ship turned in space, adjusting her course to sweep farther away from *Tornado* even as the missiles closed in.

"Mosi got the drive," Chan reported from the communications console. "She says they'll be underway in ten seconds; *Oaths* is moving to escort."

"*Finally*." Annette's attention was immediately pulled away as the impact reports from their missile salvo made it onto her screens. Like the cruisers they'd fought at Sol, the warship had *major* shields—twenty-four missiles had left the destroyer's screen flickering with light but unbroken.

"Please tell me our new shields are as strong as hers," the Terran Captain snarled.

"About twenty percent stronger," Ki!Tana replied, her voice far calmer. "Plus your antimissile suite is surprisingly effective against interface missiles."

"We didn't have shields," Annette pointed out. "Built the best alternative we had. Amandine—take us right at that bitch. Rolfson—ready the proton guns."

The destroyer's course was clearly focused on *Oaths of Secrecy* and the freighter now, but her speed advantage wouldn't be enough to avoid action if *Tornado* cut the angle.

"She'll catch them before they can open the portal," Rolfson said quietly.

"I noticed," Annette replied. "Send them another salvo, Lieutenant Commander. Let's get them looking at *us*, not Sade and Mosi."

Another twenty-four missiles blasted away, and now the distance between the two ships was dropping rapidly.

"Mosi and Wellesley have launched the cargo shuttles with the freighter's original crew," Chan reported. "They are heading for the planet as fast as they can go, getting the hell *out* of this fight."

"There could be an accident," Ki!Tana murmured to Annette. "Even a laser could take out those shuttles. You tried to let them go, but the Imperium forced a battle."

She turned a flat glare on the alien, whose skin was back to the same dark blue as earlier.

"I don't know *what* fucking *test* you think you're giving," Annette hissed, "but I will *not* fire on unarmed escape craft to make my life easier. Drop. It."

The dark blue faded to purple and then red as the big A!Tol met her eyes.

"Good," she said. "Fight your ship, Captain."

With a final glare at her far-too-pleased-with-herself alien compatriot, Annette returned her attention to the screen in time to watch their second salvo of missiles fail against the destroyer's screen. The A!Tol built even their light warships with a mind-boggling level of defenses.

"Rolfson, move to streaming the missiles," she ordered. "If we get that freighter out, we have lots of ammunition to burn. Dump everything we got from *Fang* into her."

"Yes, ma'am."

The next set of lights leaving *Tornado* formed a deadly stream, sparks of white light suicidally charging to their destruction in an orderly line.

"She's...spinning?" the tactical officer announced after a moment.

"Are you surprised there's a standard counter to that tactic?" Ki!Tana asked. "They must have dramatically underestimated your weapons' ability to seek a single target location before."

"Clearly. Time to proton beam range?"

"Ninety seconds. Ma'am...they're going to range on the freighter with their beams first."

"They will fire to disable," the big A!Tol warned them, "but they will fire."

"Keep up the missile fire, see if we can peg her with a long-range laser," Annette ordered. "Make her look at *us*, not Mosi."

They still had four of the big lasers left on *Tornado*, and while they might not *hit* at a dozen light-seconds, they would hurt if they did. Streams of invisible light started to accompany the missiles. The lasers even connected, lighting up chunks of the destroyer's shields—but only for fractions of a second before the A!Tol ship broke away.

With over ten seconds of light delay, hitting them with lasers was almost impossible.

"*Oaths* is trying to open a hyper portal," Amandine reported. He paused and sighed. "They failed; they're still too close to the star."

"Damn." Annette watched the tactical plot on the screen. Her ship was going as fast as she could. With the missiles aboard the freighter now running, she suspected she could kill the destroyer in time. Without them...the destroyer was still going to die. The only thing in question was whether or not the freighter would make it out of the system.

"Hyper portal!" Rolfson announced. "Holy mother of... It's *Of Course!*"

Lougheed's ship erupted from hyperspace less than a hundred thousand kilometers behind the A!Tol destroyer at forty percent of lightspeed. The massive laser they'd strapped to the scout ship opened fire from *inside* hyperspace, linking the tiny scout ship to the destroyer with a line of pure light.

Somehow, Lougheed kept the beam on the destroyer as his ship blasted past the A!Tol vessel, the range dropping as low as ten kilometers in the moments after launch. At that moment of insanely close range, the laser still flaring against the alien ship's shields, all eight of the rack-mounted missiles fired.

There was no perceivable flight time. The entire sphere of the A!Tol's shield lit up with white fire...and collapsed.

It was impossible to tell whether it was Lougheed's laser or Rolfson's missiles that finished the job but by the time *Of Course We're Coming Back* had been in system for two seconds, the A!Tol destroyer was nothing but fiery debris.

CHAPTER TWENTY-THREE

ALL FOUR SHIPS EMERGED FROM HYPERSPACE AT THEIR PRIMARY rendezvous point eighteen hours later and Annette breathed a sigh of relief at their apparent safe escape. Nothing had shown up on the anomaly scanners as they'd fled, and the only ship in a position to have tracked them *into* hyperspace was expanding debris and survival pods in the Messeth system.

This time, the rendezvous was farther away from Alpha Centauri, heading in the direction of the pirate station the humans had nicknamed Tortuga. It was also directly on the way to the supply route between the system Ki!Tana's data had confirmed as a major fleet base and one of the key systems supplying it.

The fleet base was beyond her little fleet's ability to engage—but the ships supplying it were a different matter entirely. Annette still wasn't sure about intercepting ships in hyperspace, but Ki!Tana seemed to think it was doable, and to be fair, *Rekiki's Fang* had intercepted *Tornado*.

"Major, Lieutenant," she greeted Wellesley and Mosi over a channel. "Any issues with our new prize?"

"The software Ki!Tana provided worked like a charm," Mosi

replied. The strange click in the A!Tol's name sounded surprisingly normal from her, not the stilted almost-right most of the human crew had mastered. "Took longer than we expected, but it was a military transport. We are now fully in control."

"And no stowaways, either," Major Wellesley added. "We've swept the ship from top to bottom. The only people aboard are us."

"Good. I'll want the triple-S company back aboard as soon as possible." She smiled at Mosi. "Sorry, Mosi, you get to stay Captain a while longer. We'll need to start offloading missiles ASAP."

"I'm guessing you want me to take her all the way to Tortuga?" Mosi asked.

"It would be unwise to send the transport on ahead," Ki!Tana interjected from behind Annette's shoulder. The Captain glared at the interruption but still gestured for the alien to continue. The old pirate knew the market better than they did.

"You are an unknown entity, Captain Bond," she said simply. "Arrive with *Tornado*, an unquestionable heavy, and a series of prizes in tow, and you will be greeted with respect. *Tornado* alone will guarantee you a fair deal.

"Send the prize ahead without the heavy to force respect and she will simply be gone when you arrive. No one will have seen her. At best, you will be able to force the return of the ship and hopefully Lieutenant Mosi's crew, but you would lose her cargo."

"I have no intention of risking Mosi's crew," Annette told her people calmly. "If the best plan is for us to show up as a pirate fleet with a flotilla of prizes, I'm willing to delay things until then.

"We'll have a full staff meeting this evening, over dinner," she continued. "Senior officers and Captains—and yes, *Captain* Mosi, that includes you until we sell that ship. Understood?"

LIKE MANY PARTS OF *TORNADO*, the Captain's dining room was large but Spartan. It doubled as the conference room for the senior officers, so it wasn't attached to Annette's quarters, and the only item to make it a "dining room" was the inclusion of a small kitchen where a steward could prepare a meal.

"Don't expect anything particularly wonderful," Annette warned the young black woman staring around at the white tablecloth and fine china laid out on the table. "The Captain's dining ware is prettier, but we're eating the same UP as everybody else."

The Universal Protein that apparently every ship in the Imperium carried was bland, tasteless, and—combined with the vitamin powders *Tornado*'s medical staff had whipped up—capable of filling the dietary requirements of humans as well as every other species aboard.

It just made *tofu* look appealing.

Mosi was the youngest and most junior of the officers invited to the dinner, so Annette had purposefully made sure the Lieutenant had made it in first. The black woman was tall and skinny, almost gaunt. She was one of Rolfson's two junior officers, normally tasked with running a shift in CIC.

Her selection to lead the prize crew was quite literally a matter of her being the Lieutenant on rotation at that moment in time, though so far, Annette was favorably impressed. Not many could keep their cool well enough to work through alien code with a warship bearing down on them.

Others began to drift in behind them as Annette gestured the prize crew's Captain to her seat at the end of the table.

They'd brought in the odd, stool-like, creation A!Tol used in place of chairs and placed Ki!Tana at one corner. Opposite her were Kurzman and Wellesley, sitting together. That caused Annette to raise an eyebrow—not least because the two men arrived together and promptly sat next to each other.

If they wanted to play footsie under the table, it wasn't *her* problem—though it was a bit of a surprise. She didn't know which of the two men would have initiated things, but they appeared to have moved quickly.

Sade and Lougheed were at the other end of the table with Mosi, both of them greeting the junior officer gently and trying to draw her out.

Amandine, Rolfson and Metharom filled the middle of the table. The bearded and stocky Rolfson made an interesting contrast placed next to the almost-elflike Sade, though the side glances the two were giving each other suggested the placement was hardly unwelcome.

Annette concealed a smile behind a napkin as the stewards brought in the food. This far away from home, pairing up was almost inevitable. So long as it didn't interfere with discipline or involve the chain of command, she was determined to turn a *very* blind eye.

There wasn't much else to take pleasure in, she realized with a sigh as the food was placed in front of her. It looked like the stewards were trying curry as a solution to the utter blandness of UP—thankfully, they were feeding Ki!Tana something else.

Glancing at the black *goo* the cooks had turned the A!Tol's protein into, she remembered there were worse things than curry.

DESPITE ANNETTE'S MISGIVINGS, the curry went over well with the human occupants of the room. To her even greater surprise, however, Ki!Tana's skin flashed the dark red of surprised pleasure when the alien bit into her own food. The cooks had managed something edible for a *completely different species.*

If she were still paying the crew, that would have been worth a raise right there.

"All right, people," she said as the dishes were cleared away. "I called you here so we could go over our plans. These are heavily shaped by Ki!Tana's intelligence and the fact that *Tornado* is our only real warship."

As the last of the stewards exited the room, Annette hit a command on her communicator to turn on the wallscreen at one end of the conference/dining room. The screen was loaded with a map of the region around them, filled in with data pulled from *Fang*'s and now Mosi's freighter's computers.

"We are here." A gold dot flashed on the map, in deep space. "The station we're calling Tortuga is here." A blue dot flashed along the border between the A!Tol and Kanzi territories. "From what Ki!Tana has said, the system has no inhabitable planets, which keeps it from the attention of both the powers around it.

"Tortuga serves as a central hub for piracy and fencing through both of the big empires out here," she continued. "We can sell anything there, and perhaps more important for our purposes, we can *buy* anything there. Improved shields. Improved power generators. Custom-built power armor for the Major's troopers. Technical specifications and designs we can provide the Weber Network back home."

She was presuming, of course, that the Weber Protocols had managed to *establish* the Network as the core of a resistance. If the survivors of the UESF *hadn't* managed that, Annette's job was probably impossible.

"With respect, ma'am," Kurzman asked, leaning forward across the table and eyeing the map. "What are we going to *buy* those things with?"

"Ki!Tana?" Annette gestured to the sole nonhuman in the room.

"Both Imperial and Kanzi currency are accepted aboard the station," the A!Tol told them. "Barter is also accepted, and you would need to acquire currency of one kind or another to make deals. If you wish to trade at A!Ko!La!Ma!, you will need something to trade. A freighter on its own has significant value. If you are prepared to sell the missiles you captured, you will find many willing to trade."

"My inclination," *Tornado*'s Captain told her people, "is to hang on to *all* of those missiles. Our long-term mission, after all, is not piracy. There will be a distinct value to us in having full magazines—and full *reloads*—of missiles that can match the A!Tol's best."

"We'll need a ship to carry them or to store them somewhere," Mosi pointed out.

"Indeed," Annette agreed. "We should have our magazines full of the new missiles by the morning. Once that's done, I want you and Captain Lougheed to return to Alpha Centauri and store all of the point seven five–rated missiles in the cache there.

"You'll swap them out for all of the point sixes Nova Industries gave us. I can't imagine they'll be worth *much* at Tortuga, but they'll be worth something if many of the Captains are as cheap as Ki!Tana suggests."

"You are correct," the tentacled alien confirmed. "They won't sell for any great amount, but they will sell."

"Everyone will rendezvous here in one week," Annette told them, highlighting a new marker on the map—about halfway between their current location and Tortuga. "*Oaths of Secrecy* and *Tornado* are going to spend the week trawling along here."

She highlighted a section of space. At one end of it was the main fleet base, the system Fleet Lord Tan!Shallegh had launched his conquest of Earth from. At the other was one of the major colonies.

"Just by tracking the speed of the hyperdrive signatures at range, we should be able to avoid engaging A!Tol warships and close with freighters," she concluded. "I'm hoping to grab one, maybe two more ships before we head to Tortuga.

"If we can pull three captures, the ships alone should cover much of the work we need to have done. Anyone have other thoughts or concerns?"

"Do we have a way to avoid engaging A!Tol military transports?" Wellesley asked. "Until we have power armor for my human troopers, I hesitate to tangle with their actual *soldiers*."

"No guarantees, unfortunately," Annette warned him. "But I have no intention of boarding ships we haven't already forced to surrender."

"A concern for the future," Metharom suggested diffidently. "We promised the former crew of *Rekiki's Fang* that they would be able to leave when we made port. How many of our new crewmembers will we lose when we reach Tortuga?"

"You will almost certainly lose all of the Rekiki," Ki!Tana said quietly. "Those who served did so due to family ties to Kikitheth. Their honor is complicated—serving the ties was more important than not becoming pirates. Keeping their oath to serve in exchange for their lives and transport to safety remained more important. But once their oath is fulfilled, they will not stay.

"Of the others...expect to lose half. You have been fair and honest with them, but they will take their coin and serve on ships with more of their race. Few, even among pirates, like being the only members of their species aboard."

"Will we be able to hire replacements?" Annette asked. While they didn't need the alien crewmembers to keep *Tornado* running, they'd been helpful in integrating the alien tech with the Terran warship. She hadn't considered that they'd likely lose people when they reached Tortuga. "What about *you*?"

"There will always be desperate sapients at the station you call Tortuga," Ki!Tana replied. "You inherited my contract; I am bound to you for fourteen long-cycles. I will help you find new crew if we need them. I am sure I have a few old friends I can trust."

"That answers my question," Rolfson said with a grin. "I was going to ask if we could *trust* anyone on Tortuga to work on our ships."

***

"PAT, CAN YOU WAIT A MOMENT?" Annette asked as the meeting started to break up. She waved her XO back to his seat at the table as the other officers slowly filtered out. Major Wellesley hung back a moment, looking at the XO with worried eyes, but followed the others out when it became clear she wanted to speak to Kurzman in private.

If she hadn't already figured it out, *that* would have been a hammer between the eyes.

The doors slid shut behind everything else and she turned to Pat

Kurzman. Her XO was a solid man, short but broad with close-cropped hair, who normally reminded her of an English bulldog. Right *now*, he reminded her of her father's dog in the gap between him peeing on the floor and them finding the puddle.

"What do you need, ma'am?" Kurzman asked in a solid imitation of his normal unflappability.

"You and James," Annette said flatly. She wasn't really asking a question. She'd known *Kurzman's* interest in men, though Wellesley's was a surprise—she was surprised by *Kurzman's* lack of wisdom.

"Um. Yeah," Kurzman replied, deflating into his chair. "Um. He's really pretty?"

Annette managed to not laugh, barely, and leveled her best glare on her executive officer, who proceeded to deflate even farther into his chair. She let the silence drag on for several moments, and then shook her head at him, concealing a smile.

"He is," she admitted. "If rather young for me." Her own tastes ran more to something like both of her junior captains, a four-poster bed, and a lot of silk rope. "I *do* hope there's rather more to it than 'he's pretty', though."

"I think so?" her XO replied slowly. "I mean...part of it is availability. There are very few people in our little flotilla not in my chain of command. Most of the gay men I could think of are junior enough that technical authority is irrelevant." He sighed. "But we're both senior officers, we can talk work, and, well...we both like football. Real football, not the American one. I *can* talk to him, which puts him ahead of at least two boyfriends I've had in the past."

"He isn't in your chain of command," Annette agreed. "But if it starts to be a problem, I will come down on you like an orbital bombardment. Are we clear, Commander?"

"Yes, ma'am!" he said crisply. He seemed to relax. "There seems to be a lot of pairing-off going on," he noted. "Sade agreed to let Rolfson buy her a drink before she goes back to her ship, for example."

"I'm not surprised," the Captain admitted. "We're a long way from home—with no *way* home. I'd be more surprised if our people weren't pairing off. That said"—she raised a hand—"I expect *you*, Mister XO, to make sure we don't have any problems.

"We can only be so military when the military we serve is gone, but if there's abuse, it needs to be stopped. If we're having bad breakups, we need to separate people. We have barely a thousand people and they might be the only free humans left in the galaxy.

"We need them happy, so I don't intend to step on anything that isn't a problem—but we need them functional, so step on anything that *is* a problem."

Looking somewhat less deflated, Kurzman nodded.

"Yes, ma'am." He paused, considering the situation and eyeing her questioningly. Given the context, Annette wasn't entirely surprised by what came next. "Do you have anyone back home, Captain?" he asked gently. "I know there can't be anyone aboard ship for you..."

"No, Commander," she told him. "To both. Whatever they say about blondes having more fun, however much action you think I've had in the last few years, you're probably guessing too high."

"Career hazard," her XO chuckled in agreement. He paused for a moment, and then asked what she knew he'd been angling for. "There were rumors about you and Casimir. Any truth to them?"

She sighed.

"Pat, is it really relevant now?"

He looked sheepish for a moment, then sighed himself.

"I'm your XO, ma'am," he reminded her. "I wouldn't expect it to be, but it might."

He was...probably right.

"Fine. I won't confirm or deny anything," she told him, "but I *will* say that Elon Casimir is a man with a lot of money. When his wife passed away, he had a distinct shortage of people he could trust to turn to for comfort. To reveal anything that happened in that time would betray that trust."

"So, more truth than most assume and less than the tabloids spewed across the world?"

Annette laughed. "Fair. Morgan, while a very sweet child, is *not* my daughter."

That had been the accusation that had actually hurt when the tabloids had found out, somehow, about that brief affair in the weeks after Leanne Casimir's funeral. Piled on top of his parents' deaths, the loss of Leanne had almost broken Elon. She'd been there and it *had*, briefly, turned into more.

Suggesting that they'd betrayed Leanne, a woman Elon had loved and who Annette had been friends with for *a decade*, before her death had stung. The affair had been long over by the time the tabloids dragged it out, but that pain had been part of why they'd carefully *not* been seen together—she had, after all, been his employee.

"Would you going back to the Force have changed anything?" her XO asked quietly and she smiled sadly as he appeared to have followed her thoughts.

"I don't know," she admitted. "And now I'll never know."

CHAPTER TWENTY-FOUR

"WELL, WE ARE NOT CATCHING *THAT* FISH," ROLFSON announced as the blip flashed on the anomaly scanner. "I'm reading her as pulling sixty percent of lightspeed!"

"What *is* she?" Kurzman asked. "That's as fast as our old missiles."

"Imperial Courier," the newest member of the bridge crew, a tall Yin named Pondar, replied. The tall blue-skinned alien was impassive as she spoke. "They are the fastest ships ever built by anyone. The Kanzi and the Core Systems have similar craft, but they are a special breed."

"Sixty percent of light?" Annette repeated. "Military ships?"

"No," Pondar replied calmly. She'd taken over Mosi's slot as junior tactical officer after impressing Rolfson in testing and was on the bridge to get experience with the systems under the tactical officer's careful eye. "Courier pilots will remind you *very* forcefully that they are not military," she continued, checking numbers on her screen. "They regard themselves as better."

"So, she's carrying news," *Tornado*'s Captain mused. "Amandine, how's our intercept looking?"

"She's a third faster than we are, ma'am," her navigator replied. "We could probably *shoot* her but we can't catch her."

"Pondar—would she surrender if we demonstrate we can destroy her?"

"No," the Yin replied. "They are *Couriers*. They will die before they fail to deliver their mail, and only death will stop them."

Annette shook her head, eyeing the featureless dot.

"That's the fastest communications the A!Tol have got, huh?" she asked.

"The big A!Tol military bases have hyperwave transmitters," Pondar replied. "They are immobile installations, but combined with the Couriers and the smaller hyperwave receivers scattered through the Imperium, they tie A!Tol territory together."

Annette nodded, slowly processing the data. They'd pulled vast quantities of data from the systems of the two ships they'd captured, but reviewing and analyzing it all was a slow process. Ki!Tana was usually around when she was on the bridge, but she was starting to realize that making sure they *always* had an alien crewmember on the bridge was important. There was so much her human crew simply didn't know—things none of the aliens might think to mention until it came up.

"Let her go," she ordered as she watched the courier cross toward the alien fleet base. "Keep your eyes open," she told Rolfson. "We want a freighter—not a warship and apparently not a Courier."

"Point four cee or less seems to be our line," he agreed. "All the watches have the notes. We'll get something, ma'am."

A HARSH BUZZING noise woke Annette up from some of the better sleep she'd had since Sol had fallen. Blinking wearily, she hit the button to accept the intercom request audio-only.

"Ma'am, this is the bridge. We have a customer—she's on course for the fleet base at point three five of lightspeed, and we have no

THE TERRAN PRIVATEER   189

other anomalies on the screen. We have twenty-two minutes in which we can launch the intercept."

She was suddenly fully awake, a predatory grin growing on her face.

"Who has the watch?" she asked.

"Lieutenant Commander Amandine, ma'am," the rating replied.

"I'll be on the bridge in five minutes. Have him take the ship to condition two," she ordered. "Wake up the senior officers—especially Major Wellesley. It looks like we have a customer."

"Yes, ma'am."

The channel closed with a click and Annette stood in her quarters for a long moment. Point three five meant it probably wasn't a military ship, but an interstellar freighter full of cargo was a prize worth taking, no matter what.

She was still grinning as she grabbed her combat vac-suit.

───────

ANNETTE WAS a minute inside her own timeline when she strode onto her bridge. Amandine stood from the command chair immediately, throwing her a brisk salute as he moved over to navigation. Rolfson had managed to beat her to the bridge somehow and was working with Pondar to try and extrapolate *some* kind of identification from the tiny amount of information the hyperspatial anomaly scanner gave them.

"Ma'am, we couldn't find Major Wellesley," the com tech standing next to her command chair reported nervously. "He's not in his quarters or answering his communicator."

Annette sighed.

"I'll let Commander Kurzman know," she said. "He'll be able to track our errant officer faster. Not your fault, Carly. Wellesley should know better than to turn his com off."

"Sorry, ma'am, thank you, ma'am," the young woman chirped as she returned to her post at communications, rapidly joined by her boss as Chan entered the bridge.

Annette pinged a private channel to her XO.

"Pat."

"Ma'am."

"Wellesley is with you."

"Yes, ma'am."

"Tell him to turn his damn communicator on and get to his shuttles," Annette snapped.

"Already on his way, ma'am," her XO said quietly. "Communicator was on. We were distracted."

"I don't want to know. Be in CIC."

"Yes, ma'am."

Killing the channel, she turned back to her bridge.

"Rolfson, what have we got?" she asked.

"Speed suggests civilian shipping," he told her. "Won't be military supplies, but there is an inhabited world in the system with the fleet base. Regular traders—could be anything, will probably be multiple things."

"How long is our intercept window?" she asked her navigator.

"If we move in the next ten minutes, we'll intercept in under twenty," Amandine replied. "If we wait more than thirty minutes, we're looking at a stern chase and we're not *that* much faster than her."

"I don't see a point in hanging around," Annette concluded, settling into her chair. "Take us out, Lieutenant Commander. Rolfson—ready a warning shot for as soon as they see us."

Moments later—a time frame that still seemed impossibly short to *Tornado*'s Captain—the warship leapt out at the freighter at forty-three percent of the speed of light.

The freighter did nothing.

"They *can* see us, right?" Annette asked as the hyperspace distance between them evaporated. They were cutting the freighter's course, gaining on it at far more than their own hundred and thirty thousand kilometers a second.

"She may not have an anomaly scanner," Ki!Tana told her, the alien having just entered the bridge. Something in how she was moving when Annette glanced at her suggested the A!Tol had been having a rough night. Her manipulators sagged and her locomotive tentacles were slow and careful in their movements.

"If she *has* a scanner, it may be old, broken, or short-ranged," the old pirate continued. "Or, well, she may see us...and realize there is nothing that they can do."

"Or it could be a trap," Rolfson noted.

"Or it could be a trap," Ki!Tana agreed.

"Spin up the antimissile suite and charge the shield," Annette ordered. "It doesn't feel like a trap. But I don't plan on dying today, either."

"Intercept time two minutes and closing," Amandine reported. "They're...still not doing anything."

"Major Wellesley." She opened a channel to the Special Space Service commander. "Are you ready to board?"

"You give the word, ma'am."

She waited. The distance was dropping rapidly—relatively quickly; they'd hit the one light-second mark where the freighter's crew would be able to see them with regular sensors. At that point, she could demand their surrender and they'd have no choice but to obey.

"Ma'am! I have an aspect change!" Rolfson reported. "New signature on the scopes."

"We have a visitor?" she demanded. "Show me!"

"No, looks like it just detached from the freighter?" he said in a confused tone. "I've got a second anomaly moving in the exact opposite direction to the original at point four five cee."

"Escape ship," Pondar said instantly.

"What?" Rolfson demanded of his new junior.

"Some captains—usually those with good insurance—have the

crew section of the ship basically built as a detachable vessel," the Yin explained. "It's surprisingly inexpensive to do, as the drive can be built to only last a week or two and usually includes the hyperdrive emitters."

"Do we need the escape ship to capture the freighter?"

"Normally, but we should be able to use *Oaths of Secrecy*'s emitters as a replacement," Ki!Tana said. "They have abandoned the freighter and will claim it on their insurance. We could, of course, capture both."

Captain Lougheed's ship was close enough to the escape ship's course to cut them off. Annette had limited ways to *communicate* with him, but given the plans they did have, if she fired a missile in parallel to the escape ship's course, he'd know to bring it in.

"No," she finally concluded. "We want the cargo and the hull. We don't need the crew—we're not slavers, and repatriating them would be a pain in the ass."

"Ma'am, we have broken the one-light-second zone," Amandine reported.

"Major—launch your boarding operation."

THE STAR FREIGHTERS that tied the A!Tol Imperium together looked odd to James's eyes. His family had kept their wealth intact the way most of the successful British aristocrats had: by investing in shipping and trade over the years. A good third of the spaceships flitting around the Sol system had a Wellesley among the investors, so the Major was very familiar with what Earth's interplanetary freighters looked like.

Each of the freighters he'd seen so far had been completely different. Even looking through the files stolen from their captures showed a vast array of different shapes and sizes, and this new ship followed the rule of looking completely different.

It consisted of four cylindrical modules linked together with a mess of gantries and wiring. The shuttle's sensors noted that the interface drive nodes were equally mounted on all four modules, probably with redundant controls as backup for the now-missing central module.

He could see where that capsule had been, a mess of broken gantries and connectors. With it missing, he wasn't entirely sure *where* to go. When in doubt, however..."

"Alpha through Delta Troops," he announced over his communicator. "Start at the top, go clockwise. Each of you takes a module and sweeps it. Echo, Golf Troops, stay out as reserve."

"What about us?" McPhail asked. With the craft stolen from *Fang*, James's headquarters section now had their own shuttle, allowing them to act as a mobile reserve.

"Take us to...that one," he indicated the one assigned to Charlie Troop. "I want to see what we're looking at with my own eyes."

"On our way, Major," the pilot told him.

THE SHIP WAS MORE than a little eerie. All of the lights in the module James Wellesley and his headquarters section boarded were still on. Indicators were flashing, computer screens running—everything aboard the ship was fully functional.

The air wasn't breathable, which was a new one on him. Most of the races they'd encountered so far breathed air with an oxygen content within a few points of Earth's. They had all been able to breathe aboard the last two ships, and their new alien crewmates could breathe aboard *Tornado*. This ship had a similar oxygen content, but its level of about six other chemicals would be almost instantly lethal to James's human Special Space Service troopers.

"Ikel," Ral, his new Yin soldier, said sharply.

"What?"

"Ikel," Ral repeated. "Carapaced hexapods, need *chlorine* in their air to survive. Would have been a pure Ikel crew—no one *else* can breathe their air."

"Works for preservation, though," someone pointed out. "Most bacteria not used to this are going to die immediately."

"Brilliant," James said with a shake of his head. "Charlie is securing the ship. Let's check on the cargo."

Most of the module was cargo space, so finding *something* to check was easy. A hatch nearby opened up to the hacking software Ki!Tana had given them, and revealed rows upon rows of stacked containers, roughly a meter wide and high by two meters long.

"What is this?" the Major asked rhetorically. He stepped over to one of the boxes and poked at it. His helmet said it had a power source but nothing significant.

"Cover me," he ordered as he identified a lock and a lid. With a sharp strike from the butt of his plasma rifle, he smashed the lock open and pushed the lid up, shining a light in.

If he hadn't known he was on an alien ship, he'd have sworn he'd opened a freezer on a ship carrying luxury food to the Mars colony. The contents were neatly packed frozen rows of what he would have sworn were steaks.

"FOOD," Annette repeated to be sure she'd understood correctly. "We captured an entire freighter full of food."

"According to the manifest, some of it is luxury edibles that about seven species can eat," Wellesley told her. "But eighty-five percent of the cargo is frozen meat and vegetables destined to be turned into Universal Protein at the Kimar system."

"No wonder they weren't willing to die for it," Rolfson announced with a chuckle. "Is it *worth* anything?"

"In quantity," Ki!Tana pointed out. "There are those at Tortuga who will buy it, though at a large reduction from its true value. The ship may be worth more, even lacking the control capsule."

"Stolen goods are never sold at a loss," Annette told her people. "Get her under control, meet up with Lougheed. Once *Oaths of Secrecy* has control of the ship, return aboard *Tornado*. We'll send them on to the rendezvous point to meet Sade and Mosi while we sweep for more prey."

"Yes, ma'am."

"Can any of our people eat the delicacies?" she asked a moment later.

"If I'm reading this right, the Rekiki can, but nobody else on our crew," Wellesley told her.

"Tell them they can take anything that appeals to them. A dozen of them isn't going to make much of a dent in a *shipment* of luxury food."

"I'll let them know, Captain."

CHAPTER TWENTY-FIVE

Annette had no luck returning to sleep after the brief excitement of the chase, fitfully tossing and turning until morning. With no new reports on her communicator when she gave up, she took extra time turning herself out.

It would never do for the crew to see the Captain at anything less than her best. The same strictures that would keep her alone while her entire crew paired up around and rationed her smiles meant she would never leave her quarters looking anything less than perfect.

There was also, she admitted to herself with a smile as she carefully covered the shadows under her eyes, a bit of ego involved.

As she finished getting ready for the day, her communicator did ping with a note. She pulled the two ends apart and reviewed the note: it was a short thank-you from Tellaki, the leader of the Rekiki aboard *Tornado*, for allowing them to raid their latest prize's cargo.

If she'd received the same note from a human, it would have included an implicit invitation to join them for breakfast. She wasn't sure if the translator was up to that level of between-the-lines detail, but she also hadn't met the centaur-like aliens for more than a moment.

Ki!Tana expected them to leave at Tortuga, but it wouldn't *hurt* to get a better feel for them regardless.

If nothing else, she understood that their race provided a disproportionate portion of the A!Tol Imperial Army's heavy ground forces. Knowing how they thought would help when the time came to retake Earth.

TORNADO'S MESS hall stewards had grown very efficient at swapping out seating arrangements for the cruiser's new alien crew. Many of the seats had been stolen from *Rekiki's Fang*; others were repurposed from what they already had on hand.

For the Rekiki, a pair of low, wide benches had been carried over from *Fang*. The four-legged aliens stepped over the bench and then dropped their lower torsos onto it, relieving their legs of much of the burden of carrying their not-insignificant weight.

"I'll be joining them," Annette murmured to the steward who approached her as soon as she entered. The Captain made a point of eating in one of the main mess halls at least one meal a day—it was, if nothing else, a period where she was away from her work computer and its infinite supply of paperwork.

"I'll have something sent over," the steward promised.

Gently waving off the young man, Annette approached the dozen aliens who had claimed one of the larger tables. The limited number of benches they had for the centaur-like aliens forced a certain degree of clustering, but she suspected that the Rekiki—who'd been an unofficial elite aboard Kikitheth's ship—would have kept to themselves regardless.

"May I join you?" she asked as she stepped up to the table.

Tellaki looked up and bared his teeth in what she *thought* was an equivalent to a smile. It was a good reminder that the Rekiki were *not* herbivores. The crocodile-like centaur's mouth was full of deadly sharp teeth.

"With pleasure, Honored Captain," he replied. "We feast on your generosity this morning."

Annette grabbed a chair from another table and pulled it up to the end of the table. She wasn't quite sure *what* the centaur-like aliens were eating, but she'd have called it "steak and eggs" back home.

"No one else aboard the ship could eat anything we captured last night," she pointed out as the steward brought her a plate with a reasonable facsimile of a North American breakfast sandwich—with egg, cheese and bacon *all* replaced with different treatments of Universal Protein.

"But you gave us that which could have been sold. We honor your generosity," Tellaki told her with a slight bow of his head. The upper bodies of the Rekiki looked even less like humans than their lower bodies looked like horses. They were covered in the same small, leathery scales as their lower torsos under very human-like uniform jackets, and their faces resembled short-muzzled crocodiles more than anything else.

"Major Wellesley speaks highly of your performance," she replied. "It is a small bonus, but all I can give until we reach Tortuga."

They had now *programmed* that translation into their software. No human was going to voluntarily try and pronounce the mouthful of clicks the program had initially transliterated the names as.

"I understand that you intend to leave us once we reach there," she continued.

Tellaki dipped his head, a strange bow-shrug gesture that managed to get across his intention.

"It is not a slight upon you, Honored Captain," he finally said. "We served Kikitheth due to ties of blood and honor, even when she chose a path we would not have. We agreed to trade service for transport from the wreck of her ship. We are vassals, not lords, and will serve a master. It is our way," he finished, raising a hand to cut off Annette's objection. "Yours is not the only race in the Imperium to find our way strange."

"I warn you now, it will take us several days to sell the cargos and prizes," Annette told him. "While you are welcome to leave as soon as we make port, I ask that you stay in communication so we can be sure to pay you your share."

Tellaki dipped his snout again, blinking rapidly.

"If we leave by our own choice..."

"You are still owed payment for your service," she cut him off. "I promised shares to every sapient who came aboard. I would not have you make me a liar, Tellaki."

Several of the other Rekiki started stamping their feet with a sharp hissing sound—that faded as Tellaki flashed his fangs at them.

They'd been *laughing*. That was a good sign.

"Your honor is appreciated, Captain. And unexpected among pirates."

"I am a naval officer charged to be a privateer, Tellaki," she reminded him gently. "Not a pirate, though I'll admit the difference is academic."

"Were you Rekiki, Honored Captain, I would consider swearing you fealty," he replied, bowing his head. "But I am a Rekiki vassal and must return to my Lady's family to tell them of her fate. This is duty."

"I will take that as an honor," she told him, bowing her head in turn. "I will not bar you from your duty, Tellaki. I regret that Kiki-theth was not prepared to surrender."

"She was a Rekiki lord," the centaur leader said. "She made her choices. I will not judge them."

Before Annette could say anything more, her communicator pinged, this time with a live call.

"Bond," she answered it.

"Ma'am, we have another customer."

ONE OF THE benefits of the—surprisingly reasonable—breakfast sandwich the mess had put together for Annette was that it could be eaten at a brisk walking pace. She dropped the wrapper in a garbage receptacle next to the bridge, quickly wiped off her face and hands with a napkin that followed it into the garbage, and then walked onto her bridge calmly.

"What am I looking at, people?" she demanded as she scanned the tactical plot and crossed to her seat.

"Single ship on course from the Tiamo system to the fleet base at Kimar," Rolfson told her. He'd had the watch but apparently had been holding it down from his regular console. "Moving at point four cee; best guess is a military freighter or high-end civilian ship."

"Ki!Tana?" Annette asked, glancing at the alien who'd arrived just after her. "Sounds right to me; any thoughts?"

"Many ships travel at that speed," Ki!Tana pointed out. "But few warships. Regardless of the value of the prize, it is no threat to *Tornado*."

"Well, then, we've sent both of our scout ships off to the rendezvous point with prizes. I'd hate to show up to the party empty-handed," the Captain told her crew. "Mister Amandine—intercept course, if you please."

"Yes, ma'am," her navigator confirmed, sliding into his chair literally as she spoke.

Amandine and Chan had been the last arrivals of her officers, though they were still short a full bridge crew.

"Lieutenant Commander Chan," Annette addressed her com officer. "If you would be so kind as to signal general quarters, I think we'll stay on the taking-no-chances plan."

"Yes, ma'am," the woman replied. There was no audible change in the bridge itself, but Annette knew that warning lights and communicators were now going off across the entire cruiser.

"Shield is up; antimissile suite is charged and active," Rolfson reported. "One missile prepped for a warning shot. Full salvo ready in the launchers just in case."

Annette nodded her acknowledgement and watched as they lunged in pursuit of their newest prey. The whole process was starting to acquire a tone of routine on her bridge. She suspected none of her UESF officers were entirely comfortable with what they were doing, but they did their jobs.

"Range is one light-minute and closing," Amandine reported. "They are turning away; we will close the range over the next twenty minutes."

"So, they see us. Rolfson: fire the warning shot."

The white light of the missile was visible on the regular scanners for barely a second. Beyond that, its light dissipated into the strange gray void of hyperspace and only the anomaly scanner showed the missile gaining on the other ship.

Finally, the two dots intersected and the missile vanished. As a warning shot, it *should* have hit the shields on an angle that couldn't have hit the ship, but it was impossible to be one hundred percent sure.

"Any reaction?" she asked.

"Not yet...wait! Shit!" Rolfson snapped. "I have anomaly separation—*missiles inbound.* I have six birds inbound, hot and closing."

"Can we take them?" Annette demanded.

"Laser suite should get most and the shields could handle the whole salvo," her tactical officer replied. "Your orders, ma'am? Do we return fire?"

"Ki!Tana?" she asked. "What kind of ship would have that speed and that armament? Six launchers is light for a warship."

"At that speed, she is unlikely to be a warship," the big alien replied. "She is potentially an armed freighter. The A!Tol Navy uses them for high-value cargos too large for Courier delivery."

"That was my first guess," Annette said calmly as the missiles bore down on them. "Hold fire, Lieutenant Commander," she told Rolfson. "If all they have is six launchers, we can take their fire while we close and disable them at close range."

"That's risky, ma'am," he warned.

"If she *is* a freighter, she's carrying something worth protecting," she replied. "We'll take the risk."

The first missile salvo broke into their visibility zone as she spoke, flashing across the single light-second their lasers could sweep in moments.

The laser antimissile suite knocked out four and the last two slammed into the shields, sending light flickering around the ship.

"Shields are holding," Rolfson reported. "More missiles incoming, Captain."

"We'll take them," she said quietly. "And hope the cargo is worth it!"

THE ARMED FREIGHTER—IF that's what it was—had a slow cycle time on her launchers. It took *Tornado* just under twenty minutes to close the range to just outside the visibility bubble around the other ship, in which time their prey only threw twenty-two missile salvos at them.

It was nerve-wracking for Annette and her crew to simply sit there and watch the missiles coming in, but firing back would likely *destroy* their target instead of disabling it.

After the first five salvos, though, Annette at least started to relax. The laser suite Nova Industries had designed and installed on the ship was proving surprisingly effective against even the A!Tol's unbelievably fast missiles.

They didn't stop all of the missiles, but only one salvo got more than two missiles through. The shield metrics Annette watched with one corner of her eye barely flickered, even when three missiles slammed into the screen at once.

"Kulap, Ki!Tana, I'm impressed," Annette told her engineer and the alien who'd worked together to install the shield. "I wasn't sure the shield would hold up to this."

"She'll have something for close range, too," Ki!Tana pointed out.

"I know. Rolfson: we're going to have to let her shoot at us, but I want the lasers on whatever close-in firepower she has. Take it out and take it out *fast*."

"Crossing the visibility bubble...*now!*" Amandine snapped.

One moment, all they could see was the gray blankness. The next, the shape of their target appeared as if popping through the side of a bubble.

She was an Imperial ship, all elegant lines and flashy technology just like the ones that had invaded Sol.

"She's firing! Proton beams on the shield!"

"Evade!" Annette snapped. "Disable those guns!"

Two massively powerful proton beams were mounted on either side of the beak-like prow of the armed freighter. Both beams smashed through space, hammering into *Tornado*'s shield, driving the metrics Annette was watching mad.

The enemy gunner was *good*, she noted absently. Amandine tore *Tornado* through an apparently impossible sequence of maneuvers, but the transport had them pinned.

"Dialed in! Returning fire!"

Tornado's proton beams and lasers returned fire in sequence as the ship spun through Amandine's maneuvers, each beam slamming into the alien until its shields finally collapsed. The stolen and upgraded proton beams holed the enemy ship's prow, shattering both enemy heavy beam weapons in a single shot.

And then *their* shields went down, overwhelmed by the sheer power of the enemy beam weapons, and missiles *flashed* across the intervening space.

The missile suite nailed two but the remainders slammed into *Tornado*'s compressed-matter armor at almost three quarters of the speed of light. The armored cruiser *rang* like a bell, safety belts and the interface drives' inherent inertial absorption preventing any injury to the crew.

Silence.

"Hit the launchers with the lasers," Rolfson said after a moment. "She has no weapons left. Your orders?"

Annette took a deep breath and slowly released it, studying the image of the elegant, damaged but functional ship a hundred thousand kilometers from her ship.

"Keep pace with her," she ordered. "Wellesley, are your teams ready to go?"

"Yes, ma'am," the Major replied over the intercom. "All shuttles locked and loaded. Do we launch?"

"Yes, but hold off a minute," she instructed. "Chan, hail them and order them to surrender."

More silence. The alien transport continued to try to evade, but *Tornado* had enough of a speed edge that that was impossible. There was no way they were getting away, but they were trying. Annette could respect that—but she wanted that ship.

"All right," she said softly. "Major Wellesley, launch your shuttles. Lieutenant Commander Rolfson, keep your lasers ready to burn out any major pockets of resistance. Chan, record me for transmission."

She leaned forward into the camera on her chair.

"A!Tol Imperial freighter, this is Captain Annette Bond of the Terran privateer *Tornado*. You have fought valiantly, but you are outgunned and outclassed. You could self-destruct and deny me your cargo at the cost of your lives, but any resistance short of that will only add to the dead.

"I don't want to kill you. You don't want to die. Surrender."

She gestured to Chan, ordering her to cut the recording and send. The *second* part of her message appeared on her scanners as she did, with Wellesley's shuttles launching from her shuttle bays.

"Give them thirty seconds, Major," she ordered. "Then..."

"Transmission incoming!" Chan interrupted.

"Put him on."

The alien that appeared on her screen was *not* an A!Tol. The speaker was a tall hairless biped with dark red skin and a seemingly immobile face, lacking both a nose and ears to human eyes.

"I am Captain Invidus of the A!Tol Imperial Priority Freighter *Songs of the Riders*," it greeted her. "Are you prepared to guarantee the safety of my crew?"

"Your crew is in no danger from me unless you resist me," Annette replied. "I will guarantee their safety and your safe return to the Tiamo system. *If* you surrender."

Invidus lowered its head, a very humanlike gesture.

"I am prepared to fight for my cargo," it said simply. "I am not prepared to order my crew to die for it. Your terms, Captain Bond?"

"You will evacuate your ship via personnel shuttles that we will take under tow," Annette told him. "You may wipe confidential and classified data from your systems, but if you wipe the operating system of the ship, the deal is off. If any of your shuttles make aggressive movements, they will be destroyed.

"Otherwise, you and your people will be delivered safely to Tiamo. Your ship and its cargo are mine."

Invidus bowed his head again.

"Your terms are acceptable."

CHAPTER TWENTY-SIX

ANOTHER DAY, ANOTHER CREEPILY ABANDONED TRANSPORT. James Wellesley was starting to think he wasn't cut out for the life of a pirate, which would have been a shock to several ancestors his family didn't talk about very much.

Invidus had been as good as its word. The local consoles were accessible when the Special Space Service people checked into them, readily disgorging an internal map of the ship that his troopers' scans confirmed to be correct.

James's headquarters section had made contact surprisingly close to the bridge. He'd allowed his two power-armored nonhumans to lead the way, but they were on the armed freighter's bridge ten minutes after they'd boarded.

The similarities to the bridges of UESF ships he'd served on were enough to bring him to a halt. The two previous prizes had been unarmed transports, civilian designs even when bought and upgraded for Imperial service. *This* ship had been built by the A!Tol Imperial Navy for its own use.

The bridge was circular as opposed to the UESF's horseshoe, with a three-dimensional hologram tank at the center instead of the big screen the Terran ships had used. A similar raised second level surrounded the bridge, full of abandoned consoles where teams would have supported the officers on the main floor.

The ship was half again *Tornado*'s size, with the armament of a destroyer. Her bridge was only slightly smaller than the privateer cruiser, and James found himself wondering just *how many* aliens they'd chased off the ship.

"Is anyone running into stragglers?" he asked over the company channel.

The responses were all negative. Invidus and his people appeared to have fully evacuated the ship—without even leaving any traps.

"Captain Bond." He raised the channel to *Tornado*. "It looks like the manifest got wiped with everything else, but the operating system is intact. You can send over your prize crew—I'm going to check out the cargo."

"I'll have Lieutenant Chou over immediately," the Captain replied. "So, you're saying Invidus figured the cargo manifest was confidential?"

"I think the red bugger erred on the side of wiping everything *except* the OS," James told her. "I'd also guess some *really* important stuff ended up on the shuttles."

"Go find out what he left us," Bond ordered. "Once we know that, I'll decide whether we'll board the shuttles to see what they took with them."

"Yes, ma'am."

"I...AM not sure what this stuff is," one of James's troopers said, staring down into the cargo container.

It had taken them five minutes to break the container open—even *with* the disturbingly effective hacking software Ki!Tana had provided them. The cargo hold nearest the bridge was full of identical containers, each a white ceramic box the size of a large suitcase with a small electronic security panel the only break in their smooth, seamless, exterior.

Now the box had opened, an invisible seam cracking the smooth exterior as one side slid up and over on silent and invisible motors. The inside was the same color, though the material looked more like packing foam than ceramic now.

Stacked in neat slots inside the packing material were translucent silver crystals. Each was the length of James's arm and a perfect octahedron.

"Ral, come take a look at this," James ordered, waving over the Yin trooper who'd joined his headquarters section.

Unlike the human SSS troopers, the Yin had powered combat armor and had been watching the door to the hold. He obediently came over, looked down into the carrying container—and promptly dropped his plasma rifle.

"*Sacred suns of holy fire.*"

The translator was still only mediocre at tone, but *that* came through.

"Check that weapon," James snapped. Whatever this stuff was, the last thing they needed was a dropped plasma weapon failing containment and vaporizing half a dozen of the containers—and half his headquarters section.

"Sorry, Major," Ral said as he reclaimed and checked over his rifle. "I...have never seen those in person and you may want to check with Ki!Tana, but I believe those are molecular circuitry cores."

James blinked. Humanity had been building nano-scale circuits for years, and the latest versions, the ones included in *Tornado*'s mind-boggling powerful computer cores, had occasionally been referred to as molecular circuits. It was more marketing than anything else, as true molecular circuitry would be a tenth the scale of even humanity's more powerful circuits.

Tornado's computer cores were each three meters tall and a meter around. If those crystals were what he thought they were, each of them matched the processing power and storage of one of those supercomputers.

"Captain?" he raised *Tornado* again. "I need a video feed to Ki!Tana. We need a confirmation on what we're looking at."

"You got into the cargo?" Bond asked.

"We did," he confirmed.

"What did you find?" Ki!Tana's translated voice came onto the channel. "We have the video feed from your helmet up now."

James looked back into the case, focusing his helmet light on the crystals.

There was a silent pause.

"I understand why this cargo had a priority freighter," the alien finally said. "Is the entire cargo these?"

The Major looked up, allowing his light and helmet camera to sweep along the entire hold and its rows upon rows of identical containers.

"What am I looking at, Ki!Tana?" Bond demanded.

"Molecular circuitry cores," the alien told her. "Each core is approximately sixty-four percent of the processing power and storage of the cores I reviewed in your systems. They are difficult to manufacture, and most Imperial systems still use nano-level circuits similar to your own."

"*Difficult to manufacture* usually means *expensive*," the Captain pointed out.

"Yes, but not unreasonably so," Ki!Tana replied. "Each of those cores costs...three times what an equivalent nano-scale computer would cost."

"The case has six," James noted. "Best guess? This hold has five hundred cases. This ship has four holds. That's *twelve thousand* cores."

"That would have built this ship four times over."

"Given that the primary use of molecular cores is to provide computer power to warships, that is a valid comparison," the alien said. "This is...the maintenance requirements for the fleet based at Kimar. For a full long-cycle for thirty-two ships of the line."

"So, this will fund the work we want done at Tortuga," Bond stated.

"Even at the cut-rate price you'll find for stolen goods, this would buy you your upgrades and another heavy," Ki!Tana told them. "Entire pirate crews have retired on lesser spoils."

"I don't think most pirates would have survived *taking* the ship," James pointed out.

"No. *Rekiki's Fang* wouldn't have even tried; we'd have broken off as soon as we realized what we'd found," the old pirate told. "Few are the pirate heavies that would knowingly tangle with a Navy Priority Freighter."

"Chou will be at the bridge in five," Bond told James. "I want you to keep at least two troops on that ship. Guard those cores, Major. They may just be the key to earning Earth's freedom."

CHAPTER TWENTY-SEVEN

"So, when we get back to Earth, I suggest we pool our funds and buy the Captain a lottery ticket," Captain Sade said with a shark-like grin as the senior officers of Annette's little privateer fleet gathered at the rendezvous point.

"Three ships and two doozies?" she continued, gesturing at the display at the end of the conference room showing the three Terran ships and their accompanying prizes. "That's luck."

"That's astrography," Ki!Tana replied. "And a willingness to take risks a regular pirate would not. The missiles? That was a fast collier called up to replace weapons no one expected to have to expend at Sol. Your possession of interface drive missiles would have been a surprise.

"As for the cores..." The alien fluttered her manipulator tentacles. "A similar armed freighter to *Song of the Riders* would arrive at the Kimar Fleet base at least once a five-cycle. The one last five-cycle might have been exotic-matter coils. The one next five-cycle could have been proton beam focusing arrays.

"Remember that we are far from the centers of Imperial power," Ki!Tana continued. "Few pirates come out this far, so the priority armed freighters are the only security likely to be assigned—and no pirate here would tangle with a priority freighter. Even among the heavies, only about half *could*, and most wouldn't take the risk. As armed freighters go"—the tentacles shivered again—"a cargo of cores is of middling value. The odds of a greater prize are there—but a pirate's livelihood is their ship."

"So, if we'd hung out there for another week and let somebody *else* shoot at us without replying, we might have stolen something more valuable?" Kurzman asked.

"Yes."

Annette managed not to chuckle as Ki!Tana completely missed her XO's point.

"Regardless of whether we were lucky or not," she told her officers, "we now have three prizes to sell. Sade, Mosi: any issues with offloading cargo at Centauri?"

"None," the young woman commanding their first prize crew replied. "The cave the cache is in is full to bursting now, though. Even with loading all the old missiles aboard the freighter, we still barely fit the new missiles into the cache."

"We will want to split those up more, given time," Sade agreed. "There are four more caches in systems around Sol, though Centauri is the biggest. Spreading the missiles around with the food and medicine stocks will reduce our point-failure sources."

"Agreed," Annette told them. "We will look into that in the future. For now, I understand all three prizes are ready to go? Lougheed?"

The half-Chinese commander of *Of Course We're Coming Back* sighed.

"We're basically using *Of Course* as a replacement for the previous command module," he pointed out. "It's...well, it's a kludge. We're holding the two ships together with duct tape and wire. I will be *ecstatic* to dump her off on anyone who wants to buy her. Does a ship that damaged actually have value, Ki!Tana?"

"Less than an intact ship," the big alien told him, flushing slightly red in pleasure at being directly addressed—Annette's officers were getting *better*, but they still tended to address questions that the A!Tol could answer best more generally and expect her to answer.

"But she is still valuable. More valuable than her cargo, in fact. Retrofitting a command center onto one of the secondary drive control nodes and adding new hyperspace emitters would be straightforward, well within Tortuga's capabilities."

"What *is* this place?" Amandine asked. "I mean, I'm envisaging some kind of rogue space station, but if they can do major starship work..."

"Perhaps most importantly," Annette said, "Tortuga is our next destination. We are, according to the chart Ki!Tana provided, seven days' hyperspace flight from the system it is hidden in. We will be flying in convoy within visibility of each other, so if anyone has any problems, we can immediately address them.

"But that said, since we are setting course for Tortuga, perhaps a better idea of where we are headed could be useful. Ki!Tana?"

The big alien flashed bright red for a moment and rose to her full, mind-boggling height.

"Tortuga's existence depends on a delicate political balance," she explained. "While this far along the galactic arm, we are mostly concerned with the A!Tol and the Kanzi, but realize that each arm of this galaxy has its own empires and local conflicts. The A!Tol and Kanzi are large by the scale of these outer empires, but it is important that there are powers in the core that equal or exceed them in technology, industry, and military might.

"These powers...do not care about the conflicts out here," Ki!Tana warned, probably catching the wave of hope that swept over Annette's crew. "The strongest are the oldest. They are insular and arrogant. Their local sports team is vastly more significant to them than the conflict out here.

"But...they are wealthy and so they are the targets of pirates. Every hundred or so long-cycles, they work together to drive the pirates from their space—and then spend the next hundred long-cycles funding privateering expeditions on each other that fuel more piracy."

"That sounds like an interesting set of international relations," Chan noted, the communication officer looking thoughtful. "Few actual wars, I'm guessing, but generally high level of tensions?"

"Exactly," the A!Tol agreed. "The peace at the core is kept by a number of treaties that call on the other powers to step in if two of the great powers go to war. There are *seven* major powers in the core.

"Key to Tortuga, though, is that three hundred long-cycles ago"— a hundred and fifty years on Terra, give or take—"there was a war between the two smallest great powers. When the other powers stepped in and imposed a peace, the terms were unacceptable to one side's military. Many of their units went rogue and became privateers —including a mobile shipyard that rivaled anything the A!Tol could build today.

"Eventually, the pirates that initially went rogue were wiped out, but the shipyard escaped. To fund the maintenance of such an immense vessel, the crew took on contracts and provided service to anyone who would pay.

"Their race—the Laians—still rule what has become Tortuga. They move the station every few long-cycles to make sure it remains undiscovered, slowly moving farther along the arm of the galaxy. Why they picked this arm, and the border between the A!Tol and the Kanzi, I don't know. But they have served me well over the years."

"So, like the place we nicknamed it for, Tortuga is a melting pot of cultures and states, beholden to no one," Annette summarized to her people. "It's lawless, so we'll need to be very careful, but it also sells *everything*—including the upgrades we want for *Tornado*."

"If you have the goods, you can purchase technology equal to or better than the A!Tol Navy's best," Ki!Tana admitted. "Few have the funds to purchase the Laians' tech, but they do offer it for sale. With what you are bringing in prizes...the funds you have reserved to upgrade your ship should allow you to acquire some select upgrades."

"So, Tortuga is a giant spaceship?" Rolfson asked. "Trying to wrap my head around that."

Ki!Tana looked at him, her skin flashing the blueish purple tones of confusion.

"Sorry," the tactical officer said, realizing she'd missed the metaphor. "It's difficult to comprehend."

"It started as a shipyard," she confirmed. "Several of the slips have now been built over and turned into living and market sections. It cannot move quickly, but it can enter hyperspace.

"Currently, it is hidden inside the rings of a gas giant in an otherwise uninhabited system. I have the pass phrases to allow us to approach unmolested."

"We will at that point probably want to allow shore leave, Captain," Kurzman suggested. "We've been away from Earth a while. It's rough on the crew."

"Everyone goes aboard armed and no one goes anywhere alone," Annette said calmly. "I don't get the impression, Ki!Tana, that Tortuga is safe."

"No," the big alien agreed. "All things can be bought at Tortuga. That includes both safety for yourself—and a lack thereof for someone else."

"COME," Annette ordered as the admittance buzzer chimed on her office. She'd been doing paperwork and watching the progress of her little convoy on the map of the A!Tol Imperium she had showing on her main wall.

That progress *looked* slow, but that was a matter of scale. The exact translation of their velocity into hyperspace was neither constant nor easily rendered, but they were going to travel over a hundred light-years in eight days.

It was mind-boggling, and the map distracted her once again as her XO stepped into the room and cleared his throat.

"Pat," she greeted him. "Have a seat. What do you need?"

"I think...I need to bend your ear as the only person I can admit doubt to," Kurzman said with a sigh as he dropped into the chair.

"Doubt, Commander?" Annette asked. She didn't have anyone to lean her doubts on at this point. He was right that she was the only one he should be showing doubts to, though she guessed that James Wellesley saw some of them.

"We're a long way from home," he told her quietly. "Like...mind-bogglingly far away and going farther. I can't help feeling that we're out of our depth. For God's sake, we're relying on one of the people who *conquered Earth* for all of our data."

"To be fair," she pointed out, "We have a lot of aliens aboard, not just Ki!Tana, and they've all been telling us much the same thing. And we did translate a bunch of the data from *Rekiki's Fang* ourselves and *that* supports her too."

"I know. But...Captain...I keep looking at the numbers, the size of the A!Tol and Kanzi Imperiums, and the data on the Kanzi...are we doing the right thing?"

Annette looked at him sharply.

"The right thing?" she asked. "We're fighting for the freedom of *our species*. Our right to determine our own fate, to stand on our own two feet and say 'We are mankind and we will not be slaves.'"

"I've been looking at the A!Tol historical records," Kurzman told her. "The species they conquer...they don't end up slaves. They end up *citizens*. It's not a fast process, but absorption into the Imperium seems to *help* people."

"Especially compared to the Kanzi."

"The alternative is not a different conqueror," Annette snapped.

"Isn't it?" her XO asked. "Let's say we upgrade *Tornado*. Return to Sol with the tech and knowledge for the Weber Network to build more ships and we somehow drive the A!Tol from Sol. What happens then?"

"We fortify and prepare. We build more ships and we defend our world."

"And when the Kanzi come?" he said quietly. "When the slavers come with ships of the line and blast whatever we build to shreds? We can't stop *either* of these empires from taking Sol, Annette."

"So, what, we should just bend our knee to the squids and hope it turns out for the best? So long as I breathe, Patrick, I will fight for my world." She shook her head at him. "If you want out, I'm sure we could hire a ship to deliver people to Sol at Tortuga."

He exhaled and shook his head, leaning back.

"No," he admitted "Sorry, that...came out with more certainty than I meant! I have my doubts, Captain, I won't deny that—but I swore an oath and put on a uniform."

"Good," she told him. *Doubts* were permitted—she had her own. But they had to be able to do the job. "Tortuga really does look like our best option," she continued. "If we can get our hands on some of the Laian tech...I *know* Casimir had plans for keeping some ship-building apparatus intact under the Weber Protocols. If we can deliver him the specs and background for gear equal to the A!Tol navy's, we have a chance—especially since we *know* they don't have compressed-matter armor."

"You think we can really do this?" Kurzman asked quietly.

"I have to," Annette told him. "And *you* have to, in public at least. If we believe we have a chance, the crew will believe. The alternative..." She sighed. "The alternative is that we end up truly being nothing but the pirate scum the A!Tol call us."

"I...think I would prefer surrender to that, ma'am."

"I suspect the warning sign is when that ceases to be the case, Commander."

CHAPTER TWENTY-EIGHT

JEAN VILLENEUVE—NO LONGER ADMIRAL JEAN VILLENEUVE, now simply another citizen of Earth—sighed and put aside the communicator as his doorbell rang. The news was...good in some ways and terrifying in others. A new industrial plant was being set up near Cherbourg, over a site that had been building surface-to-space shuttles before the occupation.

The site had been *purchased*, for a reasonable price even, from its original owners. Workers were being *hired*. He knew, through his old contacts, that there was even an active push to recruit the millions of now-ex-military personnel all around the globe into the new industrial projects.

The UESF personnel, with some notable exceptions like himself, had disappeared. But Earth's new overlords had dismantled the national militaries along with the national governments. *Millions* had been rendered unemployed overnight...and found out, a week or so later, that the promised pensions were actually real.

The Weber Network resistance formed by the Weber Protocols was starting to act, sabotage here, a small-scale attack there—but even as they started, the A!Tol were quietly undermining resistance across the planet.

Jean felt very old as he crossed the main floor of his coastal villa. It had been in his family for years, but his wife had left the villa—and him—the day their son had graduated high school and entered the UESF Academy. It was far too big for just him, but he couldn't bear to part with it.

The security robot at the door was a "gift" from Earth's new masters, a featureless doglike thing with a stun gun he didn't pretend to understand. So far as Jean could tell, it really was programmed to be loyal to him above all else, but it was a sign that much of Earth did not forgive the man who'd surrendered.

Opening the door almost stopped the old man's heart. Standing on the doorstep of his house was the squid-like form of one of the A!Tol. Hovering behind the squid, a dozen or so steps back, were a pair of power-armored centaur-like soldiers, bodyguards giving the leader space.

It *still* took Jean a minute to realize who was on his doorstep.

"Admiral Jean Villeneuve," Fleet Lord Tan!Shallegh's translator box said calmly. "We need to talk."

"I am no longer an Admiral," Jean told the alien bluntly. "You saw to that."

"Perhaps. We need to talk regardless. May I come in?"

There was something strangely prosaic about the squid-like creature standing on its four tentacles on the front porch of Jean Villeneuve's villa, the summer sun reflecting off the English Channel behind it.

That same sun reflected off the armored interface-drive aircraft and the armored soldiers behind the Fleet Lord. The A!Tol was asking—and Jean Villeneuve would not pretend the being *had* to ask.

"Very well. *Bienvenue chez moi*," he told the alien, stepping back and gesturing the creature in.

Here, in his home, he realized that the tentacled alien was actually shorter than him. All told, Tan!Shallegh stood perhaps one hundred and sixty centimeters tall on his locomotive tentacles. The bullet-shaped torso where the tentacles met was covered in a sleeve-less vest with a single platinum insignia of a pair of crossed...swords?

The design was odd to human eyes, but the fundamental sword-ness of the weapons that had become the insignia of the A!Tol military still made it through. A small commonality, though hardly enough to give Jean any connection to the being who had conquered his world.

"I have nowhere for you to sit," he told the alien. "Or your..." He realized the guards hadn't followed the Fleet Lord in. If he'd had a weapon, Jean Villeneuve could have avenged his world's conquest right there.

"A stool would work," Tan!Shallegh replied calmly. "But I do not need a seat. Feel free if you desire; this is your home."

"It's your damn planet now," Jean told him—but he took a seat in his favorite chair. "I'm too old for games, Fleet Lord. What do you want?"

"Even with the medical science you had prior to our arrival, you could expect another hundred-fifty long-cycles of relatively healthy life...I am sorry, eighty years," the Fleet Lord pointed out. "While the medical teams were highly impressed with your doctors and hospitals, they have told me they expect to be able to increase your species' average lifespan by another third beyond what you had achieved."

The A!Tol doctors thought they could get humanity to *two centuries* of average life expectancy? He was surprised that hadn't been blazoned all over the news. Earth still had a surprisingly free press, but surely their conquerors wouldn't give up that kind of propaganda coup.

"If they're right, your people will soon have a longer life expectancy than the males of my own," the alien noted. "You are by no rational standard old, Admiral."

"I told you," Jean said crossly, "I am no longer an Admiral. It is simply Mister Villeneuve now. And as I *also* told you, I have no time for games. What do you want?"

The alien's skin had turned a faint purple color, with thick dark blue streaks. Jean had encountered enough A!Tol now to know the color patterns in their skin reflected their moods—but not nearly enough to be able to *read* those patterns.

"I need information, *Mister* Villeneuve," Tan!Shallegh told him. "You sent a flotilla of hyper-capable ships outside this system during the battle." A manipulator tentacle made a brushing aside gesture that required no translation. "Do not deny it. We have detailed footage, and even if we didn't, Captain Bond has emerged again."

"For *your* information, I can receive data from the Imperium and my local fleet base, but I can only send data back to them by Courier," the Fleet Lord continued. "That is why I will shortly be returning there—our enemies have been active and I must see to the safety of my sector. Including your world.

"But it appears that a Captain Annette Bond of your United Earth Space Force has been raiding military supply ships."

"What do you expect me to say?" Jean asked flatly. "Yes, we sent out what ships we could to act as privateers and degrade your supply lines. You already know that."

"I would have expected nothing else. The only question was whether you had hyper-capable *warships*," the other sapient told him. "It is...one of the moves in the game, as my people would say. You must understand, we have played this game before."

"What, everything we do is so predictable to you? Then how did Annette escape at all?"

"Firstly, you had an unexpected group of technological advances shortly before our arrival," Tan!Shallegh told him. "Secondly, I can predict the moves of the game, but not necessarily the tentacles of the player."

That metaphor took Jean a moment to process, but he slowly nodded his understanding.

Elon Casimir's BugWorks and all of its advances had been a surprise to the A!Tol—*Tornado* had been a UESF ship for less than a *day* when they'd shown up.

Unfortunately for Earth and the Resistance the Weber Protocols had set up, Elon Casimir was *dead*, killed in a house fire the night Earth fell—a house fire Jean Villeneuve was reasonably sure had been suicide. No one was sure where his daughter had gone, though Jean had very *carefully* not looked.

He owed Casimir that much.

"I don't know what you expect from me," he repeated. "I will not betray the confidences of my service, even if you've killed it and scattered the ashes to the wind."

"I do not misestimate your honor," the alien told him. "Indeed, it is why I am here. I have studied the idioms of your people...I believe the phrase is 'to take the measure of the man.' The measure of you, to judge what kind of woman you have sent to me.

"I think a day will come," Tan!Shallegh told him with a flash of bright blue on his skin, "that you will wear this insignia"—he tapped the crossed swords—, "and I will be honored to call you *brother*."

"You'll be waiting a long time," Jean snapped, even as a shiver ran down his spine. The thought was surprisingly tempting—Earth would forever condemn him as a traitor either way, but if Earth was doomed to *remain* part of Tan!Shallegh's Imperium, how better to see to the defense of the world he'd sworn to guard?

"Perhaps," the Fleet Lord agreed. "But we have time. For today, though, Jean...I must know what kind of woman Annette Bond is."

"And why would I tell you that?" Jean snapped, suddenly angry at the use of his name, at the invasion of his space, at the demands and arrogance of this strange alien.

"Because you have sent her to my worlds to be a privateer—and we understand that concept, Jean—and there are two kinds of privateers: soldiers and murderers."

"Annette is a warrior without peer," Earth's last Admiral told his conqueror. "Her honor has never bent, never broken—not even when my service betrayed her for it. She will not waver in her mission, she will not weaken, she will dog your heels until either she is dead or Earth is free."

"I see. A soldier, then. I can fight soldiers," Tan!Shallegh said calmly. "A soldier will be hunted, will be fought, will be brought down—but if she fights us with honor, she will be met with honor. And when she is brought to bay, she will be given the chance to yield.

"But the path you have set her on is one that drags to the bottom of the deeps," the squid-like creature continued. "For all you say, Jean Villeneuve, I fear she may yet become a murderer."

"And what happens then?" Jean demanded, his heart suddenly cold.

"I believe your idiom is 'we will put her down like a mad dog.'"

CHAPTER TWENTY-NINE

THE SYSTEM WAS UNINHABITED AND UNINHABITABLE. NONE OF its five planets fell into the Goldilocks zone for liquid water to form, and if there were any species in the universe that didn't require liquid water, the A!Tol weren't aware of them—and neither were the Terrans who'd stolen their databases.

Three of the planets were barren rocks, surfaces burned to ashes long ago by their red giant primary. Two immense gas giants, super-Jovians as Earth categorized them, orbited at radii that the mind could barely comprehend as numbers, let alone distances.

There was nothing in this barren hole of a system to ever draw the eye of a stranger. A survey expedition had swept the system once a hundred years before and it had been marked in everyone's catalogs with various markers and explanations, all of which boiled down to: *this place is not worth visiting.*

As Annette's privateer flotilla emerged from hyperspace into the outer edge of the system, the massive gravity of the red giant pushing the safe zone where a portal could be formed far beyond either gas giant, they saw nothing to change that impression, either.

"All scanners are clear," Rolfson reported. "I have...nothing. Are we sure we're in the right place?"

"We are in the right place," Ki!Tana said calmly. "Set your course for the inner gas giant. The rings are dangerous: shifting, large, unpredictable. We will need updated charts to navigate them safely."

"*Tornado* could pass through with her shields and armor," Annette said quietly, studying what data the scanners were already providing on the gas giant's rings. The rings looked to have an equivalent mass to Earth's entire asteroid belt, compressed into the ring of an over-sized gas giant.

Those rings might actually approach bad-movie levels of density.

"The other vessels could not, and it would be rude," the alien told her. "Lieutenant Commander Chan, I am transferring an identification protocol to you. Once we have reached one-half of a thousandth-light-cycle from the planet, transmit it. Omnidirectional, high power."

One half of a thousandth-light-cycle was forty-two light-seconds. The translator was only so good at translating distances and measurements, though Annette had noticed it was getting better.

"I have the data packet, Captain," Chan confirmed.

"Take us in, Amandine," Annette ordered. "Let's see what a pirate base looks like."

The distance dropped away rapidly, the other five ships dropping into neat formation behind *Tornado*. *Of Course We're Coming Back* was barely separated from her prize, effectively remote-controlling the far larger vessel.

"Coming up on the designated distance," Amandine announced after several minutes of smooth flight.

"Transmitting identification protocols," Chan confirmed a few moments later.

"What do we do now?" Rolfson asked.

"Slow to a halt relative to the planet," Annette instructed. "Let's wait and see what we hear."

"It may be some time," Ki!Tana warned. "My identification

protocols are unique to me. I have not used them in some time, as Kikitheth had her own."

Moments stretched into minutes, the silence on *Tornado*'s bridge growing tighter and tighter, until Annette wondered if the station had moved. Ki!Tana said they did that sometimes.

"We have a tightbeam pulse emerging from the rings," Chan announced finally. It felt like the entire bridge let out a held breath in a single exhalation. "Source appears to be a relay beacon—the pulse is machine code. I'm not even sure our computer can read it."

"Forward it to my communicator," Ki!Tana replied. "That is odd..."

The alien's communicator was her original device, only barely linked in to *Tornado*'s network and functioning mostly through audio feedback, unlike the modern scroll-like communicators Terrans used. The flimsy display she used for visual data pinged as Chan obeyed and then Ki!Tana skimmed over it in silence, her skin a dark purplish-blue.

"It's a request for confirmation," the A!Tol finally said. "Lieutenant Commander Chan, if you can relay the packet I'm returning to you to that relay beacon."

"Of course."

More time passed. Annette understood that a pirate base on the line between two empires had to be secretive, but this was making her twitchy.

"New package," Chan announced. "Ki!Tana's translation software has got it—looks like drift charts for the rings."

"Finally," Annette breathed in relief. "Forward them to Amandine. Lieutenant Commander—take us all the way in."

TEN SECONDS after entering the rings, Annette knew that no reaction-drive ship could ever have followed the course they had been given. Inside that ten seconds, Amandine had made six separate vector changes, each of hundreds of kilometers a second.

It would *probably* have been an exaggeration to say that you could have walked through the rings, but Annette had spent a lot of time in Sol's asteroid belt. The comparison was terrifying, but Amandine took *Tornado* through the rocks with a careful hand.

"Coming up on the inner edge," he reported quietly.

"Bringing up a visual," Rolfson announced. "Sensors suggest this is going to be...my *gods*."

The screen switched from the tactical plot to a pure visual, first showing the *hundreds* of rocks inside a visual range and then showing the gap *Tornado* would dive through—and through it, the crew's first sight of Tortuga.

Ki!Tana's description of it as a mobile shipyard—a large vessel but still inherently a *ship*—had clearly thrown off Annette's expectations. She'd expected something big, bigger than even the two-kilometer-long behemoths the A!Tol had attacked Sol with.

The mobile shipyard had clearly been designed to build and maintain ships half again that size—and six of them at once. Tortuga was over twenty kilometers across, a technically mobile six-armed star. Two of the arms had been closed in at some point in the past; a metal shell wrapped the yard slips that filled the other four arms to provide living space.

The yard slip between the two enclosed arms had been subdivided into a dozen smaller slips. Two were big enough to fit *Tornado*, but the others were designed to handle smaller vessels.

The other three slips still looked like they could swallow an A!Tol battleship but held instead a small fleet of identical cruisers. Each was a smoothly lined vessel painted dark red, ten percent again *Tornado*'s size.

Twenty ships of various sizes, up to three much the same scale as *Tornado*, were docked against the enclosed arms. Four of the red cruisers orbited around the station, lazy guard dogs keeping an eye on the flock.

"We have incoming," Rolfson reported. "One of the red ships—I'm guessing those are Tortuga's owners?"

"Yes," Ki!Tana confirmed. "Remember, Captain—Tortuga's Crew are *not* pirates. They were born aboard that station; they will die for that station. They deal happily with pirates, but they look down on them."

"I'll keep that in mind," Annette told her.

"Ma'am, point of concern," her tactical officer interrupted again. "They've got powerful shields, but I still got a pretty good glimpse at their hulls as they closed. These guys have compressed-matter armor—no one else seemed to know it existed!"

"Interesting," *Tornado*'s Captain said slowly. "Are they hailing us?"

"Just now, ma'am," Chan confirmed, tossing the channel onto the main screen without needing instruction.

The being who appeared on the screen reminded her of nothing so much as an upright scarab beetle. Red cloth bandoliers had been strung across a torso covered in heavy carapace plating, each bandolier marked with insignia and medals Annette didn't even attempt to understand. A squat, beetle-like head sat atop the armored torso, massive black eyes and wavering antennae focused on the screen.

The Laian chittered for a moment, and then the translator kicked in.

"This is Captain Tidikat of the Crew," the translator told them. "You have used an old and...special access code. Identify yourself."

Ki!Tana moved into the field of vision.

"They used my code, Captain Tidikat," she replied calmly. "My contract has transferred to the Captain of this vessel and I have guided them here to do business."

The antennae whirred as Tidikat considered.

"This is acceptable to the Crew," it concluded. "Flotilla Commander, identify yourself."

Ki!Tana gestured for Annette to take over, stepping back behind the Terran Captain.

"I am Captain Annette Bond, a privateer of the United Earth Space Force," she told the alien proudly. "These ships are either under my command or legitimate prizes taken in the course of war. I am prepared to sell the prizes and their contents to fund maintenance and upgrades of my vessels."

Mandibles clicked rapidly, in something that the translator clearly didn't think was speech.

"A privateer of a fallen state," Tidikat finally said. "We are... familiar with the path you travel, Captain Bond. What cargos do you have to sell?"

"Point six cee missiles of Terran manufacture, raw protein, and molecular circuitry cores. Plus the three freighters themselves."

Tidikat's mandibles clicked rapidly again.

"Ki!Tana's presence alone would see you safely to Tortuga, Captain," the Laian told her. "Your goods will be welcome here— some more than others, as I'm sure you realize.

"The rules of Tortuga are simple," it continued. "Do not cause trouble. Obey all orders given by members of the Crew. Do not exit the marked public portions of the platform.

"We are not responsible for the security of your persons or goods. If you cause sufficient trouble, you will be ejected or terminated. If you breach the station or an order of the Command Crew, your ship will be seized as compensation.

"We do not mandate fairness in trade. Look to your own negotiations."

The mandibles snapped once, very definitively.

"Do you understand our rules, Captain Bond?"

"Perfectly," she replied flatly. "We are here to trade, not cause trouble. We will protect ourselves if needed."

"This is Tortuga," Tidikat replied, its mandibles snapping rapidly as it spoke. "This is to be expected."

CHAPTER THIRTY

"We will be docking in about five minutes," Amandine reported.

"All right, people," Annette said. "Cole, are you needed for the docking?"

"Computer systems can take it from here," her navigator admitted with a mildly disappointed look.

"Senior officers and Ki!Tana report to my office now," she ordered. "Seal the ship until we're done."

Gesturing for the officers already on the bridge to follow her, Annette strode into the Spartan office attached to the bridge. It was, as she quickly glanced around, *just* big enough for a quick planning meeting to sort out the last few details.

"We'll need Major Wellesley here," she told her officers as Chan filed in last. "He'll have to make sure we have the ship sealed first."

Working or not, it took the Special Space Service Major less than two minutes from her call to arrive and join the Space Force officers.

"What's the plan, Captain?" he asked as soon as the door slid closed behind him, forcing Annette to hide a smile at his enthusiasm.

"Ki!Tana and I have discussed what our best approach is," she told her officers, gesturing for the alien to speak.

"Your human crew has no currency that will be accepted aboard the station," the A!Tol told them. "Until we have liquidated at least one prize or its cargo, you have no funds and are operating on credit based on your relationship with me.

"Captain Bond and I will proceed to an agent of my acquaintance and negotiate the fate of our cargo," she continued. "We may need to sell the raw protein immediately to have some spending cash, but we will want to hold on to the missiles and molecular cores to get a better price. I'm sure we can negotiate a deal that puts at least some money in the ship's accounts to be distributed to the crew."

"Alien crew who are leaving us here can leave as soon as we lift the current lockdown," Annette told them. "We'll want a way to reach them to make sure we can pay them fairly. I get the feeling that building a reputation for paying fairly will help us here."

"It will with most," Ki!Tana agreed. "Some will see it as weakness."

"Then let them make that mistake," she said sweetly.

"No offense to Ki!Tana, but the two of you aren't going on the station *alone*, are you?" Wellesley asked.

"Hardly," Annette replied. "I'm bringing *you* and any two of your troopers you choose. Given the warnings we were given, I suspect powered armor and plasma weapons would be considered rude, but body armor and slugthrowers are basically casual wear aboard the station."

"Indeed," Ki!Tana replied. "Bodyguards are also expected."

"Once we've put money in our crew's hands that can actually be spent on Tortuga, I intend to allow shore leave parties to leave the ship," Annette noted. "Under *no* circumstances does anyone go anywhere alone. My preference would be for parties of six, including at least one of our nonhuman crewmembers to help our people find the lay of the land."

"Won't that stand out?" Rolfson asked. "I mean, if we moved in squads..."

"It is quite common," the big A!Tol told them. "The Laians do not spend a significant amount of time in the public area of the station. They live in the original core hull and do not mingle with their customers. They most certainly do not provide anything resembling law enforcement.

"Another thing to realize," Ki!Tana continued, "is that while the Laians do not approve of slavery, they do not intervene in slave transactions aboard the station. There is no official slave market, but you may still encounter groups of slaves. Their guards will be well armed and trigger-happy; attempting to intervene is unwise."

"Slavery? But we're talking societies with industrial robotics," Chan objected. "That makes no sense."

"Not all things are logical, Lieutenant Commander," the alien told her. "There are tasks for which a sapient creature is simply better than a machine. There is status. There is the use of enslaved skilled labor—in many cases to *run* those industrial robots.

"And there is the Kanzi religion," she continued grimly. "All other bipeds exist to serve them. Slavery is how their culture is *built*— the Kanzi race are rulers, slavers and warriors raised up on the back of an empire of slaves.

"The slavers will see your people as exotics, prizes the Kanzi will pay great sums for," Ki!Tana concluded. "Moving in groups is wise. Avoiding the slavers as much as possible is *also* wise."

"Will there be Kanzi aboard?" Rolfson asked, the big man looking hugely uncomfortable to Annette.

"Tortuga takes all comers who don't create trouble, and one of the ships docked today started life as a Kanzi armed auxiliary freighter, so yes."

"We don't start trouble," Annette ordered her people flatly. "We protect our own, but we don't start trouble. James—have your escort ready to go in ten minutes.

"We have business to complete."

ANNETTE and her escorts stopped at the airlock *Tornado*'s crew had hooked up to the massive space station they'd docked with. Both the station and the starship had more airlocks and flexible umbilicals to link them together, but the Terran crew was being cautious. One link for now was plenty.

"What's the atmosphere looking like on the other side?" she asked the SSS troopers guarding the airlock.

"Slightly higher pressure and a tad over twenty-five percent oxygen," the woman leading the team told her. "No toxins of concern; I'm only reading oxygen, nitrogen and CO-two."

Which made sense—that was the exact mix, though in different proportions, you'd find on *Tornado*. If your air was artificial, there was no purposes to putting in anything other than the requirement for life —oxygen, some specific trace gases—and a neutral buffer that all races could breathe—nitrogen.

The carbon dioxide was the result of the fact that, according to the files Annette's people now had, over ninety-nine percent of known life used *very* similar chemical reactions to life on Earth to provide energy. *Some* CO_2 was almost certainly added intentionally, Annette doubted humans were the only ones who needed a small percentage to properly function, but most appeared to be a natural by-product.

"Gravity is pegged at just under point seven gees," the Corporal continued. "High oxygen, low gravity. Sounds like it could be fun."

"Also potentially distracting," Major Wellesley pointed out over Annette's shoulder. "Watch your step; gravity shifts aren't fun."

"James, I trained on ships without artificial gravity," she pointed out. "I'll be fine." She nodded to the Corporal. "Open it up."

The inner airlock door opened and they moved in, letting it close behind them. There was a faint but perceptible change in air pressure as Tortuga's air was allowed in, overwhelming the lower-oxygen and -pressure air from *Tornado*. Once the shift was complete, the outer airlock door opened, and Annette took a deep breath of "alien" air and stepped into her second-ever alien structure.

The umbilical, sadly, was utterly prosaic. If the Laians who'd built Tortuga had used anything different from the plastic and steel Terrans would have used, it certainly didn't *look* any different.

"Lead the way, Ki!Tana," she told the big A!Tol. "You know this place better than we do."

The squid-like alien moved forward, her locomotive tentacles moving in a way that could still make Annette queasy if it took her by surprise. There was barely enough space for the massive alien to pass Annette in the tube, but they managed it.

"There is no entry scan," the A!Tol told them quietly. "All of the tubes link to one gallery with several accesses into the main bazaar. Both public arms are set up identically. The bazaar can be intimidating—even I was intimidated when I first came here."

With everything that she'd seen so far, Annette took the warning seriously. It lost some of its weight, though, as they moved through the docking gallery. There was some traffic wandering through it, aliens of a dozen stripes—she recognized a Yin and a Frole, but the rest were strange to her—but the gallery itself was prosaic and wouldn't have looked out of place on any station in Earth's orbit.

Then they exited the gallery into the bazaar and she stopped in her tracks, trying not to gape as she looked out into what the Laians had built as their main marketplace.

The shipyard slip converted into a marketplace had been six kilometers long and two wide. It had been wrapped in metal and turned into an encased environment—but they hadn't filled all of that space with corridors and rooms like a regular space station.

The open space that made up one of Tortuga's bazaars was at least a kilometer wide and four high. It had a clearly oriented "bottom" and "top", with an almost-uncountable number of galleries surrounding and rising up.

The galleries and the bottom floor were garish conglomerations of hundreds of stalls, vendors hawking an unbelievable variety of wares.

In the first five seconds, Annette lost track of the number of *species* she saw, let alone the number of sapients.

"My god," she whispered.

"I told you."

"How?"

"About two hundred thousand permanent and semi-permanent residents, *excluding* the Crew, and at least the crew of every ship you saw docked," the alien replied. "Not to mention a lot of the smaller ships are docked internally."

"There are *this* many pirates?"

"Pirates, smugglers, exiles, sapients with nowhere else to go," Ki!Tana said quietly. "The refuse of the galaxy sweeps up in places like this—but realize that even a *million* such wouldn't even be a rounding error in a census of *your* world, let alone the A!Tol Imperium."

There was a sadness to the alien's voice that the translator seemed to be picking up as the big tentacled alien surveyed the bedlam.

"When no one will have you, you go where no one will go," she explained. "The lucky join the pirates and smugglers. The unlucky starve. The *truly* unlucky fall into the hands of slavers. Do not be fooled, Captain Bond—this is the cesspit of two Empires."

Annette inhaled, letting the extra oxygen run into her system as she shivered at Ki!Tana's words, then nodded firmly.

"And it's where we must do business," she said. "Let's find this agent of yours."

───────

AS THEY MOVED into the bazaar, Annette realized it wasn't *quite* as crowded as it appeared on first glance. Their party of armed sapients barely stood out at all, though Ki!Tana's massive size compared to most of the species present definitely helped clear them a path, as most of the population moved in similar parties.

The garish stalls were fronts that led into covers hung over what had probably started life as cargo containers, now upgraded with doors and locks. The front stalls mostly either contained goods Annette judged to be cheap or were *closely* watched by armed guards.

They'd been in the bazaar for several minutes when all of the various aliens began to clear a path for someone else. Ki!Tana gestured with her manipulators for the humans to follow suit, and Annette stepped back with the crowd to see who was coming.

A squad of four aliens, one Laian, one Yin, and two from a species she didn't recognize, strode along the center of the bazaar. They clearly *expected* everyone to step aside and were clad in as close to a uniform as their three distinct body types would permit—the dark red bandoliers she'd seen on the Laian Captain when they'd arrived—and unlike anyone else she'd seen since boarding the station, all four carried plasma rifles.

"Crew," Ki!Tana said simply as the patrol past. "They don't live in the public areas, but they do make sure they get their cut. This way."

The big A!Tol ducked between two of the cargo container stalls, leading the Terrans away from the main concourse toward the back of the station. They came out into another of Tortuga's impromptu streets, but across the way from them was a surprisingly familiar-looking "outdoor" tavern.

"We will want to get your crew protein checkers," the A!Tol half-whispered. "Food here is usually UP, but drinks are at your own risk. Something that would make me mildly intoxicated would kill most humans. For now...just don't order anything."

She led the way into the bar, moving like a sapient bulldozer and assuming anyone would get out of her way. To the credit of the patrons' intelligence, they did—and anyone who might have caused trouble spotted the three Special Space Service troopers bringing up the rear and thought better of it.

Few bits of body language were universal across species, but

Annette suspected that having a hand on the grip of your firearm was one of them.

Annette caught up to her alien companion in time to hear her threaten the bartender.

"We're here to do business, Ik!It. If you want me to break the bar, fine. But I doubt Ondu would approve."

The bartender was the first cephalod-esque alien Annette had seen except for the A!Tol themselves. The vast majority of the races she'd encountered to date had, in fact, been bipedal tool-users like humans. The exceptions—the Frole, the Rekiki, the Laians themselves—had clearly been regarded as oddities even by aliens.

The bartender, however, looked like a twelve-armed octopus. He resembled an octopus, in fact, a lot more than the A!Tol resembled squids.

"Fine," it spat at Ki!Tana. "Rumor says your new friends have cargo worth dealing."

"They do," the A!Tol replied. "And I owe Ondu enough to give him the first chance. Do you really want to cost him that deal?"

The bartender hit something Annette didn't see and a panel in what had appeared to be a solid chunk of cargo-container wall next to the bar retracted into the rest of the wall and slid aside.

Ki!Tana went toward it without hesitation, and the Terrans, strangers in a strange land now, followed.

They found themselves in what appeared to be the storehouse for the bar, except that several pallets of booze were moving aside to create a clear path—and two *massive* guards clad in power armor were emerging from the shadows.

Like the Rekiki, they had four legs supporting a two-armed torso. Where the Rekiki were proportioned much like Earth horses, these guards were *not*. They both towered two and a half meters tall and fully a meter and a half around, barrel-thick bodies evenly supported on their four legs as they loomed.

"You know me," Ki!Tana told them. "We're meeting Ondu, on business."

"Weapons," the guard on the left said. "No tricks."

"Leave the guns," the A!Tol told the humans.

"What promise of safety do we have without them?" Wellesley asked, though the SSS Major was unslinging his submachine gun.

"Ondu's," the guard rumbled. "And mine. In that door, you only get hurt if we're dead."

"I think we're safe, James," Annette told him. "Let's see what this Ondu is about."

CHAPTER THIRTY-ONE

ONDU WAS YET *ANOTHER* ALIEN WHOSE SPECIES ANNETTE HAD never met before, though at least she recognized his species from the files they'd been assembling. He was a Tosumi, one of the first races conquered by the A!Tol. Grossly obese for his race, Ondu was a four-armed biped covered in short yellow feathers. He wore a tightly fitted tunic-like garment that made his obesity obvious and also pinned the vestigial wings of his race to his side.

"Ki!Tana," he snapped, clacking his night-black beak on the click in the name as he leveled jewel-like eyes on the human group and their A!Tol companion. "You are foolish to return to me."

"We have always dealt fairly with each other, Ondu," Ki!Tana replied. "Why would I not come to you with this opportunity?"

"Fairly?" the Tosumi sputtered, spraying spittle from his beak but still remaining in his chair. "You sold me *twenty thousand defective power cells*! I lost customers who'd worked with me for *two hundred years*."

Annette quickly checked her translator software. It happily confirmed that, yes, it had translated Ondu's number as well as his time unit. He'd actually said something like "three eighties of star-dances". Networked across *Tornado*'s computers and all of the hardware issued to her thousand crew, the software was getting *very* smart.

"That was Kikitheth," Ki!Tana pointed out. "And she warned you she wasn't sure of the quality of those power cells. You cut *thirty percent* off the price because of it, Ondu. You were hardly scammed."

"There's uncertain quality—and then there's cells *exploding* from casing fractures! I had to buy back all of them I could find before anyone died!" Ondu's beak clacked in what Annette suspected was feigned distress.

"I would say raise it with Kikitheth, but she's dead," Ki!Tana replied. "And, old friend, you really should have checked the cells yourself. We didn't have the tools."

"I would hope you're not expecting a good deal after that," the Tosumi grumped.

"I have brought you the best deal this station has seen in a dozen years," Annette's companion replied. "Ondu Arra Tallas, meet Captain Annette Bond, privateer of the United Earth Space Force. The flotilla that just arrived is hers—and she needs the best agent on Tortuga to liquidate her prizes.

"If you do not want to deal with me, of course, we can go talk to others. I believe Palani is still in business?"

"That amphibious reptile would not get you *half* the deal I would, and you know it, you big tentacled soft candy," Ondu snapped. "Welcome to my office, Captain Bond. Despite what it may seem, being brought here by this"—he gestured at Ki!Tana with an upper arm—"is a recommendation few can share. You even sent Kikitheth to me on her own."

"Kikitheth, I imagine, could find her own way around Tortuga," Annette demurred calmly. "Can we do business?"

"I saw your flotilla," the bird-like alien allowed. "Costa!" he shrieked, a predatory sound that made Annette's heart race. A third of the four immense hexapods, this one lacking armor and so revealing a richly furred red creature with large eyes and heavily clawed hands, emerged into the room. "Bring seats for our guests. Water as well." He glanced at Annette. "I can guarantee other things would not kill you, but not how they would taste."

The chairs that emerged—four of them slung along one mightily thewed furry arm—might not have been designed for humans, but they were close enough to be perfectly comfortable. Annette sat gingerly and faced the agent across his desk.

"We have three ships to sell, plus their cargos," she told him flatly. "I am not averse to paying a fair fee nor taking time to find the best deal, but I will find a fair deal and I will want to begin upgrades on my ships relatively quickly."

She laid a data crystal on the desk. "Details of the cargo are in there, but the high summary is one cargo of point six cee rated missiles, one cargo of raw protein, and one cargo of molecular circuitry cores."

Ondu slotted the crystal into a display unit and balanced on his chair, clicking his beak softly as he reviewed the data.

"Were I to offer to buy all of this from you right now, Ki!Tana would physically remove you from my office," the bird-like alien observed. The humor and harassment from earlier were gone. He was all business now, gesturing for Costa to lay out the drinks. "I am an agent and a broker. The most generous offer I could make you without would still be a paltry price for what you have brought—and risky for me regardless. Neither of us would benefit.

"Finding buyers will take time. Those who can purchase this quantity of missiles prefer higher quality, so they will need to be sold in smaller batches. No one aboard this station has the need for this many molecular cores, but many have a need for *some*.

"I can find a single buyer for the food," he noted. "The only value there, as I am sure you understand, is quantity. Raw protein is cheap.

"The ships...even with the damage, they can be sold, but again...I would want to line up a buyer. You need an agent, Captain, which is why Ki!Tana brought you to me. I am the best."

All four of Ondu's hands suddenly flickered into action, moving with a speed that belied his bulk. "I believe I can arrange buyers for all of your goods inside ten A!Tol cycles. For...forty percent of the gross."

Annette saw Ki!Tana's skin flash *bright* orange but raised a hand before the angry A!Tol could explode.

"I don't even need Ki!Tana to tell me that you're robbing me at that rate," she told Ondu sweetly. "Ten percent of the gross."

"That *is* robbery," Ondu shrieked.

"You know where those ships came from," she observed, carefully taking a drink of water to make the broker wait. "Believe me, Ondu, I know what robbery looks like."

The alien clacked its beak rapidly, throwing back its head in a disturbing gesture it took her a moment to realize was laughter.

"It involves more battle damage in your mind, I imagine?" he asked after a moment. "I can go to thirty, Captain Bond. You are asking a lot of work of myself and my staff."

Ki!Tana was no longer visibly furious, but Annette wasn't going to take that as solid. A!Tol showed their emotions on their skin, but it wasn't always a guaranteed thing. In this case, Ki!Tana had clearly progressed to the light red of amused pleasure. She was *enjoying* watching Annette dicker.

"Then a lower rate would motivate you to seek an even better deal for me," she told Ondo. "I can go as high as fifteen percent, I suppose, but even that seems unreasonable. We are, after all, delivering one of the most valuable cargos this station has seen in a while—and I will need to *spend* much of that money as well, a task I assume you would also be willing to help with."

Ondu paused for a moment, clearly considering.

"I can go as low as twenty-seven," he finally conceded. "Lower would not be possible."

"Really?" Annette asked. Something in her tone led Major Wellesley to have a nasty coughing fit beside her. "That's such a shame."

"A shame?"

"I can't possibly go above twenty," she told Ondu. "Though I *suppose* we could, say, sell the food cargo immediately to you at a discounted rate to assure you of a reasonable profit to start."

Which would also meet *her* need of immediate cash.

The birdlike alien stared at her unblinkingly, a state that reminded her very much of a hawk she'd met on her family farm as a child. Of course, Ondu was an overweight, flightless hawk, which robbed the glare of much of its implicit threat, and she stared right back at him.

Finally, he gave one sharp snap of his beak.

"You and I, Captain Bond, are going to be wonderful friends," he told her. "Twenty-two, please, to salve my wounded pride."

"Very well," she replied. "Shall we arrange the funds transfer for the protein cargo immediately?

BANKING ON TORTUGA was one of the services run by the Laians. They provided a secure financial database that tracked the accounts of every ship on the station, reported and recorded every transaction in a secure, confidential manner, and made sure that the Crew got their cut.

Ondu had a remote connection to the service that enabled him to confirm that an account had automatically been set up for *Tornado* on arrival and set up the transfer.

"You will want to go talk to the bank," the Tosumi noted after sending over the money for the first part of their deal. "The Crew is *very* specific on who can access accounts—and all of your crewmembers will need them too. Easier to pay their shares that way; gives them spending money on Tortuga and allows them to take cash in whatever currency they want."

"These accounts are safe?" Annette asked.

"So long as Tortuga exists, the Crew will honor your accounts here," Ondu replied. "The Laians act as arbitrators of all contracts and transactions aboard Tortuga. They are trusted to do so because they keep their word."

"Odd bunch of criminals," she noted.

Ondu laughed again, the strange clicking noise unnerving still.

"You misunderstand the Crew," he pointed out. "They are not criminals. They are exiles and sapients without state, unbeholden to any law or code but their own, but they are not criminals. They simply do not...care what others do, so long as they are paid.

"Very mercenary. But they are not pirates or slavers or murderers themselves."

"On my world, they would still be criminals," Annette pointed out. Money laundering was the politest legal term she could see applying.

"On most," Ondu agreed. "But they see it...in more complex ways." He tapped one final command and closed his holographic screen. "The sale of the food supplies is complete. I will have people by to empty the ship in three hours, if that works for you?"

"I'll let my people know," Annette agreed.

"I do suggest you talk to the Bank, though," he repeated. "Ki!Tana can take you there. The Crew will not...complain if you do not, but they will be less cooperative as time goes on if you don't play by their rules."

"Ki!Tana?" she asked.

The alien flashed a blue-purple color Annette was starting to recognize as the equivalent of a human shifting uncomfortably.

"You are less vulnerable to that than another new Captain would be," the A!Tol admitted. "My history and standing with Tortuga are...complicated, but it buys you social credit you would not otherwise have.

"But Ondu is correct. It will make your life and your human crews' life much easier—but it is also not somewhere you could have approached without money. We needed that transfer to get things set up."

"You...you had no money at all." Ondu stared at the humans and their companion for several moments, his beak hanging wide open, and then started laughing again. "Much to sell, but no cash of your own. Well played, Captain. But yes. Go to the bank, then, now that you have money. Set up accounts for your crew, pay them all their share of that sale—it may be pathetic when compared to the cost of a ship, but it will buy many luxuries here.

"I will let you know when I have buyers for the rest of your cargo."

ONE SURPRISINGLY PROSAIC and familiar bank appointment later, Annette had ship's credit accounts set up for her three ships' maintenance and supplies, a general flotilla account set up (that the money would actually flow into from the sales), and personal accounts set up for herself and every human member of her crew.

There was even money in every one of the personal accounts, including her own. The funds were denominated in A!Tol Imperial marks, of course, so she had almost no idea what the amounts really *meant*, but she had at least paid her crew—including the aliens—by the time she returned to *Tornado*.

Pat Kurzman was waiting with apparent patience as she and her escort returned aboard. She very carefully did *not* notice him and Wellesley quickly embracing while everyone *happened* to be looking the other way, and waited for her XO to join her.

"Who left?" she asked without preamble, gesturing toward the airlock with her chin.

"The Rekiki, obviously," Kurzman said. "Some of the others. Fewer than I expected—other than Tellaki and his people, we're only down twenty-six so far of the crew who came aboard with Ki!Tana."

"You are successful, Captain," that worthy inserted into the conversation. "Some may not trust your promise to pay them regardless and will remain until they are paid out for all three prizes and cargos. Many think you are lucky and will stay. I will check in with my people and let you know if any significant number still plan on leaving."

The A!Tol left along the corridor, trailed by the two members of Wellesley's escort detail. They'd been unneeded this time, though Annette had *no* intention of leaving *Tornado* without them.

"We've set up accounts for all of the human crew," she told Kurzman and passed him the data crystal. "We'll be getting a shipment of glorified charge cards shortly; I'll leave distributing them in your capable hands."

"We got the agent Ki!Tana wanted?"

"Yeah."

"Can we trust him?" her XO asked.

"I think so," Annette sighed. "It's in his interests to do well for us. His commission is going to be painful, but we'll get the money we need for the upgrades."

"Do we need them this badly, ma'am?" Kurzman said quietly. "You're talking about putting our ship—our *only* warship—into the hands of pirates. We've stood up to everything we've faced so far."

"We can't fight the A!Tol Navy on even ground yet, Pat," she pointed out. "It's a risk, I don't deny that. We're leveraging Ki!Tana's contacts to try and upgrade *Tornado* into something that can go toe-to-toe with bigger ships." She shook her head. "Ki!Tana seems to trust them. We have no choice—we're not going to free Earth by robbing freighters."

"Fair." He paused. The corridors around them were empty for the moment, but it wouldn't be long before the inevitable grind pulled them back to work. "Are we trusting her too much?" Kurzman asked finally. "We know *nothing* about her. Nothing."

"Yes, we're trusting her too much," Annette said flatly. "I just don't see an alternative. Do you?"

"No, ma'am."

"Once the charge cards are distributed, we can start doing shore leave," she told him. "You know the rules I want. Everyone watches their back. This place feels like Mos Eisley."

"That bad?" Kurzman asked.

She thought about it for a moment.

"Actually, no. It's worse."

CHAPTER THIRTY-TWO

"So, can we drink it?" one of the Service Troop Captains asked.

James ran the small scanner he'd been issued over the mugs of what *looked* like beer. It blinked for a few seconds and settled on green.

"It's alcoholic and it won't poison you," he told his junior officer as he gestured his people to the table they'd picked out in the "open-air" bar. "I don't know if I would say that means you can drink it; no one knows what it will *taste* like to humans."

"Someone has to go first," Pat Kurzman noted, grabbing one of the mugs and taking a swallow. The XO coughed, blinking rapidly as he tried to process just what he'd put in his mouth, and then shook himself.

"Whoa," he whispered. "*What* percentage did you say this was, James?"

The Special Space Service Major slipped in next to his boyfriend and slid the mugs around the table to his five Troop Captains. They were all aware of the relationship, which made them the right company to go outside the ship with.

The seventh member of the party didn't know enough about human relationships to be bothered either way. Ral, as a member of a species that was well represented on Tortuga, was also the only person in the group who *knew* he could stomach the food at the bar.

"According to the scanner, it's about twenty-two percent," James told Kurzman with a grin. "It may *look* like beer, but it's loaded like fortified wine."

"Well, the bad news is that it doesn't taste like *either*," the XO replied. "The good news is that it's surprisingly drinkable for that." Suiting actions to words, he took another mouthful of it.

With a shrug, James followed suit. The alcohol content was a shock to his system—despite his intellectual awareness, the appearance had left him expecting beer—and the flavor was another shock. It was definitely palatable, but it took a moment to wrap his brain around.

"Is it just me," he said aloud, "or does this taste like unsweetened cream soda?"

"That is *exactly* what it tastes like," Annabel Sherman noted. His Charlie Troop Captain was a blond northeastern United States citizen, a stocky woman who could have passed for the Captain's little sister—or a rogue cheerleader, when out of uniform. "God, that is *weird*."

"You are lucky," Ral told them. "My first experiment at food off my homeworld did not go so well. The result was safe but not tasty."

"We haven't got to food yet," Mumina Bousaid pointed out. Outside of her armor and in the semi-casual blue Space Force uniform, her night-black skin stood out amongst the Americans, Europeans, and Chinese that made up James's Troop Captains. Against Ral's blue skin, the four-armed Tosumi bartender, and the other aliens around them, she could have been James's sister. "The food could still be awful."

Moments after she spoke, the blue-skinned Yin waitress emerged from the back of the bar. She wore a red collar that James had been warned represented a slave and a halter top that showed off a set of breasts at odds with her avian face—in a way that suggested certain things were common for many mammalian males.

She laid a platter of roasted meat and vegetables on the table in front of them. James had discussed just what protein alignments *should* work with her when she'd made her recommendation, and everything checked out on his scanner.

As he was checking the food, though, he noticed the server leaning down next to Ral and whispering in the Yin's ear. If the two had been human, he'd have thought the waitress was hitting on him, but he'd freely admit he knew *nothing* about Yin courtship rituals.

The server swung away a moment later, leaving the humans with their food. James met Ral's gaze, hoping the alien got his questioning look.

"She suggests we stop drinking alcohol," the alien trooper said quietly. "And that we check our weapon safeties. We are being watched. Look for short aliens, one hundred sixty centimeters or so, with blue-and-white fur, that otherwise resemble you humans very closely. Six of them around the bar, with webbers and guns—though mostly out of sight from our table."

"Fuck," James breathed, checking the long-barreled slugthrower strapped to his thigh under the table. "Who are they?"

"They're Kanzi," Ral told him. "Which means they're slavers."

"THESE SPECIFICATIONS ARE DISTINCTLY INSUFFICIENT," Annette said calmly as she finished reviewing the data the shipbuilder had provided. "If I'm reading them correctly, even with the maximum power supply, this shield would barely stop two salvos from an A!Tol Navy cruiser."

"Most people, Captain Bond, don't plan for fighting Navy cruisers," the strange-looking Frole told her. The mobile fungus ran the largest and most successful shipyard—and ship parts dealership—in the public portion of Tortuga. "Pirates, even heavies, *run* from Navy cruisers."

"Piracy is merely a means to an end for me, Mister Folphe," she pointed out. "If my ship can't stand against at least her own weight in A!Tol cruisers, my long-term goals are much more difficult. The shields you've shown me simply do not meet my needs."

"The only people on this station with better gear than me are the Crew," Folphe replied. "And they do not talk to people who just drifted in from hyperspace for the first time. If you do not like what I have, Captain Bond, you may be out of luck."

"Then that will leave me with a large amount of unspent cash," she noted. They were still far short of having sold all of their cargos, but some of the cores and missiles had sold, along with the damaged hull that had held the raw protein. She had a solid idea of what the final result was going to look like—and it was starting to look like she'd be short of things to spend it on.

The fungus coughed, expelling a slew of spores in a direction away from Annette, thankfully.

"Someone looking to buy what you want comes along once in thirteen years or so," he told her, the translator slicing his native time units into English. "I do not keep units like that in stock. I do not even have schematics to build them. But." He held up a tendril in a gesture that was starting to seem universal.

"There is an individual who is often aboard this station, an Indiri named Karaz Forel, who deals in the odd and the unusual," he noted. "He is captain of a ship—a heavy—but has a sapient here who trades for him. They often deal in exotic slaves, strange sapients no one else has ever seen, but they approached me some cycles ago with *recent* A!Tol military schematics. I did not buy them, as pirates would not pay the premium to build them, but...if you bring me those schematics, I can build the units. Custom-build, even, shaped to your ships' own peculiarities."

"How long?" Annette asked. She could probably afford the *costs*, though the thought of dealing with slavers made her skin crawl, but every day she was away was a day Earth was conquered without her trying to free it.

"Fifty to sixty A!Tol cycles," Folphe told her.

Two months, most likely.

"That may be too long," she replied.

"It is the best option I can offer. Which means it is the best anyone on this station can do. Think about it, Captain. See if you can track down the schematics. It will be a week before I can open a slip, in any case."

"I appreciate your time, Mister Folphe," Annette said. "Is there any chance I could get you to arrange an introduction to the Crew yardmaster?"

"I wish," the Frole yardmaster replied. "If that worthy would let me introduce people, both I and she would be far richer."

"Shame. Thank you."

Shaking her head to clear some of the dust inevitable from being in close quarters with a Frole, Annette stepped back out into what passed for streets on Tortuga. Ki!Tana and her two Special Space Service escorts were waiting for her outside. The big A!Tol had begged off joining her conversation with Folphe, she really didn't seem to be doing well today.

Some days, Ki!Tana's skin barely moved away from the gray-black tone that Annette was learning meant pain and distress. What-ever was bothering the alien, though, she refused to not at least *try* to fulfill whatever she thought her contract required with regards to Annette.

"No luck," Annette told her. "He had some suggestions, I think I want to pull you and Kulap together to see what our best option is. For now, let's head back to the ship."

She'd lined up several potential options for replacing what was left of her ship's heavy lasers, but those were secondary. *Tornado* needed better engines, shields and power, in that order. Upgrading them was easy—getting them to a comparable level to the A!Tol warships Annette knew she was going to have to fight was *not*.

In an ideal world, *Tornado* would be able to outrun anything she couldn't outfight. In her current state, she couldn't outrun *anything* the A!Tol had in their line of battle, nor could she fight in her own weight class. Without *something* more, Annette was facing a pointless career as a powerful pirate, with no chance at liberating her world.

"Captain Bond!" a voice bellowed—in English! —across the square, shredding her distraction. *"Down!"*

The translated voice threw Annette for a moment, but her *escorts* were the best soldiers Earth had to offer, graduates of a grueling program *including* VIP protection. Even as she was starting to duck, one of the troopers slammed into her and knocked her to the ground.

Some unknown weapon coughed loudly as she hit the ground, and thick strands of sticky web slashed through the air where she'd been standing. Ki!Tana was caught, dragged to the ground by some kind of heavy capture weapon.

The SSS trooper who'd knocked Annette down was caught in the web meant for her and slammed to the ground next to the big A!Tol. The other had disappeared, diving behind cover and drawing her weapon.

Annette rolled as she hit the ground, drawing her own weapon as she came up on one knee, scanning for targets. There was nothing visible for a moment, only a scattering crowd—Tortuga's denizens could recognize a burgeoning firefight from a *long* way away.

Then a short alien, almost human-looking in a tight black uniform but with their visible skin covered in fine blue fur, emerged from the crowd with a large-bored shotgun. It was trained directly on Annette, but she'd been watching for an attack and reacted faster.

The twelve millimeter automatic coughed four times before the alien could fire its own weapon, the heavy slugs working their way diagonally up the creature's torso. The blue-furred alien went one way in a spray of blood and the weapon went the other way.

Another weapon cracked simultaneously, a double tap from the SSS trooper putting down a second alien Annette had missed.

"Get to cover!" the trooper snapped. "I'll cover you."

Annette retreated as more of the blue-furred aliens emerged, tucking herself into the doorway of Folphe's business. The second wave were not *nearly* as determined to take anyone alive, and bullets began to slam into the doorframe.

She took a deep breath, leaned around the frame and returned fire. Her first shot missed but her second took one of the aliens in the shoulder. She ducked back behind her narrow cover before she saw the result, but heard the double crack of her trooper firing again in the aliens' direction.

Then a terrifying *howling* noise echoed through the streets, followed by rapid gunfire from unfamiliar weapons. Without gunfire hitting her own position, she swung out to cover the street—if someone was helping her, she wasn't going to leave them to it without returning the favor!

A half-dozen Rekiki had joined the fight, taking cover around corners and firing on the blue aliens with deadly accurate submachine-gun fire. The attackers were trying to take cover against the new arrivals—which allowed Annette and the standing SSS trooper to open up on them again.

Several more of the aliens went down, surprisingly human-like blood scattering across the street, then the survivors bolted. Moving with an unexpected speed, half a dozen of them managed to disappear into the gap between two cargo containers before any of Annette's allies could bring them down.

They left seven dead lying in the streets behind them, and Annette turned her attention to their unexpected rescuers.

She somehow wasn't surprised to find Tellaki leading the small party of Rekiki toward her across the surprise battlefield.

CHAPTER THIRTY-THREE

"YOUR TIMING IS IMPECCABLE," ANNETTE TOLD HER ALIEN EX-crewmembers. "Thank you."

"We heard that the Kanzi had brought a hunting party onto the station, Honored Captain," the Rekiki leader told her. "Your species were the only new bipeds aboard. Given their...tastes, it was inevitable they would be hunting you."

The alien bent his upper torso to spit on the blue-furred corpses as one of his companions cut Ki!Tana and the SSS escort free.

"You are an Honored Captain," Tellaki said calmly. "We cannot serve you, as you are not Rekiki, but you have done fairly by us and we could not allow you or yours to be seized without intervention." He paused. "I have few friends aboard Tortuga," he continued after a moment. "I was only able to locate you and Major Wellesley. If you have other groups aboard the station, I may have missed them."

"Damn," Annette said mildly, pulling her communicator open. Right now, the device was linked into Tortuga's network—but she didn't *need* to link the network. The Terran-built devices were significantly more powerful than most of the communication relays used on the network.

"Shore parties, go Code Red and report," she snapped into the communicator.

"This is Wellesley with party four," the Special Space Service reported. "Was about to call you, ma'am. Local tipped us off that we're being surrounded; about to tip the waitress *very* nicely and put some holes in some slavers."

Annette waited. They had two more parties—another dozen humans and three aliens—aboard the station. Code Red should have them reporting immediately.

Only silence answered.

"Party two, party three, report," she snapped. No one responded.

"James, you have local support inbound," she told her ground force commander. "I suspect our furry friends will disappear once Tellaki's people show up. I'm linking in to Rolfson; stay on the line."

She tapped a series of commands on the communicator. The first formed a direct link to Wellesley, ignoring the local net. The second dropped her communicator completely off the local net, and the third raised *Tornado* on a priority channel.

"Commander, this is Bond."

"What do you need, Captain?" her tactical officer replied instantly. He had the watch and clearly had jumped on her call— shore leave watches were boring at best.

"I need you to ping the communicators for *everyone* we sent aboard station," she ordered. "Parties two and three are not responding; I need to know where they are."

"One second," Rolfson said crisply, his voice deadly serious. "I have your party with you and Major Wellesley's party together..."

"Where are party two and three?" she demanded.

"Looks like their communicators are together," he answered after a moment. "And nowhere near where either party reported they were heading."

"I need a location," Annette told him. "Have the Troop Captains start prepping a retrieval force—Major Wellesley, I'll meet you on the way."

"Transmitting now."

"Ma'am," the Servicewoman standing next to Annette murmured. "We have visitors."

Looking away from her communicator, *Tornado*'s Captain spotted two Yin soldiers in the red bandoliers of the Crew rapidly approaching.

The tall blue-skinned aliens surveyed the corpses of the Kanzi as they passed, standing next to them long enough for Annette to note that the Yin's skin was a far lighter shade of blue than the Kanzi's fur. The Yin's beaks and complete lack of fur made the distinction easy to draw, even if both fell into the broad category of "blue biped".

"You are responsible for this?" one of them asked Annette flatly. Her translator had enough experience with Yin now to pick up his disdain and carry it into his tone.

"They attacked my crew in an attempt to kidnap us," she told the Crewman. "They appear to have seized over a dozen of my other crew. Unless *you* intend to retrieve them, I suggest you deal with the corpses while I deal with *my* problem."

"If they initiated the attack, you will have no problem," the alien told her. "But if you initiate further violence, the Crew will be forced to become involved."

He spoke calmly, the translator picking up his complete lack of concern about the fate of the dead sapients scattered around him or the fate of Annette's crew. He approached her, his weapon moving to subtly track in her direction as he clearly attempted to intimidate her.

Annette slammed the flat of her hand into the barrel of his weapon—a light plasma weapon, exactly the kind of weapon no one *except* Crew was permitted aboard Tortuga—as it turned toward her, stopping its movement in mid-swing. *That* threw the big alien off-balance, allowing her to tear the gun from his blue hands, yanking him toward her by the heavy security strap.

Her elbow collided with the side of his head, snapping his beak shut with a resounding thud as the much larger alien soldier landed flat on his face.

He was, thankfully, still moving as Annette turned to face the other Yin. She couldn't read the alien's body language, but his complete lack of movement suggested an unwillingness to engage with her. It was dangerous to anthropomorphize aliens, but something in the cast of the Crewman's eyes suggested that he had no issue seeing his superior brought low.

"Tell your superiors you had two choices," she said flatly. "They could allow me to retrieve my crew or they could prevent my crew from being kidnapped by slavers. One of these is no longer an option."

Pulling her communicator back out, she studied the location where her people appeared to be.

"James, I'm flipping you a waypoint near to where I think these bastards are," she told Wellesley over the com. "Meet me there."

She turned to Ki!Tana, ignoring the two Crewmembers—one of whom was attending to the other while also subtly holding him down —as she focused on her people. "Are you up for this?" she asked the A!Tol, whose skin was still gray-black with pain.

"Believe me, Captain, breaking some necks will *help*," Ki!Tana told her. "Let's go."

Annette hadn't made it more than a half-dozen steps before Tellaki blocked her way. Stopping in surprise, she looked up at the crocodile-like alien as he lowered his long, *toothy* snout to meet her gaze with jet-black eyes.

"I see you, Honored Captain," he said, and something in the translated tone suggested that the words were important. "You would go this far"—he gestured toward the Yin soldier struggling to rise— "for your human crew?"

"I would go this far for *any* of my crew," she snapped. "And if the nonhumans aren't with the human crew, you'd better believe I will rip this station apart to find them."

There was some kind of communication between Tellaki and his fellows, and then the Rekiki awkwardly sank to one knee facing her.

"Honored Captain Annette Bond, if you would have this vassal's fealty, I would return to *Tornado* and take up service with you," he said calmly. "My fellows would join me in this."

"You said you could only offer fealty to a Rekiki," she replied. She didn't have *time* for this, but Tellaki's dozen well-armed, experienced troopers could make the difference between life or death for her crew.

"If you will fight for the least as few would fight for the greatest, then you may as well be Rekiki," the reptilian alien told her.

"WAIT, THE CAPTAIN DID *WHAT*?" James demanded of the Sergeant leading the Captain's protective detail.

"Put a Crew twit who told us not to go after our people on the ground with his own gun," the woman replied with a satisfied tone. "We're following the bouncing ball, with the Rekiki backing us up. See you at the rendezvous."

"Will do," he confirmed breezily before dropping the channel and looking around at his companions, cataloging his assets and liabilities. His Troop Captains were no slouches, easily capable of carrying their weight in a firefight. His *boyfriend*, however, was a naval officer.

"Can you shoot, Pat?" he asked quietly.

"I qualify," the cruiser's XO confirmed. "I'm even armed, thank you, but I'm probably not the best fit for an all-out assault on an enemy position."

"Wasn't planning on bringing you on that part," James admitted with a chuckle as he leaned back in his chair. The gesture might *look* casual, but it also allowed him to get a clear line of sight at one of the Kanzi aliens watching the exits. "Skipper said there was backup on its way, but these guys are getting antsy," he noted. "They may move before our crocodilian friends arrive."

"What are you thinking?" Sherman asked.

"If Pat is armed..." James glanced around. "We're all armed. I do *not* care about these bastards. I want to get to our crew—and if we don't move pretty quickly, we may not catch up to the Captain in time to back her up."

He bared his teeth in what someone *very* unfamiliar with humans might have called a smile.

"I have a plan."

THE PLAN STARTED with Sherman and James wobbling their way out of the bar, incoherently singing the same song...about three beats and two octaves out from each other. They gave a *wonderful* impression of being utterly drunk.

Out of the corner of his eye, James could see the Kanzi closing in on them. He'd identified six outside the restaurant, and four were now sweeping toward him and Sherman, clearly planning on taking them with the shotgun-like webbers as soon as they were out of sight of the restaurant.

Once they started to close in, though, James intentionally fell against Sherman, engaging in a level of physical contact that would probably have got him punched out in any other circumstances. They leaned against each other, clearly holding each other up as the aliens closed.

"Now?" she whispered in his ear.

"Now," he agreed.

Drawing each other's weapons, they shoved themselves apart, clearing lines of fire and opening up on several *very* surprised-looking little blue aliens. By the time the Kanzi realized *anything* was going on, James had taken one step to the side to be absolutely sure of a clear shot and opened fire.

The first Kanzi went down instantly, a solid double-tap from the standard auto-pistol ripping his torso apart. The second in James's zone managed to raise and even *fire* his webber—but rushed it, spraying the thick sticky strands across an inoffensive wall.

The alien didn't get a chance to fire a second shot as *James's* second double-tap took his head apart.

He didn't check to see if Sherman had taken down her targets—if two one-hundred-and-fifty-centimeter aliens were a danger to the woman, she wouldn't have made Troop Captain in the Special Space Service. There were at least two more Kanzi, and he needed to be sure the *rest* of his people were safe.

As James hit the ground, taking cover behind a corner, however, there was a sharp exchange of gunfire that rapidly echoed away to silence. He tapped his communicator, linking to the earbuds for his translator.

"Are we clear?"

"Three hostiles," Troop Captain Bousaid said calmly. "Neutralized."

He checked around the corner and surveyed the neat set of corpses where the aliens had rushed to back up their fellows—and run promptly into the prepared ambush of his Troop Captains.

"All right," he said crisply, gesturing his people to him. "We need to move."

"Major—looks like those friendlies finally arrived," Sherman announced from behind him.

James turned again and found a set of six Rekiki churning down the street at a disturbingly rapid pace. They came to a halt in front of him, their gazes flicking across the Kanzi bodies.

"Apologies, Major," the leader said through his translator. "We had further to go than we had thought—a passage we intended to use was blocked."

"We're fine, but it looks like two of our shore parties were captured," James told them. "Can you help us?"

"We have decided to rejoin Honored Captain Bond's crew, if she will have us," the Rekiki replied. "We are with you all the way."

The Rekiki were in light body armor and packing submachine guns. His people were in utilities and carrying sidearms. He sighed.

"We need to get the XO back to the ship," he announced. "Guo,

Bousaid," he called his Alpha and Bravo Troop Captains over. "Escort the Commander back to *Tornado* and organize the Company to come after us if needed."

"Yes, sir," the two officers chorused.

James turned an apologetic gaze on his boyfriend, who shrugged and smiled.

"I'll be a lot more use there than getting in the middle of a firefight," Kurzman reminded him. "Besides, the Captain needs someone on the bridge with the backbone to fire into this bucket of bolts if the Crew gets stroppy." He gestured. "Go!"

One quickly stolen kiss later, the commander of *Tornado*'s ground forces obeyed.

CHAPTER THIRTY-FOUR

THE RENDEZVOUS WAYPOINT ANNETTE HAD SET LED HER NEW collection of armed people deep into a section of Tortuga she hadn't seen before. Ki!Tana was surprisingly familiar with *everywhere* in the station and led them confidently through and around the various corridors and twists that led into the temporary warehousing district.

"What's your ETA, James?" she asked Wellesley, checking to see if the collection of comms had moved. They hadn't, but that didn't mean that the units were still on her people.

"We got held up and this place is a maze," the Major admitted over the comms. "I can't be sure, but I'm guessing at least ten more minutes."

Tornado's Captain looked around her companions. Six Rekiki in body armor and carrying submachine guns; two Special Space Service troopers in body armor but only carrying sidearms; herself, unarmored but with a sidearm; and Ki!Tana, who she'd *never* seen wear armor of any kind and had produced a submachine gun from within her tentacles.

Ten minutes would more than double her strength. Thirty would have two entire troops of the Special Space Service, thirty elite soldiers, backing her up.

"I'm not even sure they're still here now," she admitted to Wellesley. "I can't wait. We have to move."

There was a pregnant pause, then he sighed.

"Listen to Sergeant Lin," he told her. "Wei Lin has seen more close quarters combat than anyone else in my company. That's why she's your bodyguard."

"Understood," Annette said flatly. "My unit is set to encrypted beacon. Follow me in."

"Will comply. Good luck."

Nodding even though she knew Wellesley couldn't see her, she drew her sidearm and checked the load. She hadn't fired that many shots, but she switched to her spare magazine anyway. Better safe than sorry.

"We're going in," she told the people with her. "Sergeant Lin." She gestured to her bodyguard. "You're in charge; you make the calls. But we're going in and we're going in *now*."

"Then we go," the SSS Sergeant said calmly. "Captain, you're in the back. Tellaki, you're on point with me. Let's move."

THERE WAS ALMOST no one in the open spaces in the warehousing district—people would presumably only come there when loading or offloading a ship—and the handful of beings that they did encounter rapidly cleared out of the way of an armed party on a clear warpath.

The beacons on the communicators led them off the main thoroughfare into a dingier, clearly less well-maintained section of the district, and finally to a loading dock door that wouldn't have looked out of place on Earth.

"Can we open this?" Annette asked Ki!Tana as they approached it.

"Of course."

"Everyone move back to cover her," Lin ordered as the big A!Tol removed her communicator's paper-like display and started checking into the door's software. "If they're smart, they're waiting for us."

"They are smart," Tellaki replied as he gestured for his people to obey. "They were not expecting others to intervene; they see great value in your people as stock and will protect them."

"Why *us*?" Annette asked.

"Because you are new and exotic, and there are many wealthy Kanzi who will pay well for new and exotic slaves," the Rekiki said simply.

"Slaves *still* don't make sense to me," she noted.

"In this case, it is about power and sex," Tellaki said. "The Kanzi believe all bipeds but them were created to serve them. There is a section of their population—with many members in their leadership —that..."

"Takes that in a very specific way," Annette concluded. "I'm starting to *really* dislike them."

"You are hardly alone," Ki!Tana replied. "The A!Tol Imperium are their deadly enemies, and slavers caught inside Imperial borders are sentenced to death if it can be proven." She fluttered her manipulator tentacles toward the door. "I am ready. Shall we?"

"Go," Wei Lin snapped.

The big docking door smoothly opened, sliding up into the roof without even a whisper of a sound. The space on the other side was smaller than Annette had expected, barely thirty meters wide and forty deep, and filled with crates and containers. An upper catwalk linked into a suspended second floor and two sets of stairs.

Two Kanzi guarded the visible entrance to the second floor. Another six were working amongst the containers, checking numbers against a sheet of electronic flimsy. All of them looked up as the door opened—and went for weapons.

The two guards were carrying rifles, probably slugthrowers but potentially plasma weapons. Annette quickly classed them as the key threat and opened fire at them.

By the time her bullets slammed into the catwalk next to the closer guard, both of them were already going down. Wei Lin and the other SSS trooper had made the same assessment as Annette—and acted faster and more effectively.

Annette hung back, trying to take stock of the situation and failing as the two troopers moved through the door. Their Rekiki backup had put down half of the Kanzi on the ground, but the remainder had managed to take cover and acquire their own weapons.

Bullets cracked into the wall next to Annette and she dove forward for cover of her own. Leaving the Kanzi on the ground to the SSS troopers who were rapidly outflanking their position, she focused on the door the two more heavily armed aliens had been guarding.

"With you, Captain," Tellaki told her, clearly recognizing her intent. She glanced back to nod at him and then charged the stairs with two of the Rekiki right on her heels.

Part of her mind noticed the last Kanzi on the ground throwing up its blue-furred arms in surrender as she charged up the stairs, but her priority was her crew—and the locator beacons said the communicators were in the second-floor office.

She hit the door hard, throwing it open into the Kanzi behind it. He was thrown off-balance, but unlike any of the others they'd encountered so far today, this one had managed to put on *part* of a suit of powered armor. His head and legs were uncovered, but the breastplate, arms and gauntlets wrapped around his torso to protect him.

An armored forearm slammed back into the door, crashing it shut behind Annette.

"Who the hell are you?" the armored Kanzi demanded.

"I'm the queen bitch whose crew you kidnapped," Annette snapped, ramming her pistol into his face. His armored gauntlet grabbed the weapon in time to interpose his palm in front of the barrel, catching the bullet with an audible grunt as she fired.

"The Crew will kill you for this," he told her. "Attacking a warehouse without sanction? Whatever you wanted, your only chance of living through this is to surrender." Somehow, the leer got across the species body-language barrier easily. "You'll be valuable enough to keep alive, after all."

"I'll deal with them later," she said sweetly, flicking the pistol from slug to rocket rounds and firing again. He caught the bullet again, bared sharpened teeth at her, and then blinked in surprise when the rocket engine fired.

It didn't throw him off much—just enough for Annette to pump four more rounds into his unarmored head.

MOMENTS LATER, the door came apart as Tellaki hit it with every ounce of force a four-hundred-kilo crocodile equivalent in full body armor could muster. He careened into the room, his submachine gun covering every corner of the utilitarian office until it came to rest level with the gory mess that *had* been a Kanzi.

"Honored Captain, are you all right?" he demanded.

Taking a deep breath and looking around the room, Annette nodded. Realizing that the Rekiki was unlikely to be able to read the gesture, she swallowed hard before speaking.

"I'm fine," she told him. "The communicators are...there." Following the image on her communicator, she pointed at an assembly of storage cabinets. "Shit. Search the rest of the warehouse for our people."

Stepping over the blue-furred corpse, Annette ripped open the cabinet. A plastic bin on the bottom shelf spilled over when she grabbed it, scattering the scroll-like communication devices her people had been issued across the floor.

The utilitarian office she stood in wouldn't have been out of place in any warehousing district on Earth. Four plain metal desks with roll-up monitors designed to interface with portable computing devices. A small food counter with what would have been a coffee machine on Earth. An entire wall of storage cabinets, two exits back into the warehouse—and two doors leading into other sections of the suspended second floor.

"Do you hear anything?" she asked Tellaki, gesturing toward the doors.

"No."

"Right." Annette paused, eyeing the doors. Presumably, if there were more Kanzi, they'd have emerged by now. If her people weren't in the cargo containers on the main floor of the warehouse, they were up here—or had been moved already.

"The Crew will likely be on their way," the Rekiki told her. "We are short of time."

"Right," she repeated. Picking a door at random, she shoved open the one closest to the entrance she'd come in. Instead of a set of offices or a bathroom, she found a small airlock-esque room—with an armory of unfamiliar weapons.

"What are these?" she asked, gesturing.

"Stunners and shock prods," Tellaki replied instantly. "This has to be their holding area. It will be soundproofed—there may be more Kanzi inside who haven't heard anything. I will go first."

Stepping back to cover him, Annette gestured for him to go ahead. The crocodilian alien stepped up to the inner door, bracing himself on all four legs and then slammed a hand onto the panel next to the door. It whirred for a moment and then slid apart on smooth magnetic bearings.

"Fuck you!" a female voice bellowed. "Fuck you all and the fucking horses you fucking rode in on!"

An unfamiliar sound buzzed through the air and Tellaki winced, lurching back as the air around him shimmered like a warm day.

Before whatever weapon was being used managed to cause actual damage, Annette charged into the open space next to the Rekiki.

"Stand down!" she snapped.

Thankfully, the naked young woman holding the stunner had seen Annette and jerked the weapon away.

"Captain!"

It took Annette a moment to place her: she was Sarah Amita, one of the engineering specialists who'd been assigned to Lieutenant Mosi's prize crew. She'd ordered that prize crew to take one of the first shore leaves as a reward for their hard work.

That was a decision she was starting to regret as she took in the full scene inside the holding cell. All of her missing crew were present—including the nonhumans, thankfully—but the humans had been stripped naked. All of them but Amita and Mosi were locked away in cages that covered the walls of the room. The single Kanzi in the room was *also* naked—and dead.

Very dead, his eyes bulging out of his skull and Mosi's hands still locked around his throat. The black officer's naked body was covered in stab wounds where the Kanzi had repeatedly attacked her to try and save his own life.

"She's still alive, Captain," the young specialist standing over her officer said desperately. "We've got to help her!"

Annette looked at the young woman. She'd killed her attacker—and from the Kanzi's state of undress, *his* intentions were disturbingly obvious—but Mosi had already passed out from loss of blood.

"Tellaki. You have some kind of medkit, right?" she asked desperately.

The alien had already starting unstrapping various supplies from within his armor but didn't step past Annette as he met the survivors' gaze.

"I do not have antibiotics or painkillers for your species," he said quietly. "But I can bandage her wounds if you will let me."

Amita trained the stunner on him, but then Mosi shifted, her hands finally releasing the Kanzi's neck as more blood leaked from her. The young specialist nodded sharply, allowing the big alien to approach Mosi with his bandages.

"Ma'am," Wei Lin said quietly from the door. "My god..."

"Sergeant—help Tellaki," Annette ordered as soon as she realized her guard was there. "Have his people break ours out. Their uniforms have to be around here somewhere."

"I'll help her," Lin promised as she crossed the room. "We'll get it sorted. But you're needed—the Crew are here."

All Annette wanted to do was tear the entire station apart, bolt by bolt and rivet and rivet, and destroy every goddamned alien who'd ever crossed her path. She wanted to pull up her communicator and order Kurzman to fire up the proton beams and rip the station to pieces.

Instead, she nodded and stepped back, letting the Sergeant get to work while she stepped out into the main warehouse to see how bad the situation had become.

* * *

THE REKIKI who had rejoined her crew were forming a rough blockade across the entrance, resolutely barring entry to the warehouse to the squad of power-armored Crew soldiers. All of *these* soldiers, Annette noted as she approached the standoff, were Laian. None of their recruits from other races; these were born and bred Crew.

"Are you in charge here?" asked one of them, presumably the leader as his armor was marked with gold symbols that meant nothing to Annette. He was apparently making the same judgment on the fact that she was the *only* one in a uniform, battered as it was.

"These are my crew, yes," she replied as calmly as she could. The translator would lose most of her emotion, but homicidal rage was no answer to battle armor.

"This facility is not registered to you," the Laian commander told

THE TERRAN PRIVATEER   277

her. "Weapons have been fired, people are dead, and you do not belong here. Your explanation?"

"Fifteen members of my crew were kidnapped by the *scum* that owned this place," she replied, managing to only spit the one word. "Since you failed to protect them, we acted to retrieve them."

"You are not permitted to engage in lethal force except in immediate self-defense," the Laian officer reminded her. "This should have been reported."

"I was told to do nothing," she said coldly. "These people tried to rape one of my crew, who is now dying. Had I waited longer, more of my crew would have died. If you want to make an issue of my protecting my crew, you're going to have to fight me for it."

She was familiar with the body language of neither species around her and she could *still* feel the tension ratcheting up. Defiance wouldn't help—even with Tellaki's people, she had light body armor and submachine guns versus power armor and plasma weapons.

"This situation has already passed simple solutions, Captain Bond," the Laian said after a long moment. "It seems the owners of this facility have remote access to the security systems. Captain Ikwal of the Kanzi vessel *Faces of God* is apparently dead, but his second-in-command has filed a formal complaint against you for an illegal assault and the murder of his Captain."

He paused, seeming to wait for a response from her. She stared at him for a long moment until he made a distinct "come on" gesture and she realized what he needed.

"Where, sir, would I be able to file an official complaint against *them* for kidnapping and murder of my crew?" she demanded.

"As it happens, you would need to file that report with an officer of the Crew such as myself," he said smoothly. "Contrasting complaints would require arbitration by the High Captain. If you are prepared to surrender yourself as security for the good behavior of your crew, I can place this facility under lockdown but allow your crew to return to your ship unimpeded."

"May I bring a companion?" she asked, glancing around for Ki!Tana. The big alien wasn't part of the blockade at the door—apparently because she'd found cover big enough to protect her. Bond waved the A!Tol over to join them.

"Ah, Ki!Tana," the Laian officer greeted the alien. "I was warned you would be involved." He turned to Annette. "The Ki! will not be permitted into the arbitration process, as it is only for Captains, but she may accompany you until then if you surrender and make that complaint." He paused, glancing up at the suspended second floor, where the holding cells had been concealed. "I will also have our doctors see if we can assist with your wounded crew."

Annette nodded swiftly before she could change her mind.

"Very well."

CHAPTER THIRTY-FIVE

Major James Wellesley arrived at the warehouse at a much slower pace and with much less shooting than he'd originally planned. He and his Troop Captains had paused at the original rendezvous point for two of his troops to catch up with them, and they now approached the Crew soldiers guarding the warehouse with the somewhat-illusory advantage of numbers.

Without power armor for his humans and unwilling to break their restriction on weapons, his thirty-odd troopers were no match for the ten Laians in power armor. That was not really the point: the point was to impress on the Crew how seriously *Tornado's* crew took recovering their people.

The status of the power-armored insectoids, though, was *nothing* like what he expected. While two were maintaining a very clear, alert guard, most of them had doffed their helmets and appeared to be relatively relaxed.

They also didn't react to the humans showing up with thirty more armed troops at all.

With a sigh, James approached the Laian with the most gold filigree on his armor and threw a crisp salute.

"Major James Wellesley, *Tornado*," he introduced himself. "I'm here to escort our people back to my ship."

"Of course, Major," the Laian replied. "I am Second Lance Pekelon. All of your people are inside, except for your Lieutenant Mosi, who has been transferred to the main medical facility in the Crew section of the ship, and Sergeant Lin who insisted on accompanying her.

"Well, and Captain Bond and Ki!Tana, of course, who will shortly be facing the High Captain to decide the fate of your ship for this action," he added, a minor and apparently unimportant addition.

"Thank you," James said slowly. "Am I permitted to retrieve them, Second Lance?"

"You are," the...junior noncommissioned officer, he thought, told him. "I do need to otherwise maintain lockdown of this facility until the High Captain has completed his judgment. I can only spare two troopers to escort you."

"I appreciate the assistance," he said gravely. Sadly, two power-armored and plasma weapon–armed troopers probably *were* more of an escort than his thirty-plus humans with assault rifles.

"I never said anything, Major," Pekelon said quietly, "but the Kanzi deserved to be driven from our station a long time ago. You will not find many Crew mourning their shed blood."

He stepped back, waving for James to lead his people in and rescue their fellows.

THE LAIAN COMMANDER took Annette's statement and complaint with quickly efficient questions, clearly processing a translated version of her comments into their system via software in his helmet, as his troops escorted them through the warehouse district, through an unprepossessing hatch, and into a concealed rapid transit system.

A small pod whisked them away to the original central hull of

Tortuga, where they were led to a small waiting room carefully painted with murals of a strange and unfamiliar world.

"The seat is for a Yin," the Laian told Annette, gesturing to one of the two chairs. "It should work for your species. There is a cupboard with water over there." He gestured with an armored claw. "Please make yourself comfortable."

The armored insect-like alien bowed, a weird bending movement in his case, and left the room—leaving Annette and Ki!Tana alone for the moment. The big A!Tol settled onto the odd curved bench her race used as seats and shivered slightly, her skin *still* the gray-black of minor distress.

"Are you all right, Ki!Tana?" Annette asked as she settled into her own chair. "You seem to have been in pain all day."

"It is a long explanation," her companion replied. "One we will not have time for today, but some days are worse for me than others. I have carried my burden for a long time, Captain Bond, and I will carry it for some long cycles yet."

"Your burden?"

"We don't have time," Ki!Tana repeated. "Realize before you go into this meeting that the High Captain can seize your ships and all of your accounts. You do not have the force to stop him."

A chill ran down Annette's spine.

"Would he do that?" she asked, realizing at last how much danger her instinctive reaction to protect her crew had put them all in.

Ki!Tana made a small grinding noise and Annette realized she was quite literally grinding her beak against itself. Whatever was wrong with the A!Tol, it was getting worse.

"I don't know," she finally admitted. "If it remains Ridotak, you benefit from knowing me. He *should* be, but changes of High Captain are not announced or advertised.

"Even if not, you merely defied a Crew giving an order on the spot. The Kanzi have broken a longstanding Crew dictate, one the Crew values highly. So long as you do not anger the High Captain, the odds are in your favor. Just...remember that this being could end your campaign with a word."

"I will," Annette promised. "Are you sure you're okay?"

"I have overexerted myself, given my state," the alien admitted. "I will be fine, but if you would be so kind as to fetch me water? Moving would be...difficult."

Annette grabbed a bottle of water, clearly designed to be easily drunk from by as many species as possible, for the other sapient and passed it over.

"If they don't talk about the High Captain, how do you know who it is?" she asked. "For that matter, *they* knew you."

Ki!Tana swallowed the entire contents of the water bottle in a single extended gulp, and turned her black eyes on Annette, flashes of red and blue barely visible on her skin despite the overwhelming gray of her current state.

"If Ridotak remains High Captain, he will tell you anyway," she admitted. "There was a time, Captain Bond, before I served Kiki-theth, when *I* was Crew. And at the end of that time, before I set out into the galaxy to see if there were other paths for me to walk, Ridotak was my Captain."

THEY WERE MOST of the way back to *Tornado* when James's finely tuned professional paranoia exploded. His lead element, a five-man patrol from his Alpha Troop, had entered the long gallery linking all of the docking tubes on this side of the station. The gallery was empty, with even less traffic than when they'd arrived. The access corridor most of the group were still in was still lightly occupied, with a couple of cargo movers moving toward the gallery access...

"Everybody to the walls!" he bellowed. "Ambush close!"

The SSS troopers knew the meaning of *that* command and bodily grabbed the still-shaky ship crewmen and -women who *weren't* trained in the Special Space Service's lexicon of danger commands.

Even before the two cargo movers had reached his people, all of the spacers were against the walls and down, with kneeling SSS troopers covering them and aiming at the vehicles.

The two Laian escorts seemed to freeze in the confusion. One realized what James had seen as a threat and stepped out to challenge the two cargo movers. They were unmanned vehicles, normally, and sensors and safety protocols meant they supposedly *couldn't* hit anything, let alone a sapient.

So, of course the multi-ton transport vehicle drove straight over him, smashing the insectoid alien to the ground and grinding to a halt on his power armor. The vehicle's engine whirred, unable to push farther as the armor wasn't going to be damaged or flattened by a civilian cargo hauler.

The second Laian reacted to *that*—by putting three plasma bolts into the engine block of the second hauler. It careened to a halt in a crashing ball of flame.

And then the gunfire started. Kanzi in body armor—only two, thankfully, in *power* armor—swarmed out of the first hauler and opened fire. Plasma fire slammed into the still-standing Crew trooper in a hail of superheated white flame. Power armor was tough, tough stuff, but not *that* tough.

The Laian still managed to spray fire back at his attackers, fire burning through regular body armor like it wasn't even there, before collapsing backward, cooked in his own suit.

He had bought James's people precious seconds. Seconds they put to deadly use.

James hadn't expected to fight the Crew when they caught up to them, but they hadn't *known* that—or that the Kanzi wouldn't have power armor—when they left the ship. The two troops who'd caught up with him had under-barrel grenade launchers strapped to their rifles.

In the seconds the Laian's sacrifice bought them, they carefully targeted the launchers and opened fire with a salvo of armor-piercing grenades "liberated" from the armories of A!Tol military freighters. A dozen Kanzi from the jammed hauler were still standing, and two power-armored figures were hauling themselves out of the burning wreckage of the other.

Each took at least one grenade, and then James's people followed up a fusillade of armor-piercing bullets. The rounds were *far* from enough to threaten the power-armored soldiers...but they proved entirely redundant.

Thirty grenades went off in an ear-crashing cacophony of bright flashes from the deadly spikes of plasma the weapons flashed into the nearest mass when they triggered.

When the noise and the light cleared, none of the Kanzi were still standing. Blood and bits of blue fur were splattered across the remaining hauler, the walls, the roof.

"Get the hauler off our armored friend," James snapped, swallowing his stomach's attempt to empty itself at the smell of burnt fur and flesh. The grenades had been designed to kill power armor. Against regular infantry, they'd been pure overkill. "I think the blue-furred bastards just cut their own throats, but let's earn ourselves some goodwill."

CHAPTER THIRTY-SIX

THE ROOM THEY WERE IN WAS APPARENTLY SUFFICIENTLY shielded to prevent Annette from linking in to either the station's network or her direct connection to *Tornado*. Nonetheless, her communicator at least gave her the time, which let her know that it was a little over forty minutes before the door to their comfortable holding area opened again.

Two Laians entered, clad in the red bandoliers that seemed to serve as regular working uniforms for the Crew, but with somewhat more gold embroidery. The lead, somewhat larger than the other—so female, as Annette understood Laian physiology—bowed to Annette and Ki!Tana.

"I am First Spear Podule," she greeted Annette. "We are your escort to the hearing."

"The hearing was put together that quickly?" Annette asked, somewhat surprised. The High Captain ran a space station that rivaled a small city. She would have expected it to take more than an hour to pull him free to organize a hearing.

Tornado was a lot smaller, and she was pretty sure *she'd* need more than an hour to sort out a hearing for infractions by her people unless...well, unless it was something extremely serious.

"The situation is unusual and of high priority," Podule told her as she finished her thought. "It has been some time since a series of incidents of this scale and severity has occurred aboard Tortuga."

The insectoid alien gestured for Annette to follow her and left. With no choice but to obey, Annette nodded to Ki!Tana and followed, the second Laian falling in behind her.

Annette's sense of direction was good even in three-dimensional space, but as the Laians led her deeper into the central hub of the old shipyard, she quickly lost track of her location. The hub was laid out in a series of concentric circular corridors that spiraled up and down to reach new levels. Rooms were presumably sandwiched between, but Annette only saw connecting corridors and stairwells.

Finally, well after they'd managed to get *Tornado*'s Captain completely lost, the latest gently curving corridor terminated at a massive security hatch, a heavy black metal blast door that likely protected either Tortuga's bridge or a similar nerve center.

Their exit was about five meters before the hatch, a side door that slid aside to allow them access into a mid-sized conference room that, other than the chairs and the occupants, would have looked perfectly normal anywhere in Sol.

The tables had been set up in a rough U shape. The top of the table was already occupied by three Laians, one absolutely immense one in a bandolier that eschewed gold embroidery for simply *being* gold, clearly marking its wearer as the leader of the Laians, the High Captain of Tortuga.

Either the pickup, the trip up, or both, had clearly been very carefully timed. At the same moment as Podule led Annette into the room and gestured her to a chair that would fit her physiology, a Kanzi with pure dark blue fur was led in the other side of the conference room and placed in the seat exactly opposite Annette.

This was the first chance she'd had to study a living Kanzi, and she was almost disturbed by how humanlike the alien's features were.

Despite being barely a hundred and fifty centimeters tall and covered in blue fur, the being across from her was one of the most human-looking sapients she'd seen so far.

"Captain Annette Bond, Oath Keeper Waltan Cawl, you have left me with an aggravating dilemma," the gold-clad Laian told them. "I am High Captain Ridotak, the leader of the Crew and the ruler of Tortuga. It has been many years since such a series of crimes has been committed on my station. What am I to do with you?"

"That *thing* murdered my Captain!" the Kanzi Oath Keeper—presumably a rank of some kind—bellowed, pointing at Annette. "Shot him in the head with her own hands."

"Your Captain kidnapped my crew and *killed* one of my people," Annette snapped back.

"A point of minor correction, Captain Bond," Ridotak interjected calmly. "Your Lieutenant Mosi is now in the care of the Crew. Luckily, we appear to *have* a physiological profile on your species, and she is responding well to treatment. I am told she will live."

That stopped Annette's rant in its tracks and drew a sigh of relief. She hadn't expected Mosi to live.

"Thank you," she told Ridotak.

"You're *treating their wounds?*" Cawl demanded. "Wounds acquired *attacking my people?*"

"Actually, no," the High Captain replied mildly. "We are treating wounds acquired when one of your people attempted interspecies rape on a female who had been kidnapped by armed force aboard my station."

That finally silenced Cawl.

"We have permitted that disgusting trade to continue on our station due to the high overlap between slave traders, smugglers, and pirates," Ridotak continued. "Part of the deal, however, was that there would be *no* slave-taking on the station itself."

He turned to Annette with a wide, expansive gesture of his closer claw.

"That said, Captain Bond, it is *also* the rule of this station that orders given by Crew are to be followed," he reminded her. "You were ordered not to get involved, as we try to avoid this scale of violence. Your actions, while understandable, were a violation of the peace of this station. You will be required to pay a penalty of one million A!Tol Imperial Marks or an equivalent amount in trade or alternative currency before you will be allowed to recommence trade on Tortuga.

"Do you understand, Captain Bond of *Tornado*?"

Annette swallowed hard. That was actually *more* than was currently in *Tornado*'s accounts, even with her own funds included. Once they sold the remaining prizes and cargo, though, they could cover that and still probably fund their upgrades.

"Yes, High Captain Ridotak," she told him. "Will my agent be permitted to continue selling my cargo to help us raise the funds?"

"Yes," Ridotak replied with a tossing gesture with his arm. "But wait before you make plans, Captain Bond. I am not yet done with you."

Cawl clearly wasn't sure what to make of this. Annette suspected that the punishment was severe enough that he probably *did* think it was enough, but he was also furious that his Captain and crewmates were dead.

"Sir, wait one moment," one of the other Laians suddenly said, just as Ridotak was turning back to Cawl. He slid what appeared to be a flimsy across the table, suggesting that the High Captain didn't have a communicator with him.

Something in Ridotak's manner changed. Annette wasn't entirely sure, but she'd guess from his gestures that the High Captain had been more amused than anything else up to this point. Now his upper claws snapped together and then rested on the table in front of him as he leveled his gaze on Waltan Cawl.

"Did you think that I was stupid, Oath Keeper Waltan Cawl?" he demanded. "Did you think we were blind in our own station? Crawling fools you could befuddle with one claw and betray with the other?"

Something had happened, and it was *not* to the Kanzi's benefit. He also clearly knew exactly what Ridotak was talking about, and quivered back in his chair.

"Since you have been blocked from communicating since you arrived here, it falls to me to explain the result of your attack on Captain Bond's people," the High Captain continued. "None of the humans or the other races serving Bond were injured. Your entire team of slavers was killed.

"But not," Ridotak noted, the mandibles on his jaw started to click rapidly as they trembled with rage, "before you killed one of *my* people. Do you know the penalty for the murder of Crew, Oath Keeper Cawl?"

"I didn't kill them!" Cawl snapped, but if his body language was as human as his appearance, his half-bowed position and trembling frame suggested that he was utterly terrified. "Mercy!" he whimpered after a moment.

"Your Captain broke a longstanding Crew decree," the High Captain told him. "The punishment for that alone would have been legendary, but now? Now you will be an *example*, Oath Keeper Cawl!"

Ridotak rose to his feet, all four arms in front of him as the two-and-a-half-meter tall insectoid stretched the full length of his carapace. The old Laian was *huge*; only Ondu's bodyguards and Ki!Tana had been larger among the aliens Annette had met.

"Your ship, *Faces of God*, and all associated accounts will be seized," he mandated. "The personal accounts of Captain Ikwal and Oath Keeper Cawl will be seized. All crew from the *Faces of God* have sixty-six hours to leave Tortuga or will be sold to whatever *other* slaver scum are left on my station.

"The only *mercy* I am prepared to offer is that *you* will be spared to suffer under the same order," he concluded. "I hope you have friends who value you enough to buy you a ticket home, Waltan Cawl."

The Kanzi was now melted into his chair, barely swallowing

what would have been hyperventilating sobs in a human—and didn't look much different on a Kanzi.

"Captain Bond," Ridotak addressed Annette again. "As the victim of the violation of our decree, *Faces of God* and one half of the confiscated accounts will be turned over to you as compensation, less the one-million-mark penalty for your own violations of our orders.

"Money does not wash away blood in my experience," he noted, "but I must ask you to promise that this suffices as punishment for your purposes and you will not pursue further action against Ikwal's crew except in immediate self-defense."

Annette paused in shock. *That* hadn't been expected. If they planned to deduct the fine from the seized accounts, the accounts would likely still make a noticeable contribution to her little squadron's needs.

"Yes," she finally agreed. "I accept this as sufficient punishment and will pursue no further action."

"Good," Ridotak said briskly. "We must talk in private, Captain. This hearing is dismissed!"

The massive Laian moved slowly and carefully but with the momentum of a falling mountain. Annette's escorts chivvied her to her feet and gestured for her to come with them as they followed the High Captain.

Cawl's escorts were having a *much* harder time mobilizing him.

RIDOTAK'S PATH took him out the other side of the meeting room, past a second set of security hatches presumably leading to the same place as the first, and down another gently curving and sloping corridor to a set of offices tucked away from the main bustle.

At the door to what looked like the largest office, Annette's escort waved off and Annette stepped through to find herself alone with the unquestioned ruler of the largest pirate port in her arm of the galaxy.

"This was not done for your benefit, Captain Bond," Ridotak noted. "Please, have a seat." He gestured to a quartet of chairs organized around a table. Two were clearly designed for Laians, but the other two looked to have been swapped out for ones suitable for a human-sized biped.

The room itself looked surprisingly plebeian. The walls were a soft gray tone, the furniture in black metal. A massive desk with what looked like half a dozen adjustable screens filled a good third of the office, but the chairs looked comfortable even to Annette.

"You just handed me a ship—that I know nothing about, admittedly—and a currently undetermined amount of money," she replied. "If it wasn't done for my benefit, I have still benefited."

"The Crew generally allows the public areas of the station to sort out their own affairs unless they interfere with ours," Ridotak explained. "Corpses in the street are not uncommon. People sell themselves into slavery or various lesser forms of indentured servitude every day. There is no other recourse for the desperate here but death."

"This doesn't bother you?" Annette asked.

"It did once," he admitted. "But the Crew are a small force in a large universe, Captain, adrift because no one helped us. Those of the lost and desperate who come to us with value, we recruit. The rest must choose their own paths. We of all beings are not qualified to guide them."

Fatalistic and stupid as the philosophy sounded to Annette, she could see how that, combined with the Crew being utterly without nation as she understood it, allowed Tortuga to function as it did.

"You did all of this just to tell people not to cause you trouble?" she asked.

"Yes," he confirmed. He tossed a flimsy across the table to her. "I believe that should be readable for you," he told her. "I am uncertain of the reliability of the translation software the A!Tol had nineteen months ago."

Annette glanced it over. It was a summary of the accounts seized, the amount deeded to her, the deduction for the fine, and the—signifi-cant—remainder deposited to her flotilla account.

"Realize that, as Captain, the accounts for your flotilla are exten-sions of your personal account," Ridotak observed. "If you are wondering, that sum would be enough for you, at least, to purchase a mansion in a quieter Core system, stock it with food custom-made to your biology, and live like a queen for the rest of your life."

"But not enough for my entire crew to do so," Annette guessed.

"No. Your loyalty to your crew does you credit, Captain Bond, as does your alliance with Ki!Tana. But tell me, are you not tempted? To just...walk away from the impossible course your oaths have set you upon?"

"I do not yet believe the course is impossible," she replied firmly. Her doubts were a private thing, better studied in the dark of her own office, not this softly gray space controlled by this strange sapient. "Even if it was, I swore an oath, High Captain."

"Ah," he breathed. "So, it is not merely Ki!Tana's influence. You *are* this stubborn."

"Ki!Tana's influence?" Annette asked. "She did say she knew you. Worked for you."

"Do you have any idea, Captain Bond, what kind of trickster demon you have bound to yourself?" Ridotak asked. "The Ki!Tol are wise and knowledgeable, but realize that they are all, to a being, utterly insane."

The Ki!Tol? Annette had assumed that Ki!Tana was a name, but it was starting to sound like the Ki! part meant something *else*. Some-thing she was going to have to ask the alien about.

"She has been of great help to us," she said carefully.

"As she was once of great help to me," the High Captain agreed. "Understand that however old you think your friend is, she is older. Understand that whatever you think she is at all, you are wrong. It is not my place to share her story. Ask her, if you must know it."

"A trickster demon, though?" Annette asked.

"Ki!Tana will never lie to you," Ridotak told her. "She will never do more than present options—honest ones. She will never mislead you or deceive you or fail to answer a direct question; these are not things the A!Tol have in them.

"But her advice has layers within layers, Captain Bond. Those the Ki!Tol attach themselves to are never meant for ordinary things. If you stand with her, you will end a criminal, a king, or a corpse."

"It seems she delivered both of the first two for you," Annette pointed out, and Ridotak's mandibles clicked rapidly in chittering laughter.

"Age and fine food will arrange for the latter more quickly than anyone not familiar with my race would guess," he noted. "If you accept that your life will never be calm, then stay with Ki!Tana, Captain. It may well kill you, but it will not be *boring*."

He gestured toward the door, a clear dismissal, but Annette stopped, eyeing him.

"Sir, one final request, if you will permit," she said.

"From one of Ki!Tana's students to another, I can at least listen," he allowed.

"I understand that the Crew have repair docks and technology unrivaled by any in this sector of space. I want to buy that tech and pay for what I fear may be the only reliable docks on this station to install it."

Ridotak lurched to standing, looming over Annette with every kilo of his impressive bulk in silence for a long moment.

"You have courage, honor, and fight for your crew when they need you. I would be proud to have you as a Captain of mine," he told her. "I will put you in touch with our Dockmaster. Be warned, however," he concluded with that chittering laugh, "if you wish to buy *our* systems, Captain Bond, you will probably be selling that ship I just gave you back to us."

CHAPTER THIRTY-SEVEN

JAMES AND KURZMAN WERE SITTING OUTSIDE THE SHIP WHEN the Captain returned. Theoretically, James had assigned himself command of the guard detachment—currently *inside* the ship, with plasma rifles—but once he'd got Captain Bond's update, he'd relaxed significantly.

Instead, he and his boyfriend were sitting on lawn chairs, drinking beer and watching the aliens go by.

Those aliens didn't need to know that James's beer was non-alcoholic and there was a plasma rifle under his chair.

The Captain and Ki!Tana arrived together, via a floating hover platform driven by a four-armed Tosumi in Crew red. He stopped, letting them off, and then whizzed away again without a word.

Ki!Tana's skin had gone pure black and James was on his feet immediately. He'd *never* seen the A!Tol that color.

"Are you all right?" he demanded.

"I need rest," the alien replied. "That's all." She paused, one support tentacle half-buckling under her. "I would not object to assistance," she admitted.

The Captain was already there, but James joined her immediately, the two of them slipping under Ki!Tana's manipulator tentacles to help support her. He realized, as the leathery limbs settled onto his shoulders, that it was actually the first time he'd *touched* the A!Tol.

The unconscious part of his mind had expected the squid-like alien to be wet, slimy and cold. Instead, her tentacles were warm and leathery as he grabbed hold to support her. She was also *huge* and a lot denser than he'd have guessed.

"Thank you," she told them. This close, it was a lot easier to hear her *actual* speech, a mix of sibilant vowels, harsh consonants and beak-snapping clicks normally blocked by his translator earbuds.

"I've got the outside," Kurzman told them, and James gave his boyfriend a grateful smile. "Get her in."

Slowly and carefully, they eased the big alien through the cruiser to her quarters.

"Are you going to be all right?" James asked, hitting the panel to open the door.

"Yes," Ki!Tana told them. "Today was a bad day and I pushed too hard. I need rest, but I will be fine."

"If this is a recurring condition, I need to know," the Captain told her. "Especially if there's something we can do."

The tiniest flecks of red appeared in the black of her skin for the moment as Ki!Tana turned her gaze on Captain Bond.

"We need to talk on several things, Captain Bond," she finally said. "But not tonight. Soon."

The alien carefully lurched into her quarters and James looked over at the Captain. She met his gaze levelly, then quirked her lips in a half-smile.

"You and Pat didn't need to wait up for me," she told him. "I sent you an update."

"We saw," he acknowledged. "But...I wasn't going to believe it until I saw you with my own eyes. You're all right?"

"I am," she confirmed. "So is Mosi. I checked in on her before we left; she's responding well to their treatments. And while the price was very nearly higher than I'd be prepared to pay, we also have an appointment with the Laian Dockmaster in the morning."

He knew she wasn't talking about money. The appointment with the Laian Dockmaster would cost them money—a lot of it, as he understood it—but the *price* of the appointment had nearly been the lives of their crew.

"So, don't plan on spending any of the ship's money until that deal is closed, huh?" James noted consideringly.

"I'm not even planning on spending *my* money," Bond said dryly. "Why?"

"I want some bloody power armor," the British officer said flatly. "This morning would have been preferable; tomorrow will have to do."

Without power armor, he was forced to resort to massive overkill to stand a chance, a stance that was dangerous aboard a space station and offended his own sense of elegance.

"I can see your point." The Captain sighed. "We should be able to afford it when everything settles, but the ship upgrades have to come first."

"I get that," he admitted. "But we're looking at being at an ugly disadvantage if we ever have to board an A!Tol warship—not to mention landing parties when we return to Earth." He sighed. "I'll pool funds with the Troop Captains; we'll see if we can afford it ourselves."

"If you do, we *will* repay you," Bond assured him. "Either from sales or from our next operations."

"If the Laians charge what I think they will, the next operation is going to need to be impressive," the Major pointed out. "And after the last one, *impressive* may get harder."

"Believe me," his Captain said fervently, "I know."

THEIR REKIKI DID HAVE power armor, which meant that two of Tellaki's troopers were assigned to Annette's escorts the next day. Wellesley didn't, however, remove Sergeant Lin or her human companion from the escort, which left *Tornado*'s Captain feeling like she was leading a small army through Tortuga's corridors.

Ki!Tana's absence helped reduce the impact, as the two Rekiki, while larger than humans, didn't match the A!Tol female's massive bulk. After her poor state last night, Annette hadn't been surprised when the alien didn't respond to being pinged for the meeting, and had coopted Kurzman to act as her "informed backup".

The two humans might not know as much about what counted as top-tier weapons and shields in the galaxy as they'd *like*, but they had a pretty solid idea of the numbers they wanted for *Tornado*. If the Laians could offer improvements from there, great. If not, they were reasonably sure the Crew could still get them what they wanted.

With two crocodile-centaurs in full powered armor, if only armed with battle rifles instead of the standard plasma weapons, their path through the station was unsurprisingly smooth. Crowds parted, the roving parties of ships' crews dodged aside, and Annette was *certain* she saw at least one slaver outright *panic* when the sapient saw humans coming, turning his people and his shackled "cargo" around in the opposite direction as quickly as they could.

No one was trying to sell them anything, either. It was a far quieter trip through Tortuga than she'd had before, and it wasn't just due to the power armor.

"Did I *miss* something?" she muttered into the channel. "Did I accidentally install spikes and skulls on my uniform last night and not notice?"

"Respect on Tortuga only truly comes in one flavor, Captain," one of the Rekiki replied after a moment. "You *destroyed* Captain Ikwal and his crew—by the fire of your soldiers and your own words in the High Captain's court. That you killed him with your own hand only adds to the legend already spreading about the new Terran privateer."

"So, they're afraid," she said grimly. "The slavers seem to think I'm about to go shoot them in the head and steal their slaves."

The soldier paused. "Would you like me to?"

"Like? Yes," she admitted. "But the Crew wants to continue in their apathy and I continue to need the Crew. So, not today."

The armored centaur glanced at where the slaver was chivvying his pathetic victims back out of sight.

"Pity."

WHEN THEY REACHED the connection from the closed-in shipyards that served as Tortuga's public markets to the main hub of the original repair ship, Annette had to leave the bodyguards behind. The only people with power armor and guns allowed in the Crew spaces were the Crew themselves.

She was met, however, by a trio of armed Laians, who escorted her and her executive officer through the confusing, hive-like structure of the hub to the Dockmaster's office on the opposite side of the station. They stopped upon reaching the door, gave her a silent, strange, four-arms-crossed-across-the-carapace salute, then allowed them into the office.

Stepping into the room, Annette stopped in surprise, causing Kurzman to have to dodge briskly sideways to avoid running into her. The Dockmaster's office was a large room with the door in the middle of its inner wall—and the outer wall entirely consumed with a massive window over the three yard slips of the station that the Crew's Dockmaster controlled.

Like the yard slip available to rent to most customers, two of these had been subdivided from yards designed to handle capital ships to yards designed to handle multiple cruiser-sized vessels. Many of those slips were full, though there didn't seem to be any active work going on. There were more of the red-painted cruisers sitting in dock than it had looked like from the outside—another fifteen at least.

Anyone who tangled with Tortuga was going to find *that* fleet an unpleasant surprise—assuming the Crew could man them. She didn't know how many Laians were aboard Tortuga, but forty cruiser-sized vessels would require a *lot* of personnel.

"Welcome to my office, Captain Bond," said a small Laian, the tiniest of their adults she'd seen yet at barely a hundred and sixty centimeters tall, with a carapace that shimmered a pearlescent blue hue she hadn't seen before. The combination suggested to Annette that the Dockmaster was actually the first *female* Laian she'd seen yet —outside of power armor, anyway.

"I am Dockmaster Orentel of the Crew of *Builder of Sorrows*," she greeted Annette. "Please, come in, come in. I have seats for you and Commander Kurzman, but if you wish to enjoy the view, you are welcome to stand by the window. Most of my guests do."

Annette inclined her head to the tiny alien with her glittering carapace, and walked over to the window. The initial shock past, she now looked past the yards, "up" to the massive gas giant Tortuga orbited.

"*Builder of Sorrows*?" she asked.

"Surely you do not think we were always called Tortuga?" Orentel asked. "It is an A!Tol word for 'insect hive.' While we have adopted it as our own, it was hardly complimentary when given."

Of course, the A!Tol word for insect hive was actually the mouthful of beak snaps the humans had decided not to use.

"*Builder of Sorrows* is a nicer name," Annette agreed, "if a sad one."

"We are exiles, Captain Bond, children of a Navy flotilla scattered to the interstellar winds," the Dockmaster said quietly. "We have little to our culture, I fear, but sadness. We know the path you walk, Captain, that of a privateer without a world."

"I intend to retake my world," Annette said fiercely.

"Your intention is not in doubt," the Laian agreed. "You are here because my High Captain sees the mirror of our sorrows in your future, Captain Bond. And because Ki!Tana brought you, and my

High Captain owes her still. And because when the Kanzi attacked your people, they broke a longstanding decree of our High Captains. Showing you favor makes a point."

That brought a wince, for multiple reasons. Annette didn't *want* her people to end up like the Laian Crew, an exiled remnant whose continued survival was utterly reliant on criminal activity. It also wasn't pleasant to be reminded that they were largely helping her to make a point to anyone who would be tempted to follow Ikwal's example in defying their orders.

"Somehow, I imagine none of that means you are doing work for free," Annette replied dryly.

"Of course not," Orentel confirmed. "That would be entirely inappropriate for a marketplace such as that which Tortuga has become." She gestured with a pincer, and Annette saw that the Laian now held four small ivory sticks in her pincers—some form of data-manipulation tool, she guessed.

A hologram appeared in the middle of the large office, showing *Tornado* in more detail than even Annette had seen her since they'd finished recommissioning her into United Earth Space Force service.

"Your ship, Captain Bond," the Laian said as the wands in her pincers flickered. "I ran the data you provided us through our modeling programs and collated our own cruisers' close scans. Compressed-matter armor—built into the hull, not an upgrade. The tubes, oversized, designed for cruder missiles than you're using. The proton beams, stolen. Same with the shield generator. The lasers, surprisingly efficient, though with inherent limits as a weapon system. The defense suite, *extremely* impressive given your apparent tech limits. Intelligent to include; too many lesser powers rely on the shield."

Each section flashed red as Orentel spoke.

"No one in this sector has developed compressed-matter armor," she noted. "The Core Powers regard it as one of their advantages over the outer empires. Your people discovered it?"

"An accident while building exotic-matter emitters for hyper-drive arrays," Annette admitted.

"That is how *everyone* discovers it," the Dockmaster replied. "Your hull is solid. The ship design is useful for the sort of upgrade you want. It appears that we can even physically relocate the crew quarters and command sections if needed?"

"She was built as a test bed for rapid modification and iteration," *Tornado*'s Captain agreed.

"There is much I can do to your ship," Orentel finally noted, walking around the model and studying it. "Inefficient to upgrade the launchers, have to cut new holes in armor, *never* easy with compressed matter. Take hundreds, possibly thousands, of hours."

The wands whirred and huge chunks of the ship lit up.

"Beams. Engines. Shields. All require power," she concluded. "It all depends, Captain Bond, on what you can afford."

Annette had been waiting for that and quickly checked her communicator screen. It had the latest estimate from Ondu of what he'd be able to sell their remaining prizes and cargo for and how much would go to her and the ship's accounts.

"And that, Dockmaster, depends on how good of a price you're going to give us," she said, leaning forward to start the inevitable dickering.

CHAPTER THIRTY-EIGHT

They had been hectic, terrifying, dangerous days, but *Tornado* had been docked at Tortuga for only five days when Annette called all of her senior officers into a meeting on her return from the Crew's portion of Tortuga.

Ki!Tana had apparently only just left her room, but there was more vibrancy to her skin now, a few more spots of color in the hazy gray of her normal calm. The gray-black pained tones of the previous day were muted, only an occasional flicker of darker gray to suggest she wasn't fully back to normal.

Annette studied her officers, concealing a smile at changes in the seating arrangements that no one had discussed and carried notable implications. Captain Elizabeth Sade—a civilian, technically, and also completely out of anyone's chain of command—had shifted to sit next to Commander Rolfson. Lieutenant Commanders Chan and Metharom—communications and engineering respectively, so out of each other's chain of command—had been shifted together by the change and seemed completely unconcerned.

Wellesley and Kurzman had been sitting together before, so no change there. The changes had shifted Amandine and Lougheed together and that pair seemed bemused more than anything else.

As she and Kurzman had discussed, everyone appeared to be pairing off. While none of the relationships violated protocol, several Annette was aware of came close. Were they in Sol and she was seeing this many couples forming up, she'd endeavor to transfer some of them to other ships just to minimize the number of distracted crew.

In their current state, however, anything that tied their crew together more tightly was to her benefit. They would fight harder for each other, and the pressures of their exiled existence would probably prevent too many ugly breakups.

"All right, people," she announced once everyone had settled in. "I have good news and bad news. The good news is that we have a deal with the Crew and will be shifting over to a slip in their yards in" —she checked her watch—"twenty-seven hours.

"They will be installing two brand-new antimatter power cores in our currently empty spaces, upgrading four of our existing fusion cores to approximately five times their original power density, and ripping out the last three cores to free up volume," she noted.

"They're going to use that free volume to enable them to completely rearrange the existing internal crew and power modules to allow for a significant increase in beam-weapon volume. We're losing the last of our lasers in favor of more proton beams, and they'll upgrade our existing two beams to the same standard—again, one superior to that of current generation A!Tol cruisers."

She smiled grimly.

"Lastly, while the Laians are impressed that we *had* a missile defense suite, they think ours is *adorable*. They're going to rip it out completely and replace it with something that translates, roughly, as 'deadly rainshower defenders'. I have no idea what that means, but it's supposed to be more effective."

"They are rapid-fire, close-range plasma cannons," Ki!Tana explained. "If they are providing the full suite, it should come with a number of similarly equipped autonomous drones."

"It's the full suite," Annette confirmed, "though I'm warned replacement drones will cost us an arm and a leg, which brings me to our bad news."

She surveyed her officers, watching them lean forward, wondering what other shoe was going to drop—except for Kurzman, who knew, and Ki!Tana, who clearly guessed.

"We are officially broke," she said flatly. "If Ondu sells significantly below his estimates, we will actually be in *debt* to the Crew when the work is done, which I doubt is a good idea. My own personal accounts are also gone, as are the XO's, and we sold *Faces of God* right back to them without even *looking* at the ship they handed us.

"Sorry, Major," she nodded to Wellesley, "but *Tornado* cannot afford to acquire power armor for your people. Or, well, anything. If anyone of you want to offer the flotilla a loan from your own accounts, it would be very much appreciated," she finished dryly.

"I've already pooled resources with my Troop Captains," the SSS Major replied. "We have an appointment with an armorer tomorrow. I am *not* sending my troops up against power armor without matching gear again."

"I appreciate it, Major," Annette told him honestly. "I wasn't looking forward to asking you to. We *will* repay you—as soon as *Tornado* is upgraded and we can go hunting again."

"How long will that be?" Lougheed asked.

"Thirty days, give or take a few hours," she replied. "The translator turned whatever units they used into seven hundred and twenty-six hours. Another downside of this deal is that we won't have schematics, so there's no point sneaking back into Sol to send the designs to the Weber cells. I asked," she noted dryly.

Of Course We're Coming Back's Captain glanced at Sade, who nodded to him.

"I think Elizabeth and I can fund whatever costs we run until then," he offered. As junior Captains, they'd received significant shares in the prizes taken. More than enough to cover the maintenance costs and food that would arise for all three ships for thirty days.

"Thank you," Annette said softly. "At least, not needing to go home means we can start hunting again as soon as we're good to go. The Network may be able to reverse engineer the Laian work, but they'll need time—time in which we need this ship if we're to make a difference."

She glanced around her officers.

"We're going to have an odd month ahead of us," she told them. "I'm not comfortable sending *Of Course* or *Oaths* out without *Tornado* for backup, so we're all going to be sitting around Tortuga. Let's try to keep our people out of trouble, shall we?"

"If you have more questions or concerns, now is the time."

Thoughtful gazes suggested she'd have more questions later, but for now, everyone was silent.

"All right. Ki!Tana." She glanced at the strange alien who'd attached herself to Annette. "Meet me in my office," she ordered. "Everyone else, dismissed."

BACK IN ANNETTE'S OFFICE, she gestured Ki!Tana to the specially designed couch she now kept there for the big alien. The A!Tol dropped herself over it with a slight flush of pleasure and gestured with a manipulator tentacle for the Captain to speak.

"Are you all right, Ki!Tana?" Annette asked. She looked better than the previous day, but the alien had been pretty far gone by the evening.

"It is...complicated," her companion said slowly. "In a purely medical sense, I am no better off than I was yesterday. Some days are easier than others, but the underlying conditions remain. Were I to be tested by a physician qualified in A!Tol physiology who did not know what I was, they would recommend you say your final goodbyes."

That was not what Annette had expected to hear. So much of what she'd heard of the strange alien companion that she'd acquired suggested that Ki!Tana had been around for a very long time, and she'd subconsciously assumed that the A!Tol would *be* around for a long time.

"Are you dying?" she asked.

"No," Ki!Tana said crisply. "I am Ki!Tol. I have already died and a new soul risen from who I was."

"I am lost," Annette admitted. "Start at the beginning, I guess?"

"The beginning is the physiology of the A!Tol, of which you know almost nothing," the alien told her. "Our males live and die as you would, growing slower with time. They are...not so bright to begin with. But that is an outdated attitude, I suppose," she continued with a flush of yellow in her skin.

"We have...more distinct differences between our two genders than you humans do," she noted, "though our males are more capable than we allowed them to be once. They are still rare among our senior military and top scientists."

"I thought the A!Tol who conquered Earth was male?" Annette asked, curious.

"Tan!Shallegh is, yes," Ki!Tana agreed. "The Tan! marks him as a first-degree relation of the Empress, born from the brood of one of the Empress's brood-sisters. He has advantages to offset our gender prejudice. Were he female, he would be on the list of potential heirs to our current Empress." Her manipulators fluttered in a shrug. "But he is not, and we are not *that* enlightened with our males."

"Your females are bigger on average, as I understand," Annette said slowly. "That can't help."

"It does not. We are larger, stronger, heal *much* faster, and we regard ourselves as smarter," the alien said calmly. "Unlike our males, our females grow until we die. We can even replace lost tentacles, where our males cannot."

Tornado's Captain considered what all of that would have meant for, say, medieval or early gunpowder combat troops, and shivered.

She could see why males had become the sheltered, "gentler" sex for the A!Tol.

"What we *lack*," Ki!Tana continued, "is an internal gestation chamber. We do not have any mechanism in our bodies to feed our young while they grow—and we do not lay eggs."

Annette looked at her alien friend in confusion—then in horror as just what that meant sunk in.

"Our embryos literally consume us from the inside out," the A!Tol said flatly, her skin flushing purple with sadness. "We have, in thousands of years of study and science, never found a way to prevent carrying our young to term internally from being fatal."

"Surely, by now you can get around that?" Annette asked. Even humans had mastered ex-vivo gestation by the end of the twenty-first century—an invention that had dramatically slowed the decrease in births in the world's middle class.

"We had the ability to extract gametes, artificially fertilize them, and bring them to live birth externally before we had *computers*, Captain Bond," Ki!Tana told her. "Which led us to the most horrifying scientific side effect our species has ever encountered."

Annette waited in silence. This was something she probably could have researched, now that they were at Tortuga and had access to galaxy-wide databases. Hearing it from her *friend*, which was what Ki!Tana had somehow become, made it so much more immediate.

"If we remove the ability to conceive by removing the gametes, this does not remove our hormonal *urge* to conceive," Ki!Tana explained. "Our males have no sex drive unless activated by a female's pheromones, but we females enter a phase where our bodies demand that we conceive. And since conception is fatal to us, that phase does not end."

Heat. She was basically talking about a sapient species going into an inescapable, unending heat of the kind that caused dogs to jump walls and cats to squeeze through impossibly small cracks. A heat that could only be stopped by a pregnancy that would be *fatal*.

Annette couldn't help herself. She stared at Ki!Tana in open horror.

"We have found ways," her companion continued, clearly aware of Annette's reaction, "to postpone what we now call 'the birthing madness'. Drugs. Treatments. Removing the gametes early helps. We avoid all A!Tol young until they are mature, leaving their care to immature females and related males. We have managed to push its onset past three hundred long-cycles, aligning our lives with what our doctors can allow our males.

"But the madness takes us all and it does not leave," she said flatly. "Some choose not to have their gametes fertilized until it does, and have them reimplanted, dying as their foremothers did. We have ways to make it less painful, but it remains a minority choice. Most see their broods raised while they live, even if they don't *meet* them until they are adults.

"And then, when the madness begins to take them, they quietly arrange their affairs—and then calmly arrange their deaths."

The office was silent.

"And you are in this 'birthing madness', I take it?" Annette finally asked, once the mind-boggling horror of being an A!Tol female had at least partially processed.

Ki!Tana's skin flashed a wan red, tired pleasure and acceptance.

"A small fraction of us refuse to die," she said simply. "We make arrangements. We lock ourselves away in isolated places of meditation. Only the rich can even try, as the madness grows stronger for many long-cycles. Even among those who try, many choose to die in the end.

"Eventually, and how long varies from person to person, the madness stops getting *worse*. The body can regenerate removed glands, but it will eventually reach the highest production of the hormones it possibly can."

Manipulator tentacles flutter.

"Then you adapt," she said simply. "You rebuild your mind and soul from the fragments left behind. Understand, Captain, that I do not know who I was before I entered that cell on the side of a mountain. Even her name is lost to me; I have only fragments of her memories.

"Eventually, you walk free," Ki!Tana concluded. "I suffer from the birthing madness every day, Captain. I am Ki!Tol: Elder. I can only barely deal with my own people, but aliens do not trigger the same issues. Most Ki!Tol eventually give in. We choose to die."

"Ridotak called you a trickster demon," Annette noted.

"Ki!Tol have a reputation as wise beings," her friend concluded with a flutter of tentacles. "I give advice, guidance. It has led some I have worked with to great things. Others I have made mistakes, and they have listened with insufficient question.

"I am very old, Captain, but I am not infallible. I have placed my knowledge at your service, but do not forget that I am merely...experienced, not always wise."

"And what is your agenda here, Ki!Tana?" Annette asked softly.

"I have walked this galaxy for multiple times what my kin would call my allotted cycle, Captain Bond. Ridotak calls me a demon advisedly: my main agenda is to not be bored."

CHAPTER THIRTY-NINE

THE LIFE OF A RETIRED COLLABORATOR WAS A QUIET ONE, JEAN Villeneuve reflected. No one expected him to do anything anymore. He knew nothing about the Weber Protocols, and the Resistance they were supposed to assemble had done very little in the months of occupation so far.

His neighbors in the villa on the beach knew who he was. They probably understood—the community along the southern French coast he lived in was a place for the wealthy, not the young or the non-pragmatic—but they avoided him regardless. The wealth he'd inherited from his wife's long-dead family and the generous pension the A!Tol paid him—in Imperial marks, even!—left him with few worries.

That meant he got to sit on the top of the cliffs a few hundred meters from his house and watch the waves crash on the beach in silence. That his life contained no worries did not mean the man once charged with the defense of Earth had no worries.

The first industrial plants in Cherbourg, a hundred kilometers up the coast, had come online. A!Tol technology was starting to become available on Earth—and it was most easily purchased with Imperial marks. The aliens had set what seemed like fair exchange rates to Earth's currencies...but the direction was clear.

If you work with us, your life will be better.

That's what those luxuries told Earth's people. The many millions of soldiers the A!Tol had decommissioned received pensions in marks. If those soldiers stayed decommissioned, they lived well and had access to the alien tech making life simpler.

If they didn't...well, the A!Tol didn't seem to go in for reprisals, but resistance was not tolerated. The Weber Network attacks so far had been met with targeted responses. UESF personnel Jean had known his entire life had died, but they'd died facing their enemies with guns in their hands. He couldn't blame his friends, but to his surprise, he couldn't blame the A!Tol, either. He had no illusions about Earth's new overlords: they were here for their own reasons and their own benefit. But he'd give them the credit for their follow-up: no one was dying who hadn't raised arms against them. Their counterinsurgency forces' hands were pretty clean.

So far.

He sighed and shook his head, spotting an old car rolling up to the villa's front door. That was...odd. A few of his old friends, mostly UESF officers retired before the invasion, still visited him, but they had nice cars. The A!Tol Imperial Governor had made a courtesy visit shortly after Tan!Shallegh had left Earth, but she'd come in an air-car.

The car was really old. Not much more than a beater—a cheap rental? Strange. A young woman, dark-haired and wearing a shawl and sunglasses, got out and knocked on his door. She waited a moment, then knocked again. Stubborn. Or desperate?

Jean Villeneuve's bones weren't as old as he sometimes pretended. He rose with ease and started swiftly striding toward the house. Whatever was going on, it was going to be more interesting than staring at the ocean, getting depressed.

BY THE TIME he reached the house, the young woman had knocked repeatedly, hit the announcer plate, pounded on the door, tried the handle, and settled herself relatively calmly on the steps, looking as if none of the previous activities had happened.

She managed all of this in a little under five minutes. Jean hadn't been *that* far away. When he stepped around the corner of the house, however, she scrambled back to her feet and faced him, her body language twitchy, nervous.

"I am guessing, mademoiselle, you did not end up at my door by accident," he greeted her. "So, I presume you are looking for me. I warn you," he continued, "that you have probably caused the security bot to upgrade your threat level. If you were to, say, draw a weapon on me, it would disable you."

"I'm not here to hurt anyone," she told him in a soft southern American drawl—Louisiana, unless he missed his guess, "I just... didn't know where else to turn. They say the aliens still talk to you. I need someone who can get them to listen."

"Mademoiselle," Jean said quietly, "I am the man who surrendered Earth to the A!Tol. *Nobody* talks to me anymore unless we have been friends for a long time. I don't know why you would come to me."

"Because nobody listens!" she snapped. "My brother, my husband—they're both gone, but *no one* believes me. If anyone does..." She shivered. "I think they think the A-tuck-Tol did it and don't want to cause trouble. Please, Admiral, I'm...desperate."

Jean Villeneuve was prepared to give the A!Tol *some* credit—enough to think they weren't kidnapping or disappearing people at random, at least.

"Why me?" he finally asked.

The woman swallowed hard. "My name is Amy McQueen," she told him firmly. "My father served with you aboard *Endeavor*. He said you were trustworthy, the best. And the aliens *talk* to you. It seemed...it seemed...I didn't know what else to try."

Jean sighed. There had been eleven hundred men and women

aboard *Endeavor*, the first battleship the UESF had even built, and he *still* remembered Steve McQueen. He'd been an enlisted spacer, a career *maladroit* determined to do his job and unable to do it *right*.

"Come in, Mademoiselle McQueen," he said quietly, opening the door.

"How is your father?" he asked a moment later, as he deftly guided her past the doglike security robot to the front sitting area.

"No longer with us," she admitted. "Work accident about five years back."

Jean nodded sadly. That did not surprise him. That McQueen had managed to live long enough to have two children almost did.

"All right," he said to the young woman as he passed her a glass of wine—this was France, after all, and she'd come a long way for him to be inhospitable. "You said your brother and husband were missing? What do you mean?"

"They're both soldiers, US Army, in the same company," she told him. "They were in the bayou for exercises when the aliens arrived. They were out of touch with the outside world until they got back to base to find out that world had changed around them.

"I got notes from both of them the day they got back to base," McQueen continued. "Then...nothing. They should have been mustered out with everyone else and sent home. I took a week off of work to build a small extension to our house for Dave; without knowing what the pension would be, I figured he'd need a place to live.

"Then I realized I hadn't heard from either of them and they should have been home," she said in a rush.

Jean eyed the young woman sitting in his living room carefully. With long, well-taken-care-of black hair and clad in a demure suit, she didn't look like the type to engage in carpentry, but apparently, looks were deceiving.

She was right in her timeline. The A!Tol had been *very* careful to make sure all of the soldiers they decommissioned made it home within a week, in some cases deploying their own military shuttles to provide transport.

"What did you do?" he asked.

"I told my firm I was going to need more time off," she replied. "I'm the most junior lawyer there, and with no one quite sure how the legal system is going to shake out under A-tuck-Tol rule, they could spare me. At a reduced sabbatical rate," she noted, somewhat bitterly.

"I drove down to their base," she continued after a moment. "It was empty. Everyone was gone—most of the brigade had been sent home before they got out of the bayou. Dave had told me the place was just them and a few administrators turning off lights."

She shook her head.

"I ran into another woman there," she said softly. "A lady I knew a little: Harry's platoon lieutenant's wife." McQueen swallowed. "She was there for the same reason I was, Admiral. Her husband never came home."

The dark-haired young woman looked down at her hands, focusing on them as they clenched around her still-full wine glass.

"Bank says Harry's pension from the aliens is coming in," she said. "They don't seem to know he's gone. Nobody seems to know where he went.

"Started poking. I'm a *lawyer*, Admiral. I know how to research. No one's admitting anything, but the stories are out there if you look. A company of US soldiers from the bayou here. A ballerina troupe in a plane flying home to Australia there. Hundreds of people, Admiral. Missing."

She produced a datachip, holding it out to him.

"Everything I found is on here," she said. "I tried to take it to the police, but they're all scared. I think they're afraid it's the A!Tol, and all the high-level police systems are through them now. If the aliens are stealing people, how can we stop them?"

"That was my job, Amy," Jean said quietly. "And I failed."

"No!" she snapped, her voice suddenly hoarse. "You did what

you had to do. This...this doesn't make *sense* to be the aliens. Too few, too scattered. If they'd wanted ten thousand people, they'd have just loaded them up out of the Army divisions they knocked out.

"I..." She paused, swallowing and lifting her head to meet Jean's gaze. "I want you to take this *to* them," she admitted. "If it *is* them, we can't stop it. But if it isn't, our fear might be holding us back from the only people who can *help* us."

Jean sighed, eyeing the small chip in the woman's hand for a long moment. Then he took it.

"I have a contact number," he admitted. "I don't know if..."

The rumble of aircraft cut off the rest of his self-effacing statement, and shadows crossed over the windows. Out of the nearest window, he could see an orbital shuttle—an Imperial design, he thought, but the interface drive UESF ships hadn't looked that different—settling onto his landscaping, crushing an expensive hedge.

"Mademoiselle McQueen," he said softly, "I hope you do not take this the wrong way, but I think you should go into the bedroom."

With a practiced hand, he flipped open his coffee table to reveal the ugly shape of a UESF twelve-millimeter submachine-gun.

"Go!" he snapped, and with a surprised look at the gun, the young lawyer went.

BY THE TIME McQueen had completely disappeared and Jean had fully checked over the SMG, the sound of landing aircraft had passed. A quick glance out the window showed that the shuttles had disgorged power-armored troops, bipedal, roughly human-sized soldiers.

From what he'd seen on the news, a significant portion of the A!Tol soldiers were bipeds of some kind, some of them human-sized, some smaller or larger. He was *probably* looking at Earth's conquerors, if only because the Resistance was unlikely to have access to powered battle armor.

The soldiers were spreading out, forming a perimeter—an outward-facing one, which was probably a good sign—and then his thoughts were interrupted by a calm rap on the door.

Slowly, concealing the gun with his body, he approached the door.

"Yes?" he called out as whoever was outside knocked on the door.

"Admiral Villeneuve, this is Company Commander Kital," a translated voice said through the door. "I apologize for interrupting you with your guest, but I have orders to evacuate you into orbit. We believe your life may be in danger."

Sighing, he threw the door open, looking out at the massive, four-legged, centaur-like suit of armor standing on his doorstep. Kital had removed his helmet, presumably out of some false attempt to appear less threatening. Since the alien's head looked like a snub-nosed but *very* toothy crocodile's, it wasn't really an improvement.

"The young lady is no threat," Jean said quietly. "In fact, *she* needs to talk to the Governor."

If they were going to drop interface drive shuttles over his property, they could look into why people were going missing.

Kital cocked his head, a gesture that looked more like it belonged on an inquisitive puppy than a two-hundred-kilo sapient carnivore.

"We can arrange that, Admiral, but you need to come with us *right now*," he insisted.

"Why?" Jean demanded. "What happened?"

"The Cherbourg complex has been destroyed," the alien said flatly. "A wave of other terrorist attacks is triggering worldwide. The Governor believes that, as the being who surrendered to us, you are in danger."

Jean swallowed, then sighed.

The Weber Network appeared to have finally begun its full-scale movements. He knew very little about what the Protocols called for the Resistance to do, but he was quite certain assassinating him *wasn't* on the agenda.

Telling the company of armed aliens that had just crushed his roses that wouldn't help though.

"Let me fetch McQueen," he said finally. "And then I want to be taken to the Governor as soon as she is available. I understand," he noted, raising a hand to forestall any comment by Kital, "that won't be immediately, but I think what this young lady has found may be hugely important to the relations between humans and the Imperium."

FROM AMY MCQUEEN'S wide eyes as they were loaded on to the shuttle, she'd never ridden in a spacecraft before, let alone an alien one. Even now, most people on Earth had never truly left the surface of their planet, though one of the things the Cherbourg industrial plant had been supposed to manufacture was small-scale interface drive units to help change that.

And now it was gone. Jean still had his UESF communicator, though it was in many ways worse than a civilian handset now that it had to run on the same networks. Its unrolled screen, though, showed him all he needed to know.

Cherbourg was the worst, fires still raging through the industrial site. Reporters were desperately trying to assess casualties even as mixed Imperial and human teams worked to contain and suppress the fires. The only difference from before the invasion was the lack of ambulances with brightly flashing lights—night-black military shuttles waited to whisk the injured away to A!Tol ship hospitals as soon as they were rescued from the rubble.

The shuttles were designed to be intimidating, but today, their speed would save lives.

Across the Channel, in London, fires were rising from City Hall. None of the reporters were sure if the London Assembly had been meeting when the bombs had gone off, but they were reporting on rumors saying an A!Tol had been meeting with the Mayor at the time.

North America. South America. Africa. Asia. Every continent had seen at least one attack, most of them two, in the two hours since Cherbourg had been blown to hell. The Weber Protocol–spawned Resistance Network had turned to their job with a vengeance—and a level of violence that sickened Jean.

"The Governor is going to speak," Kital told Jean moments before the news feeds he was watching lit up with the same announcement. A few seconds later, the cameras cut to the many-tentacled alien, standing behind a podium with no labels or symbols.

Medit! was larger than many A!Tol Jean had met, though most of Earth didn't have the experience to judge. When he'd met her, her skin had been a neutral gray through their entire conversation, but that self-control had apparently fled her tonight. While her tentacles remained neutral gray, the bullet shape of her torso glittered in orange, purple, and black.

It wasn't a pleasant set of colors to human eyes, and he doubted the emotions it represented were any better.

"People of Terra," she began, her words being replaced by the translator box she wore on her chest. "Today, we have seen a grievous assault on A!Tol personnel across your planet and the destruction of several facilities meant to bring your medicine and industry closer to Imperial standards.

"I must note that in many cases, warnings were delivered to the targets sufficiently in advance to prevent massive collateral damage. Many people are alive who would not be if these attackers had not taken these steps.

"We are uncertain of the total death toll. More information will be provided to the local media as we learn it.

"Given the scale of these attacks, I must assure you that all of our resources will be dedicated to bringing the perpetrators to justice," Medit! told the cameras. "We will find the guilty and punish them. We can do no less. We will do no more.

"The innocent have nothing to fear. The guilty should start watching the shadows."

The video feed cut off, Jean's news feed disintegrating into rapidly assembling articles and live analyst feeds.

"You may want to close that and look out the window," Kital told him. "I know you fought them, but I don't think you've seen one of our battleships up close."

The news media remained surprisingly open and free under Earth's new management, and had happily informed everyone that two A!Tol battleships remained in orbit. It appeared that the Governor had retreated aboard one at the beginning of the attacks, and that was where Jean and McQueen were being taken.

He heard McQueen inhale sharply next to him. Her father had served on Earth's first battleship, but that would have been smaller than an A!Tol *cruiser*, let alone this leviathan of the stars. The ship was two kilometers long, a multi-megaton monster with an odd organic feel to it. In many ways, it almost resembled an A!Tol, with a central hull and a number of nacelles reaching forward with her energy weapons.

It was painted bright white, glittering in the Sun as the shuttle whipped around it at a mind-boggling speed now they were clear of atmosphere.

"*Shield of Innocents*," Kital said quietly. "She is an older ship, but her crew will die before she leaves this system to the Kanzi. Someday, you may give us credit for that, Admiral Villeneuve."

JEAN AND MCQUEEN were hustled off the shuttle by their escorts, the power-armored soldiers all unhelmeted now. Without the helmets, the distinctions between the various bipeds became a lot clearer. Height was one divider, but the category of "bipedal soldier" that made up a surprisingly large chunk of the alien ground troops on Earth appeared to include everything from aliens with three eyes, no visible ears, and skin that looked like soft metal, to squat creatures with red fur and wide, toad-like faces.

The rest of the company were saurian centaurs like Kital, all members of the same species with different colors and complexions of scales.

The escort dissipated quickly as they moved into the ship, most of the troops heading in different directions while Kital and a single other saurian trooper led the two humans deeper into the ship.

The interior of the vessel was much smoother than an equivalent UESF ship would have been. Jean's practiced eye easily picked out where access panels had been tucked away in the smooth lines, but the calm white walls and concealed panels were a far cry from the plain steel and open hatches of Earth's crude ships.

Shield of Innocents' shuttle bay was a busy swarm of small space-craft arriving and leaving, many of the arrivals disgorging injured human civilians into the hands, tentacles, claws, and other manipulators of the waiting medical teams.

"Each of the battleships can handle three thousand wounded," Jean's escort told them quietly. "The cruisers another three thousand between them. The less critically injured will probably get shifted to planetside facilities relatively quickly, but since the worst cases will need to be treated up here, we're planning to bring all of the wounded up for triage."

The Governor may have given the Resistance credit for trying to minimize collateral damage, but that likely meant there were only thousands of injured instead of thousands of dead. The Imperial troops and government appeared to be pulling out all of the stops in disaster relief in response.

Jean sighed as they left the shuttle bay, shaking his head. Every target he'd seen made sense, and this was exactly the kind of operation the Resistance had been created for, but instead of making the A!Tol look *bad*, they appeared to have handed them the propaganda coup of the century.

The worst part was that he wasn't even entirely sure the A!Tol were helping people for any kind of ulterior motive. They really did seem to be just...trying to help.

"The Governor is waiting," Kital told him, bringing them to a door even Jean had almost missed. "Should your companion wait with me?"

"No," Jean said shortly. "The Governor needs to see Miss McQueen's data. I'm just the door opener."

With a firm nod to the panicked-looking young woman he'd dragged this far, Jean Villeneuve stepped through the door into the office of the A!Tol Governor of Earth.

THE OFFICE DIDN'T LOOK like a permanent fixture for Medit!. There were no decorations. A utilitarian desk and couch had been added for the Governor to work from, and someone had recently provided two human chairs for her guests. A massive screen was set up next to the desk and couch, and the Governor was scrolling through dozens of images at a time, a haptic field over the screen responding to commands from her fluttering manipulator tentacles.

"Ah, Admiral Villeneuve," she greeted him. "And Miss Amy McQueen."

"Not an Admiral anymore," Jean reminded the Governor. "Not an officer of any kind."

"We could fix that," Medit! pointed out. "My staff could have an appropriate uniform and insignia done up by the end of the day. Lesser Fleet Lord would be a small demotion for you, equivalent to your Vice Admiral, I think, but give some time for retraining and we could have you in command of your own cruiser squadron inside a Terran year."

He shook his head.

"No offense, Governor, but I have no intention of serving the people who conquered my world," he said dryly. "I have to decline your generous offer."

Her skin was still torn up in colors of orange, purple, and black—but streaks of blue and red appeared as she offered and he responded. Jean wondered if the Imperial databases that had been made publically available on Earth included a translation guide for their conquerors' skin tones. He would have looked it up if he hadn't expected to remain retired.

"Shame," she told him.

"Every time I talk to one of you tentacled *bouffon*, I feel like I'm being tested," Jean pointed out grumpily. "I'm just here to deliver Miss McQueen—something is going on on Earth that either says you're *lying* to us or you have a problem."

Medit!'s skin flashed bright orange before quickly returning to its mottled tones.

"The Imperium does not, as a rule, lie," she said, her translator picking up a level of flatness that Jean suspected was not due to a software failure.

"We *are* testing you, Jean Villeneuve," she continued after a long moment of silence. "In time, we may even tell you why. What did Miss McQueen find that was so important?"

At least they weren't going to *lie* to him, he guessed. He gestured the young woman forward.

"Tell her what you told me," he instructed.

Haltingly, McQueen started. Medit! waited calmly for her to finish, and the young lawyer rapidly regained her confidence, likely mentally classifying the Governor in the same category as a human judge.

When she finished the recitation she'd given Jean, the A!Tol gestured with a manipulator tentacle.

"May I see this data?"

McQueen glanced at Jean, who still had the original chip she'd given him, then produced another copy of the chip from her suit jacket. *Smart* girl.

Medit! took the chip and dropped it onto a small plate next to the big screen that Jean had completely missed. The plate lit up in colors beneath the chip, flickering for a couple of moments. The datachip was designed to be accessed by slotting it into a reader, but it appeared that the A!Tol tech it was sitting on could read it regardless as a directory appeared on the big screen.

All of the labels were in English, but the Governor flipped an icon from the screen onto the directory and everything changed over into a completely different iconography and language—the computer was translating the Terran files, file structure and even language in real time.

Jean was impressed. The top-line computer hardware Nova Industries had acquired for the XC units like *Tornado* probably had the processing power to do that, but nobody on Earth had written *software* capable of that. And this was just a secondary demand on the battleship's computers.

As video streams and text started to flash onto the screen, it rapidly began collating past what Jean could follow. He suspected there had to some kind of AI routine that was organizing the data in a manner Medit! was used to working with, but it was still impressive how quickly the A!Tol cut through all of the data, her skin shifting to darker and darker orange as she worked.

"Miss McQueen," the Governor said, the translator applying an impressive amount of graveness to her voice. "May I keep this chip?"

"I have copies," McQueen said calmly.

"I would hope so," Medit! agreed, a momentary flash of blue cutting through her current burnt umber tone. "This should *not* be happening," she noted. "We do *not* engage in kidnapping or murders. It undermines the entire uplift effort."

Uplift. Jean didn't think the translator had chosen that word at random. Uplift was...very different than conquest, if they meant it the way he suspected they did. Of course, what the *colonizer* thought was 'uplifting' could be very different than what the *colonized* would think.

Medit! stepped away from the haptic interface, her black eyes turning back to the two humans.

"You were correct to bring this to me, Jean Villeneuve," she told him. "This is a greater threat to the integration of Earth than the Weber Network attacks."

Jean tried not to wince at her revelation that she knew about the Weber Protocols. He probably failed. *That* was unexpected—all of the records he'd been aware of were destroyed.

"How?" he asked, not bothering to pretend he didn't know what she meant.

"There is always a Resistance," Medit! told him. "We have swum these currents before; we know their rocks and reefs. All sapients are different, and yet so often very similar. We know how to handle armed rebellion.

"But this represents corruption within our own ranks," she admitted. "These people could only have been kidnapped by the officers and soldiers of our invasion force. Sadly, they have almost certainly been removed from Earth and funneled into the supply chain already."

"The supply chain?" McQueen demanded. "What has happened to my brother? My husband?!"

"Kanzi slavers operate in our space despite our best efforts," Medit! said quietly. "They believe that other bipeds were put in this universe to serve them, and would likely happily purchase your people as 'exotics'.

"I cannot guarantee that we will find your family," the Governor told McQueen. "I *will* swear to you, upon the honor of my Empress, that we will find those who stole them. We will move the stars and seas to try to find your family and the other victims.

"We swore protection for Terra when we came here," Medit! reminded them. "If that oath has been forsworn by our own soldiers, I will hunt them. I will break them. If any power in this universe can return your family to you, we will.

"And if we cannot, I swear to you we will avenge them."

CHAPTER FORTY

FOUR WEEKS WAS A *LONG* TIME TO SIT STILL, EVEN ON A STATION with as many and varied entertainments as Tortuga. Those entertainments seemed to be keeping Annette's crew busy, though her own complete lack of funds had dramatically limited her own ability to enjoy herself.

Despite all of the work, *Tornado*'s crew compartments had been shifted around in one single piece, and her artificial gravity was efficient enough that there hadn't even been a spilled drink during the process. Annette had remained aboard through almost the entire work, quietly watching video feeds from her office.

Part of her felt guilty. Every day she spent sitting in dry dock, doing nothing, was a day Earth remained under the heel of an alien overlord. Every day she was here was a day she was asking her crew to spend away from their families and their homes for no certain goal.

But they needed the upgrades, and every day they were away from Earth *at all* was the same. In quiet moments like this, as she sat alone in her office, it was easy to admit that she didn't *have* a plan. Not one she believed in.

The only plan she had was to steal technology and plans for technology from the A!Tol and funnel it back to Earth, where hopefully the Weber Network could do something with it. She didn't have schematics for the Laian tech, so that didn't work, but *Tornado's* upgrades would finally put her in the same weight class as the A!Tol Navy.

Capturing military logistics vessels and civilian ships wouldn't get her what she needed. She could buy some of the schematics here on Tortuga, but anything she bought would be inferior to the aliens' top-line military gear—even more so once the Network managed to somehow assemble a hidden yard to *build* anything and finished building ships in secret.

Plus, the more she learned of the Kanzi—and of Tortuga itself, for that matter!—the more she realized driving the A!Tol out would only be the beginning. If they drove the Imperium out, the Kanzi would try and move in. If the Kanzi didn't...the pirates and raiders who operated through Tortuga would be perfectly willing to raid a weak independent world for slaves and resources.

Even if she somehow managed to free Earth, they wouldn't magically be stronger than they had been before. And freeing Earth wouldn't be without a cost. Whatever fleet they built would take losses, have damaged ships.

She could free her world from one conqueror only to make them vulnerable to another.

A pile of money so large she could barely comprehend it had allowed her to upgrade her ship to be able to take on any A!Tol ship in her own weight range and win, but she only had one ship. The Imperium and their enemies had hundreds.

The screen in front of her showed Crew workers and drones closing up the gaps around the last of *Tornado's* new proton beams. They were slightly ahead of schedule and would finish everything up in the next day or so.

But Captain Annette Bond had to admit, to herself if no one else, that she wasn't quite sure what to *do* once her ship was ready for war again.

ANNETTE'S BRAINSTORMING SESSION, an attempt to find a solution to her problems that had once again devolved into brooding, was interrupted by a chime on her communicator.

"Captain, this is Chan," her communication officer told her brightly. The woman had been *far* more cheerful since she and the chief engineer had settled into a quietly solid relationship. Annette, with her lack of available options, was quietly envious of the two women's obvious luck and contentment.

And surprised, since she doubted they would even have looked at each other without being stranded light-years and light-years from Sol.

"What is it, Yahui?" she asked.

"We have a caller for you," Chan reported. "Video link, from the Captain of the new ship that just arrived last night: an Indiri named Karaz Forel."

Annette sat up straighter. *That* was the man the first yardmaster she'd spoken to had said could get her recent A!Tol military schematics—those and exotic slaves, which weren't much use to her.

"What was his ship?" she asked. "I didn't pay that much attention, to be honest."

"I'll forward you Rolfson's assessment," Chan promised. "She's a heavy, though: even bigger than *Tornado* and a nasty pile of scrap."

"I'll take a look," Annette said. "You may as well put Captain Forel through. Visual to the wallscreen in my office, please."

She'd been using the screen as a pseudo-window, looking through the video feeds at the work being done on her ship. Now she quickly made sure her uniform and braided blond hair were straight, and faced the screen as it flickered and then formed into the image of the first Indiri she'd ever taken a solid look at.

The translators the humans used had originally been built for Indiri, and so her eyes were drawn first to Karaz Forel's ears. They looked surprisingly humanlike, despite having black skin and emerging from a broad, wide-mouthed face covered in slickly moist short red fur.

Despite the fur, the Indiri reminded her of nothing so much as a frog. Big bulging eyes protruded from the wide triangular head, and a long tongue flickered around the alien's disturbingly open, dark-interiored, mouth.

"Captain Karaz Forel," she greeted him. By now she had a *lot* of practice at not letting her initial reaction to strange aliens show. "To what do I owe the pleasure?"

"Captain Bond of *Tornado*," he returned the greeting. "You have made quite an impression on Tortuga. I always fear when I return that I will find the entire star system gone, but the havoc this time is almost as impressive! I wanted to meet the spawn-source of such chaos."

"I'm certainly not able to destroy stars, Captain Forel," Annette told the pirate captain. "Otherwise, I am as you see: a privateer in command of a handful of ships. Beyond that"—she smiled—"my secrets are my own."

Forel's long tongue flickered in a twisting spiral accompanied by a sharp barking noise. She *thought* he was laughing. It was always hard to tell, and the translator didn't tend to concern itself with anything but words.

"It is the A!Tol I fear would destroy this star," he warned her. "It is within their power and they wisely fear the Laian exiles of the Crew. I do not mean to swim into your secrets, Captain Bond. Your ship and her exploits are impressive."

"We have worked hard and achieved much," Annette said carefully. The A!Tol could destroy star systems? She was going to have to find out if the alien was being metaphorical. If not...that was something *else* to consider in her strategies.

"Indeed. Wisdom and firepower create many opportunities, do they not?" Forel asked. "My...wise friends in the A!Tol Navy have delivered such an opportunity to me, Captain Bond, but I fear I lack the firepower to fully swim the currents."

"There are many ships here open for hire, I presume," she pointed out. "*Tornado* is but one ship. My scout ships aren't worth much in a fight."

"And most of the pirates here are not worth much more," the Indiri agreed. "With *Tornado* matched to my *Subjugator,* they will be *useful,* but without *Tornado,* every ship in Tortuga would not be enough."

"Unless you could recruit the Crew."

"Unless I could recruit the Crew," he allowed. "Which we both know will not happen. Tradition says the heavies split half the spoils, Captain," he told her. "The other pirates share the rest amidst them, but you and I would walk away with a quarter of the prize each. Hear me out, Captain Bond."

She wanted to shut the disturbingly moist alien down and send him on his way. Forel was a slaver, the type of sapient who would capture others and force them into servitude for his own profit—the *name of his ship* said as much.

But.

The sales of their cargo and prizes had ended lower than she'd hoped or Ondu had predicted. They'd covered the payments to the Crew, but only because Annette's senior officers didn't have much more use for the money than she did. They'd pooled their funds, made the last payment on the upgrades, and covered the maintenance fees, docking fees, and food resupply.

But now not only was Annette broke and the flotilla account empty, she owed her senior officers over a million marks. She wasn't, quite, desperate—but a score large enough that Forel would accept a quarter would rebuild their accounts, enable them to buy the tech to deliver to Earth so that *Tornado* wouldn't stand alone against the A!Tol.

"All right," she said finally. "You have my attention, Captain Forel."

The wide mouth opened even farther, thick lips pulling back disgustingly to reveal rows of deadly sharp teeth in a disturbing attempt at a smile—and how did Forel know humans well enough to make even that pathetic attempt at the gesture?

With a gesture of a hand she half-expected to be webbed, Forel brought up a star chart of the region.

"The A!Tol maintain a series of logistics bases along the border with the Kanzi," he explained swiftly, highlighting a number of stars in green. "This one is their newest in this sector, positioned to support their operation against your system." The farthest green star along the spiral arm flashed.

"They have completed the full supply loadout for the facility," he noted. "Food, missiles, repair parts, molecular circuitry cores—everything you captured on your way to Tortuga, in even vaster quantities. Because piracy in this sector has grown worse lately, with some high-profile captures, they have pulled a lot of ships back to the main Navy base in the region, here at Kimar."

A star flashed red. It was the same one their intel said was the Navy base where Earth's conqueror, Fleet Lord Tan!Shallegh, was based.

"The logistics base has significant *fixed* defenses, but I have acquired the codes for the orbital constellation," Forel noted. "There are also a cruiser and several destroyers. Even with the control codes, I cannot take even the cruiser on my own.

"But with *two* heavies," he gestured to Annette, "we can blow the constellation, trap the defending ships, and take control of the system. The loot from a Navy logistics depot will set up every being involved as a king, swimming in females or jewels or whatever they choose!"

He was practically...no, he *was* salivating at the thought. She wasn't sure if it was Indiri in general or just Forel who was this disgusting. She had her suspicions, though, and they were relatively complimentary to the species.

"That's a lot of cargo," she pointed out carefully. "That won't fit on the pirate ships."

"The choicest loot will," Forel replied. "For the rest, the base is supplied with a small fleet of automated ships, designed to deliver cargo to formations in need as quickly as possible. We will load the rest onto those and send them to Tortuga to be sold and divided.

"Even a quarter of this will make you and me rich beyond dreams, Captain Bond," he told her. "But if you need more incentive..."

She waited in silence. It was a lucrative operation, one that could set her up to pull a lot of resources Earth's way, but she wasn't sure that she wanted to work with Karaz Forel.

She wasn't sure she *could* work with Karaz Forel.

"I'm listening," she said shortly.

"I know from Yardmaster Folphe that you are looking for schematics of military hardware," he noted. "Shields, missiles, proton beams—I'm guessing you humans have a hidden shipyard somewhere."

Annette said nothing. He was far closer to the truth than she liked, though she *did* like where his hint was going.

"I have the latest schematics of A!Tol military hardware, acquired from my...wise friends in the Navy," Forel told her. "While those schematics are *worth* much, let's be honest, *copying* them doesn't *cost* much. If you sign on to this operation, I will back your twenty-five percent share, I will bring the codes for the defense constellation, *and* I will give you the full schematics for the latest generation of A!Tol weapons, engines, power generators...and the cruisers and super-battleships they mount them on."

His horrible fake smile appeared again as she blinked at that.

"You have not even *met* their super-battleships yet," he pointed out. "Just their battleships. Just *one* super-battleship would make *everyone* hesitate to tangle with Earth. I do not know if whatever yard you have hidden in murky waters could build it, but the designs may have value regardless."

She sighed.

"You make an offer I would be a fool to refuse, Captain Forel," she admitted. "Very well. *Tornado* will need another day to finish her yard work, but we're in."

"Warm waters!" he exclaimed. "I will reach out to the other Captains. This will be a pirate armada such as this corner of the galaxy has *never* seen!"

***

JAMES WELLESLEY HAD no idea what kind of creature the egg was from. Even cooked, his little portable scanner told him the things would easily kill him. It was a pretty thing in speckled blue, a little under five centimeters long, and it shivered slightly in the fingers of his power armor gauntlet.

"Good job, Major," Ral told him. The Yin who'd attached himself to the Special Space Service Fifty-Second Company's headquarters section was something of a lucky find. While he hadn't been formally trained as an armorer, he'd apparently done enough of the tuning of previous sets that he was able to handle the final calibrations for *Tornado*'s troopers new power armor.

"Now," the sharp-beaked blue biped continued, "rotate, walk over to the bench and put the egg down."

James grimaced. The floor of the room was covered in little blue eggshells where troopers had lost control of the gauntlets, or dropped the egg while turning, or failed to hold tightly enough while walking, or... There was a cleaning bot in the closet of *Tornado*'s armory. Ral was leaving the mess on the floor intentionally, to make the apparently simple challenge even harder.

Carefully, ever so carefully, he turned. He *felt* the servos and powered musculature shift with him, moving the hundred-and-fifty-kilogram mass of the suit of armor while putting only the slightest of strain on his own muscle.

He crossed the room, put the egg down amidst the others there—and then twitched, crushing the egg into a thousand pieces as the communicator in the armor helmet buzzed. He sighed.

"I should have left the communicator turned off," he complained to Yin, then glanced at the icon on his heads-up display. The suit read his eye motion, confirmed his hold to make it an order, and then opened the channel.

"Wellesley," he said snappily. "What is it?"

"Major," Captain Bond's cool tones responded, and James swallowed the rest of his tirade. Things were getting flexible aboard *Tornado*, but not *that* flexible.

"I need to know if your troopers are ready to deploy," she asked calmly.

James surveyed the room covered in eggshells. They'd expanded the armory by the simple expedient of cutting out the walls for several other surrounding rooms and welding their doors shut. This section, with the power armor, had been nicknamed the morgue—and next to it, just clear of the egg debris, were the racked plasma cannons, automatic grenade launchers, and multi-drum shotguns that were designed to link to the suits.

They were still fine-tuning the suits, but *every* member of his company was now rated on one of those weapons.

"We're at seventy-five percent on the suits," he admitted. "Some fine-tuning work to do, but my company can drop and my company can fight. What do you need, Captain?"

"We appear to have signed on for the biggest pirate raid in recent history, Major," Bond told him. "We're getting a quarter of the loot and all of the schematics we need for Earth out of it," she continued, "but I don't trust our partners.

"I want your company ready to make ground landings and make sure we get our share of the goods," she continued. "I *also* want you to have at least a troop prepped for a boarding action, just in case we need to make sure our *friends* keep their promises.

"Can you do it?"

Inside the helmet, James grinned as he continued to look at the weapons, each of them flickering up ghostly overlay data in his screens as their encrypted chips responded to his suit.

"We can do that," he confirmed. "Not a problem."

"Good. I'll have more data soon. We'll be on our way within seventy-two hours."

"We'll be ready," James promised. Letting the channel close, he removed the helmet and met Ral's gaze.

"What do you need?" the Yin asked.

"Everyone in the company to the highest calibration you can get as quickly as possible," James ordered. "Speed prioritized over hundred percent, understood?

"*Tornado* is going back to war."

CHAPTER FORTY-ONE

"Dock reports all umbilicals retracted," Amandine reported. "I confirm. *Tornado* is floating free, ready to activate the gravitational-hyperspatial interface momentum engine."

Annette felt a huge sense of relief sweep over her and stretched with a rare brilliant smile at her bridge crew as her ship *finally* edged its way free of the construction slip that had been her home for the last thirty days.

"Take us out, Lieutenant Commander," she ordered.

"I have a clear entry zone; bringing the drive up at one kilometer per second," Amandine said calmly. There was no perceptible change on *Tornado*'s bridge—indeed, none of the work done over the last month had noticeably changed the bridge—but the gantries of the yard disappeared almost instantly.

"We are clear of Tortuga and inside the rings," he stated a moment later. "Self-tests on the drive are showing clear and green, but we don't have the space in here to test them out."

Tornado's drive was now supposed to be able to reach half of lightspeed, but the space Tortuga was hidden within was only a hundred thousand kilometers or so across.

"That's all right," Annette told him. "I don't like it, but we're going to have to go on self-tests and the Crew's word. We don't really *want* to show off in front of our new friends. Rolfson—weapon and defense status?"

"Beams, launchers and shields all show green on self-test," he confirmed. "Self-tests on the plasma antimissile suite are showing some cyclic issues on the hydrogen feeds. Metharom is looking into it."

Annette threw a readiness display up on her command chair's miniscreens, studying her ship's status. Everything checked out, though her only source on the capabilities of her upgraded command was the Laian Crew themselves.

"So, Ki!Tana," she said conversationally, turning her head to look at the big A!Tol's now-permanent bench in the nook beside her, "have the Laians played straight with us?"

"I have been going over the work with Metharom as everything was installed," her alien companion told her. "They have installed technology on your vessel I have never seen outside of their own ships. They have held some things back, but they have installed everything they promised you. You would likely lose against a modern ship from the Core powers, but against the empires in the spiral arms? They will never see you coming."

Annette glanced at a collection of icons on her screen.

"So," she murmured, "do we think they sold our new specs to our Indiri friend?"

Ki!Tana clacked her beak, her skin streaking red in amusement.

"My dear Captain, I know the Crew didn't sell Karaz Forel the specs for your ship, because *I* sold him the specs for this ship," she told Annette. "They may have been the specs before the refit, but he did not specify—and he paid richly."

Tornado's Captain stared at the strange, apparently potentially immortal alien on her bridge in surprise as a round of chuckles went around the bridge.

"You had a powerful ship when you reached Tortuga, Captain,"

Ki!Tana finished. "He underestimates you now. He also lacks the experience to understand what the armor means: few outside the Core had seen armor such as yours in action."

"Well, then, let's not keep our new friends waiting," Annette said with a smile. "Amandine, take us out to join them. We have an armada to lead!"

ANNETTE WATCHED with cautious eyes as Amandine skillfully cut around the massive bulk of Tortuga to join Karaz Forel's fleet. With shares in as massive a score as the amphibious pirate was promising, he'd managed to talk almost every ship in the pirate station out of their hiding places for this operation.

It was more ships than Annette had expected. *Subjugator* and *Tornado* were the heavy hitters, Forel's ship half a megaton heavier than *Tornado*'s own two million tons.

The Indiri ship was the first big pirate ship they'd seen since *Rekiki's Fang,* and it was clear that unlike *Fang, Subjugator* had been built for this purpose. While she was heavier and wider than *Tornado,* much of her mass was focused in a heavily armored central sphere, with three interlocked rings holding much of her weaponry, while the central structure protected her cargo and engines. Part of the sphere was a massive hatch, clearly designed to scoop up smaller vessels like a swooping bird of prey.

If Annette had built a ship to *be* a privateer and a raider, it might not have *looked* much like the Indiri ship, but the same points of "protected cargo space", "capture capability" and "heavy armaments" would have been ticked off.

The rest of the pirate fleet was a far more motley mix. Fifty-six ships, including Annette's two scout ships, formed a rough sphere around the two heavies. They varied from ships even *smaller* than her scouts, mostly designed to ram and board slower ships with their entire crews, to ships the size of old UESF battleships with significant weapons and armor that were still barely a match for an A!Tol destroyer.

There was no uniformity, discipline or organization to Karaz Forel's pirate armada, but the fifty-eight ships represented an incredible amount of firepower. Annette was impressed.

Her cruiser finally slotted into its place at the center of the rough formation, alongside *Subjugator,* and Annette reviewed the whole situation grimly. This wasn't what she'd envisaged when she'd been sent away from Sol. She hadn't known enough to plan for victory, but she certainly hadn't expected making allies with a slaver and a fleet of pirates.

The attack would provide resources to help liberate Earth and weaken the A!Tol presence in the area around Sol, both high on her objectives, but she couldn't help feeling they were missing something when *these* were the allies they found in their quest.

"Ma'am, we have Forel on the channel for you," Chan reported.

"Put him on the main screen," she ordered, swallowing her discomfort as she faced the disgusting creature she'd tied her mission to for now.

Karaz Forel appeared on the screen, his face split in his grotesque imitation of a human smile. The camera was surprisingly tightly focused, showing only the Indiri and his command chair. A faint mist sprayed down from above the alien, slicking his fur with moisture and somehow managing to make him look even *less* clean and organized.

"Captain Bond. Your ship is most impressive," he smarmed at her. "Is your dock work complete?"

"It is," she told him. "Are any of this collection going to break down before we leave the system?"

He laughed, his tongue twisting in that disturbing spiral again.

"If any of them do, we'll leave them behind!" he told her. "With your *Tornado* and my *Subjugator,* the rest are just to keep the small fish off of our backs while we finish the job. If you're ready, I see no reason not to find the current, do you?"

Annette took a moment to mentally translate the metaphor to

"get started", then returned his obviously fake smile. She was reasonably sure that Forel was calculating the best moment to betray her, but for now, he was treating her as the only equal partner in this endeavor.

"I do not," she agreed. "Let's be about it."

She gestured for Chan to cut the channel, then laced her fingers together as she watched the formation begin to move toward the channels out of the gas giant's rings.

"He is hiding something from you, Captain Bond," Ki!Tana told her. "I am not certain what."

"I *think* this deal is honest," Annette replied, "but I agree. He's only waiting for the best moment to sell us out. I can't trust a slaver."

"Forel is as crazy for his race as I am for mine," the A!Tol said. "He will not hesitate to betray you, sell you into slavery, or attempt to steal your ship. *Subjugator* was a Kanzi vessel, built for cross-border slave-raiding. They were buying slaves from him when he broke the deal, murdered them all, and stole their ship."

"I have no intention of trusting him," Annette repeated. "But damn. He doesn't like Kanzi?"

"He hates *everyone*," Ki!Tana told her. "But the A!Tol and the Kanzi are at the top of his list. Watch your blind spots, Captain Bond. These are dangerous waters you swim in."

"Murky ones too," she told the alien. "He keeps faking human body language—badly, but how does he even know us well enough to do that? You're right. He's hiding something."

CHAPTER FORTY-TWO

OF COURSE WE'RE COMING BACK'S MAIN VIEWSCREEN flickered with the radiation burst of the opening hyperspace portal, then stabilized as the scout ship slipped through the gap in reality back into regular space. Despite only having a minor upgrade to their speed, the two Terran scout ships were still the *stealthiest* ships in the pirate armada.

Of course, hyperspace portals weren't particularly stealthy at the best of times. There were solutions to that.

"How are our decoying friends, Sarah?" Andrew Lougheed asked, studying the screens. *Of Course* and *Oaths of Secrecy* had cut their drives just before opening the portal, and were now moving entirely on cold gas jets. Compared to the interface drive's near-instantaneous acceleration to large chunks of lightspeed, the jets' single gravity felt glacial.

"Our pirate friends are screaming across the system at forty-five percent of the speed of light," his tactical officer reported, directing a smile Andrew's way that skittered the edge of professionalism. He *probably* needed to talk to her about that, but they *were* privateers now.

How much of the old rules really still applied?

For the moment, however, his focus was on the two pirate ships, each roughly two thirds the size of an A!Tol destroyer, screaming across the star system in front of him. They would get a clear initial scan of the system and its contents, but details took time—and so fell to the two Terran ships that could drift through the system without being seen.

"They have *someone's* attention," Sarah Laurent pointed out. "Check out planet four."

The system, Lambda Aurigae on the old Terran charts and Orsav on the A!Tol charts, had no gas giants or asteroid belts. It did have fifteen small planets, ranging from the size of Mars to five times the size of Earth, that got icier and icier as you moved farther out-system. None were habitable, however, making Orsav spectacularly useless for everything except its location.

Planet four was the *closest* to being habitable, with an orbit that gave it liquid water on some parts of its surface for roughly one quarter of its twenty-three-month orbit. Without much in terms of atmosphere, however, that water didn't do much other than sit there and boil off.

Right *now*, however, the main point of attention was that someone had just booted up an interface drive and gone charging out after the two pirate ships. Size was difficult to tell at this distance, but the ship was moving at a full half of lightspeed, rapidly closing on the slower pirate ships.

"Are they going to make it out?" he asked slowly.

"Scans make our new friend a destroyer," Laurent replied. "She could take either of our decoys without even breaking a sweat, but against both of them...I'm not sure she *wants* to catch them. Just make them run."

She shrugged.

"Either way, I'm not shedding tears for our local pirate scum," she pointed out.

"Fair," he admitted with a chuckle. "Just remember that category *includes* us now!"

"We may be pirates," Laurent said softly, "but we're *not* scum. You've seen this bunch."

Andrew shook his head and pressed his finger to his lips.

"I have, but they're our allies today," he reminded her. "What do we have on planet four?"

"Focusing the passives as we close," she confirmed. Laser linkages to *Oaths of Secrecy* allowed them to get data from different angles, dramatically expanding their effectiveness.

"Defensive constellation detected," Laurent reported a moment later. Additional red icons started to flash onto the screen. "Estimating in excess of five hundred contacts, missile and beam platforms." She shook her head. "I hope Forel isn't lying about that code, sir. We're resolving more contacts by the second. That constellation would eat the entire armada."

"What about the base itself? And the ships, for that matter?"

"We got a *big* thermal signature on the planet," she replied after focusing on her data. "Looks like half a dozen or more *massive* fusion plants fueling some kind of facility; that won't be small, sir."

"If it were small, this whole endeavor would be a waste of time and money," Andrew pointed out. "And the ships?" he repeated.

"I've got two more heat signatures in orbit; I *think* they're destroyers," she reported. "No sign of the cruiser Forel expected."

"Keep an eye open as we close," he ordered. "We'll need to relay everything to Captain Bond and the others when they arrive. If the cruiser is missing, no one will mind. If *we* miss *her*, the armada might be in for a world of hurt."

THE TWO TERRAN scout ships continued on their slow way deeper into the system, watching with a careful eye as the A!Tol destroyer overhauled the two pirate ships.

The details of the logistics base resolved with further clarity as the ships approached. The constellation had been assembled to stand an attack by a full Kanzi battle group based around at least one ship of the line. It was impossible to get an *exact* count without getting far closer than Andrew or Captain Sade planned on getting, but it was somewhere between seven hundred and one thousand platforms.

"Datapulse from our decoys," Laurent announced. "I'm incorporating it, but I'm not seeing anything new. A little bit more resolution: I've got a third destroyer in orbit. That gets us to four total."

Which was about what Forel had told them and, apparently, a standard subunit used for A!Tol Imperial Navy light warships. That still left them missing a cruiser, a warship supposedly a match for either of their heavies—though Andrew had his suspicions about what *Tornado*'s upgrades would mean for any cruiser unfortunate to tangle with her.

"Destroyer is opening fire," Laurent continued. "Missiles closing on one of our friends—she fell about a half-light-second behind the other, and it looks like she's going to pay for it."

His tactical officer didn't sound particularly bothered by this at all. She hadn't been one of the people grabbed by the Kanzi slavers, but she was good friends with Lieutenant Mosi. Mosi had recovered from her *physical* injuries, but that didn't stop the entire flotilla being coldly furious with the very *concept* of slavers.

And too many of their erstwhile allies dabbled in slavery, for disposing of captives no one would ransom if nothing else.

Andrew couldn't bring himself to rebuke her for her apathy regarding the fate of their allies. He didn't particularly disagree with her.

"Are they going to catch them?" he asked.

"Missiles will," she confirmed. "Impact in sixty seconds, hyper portal safe distance in one hundred and thirty-six seconds. I don't think our laggard friend will make it."

"Turn the passive sensors up to maximum sensitivity," Andrew ordered. "If she goes up, that will give us one *heck* of a hard radiation blast to bounce off everything in the system."

"I thought I *wasn't* supposed to be happy they were about to die?" she asked with a smirk.

"I am shocked and saddened by their imminent demise," he replied virtuously. "But let's use it to our advantage regardless."

He settled into his command chair to watch the show. Laurent had estimated the time perfectly, and the first salvo of missiles slammed into the trailing pirate exactly on time. Like most ships this far out the spiral arms, apparently, the pirate ship lacked any kind of active antimissile defense, but her shields absorbed the impact.

The second salvo suffered the same fate, and Andrew mentally saluted the pirate captain. Whoever they were, they hadn't skimped on the defenses for their ship. Those were impressive shields for a ship of its size.

The captain clearly didn't trust their ship's shields to hold through another salvo, and *Of Course*'s sensors announced an ugly burst of radiation as the pirate ship tried to open a hyperspace portal, still over a dozen light-seconds inside the safety zone.

The portal failed in a flash of light and energy that slammed back into the pirate's shield, setting them to flickering with energy overload —and then the Imperial destroyer's missiles arrived. The shields wouldn't have held either way, but with the energy flare from the failed portal, they never stood a chance.

The scout ships were too far away for Andrew Lougheed to even be sure how many missiles the destroyer had launched, let alone how many had hit home. Enough made it through that the four-hundred-thousand-ton starship vanished in a ball of flame and hard radiation, energy ripping apart antimatter and fusion power plants in a burst of destruction.

"Hyper portal open," Laurent announced. "Our other decoy is clear."

"Is the destroyer pursuing?" Andrew asked. "And is that pulse giving us any data yet?"

"We're a good two light-minutes away," she pointed out. "We're still waiting on the reflections from everywhere else." She checked something in response to his first question as well, then shook her head. "Destroyer is not pursuing; she is coming about to return to orbit."

Andrew nodded. No one—except the decoy ship's crew themselves—would have minded if the destroyer had gone into hyperspace after the decoy. The prize wasn't going to shrink if the defenders weakened themselves.

"Gotcha!" Laurent suddenly snapped. "Radiation pulse is pinging off artificial material in orbit of the fifth planet. I can't resolve a *lot* of detail, but it looks like we've got a major starship hiding behind the moon."

"Sneaky tentacled bastards," *Of Course*'s Captain noted aloud. "Make sure it's in the data packet and fire it at *Tornado*'s emergence time and location."

"Data packet on its own way, sir," she confirmed. "What now?

CHAPTER FORTY-THREE

COMBINING THE EXOTIC-MATTER ARRAYS OF THE EIGHT LARGEST ships in the pirate armada allowed the fleet to rip open a portal over a hundred times bigger than the usual one *Tornado* created. Instead of being slightly larger than the opening ship, barely large enough for a second ship to slip through if you were clever, this portal was a full light-second across.

Fifty-four pirate ships, with *Subjugator* and *Tornado* in the lead, passed through the portal at forty-five percent of the speed of light. There was no subtlety, no attempts at tricks or stealth. With this many ships, it would have been wasted time.

"We are receiving datapulses from the scout ships," Chan announced. "Relaying to Rolfson. Looks like four destroyers in orbit of planet four with the base and the defense constellation, and a fifth ship, probably our cruiser, hiding in orbit of planet five."

"Forward the data on to the armada," Annette ordered. She studied the tactical plot as Rolfson started to update it. The defensive constellation was the joker in the deck. The defensive plan, if she were generous enough to call it a plan, was clearly to pin any attacker between the cruiser and the constellation.

"New orders for the scout ships," she continued after a moment. "They are to exit the system as soon as practical and proceed to Rendezvous Point Sigma Three."

Sigma Three was a rendezvous they had *not* shared with Forel or his friends, a point in deep space on the route back to Alpha Centauri. An easy spot for Annette to swing through on the way to Tortuga or back to their cache in Alpha Centauri system.

Somewhere safe from any treachery or betrayal Forel had planned.

"Now get me Captain Forel," she instructed. "Time to get this show on the road."

"A moment, ma'am," Rolfson interrupted. "I should note that our own sensor sweeps cannot confirm the presence of a ship at planet five."

"Lougheed and Sade did say it was hiding," Annette pointed out with a nod. "Better to assume they're trying to sneak up behind than that they don't exist, yes?"

"Yes, ma'am," he conceded.

A moment later, Chan opened the link to *Subjugator*. Once again, Forel sat moistly at the center of a very narrow view excluding the rest of his bridge. She knew, intellectually, that his race was amphibious and his fur and skin had to be *much* more comfortable damp.

It still felt like she was looking at a sweaty used car salesman with a damp comb-over.

"Captain Bond."

"Captain Forel. If you don't have those constellation codes you promised us all, this is going to be a very short and painful operation," she reminded him. "Shall we open the dance?"

"I think we should give our tentacled overlords time to feel the water heating up," Forel told her with his horrible fake smile. "Let us see if we can lure our cruiser friend out to play before we demonstrate our toys."

"It's your code," Annette said sweetly. "I'll just remind you your ship *is* in proton-beam range of mine if I think you've lied to me."

She smiled at him, an expression that none of her crew would have thought was genuine for a moment.

Forel sucked his tongue fully into the back of his mouth in a convulsive gesture, pausing for a moment before responding.

"I do see your concern," he finally said. "But such actions will not be necessary."

"Of course not," she told him. "Your lead, Captain Forel."

She made a sharp gesture and Chan shut the channel.

Moments later—probably enough time for Forel to unswallow his tongue—*Subjugator* turned in space, shaping a direct course for planet four and the logistics base. Over the course of the next several seconds, the rest of the armada began to follow in a disorganized gaggle.

"Keep us on *Subjugator*'s flank," Annette ordered. "Watch for the cruiser and keep an eye on that constellation. Let me know a minimum of ten seconds before we enter its weapons range."

The pirate fleet continued on its course, barely in anything remotely resembling a formation to Annette's eyes. She sighed. There was only so much competence or discipline she expected from a set of pirate ships, but at least some basic station-keeping would have been helpful.

"Forel is transmitting to everyone," Chan advised.

"On screen."

Once again, Forel appeared on the screen. This time, only his face was visible, in a screen-within-a-screen as the rest of the transmission was a tactical view of the defensive constellation. Proton-beam satellites and missile launchers filled the sky over their target, each satellite surrounded by a force field stronger than many of the smaller pirate ships.

"This is the moment you have been waiting so impatiently for," he told them all. "Look at this. An A!Tol Imperial Class Four Defense Constellation. Capable of standing off a *ship of the line*. We have mustered one of the most powerful collections of pirate vessels ever seen in this arm of the galaxy, and that constellation alone could fight us to a standstill.

"But you came because I promised you an answer, and so I shall deliver the rising tide of our victory!"

Forel did something out of the scope of his screen and the lights representing the constellation flickered on the display for a moment, and then returned to full strength.

"Wait for it," he ordered calmly. "And when the shields go down, target the constellation and fire every missile you have. The A!Tol are perfectly capable of overriding the code, given enough time."

"Now, *that* is something I'd like to have known in advance," Rolfson snapped, his hands suddenly flying over his controls as he queued up *Tornado*'s missile batteries.

"And...now," Forel announced. A moment later, the constellation satellites icons flickered again—and this time stayed dark. "Their shields are down," he informed his followers. "Take them out."

"Kill the channel and confirm that," Annette snapped.

The screen cut back to *Tornado*'s standard tactical plot as Rolfson and his computers tore through their scanner data, seeking the tiny imperfections and twists of light that marked the presence of an active energy shield.

"He's right," Kurzman confirmed. "Constellation shields are down. Launch when ready, Commander Rolfson."

Subjugator had fired first, but *Tornado*'s computers and sensors were the best in the armada now. Many of the other pirates apparently took *Tornado* firing as proof of Forel's claims and joined in. Moments after Forel had declared the constellation disabled, *hundreds* of missiles were flashing toward planet four and the defensive constellation.

There were multiple different speeds amongst the missiles—in fact, Annette was relatively sure some of the missiles she was seeing fired were the Terran-built point six cee weapons she'd sold at Tortuga—spreading the attack out over almost a full minute.

By the time *Tornado* and *Subjugator*'s second salvos arrived, hundreds of the platforms making up the constellation were gone and the A!Tol ships clearly realized there was a problem. All four destroyers charged out, actively trying to shoot down missiles with their own weapons.

"Ma'am, we have a ping from the fifth planet," Rolfson announced. "Looks like the cruiser is coming out to play."

"Leave the constellation and the destroyers for the smaller ships," she ordered. "Bring us about and take us at that cruiser."

She glanced at the screen and confirmed she didn't need to reach out to Forel: *Subjugator* was making the same course correction. Both of the pirate heavies were turning to face the largest of their opponents, leaving their lesser companions to deal with the four destroyers —at over twelve-to-one odds, the smaller ships should at least be able to keep the destroyers occupied.

"Ma'am, you need to take a look at this," Kurzman suddenly told her quietly over the link from CIC. "We've got a solid scan on the ship leaving that planet and we may be in trouble—that's no cruiser."

ANNETTE BOND RAN over the numbers the ship's computer was assembling on the newcomer and a chill ran down her spine. An A!Tol Imperial Navy cruiser was a two-million-ton ship half a kilometer long, roughly the same size and mass as *Tornado*.

The ship now pulling fifty percent of lightspeed toward them was easily twice *Tornado*'s mass. It was an elegant thing, all curves and lines and extending nacelles, over eight hundred meters long and three hundred wide, with an energy signature that suggested she was going to be a headache.

"What am I looking at, Harold?" she asked her tactical officer.

"I'm not sure," he replied. "We don't *have* a lot of detailed files on the A!Tol Navy; she's smaller than the battleships they showed up at Earth with but bigger than the cruisers. Ki!Tana?"

"It did not occur to me to arrange more detailed files," the A!Tol admitted. "Most piracy avoids heavier warships. It is likely one of their fast battleship units, designed for rapid deployment."

"So, a battlecruiser," Annette noted, mentally slotting it into a class she could hold easily in her head. "Heavier weapons or defenses?"

"Depends on the class," Ki!Tana replied. "If they've assigned it as the lead defensive unit for a post like this, it likely has heavy shields and a lighter armament—but still heavier than a cruiser's."

"And shields are vulnerable to beams," *Tornado*'s Captain noted. "Chan, link us in to Forel. We're going to need closer coordination with *Subjugator* than planned. Amandine, set us on a direct intercept course; I want to force her into proton-beam range. Rolfson...she's going to have more beams than we do. Kill her first."

Her bridge crew leapt into action, a reassuring sign of competence and confidence as her ship went into action against a superior A!Tol warship for the first time since they'd fled Sol.

Annette herself carefully wiped her palms against her uniform pants, hoping none of her people spotted her sweaty palms. The last time they'd faced a real A!Tol military force, they'd been forced to flee their home. This time would have to end better.

"Captain Bond, my friends did not warn me about a vessel of this scale," Forel admitted, his red-furred face appearing on her command chair's small screen. "This is..."

"Within the capacity of our vessels combined," she said swiftly. "We need to close together, force the battlecruiser to split her fire. She's bigger than we expected, but we've come this far, Karaz Forel. Will you give up the prize now?"

The amphibious alien shivered, droplets of water flickering off of his fur onto the camera, then once again gave her a wide fake grin.

"You are correct, of course," he told her. "We share the current, Captain Bond. Let us strike as one!"

THE TWO CRUISERS shot toward the battlecruiser at half the speed of light, and the battlecruiser charged toward them at the same velocity, both calculated relative to the local star. The *relative* velocity between the three ships was only eighty percent of light-speed, but it was still enough for the five-light-minute distance to melt away as they closed.

Both sides opened up with missiles while still two light-minutes apart. All three ships were carrying modern point seven five cee missiles, which meant they had effective closing rates of over ninety percent of lightspeed.

"Bogey is focusing fire on *Subjugator*," Rolfson reported. "She has over fifty missiles inbound. I can deploy rainshower drones to protect her?"

"Negative," Annette ordered. "Let's not flash *all* of our new toys where Mister Forel can see them. Focus missile fire and charge the proton beams."

The two pirate heavies had fewer launchers between them than the battlecruiser did. The battlecruiser was throwing over fifty missiles a salvo, but the pirates were only replying with forty-six. As the seconds flickered away, that still turned into *hundreds* of missiles flying each way—and the A!Tol missiles were focused on *Subjugator*.

"Let's see how our friend holds up," Annette murmured as both sets of missiles closed on their respective targets. "Let me know if any of those missiles start turning our way," she ordered.

"Yes, ma'am."

The first missiles slammed home, dozens of weapons unleashing unimaginable kinetic energy as they hammered into each ship's shields. Both ships took the beating with unsurprising grace, even these massive salvos insufficient to bring down heavy shields in a single strike.

Forel's face once again popped back up on her command chair screen.

"Captain Bond, *Subjugator* will not survive many hits like that," he said flatly. "I need your assistance."

"We will see what we can do," Annette promised, eyeing the tactical screen. "Rolfson!"

"Ma'am!"

"Redirect our offensive fire," she ordered. "Intercept as many of the Imperial missiles as possible; let's clear our friends a little breathing room!"

"On it," he promised.

There was a limit to how effective that strategy could be, she knew. If nothing else, command and control were...problematic with lightspeed links, and missiles traveled at three quarters of the speed of light. But it should buy the furred toad on her screen *enough* of a breather to get him into beam range.

"My thanks," Forel murmured before his image disappeared again.

"Keep the toad alive," Annette told her crew with a sigh. *Tornado* had the heavier missile armament of the two pirate ships, but neither of them was planning on battering down the battlecruiser's shields with missiles.

"Bogey is evading," Rolfson reported. "She's adjusting course to try and loop around us and support the destroyers."

"Smart," she acknowledged. She'd do the same in the A!Tol captain's place: the battlecruiser could crush half of the smaller ships in a single pass, freeing up the destroyers to support the bogey against the pirate heavies that *could* threaten her.

"Let's not let her do that," she continued. "Amandine, take us in!"

"Do we go faster?" her navigator asked.

They'd been matching the same point five cee speed *Subjugator* was putting out. With their Laian upgrades, they now had a short-duration sprint ability of another five percent of lightspeed—something the A!Tol ship couldn't match.

"No," she finally decided. "We'll cut her off well before she's clear, anyway. Beam range?"

"Thirty seconds and counting."

Again, Annette wiped her sweaty palms on her trousers and

hoped none of her crew saw her nervousness. Unless the battlecruiser had lighter beams than she expected, the moment they hit range was going to be *painful* for everybody, including *Tornado* and *Subjugator*.

"I'm showing shield flickers on *Subjugator*," Rolfson reported. "Wait, *shit*: her shields are down, she's hit!"

There was a flash of energy release, a blast of atmosphere—then the other pirate ship's engines cut out while she was still five seconds short of the battlecruiser's beam range.

Annette swore loudly as she realized that Forel had abandoned *Tornado* to enter proton-beam range, the deadliest aspect of space combat, alone.

"Kill her!" she snapped as *Tornado* flashed across an invisible line in space and the deadly streams of energy flashed out from both vessels.

For a moment, both sets of proton beams flailed impotently into empty space, and then *Tornado* found her enemy's measure. Multiple beams connected the two ships, invisible streams drawn in white on the tactical plot, pulsing vast quantities of energy into the A!Tol ship's shields.

Barely a second more passed before the *Imperial* ship's beams latched onto *Tornado* and returned the favor.

"Her beams are weaker than ours," Rolfson crowed after a second. "We may just make it..."

The battlecruiser had *more* beams, though, and the first of them punched through *Tornado*'s shield as the tactical officer spoke, sending the ship lurching away as energy transferred into her armor with crushing force.

"Firing missiles!" the tactical officer snapped. "Intercepting the beam!"

Icons flickered on the screen as interface drive missiles flashed out of their launchers, interposing themselves in the path of the beams that were cutting through the cruiser's shields. Without shields or compressed-matter armor of their own, the missiles lasted mere fractions of a second.

They were *enough* fractions. *Tornado*'s own beams broke through, the Imperial ship's shields flickering and *collapsing* as the two ships closed—and Rolfson sent two missiles that hadn't been sacrificed to defend the ship screaming across the gap at an unimaginable speed.

Compressed-matter armor had saved *Tornado* but the A!Tol didn't have that defensive layer. Proton beams tore massive gouges in the battlecruiser's hull, ripping out the responding weapons—and then those two missiles arrived, hammers traveling at three quarters of the speed of light that released their kinetic energy in blinding flashes.

When the light cleared, all that remained of the battlecruiser was drifting fragments.

CHAPTER FORTY-FOUR

"STATUS REPORT!" ANNETTE BARKED, RUBBING HER SHOULDER carefully where the impact had slammed it into the edge of her chair.

"Armor held, barely," Ki!Tana—acting as bridge engineering officer—reported. "Metharom's teams are reporting minor vibration damage throughout the ship but nothing critical. Bruises, basically—to both people and machinery."

"Good to hear," she replied. "What about our moist friend?"

"*Subjugator*'s shields are back up but her drive is still down," Rolfson reported after a moment. "Not picking up any more atmosphere venting."

"Ki!Tana, Rolfson...what are the odds that engine failure was real?" she asked quietly.

"His shields went down and he took a single nonfatal hit?" the A!Tol asked. "If that was real, the Empress is my mother."

That confused Annette for a moment, then she remembered that, if nothing else, Ki!Tana was at least four or five times the A!Tol Empress's age.

"Rolfson?"

"I concur," the tactical officer said after a quick glance over at

Amandine, who nodded as well. "The drive is heavily distributed. A single hit could reduce her speed but couldn't take out her drive, not without her being *very* badly designed. If that hit actually took out her engines, *my* mother is a *virgin*."

That got chuckles from the human crewmembers, though Pondar, the only alien on the bridge other than Ki!Tana, looked thoroughly confused by *both* metaphors.

"Raise Forel for me," Annette ordered.

A moment later the Indiri reappeared on the main screen, back in his regular focused view.

"Apologies, Captain Bond," he began. "We had an unexpected power surge. We should have our engines back online in a minute or two."

Annette gave the alien who'd tried to abandon her to her death a large fake smile.

"We took some damage ourselves," she lied. "We're in pretty rough shape, but we can still support the ground assault. As soon as your engines are online, we should both move to back up the rest of the armada against the destroyers."

A quick glance at the tactical plot confirmed that at least some of the A!Tol destroyers were still intact, the smaller pirate ships engaging in a long-range, low-risk missile duel that had still managed to cost them eight ships so far.

"Agreed," Forel said calmly. "Give me one hundred seconds, Captain, then we can be on our way."

He cut the channel, and Annette turned back to her crew. "Close us up with *Subjugator*," she ordered Amandine. "Keep our scorched side away from her, make it look like we're being super-protective of a damaged section."

"I can do that," the navigator replied. "Can I just be super-protective of the whole *ship*? It *does* have my own personal skin aboard!"

WITH UNSURPRISING CONVENIENCE, *Subjugator*'s interface drive came back online just as *Tornado* was passing her, allowing the other pirate heavy to fall in a few tens of thousands of kilometers behind the Terran ship.

As the two heavies returned toward planet four and its orbiting duel, Annette studied the last ten minutes of the fight on fast-forward and realized that the pirates really had *no* clue how to fight a fleet action. They had, intelligently given the superiority of Imperial beam weapons to those most of the pirates had, refused to close, maintained a long range missile engagement.

Given that Imperial *missiles* were superior to those in the pirate magazines, it would have been a more even match than the numbers suggested, no matter what. To make matters worse, however, the pirates had split their fire across all four targets, and done so unevenly. One of the destroyers had taken over a third of the pirate fire, and had *eventually* come apart under the battering—but the four A!Tol ships had focused their fire on one pirate at a time, and six pirate ships had died before the first destroyer had been eliminated.

Now the three remaining destroyers had closed up their formation as tightly as possible and continued to focus their fire on a single pirate ship at a time.

"They started with the weakest-looking ships and are working their way up," Rolfson noted, following the same data she was. "Scarily competent bastards."

"So are we," Annette replied. "Hold back four launchers around where we were hit, but open up with the rest. Pick one target, send it to *Subjugator*, then pound her to pieces."

A minute later, the ship vibrated as twenty missiles flashed away, diving toward the most damaged of the destroyers. A few seconds later, *Subjugator* entered her own range and followed suit.

The two heavies' faster missiles dove through the formation of smaller ships, hammering home on the weakest destroyer, plowing through her already-depleted shields and shattering the half-million-ton starship into tiny pieces.

"Destroyers are switching target to us," Rolfson announced. "And *moving*; they're trying to close to beam range!"

"Amandine, go evasive," Annette ordered. "Harold: kill them for me?"

"On it," he confirmed. "Transmitting next target to the entire flotilla. Let's see if they get the idea!"

Tornado vibrated again as more missiles left the hull, and the tactical display flickered for a second before stabilizing, accounting for evasive maneuvers.

"We have three salvos inbound, twenty missiles each," Amandine announced. "Permission to deploy rainshower defenders?"

"No drones," Annette told him. "You are cleared to engage with hull-mounted plasma systems."

"Yes, ma'am," he confirmed, his attention already lost in the systems. Moments later, the new suite of antimissile defenses, the poetically named "deadly rainshower defenders" activated. In a sense, the weapons were glorified plasma shotguns, firing hundreds of electromagnetically charged, superheated packets of hydrogen into space.

In a few moments, the space in front of the incoming missiles was filled with balls of deadly plasma, each individually magnetically attracted to anything metal in front of them. They couldn't move far to impact with the missiles, not given the super-high velocities involved—but they could move far *enough*.

Missiles started exploding well short of *Tornado*'s shield, and the destroyers had no such system. While not all of the pirates obeyed Rolfson's targeting instructions, enough did to send a crashing tsunami of over three hundred missiles crashing down on the targeted destroyer.

By the time the destroyers' third salvo ran into the plasma shower and disintegrated without even reaching *Tornado*'s shields, both of the ships that had launched it were nothing but debris.

Captain Karaz Forel's pirate armada now controlled the Orsav system. Eleven of the smaller pirate ships had died dueling the destroyers, but the entire defending task group was gone.

"Major Wellesley," Annette said calmly, opening a channel to the Special Space Service officer waiting in his landing shuttle. "You are clear to deploy. You know the drill: secure the target, set up for cargo extraction. Watch your back.

"Stay alive."

CHAPTER FORTY-FIVE

JAMES WELLESLEY SMILED AS BOND'S COMMAND ECHOED through his helmet.

"Are we ready to go?" he asked his people.

"Yes, sir!" they chorused.

"McPhail," he addressed the pilot. "Take us down. All of our shuttles should be hitting the northwestern corner; the big hangars there should have the automated freighters."

"Roger."

While the Terran-built shuttles *Tornado* carried were slower than many of the other landing craft in the armada, it wasn't like most of that speed could be *used* on approach to a planet. James's people would reach the planet last by a few seconds, but since none of the shuttles could approach the planet at forty or forty-five percent of lightspeed, the final few thousand kilometers would be crossed at a minuscule fraction of the spacecraft's maximum speeds.

In effect, the final arrival time would be decided more by their shuttle pilots' skill and bravery than by the maximum velocity of their interface drives—and James *knew* his pilots.

He watched the planet approach at a blistering speed, a tiny display inside his power armor's helmet showing him the position of all of the several hundred shuttles descending from the remaining pirate ships. The division of targets was haphazard at best, with *Tornado*'s troops arriving at the opposite corner from *Subjugator*'s.

Five thousand kilometers from the planet, the shuttles slowed dramatically, dropping from nearly half of lightspeed to a few kilometers a second at best.

James grinned inside his helmet as *his* pilots blasted right past that mark, closing the distance with the earlier wave by the simple method of running the drive at full for a few seconds more. The other Terran pilots followed McPhail's example in cutting speed *right* behind the rest of the pirates, and he nodded approvingly.

Normally, he would disapprove of using his allies as ablative meat —but given that in this case those allies *wanted* to be first to steal the best of the portable loot, his sympathy was surprisingly limited.

"Altitude three thousand kilometers; we are dropping at fifty kilometers a second," McPhail reported. "We'll have to slow for landing; estimated time to target ninety-two seconds."

"Watch for ground fire," James ordered. "Evade as you feel necessary."

"Go teach your grandmother to suck eggs, sir," she replied. "If you *want*, I'm pretty sure that shiny suit would survive being dropped from this high; want to test?"

"I'll pass," he said dryly. "I'm hoping for a nice, easy landing and some mass surrenders."

His pilot opened her mouth to reply but stopped as warning lights started flashing across her panel.

"*Shit!* Interface missile launch!"

There was no time to dodge. There was no atmosphere over the logistics base and no need for the missiles to slow down to avoid hitting the planet. The weapons shot up at over seventy percent of the speed of light, crossing the few thousand kilometers between them in fractions of a second.

Shuttles started exploding, the defenders targeting each craft with three missiles to make sure they overwhelmed the tiny spacecraft's shields.

James's shuttles didn't even *have* shields.

"Get us *down*," he snapped. "I don't care where; just put us on the ground!"

"Hang the fuck on," McPhail snapped back and the screen began to spin as she brought the interface drive back up to power.

No matter how desperate, they couldn't go down at top speed, but they could go down a *lot* faster. Fifty kilometers a second became a *thousand* and suddenly the ground was *there*, McPhail slamming the engine into a complete stop as the shuttle came screaming down at the roof of the complex.

Only computers could try and judge that timing—and even computers couldn't always get it right. McPhail cut the drive at the last moment, but the landing craft was still traveling at over a kilometer a second when they hit the armored roof of the base and crashed clean through the roof, the next two floors, and came to halt thirty meters *into* the base.

The shuttle was silent for a long moment.

"We're *in* the ground," McPhail finally noted. "Close enough?"

FORTUNATELY, the exit from the shuttle had managed to align with the corridors of the station, and James's headquarters section were able to shove their way out of the shuttle into the base. Checking his map, James realized they were on the completely opposite side of the base from where they were supposed to land, smack dab in the area *Subjugator*'s troops were supposed to handle.

"Guo," he pinged his Alpha Troop Captain. "What's your status?"

"We are down at the target," Jie Guo replied. "Coming under fire from A!Tol security forces, but I've got three troops here. Where are you?!"

"Opposite end of the complex," he replied, bringing up a map showing his people's drop zones. They'd been scattered across the complex—he wasn't sure *how* Alpha, Delta and Echo had all managed to land at the hangars—but most of them were nearer to Guo than to him.

"All troops, make your way to the hangars and rendezvous with Guo," he ordered. "We need those robot freighters."

"What about you, sir?" Tellaki demanded.

"We're going to secure the local area and see if McPhail can pull the ship out of her new crater," James told them. "I believe this is a storage section; resistance should be light."

"Don't tempt fate, sir," Guo told him. "We'll see you when the dust settles—these tentacled bastards are *determined* to fight for these ships."

"Good luck," James said.

Cutting the channel, he looked around the empty corridor they found themselves in.

"Well, folks, in the absence of better data, I suggest we go that way," he ordered, gesturing in the only direction they *could* go. "Let's see what trouble we can find."

THERE WAS MORE trouble in this segment of the base than he'd expected. The maps that Forel had provided marked the region the alien had targeted his own landing in as a storage area, likely containing high-value but low-use items like computer parts—a logical place for him to claim first dibs on but unlikely to see heavy defenders.

James's people hit the first defensive position less than fifty meters "north" of their original landing site. It was a security checkpoint, four aliens—all Rekiki, he noted—with light body armor and plasma weapons guarding a set of scanners and a built-in barricade.

A fusillade of plasma fire forced his point man back into the corridor, scorch marks on the front of his power armor. Without the armor, the man would have been *dead*, which made James *very* pleased with the expense.

"Grenades and charge," he ordered. "We have *no* time."

A dispenser on his wrist popped a small explosive device into his free hand. He quickly checked to be sure the rest of his team were ready and then threw it on a careful arc that bounced it around the corner.

One. Two. *Three.*

On three, ten hundred-gram hypervelocity fragmentation grenades went off, spraying the security checkpoint with deadly shrapnel.

A moment after the weapons detonated, James started forward with his team, following the explosives around the corner with his weapon extended. The computer in his power armor flashed analysis of the targets: one guard down, the other three wounded but still up.

His people opened fire, a spray of plasma bolts that ripped the barricade to pieces along with the guards behind it.

"Clear!" James snapped. "Confirm!"

Two of his people carefully stepped forward, covered by the rest of the team while they checked to be sure there were no automated defenses and examined the security door.

"The door is locked down," Ral, his Yin trooper, reported. "Tight security code—I'm not sure even the guards would have access."

"I'm not slowing down to hack it open," James replied. "Kara—set charges."

Kara Hughes was his headquarters section demolition specialist, and she leapt forward with a will to examine the door.

"I can blow it, but it's going to be one hell of a boom," she said quickly. "Clear the zone; I'll need a couple of minutes."

"Everybody back," he ordered. "Let us know if you need anything."

"I've got the charges; just need to be sure I won't blow anybody I don't mean to, sir."

That was about as blatant a hint as she could get away with, and he nodded as he stepped back with the rest of the team.

"Space Service troops, report," he ordered calmly once he was clear of the checkpoint room.

"This is Guo," Alpha's Captain replied. "I have Alpha, Bravo, Delta and Echo with me. We have secured four of the ten hangars for these robot freighters. They're impressive-looking ships, everything we were told they would be."

"How many are we looking at?"

"I'm seeing five per hangar so far," Guo confirmed. "Each *Tornado*'s size; these hangars are *huge*."

"Take 'em and hold 'em, Troop Captains," James told them. "They're the key to us getting *paid* for this stunt."

"Sir, this is Sherman," his Charlie Troop Captain reported. "We have a problem."

"What kind of problem, Annabel?"

"We're moving through the admin section of this base," she told him. "Civilians, some uniformed, some not. They're all dead and we didn't kill them."

"Someone was there before you?"

"One of the pirate ships closest to Forel," Sherman confirmed. "I don't recall a 'no prisoners' order, boss."

"Because there wasn't one," James said flatly. "Tellaki, your status?"

"Echo is with me now, Honored Major," the Rekiki replied. "Apologies for delay; we were discussing that exact lack of order with some of our pirate friends." He paused. "We may need support from on high. Am I authorized to terminate our 'allies'?"

James winced.

"That bad?" he asked, then sighed. "That's the Captain's call, not mine. I'll bounce it."

"EXPLAIN," Annette ordered as soon as she'd been updated and linked to Tellaki.

"My honor does not permit me to allow the slaughter of surrendered enemies or the unarmed without direct orders," the Rekiki vassal who'd ended up sworn to her told her. "The pirates we are sharing this section of the complex with have no such honor. We are... in disagreement."

Tellaki's helmet started relaying his footage to her. The space looked like a cafeteria with an attached atrium, though the plants in the atrium were *purple* instead of green. There had already been a firefight of some kind, as scorch marks marred the pale blue walls.

At least fifteen aliens with no armor or weapons had been herded along one wall, guarded by four of Golf Troop's Rekiki soldiers. The other members of Golf Troop were standing with Tellaki and had their weapons trained on an eclectic group of aliens, including several Yin and a Tosumi led by an Indiri, who had their own weapons trained on Tellaki's men.

"They have no armor," the Rekiki said calmly. "I can end this disagreement immediately with your permission."

All of the prisoners were in Imperium uniforms, which *did* make them enemy combatants. For a moment of dark rage, Annette was tempted to simply tell Tellaki to walk away. If they'd all been A!Tol, she might even have given in—but only two of the prisoners were the tentacled aliens. The rest were a mix of other species, including at least two she hadn't seen yet.

"No," she told Tellaki. "*Nobody* dies; do you understand me?"

"I am sworn to you, Honored Captain," the alien replied. "Your command?"

"Tell them that we are taking these prisoners and they will receive a portion of any sale or ransom," she ordered.

The saurian alien turned his attention back to the pirates and snapped at them, a hissing and sibilant speech her translator confirmed as roughly what she'd said.

"Our orders from Forel are no prisoners," the Indiri replied. "No slaves.

"Relay me?" Annette asked Tellaki, and a flashing light informed her that he had linked her to her speakers.

"Forel passed no orders to me and has no authority to command me," she told the Indiri coldly. "These prisoners belong to *Tornado*, and my troops *will* kill you if you defy me. Do you understand me?"

The amphibious alien wilted and slowly backed away, leading his troops out of the room.

"Don't pick fights, Tellaki," she told him quietly. She wasn't willing to order her people to stand by and watch murder, but stopping *all* of them would start a fight with the rest of the pirates they didn't need. "I won't ask you to stand by, but don't go looking for fights. We still need to work with these...people."

"I will see these prisoners safely to the hangar, where Guo can protect them," he replied. "We will take what prisoners we can, but I accept your command, Honored Captain."

Annette felt strangely dirty. This very base had enabled the conquest of Earth. There was no question that these people were her enemies. It still felt wrong to let her "allies" carry out mass murder so long as it wasn't directly in front of her people.

Right now, however, she needed the allies more than she needed to feel clean.

CHAPTER FORTY-SIX

"FIRE IN THE HOLE!"

The moment after Hughes gave the radioed warning, James felt the ground and walls shudder from the impact of the explosives—and *keep* shuddering for several seconds.

"How big a charge *was* that?" he demanded.

The demo specialist shrugged, the gesture barely visible in power armor.

"It was a *very* secure door," she replied.

Shaking his head, James gestured Ral forward, the Yin back on point as they moved deeper into the A!Tol base. Despite the impact of the explosives, Hughes's charges had only managed to detach the door itself. It lay on the ground, a disturbingly intact, if warped, hunk of metal.

Beyond it was some kind of administration and control center, half a dozen seats for various races in front of computer screens, and a few desks with organized stacks of paper-like flimsy computers. There was no one *in* the room, however, and the screens were disabled.

It had been neatly shut down, not a result of the attack—and yet this calmly shut-down control center was behind a highly secured, guarded checkpoint and door.

"What the hell?" he murmured. Three exits. "That way," he ordered, picking the one directly ahead. "Let's see just what Forel's people were looking for."

Stepping through the door at the end of the short corridor gave James part of the answer—and sent a chill down his spine. The door opened out onto a catwalk that wrapped around a massive storage warehouse, easily a quarter-kilometer on each side.

The floor was full of...cages. Portable cells of some kind, with opaque walls but open tops to allow guards to secure them from above. *Thousands* of them.

"That is wrong," Ral said slowly. "This is a slave-holding facility. It does not belong in an A!Tol military base!"

"Which is why it's secured and the control center is unmanned," James said grimly. "Are they occupied?"

All ten men, women and aliens of his HQ section were now out on the catwalk, their power-armor scanners linking together to sweep the thousands of cells for life.

"No," he finally concluded. "That makes no sense."

"If they were prepared for more prisoners from whatever source than they got," Hughes said slowly, "then there are other warehouses like this."

"We need to find them," James ordered. "There's an exit that way," he said, gesturing toward a door leading off from the catwalk. "Something is *very* wrong here."

Ral led the way once more, with the rest of the section following him—closer than doctrine called for, but James's people were picking up the same vibe he was. Not only was something wrong, but it was *important*.

The corridor linked them to another control station. This one clearly *had* still been operational when the attack began, with two bodies lying on the floor—both A!Tol, both clearly shot at point-blank range.

"Look at where they fell," James said softly. "They were shot in the back while at their workstations. They weren't killed by troops from the armada. They were killed by their *coworkers.*"

"As soon as the defenses were gone," Hughes commented. "Someone was *waiting* for our attack."

"Check these screens," James ordered. "One of these spaces has to be occupied. *Find it.*"

His helmet could translate the A!Tol text on the screen into English, but it was a slow process and he wasn't practiced at it. Pophe and Ral, his two alien teammates, were *far* more practiced at it and got to work immediately.

"There are four cargo warehouses behind the security seal," Pophe reported after a moment. "The one we passed through is the only one without life signs." The strange mobile fungus turned its eye stalks toward James. "The other security door is open; it was not breached," it continued. "There are power-armor units moving toward warehouse C."

"I suspect our red-furred friend knows *exactly* what's going on," James observed. "Let's go break up his party."

THEY FOUND the rest of the team that had been running the warehouse sector before they found Forel's people. Five aliens—two Tosumi, two Yin, and one A!Tol—had clearly met up with Forel's people—and then been shot down by surprise.

Unlike the execution-like murders in the control center, these were plasma bursts to the front from high-powered weaponry—plasma cannons equivalent to those James and his people were carrying.

"They were not expecting that," Ral said softly, the Yin kneeling over the bodies of the Imperial technicians. "All were armed but never drew their weapons."

"So Forel was working with people here and betrayed them," James agreed. "The order wasn't 'no prisoners' it was 'no *witnesses*'."

"That's not good for us," Hughes noted.

"No." James gestured for the team to move out. "Let's catch up to Forel's people. This whole thing stinks, and the more we know, the better informed the *Captain* is."

"Can't be far," Ral noted. "The bodies are still warm."

They moved, another door falling behind them as they traced the path the map said would lead to one of the occupied warehouses. An icon on his helmet marked the likely location of the other pirate group as James's people moved as quickly as they could.

Finally, they reached another catwalk, standing out above another massive array of portable cells. This time, they weren't alone. A dozen power armored bipeds, potentially any one of a dozen or more two-legged races inside the armor, stood on top of the cells and turned to face them as they stepped out onto the catwalk.

"You are not supposed to be here," one of them said immediately. "Leave."

"We came down off-course by accident," James said calmly. "We are supposed to be working together, we can help you."

He stepped forward, trying to get a look into the cells, to see just *what* Forel was looking for that had been worth all of this trickery, deception and murder to achieve.

Twelve plasma cannons suddenly leveled themselves on his team.

"Leave," the leader repeated. "Your help is unneeded and none of your people should be here. We will kill you if you do not go."

James wasn't *quite* far enough forward to see through the tops of the cages and hesitated. Instinct told him not to retreat, but if he started a firefight without a *reason* things could go very wrong. If he fired first, he would bring the entire alliance crashing down in flames.

"Wait?" a voice exclaimed from below. "Someone speaks English?! Help us! We've been kidnapped!"

"Be silent," the pirate leader bellowed, his translator directly outputting English as he stomped a power armored foot on the top of the cage and pointed a plasma weapon down at the speaker. "You will learn your place."

A sudden tiny screen flashed up in the corner of James's visor—Kara Hughes had tossed a sensor ball, a rolling drone with a tiny camera, over the side of the catwalk. It landed with a clatter, rolling across the top of the cages and attracting *everyone's* attention as it threw its video feed back to the Terran Special Space Service troopers.

The cages were full of people—*humans*. Ragged and exhausted-looking, manacled with chains that were primitive and out of place amidst the glittering white and complex technology of the A!Tol Imperial base.

"Yeah," James said quietly, leveling his own plasma cannon at the pirate troops. "Not a chance in hell. Walk away or burn, but these are *our* people and I am *not* leaving them with you."

"Wait!" the alien shouted. "Our captains are allied. This was always the—"

James's first shot arrived before the pirate finished speaking. The plasma cannons he'd issued his people were designed for many purposes—and one of their modes was a deadly narrow beam of superheated hydrogen intended to take down power armor.

Fired by surprise, it worked like a charm. The lance of fire took the alien in the throat, burning clean through his armor and killing him before he finished the sentence.

James followed his plasma bolt over the catwalk railing, slamming down on the top of the cells with a resounding crunch. The first counter-fire went over his head as he landed, and his second shot took down another pirate trooper—and then his own people joined in.

A blast of plasma slammed into his shoulder, freezing his arm in place and spinning him backward. More fire came down from the catwalk, his people carefully sweeping the top of the cells with fire angled not to enter the cells.

The SSS officer fell off the top of the cells, slamming into the floor of the warehouse with a crushing thump before struggling back to his feet and putting a bolt of plasma through another pirate.

Then it was over, the last two pirates throwing their weapons down and raising their armored gauntlets in the air.

"Get out of the armor," James ordered, covering them with his own weapon. "Report!"

"Ral is down, hurt bad," Hughes report. "We lost Rogers, too."

James nodded, swallowing his pain as he surveyed the cells around him. There were at least five thousand cells in this warehouse alone, each holding a single human in barely tolerable conditions.

"Ma'am," he said quietly as he raised Annette. "We have at least *fifteen thousand* human prisoners in this base—and Forel's people were trying to pull them out as slaves."

"I was watching," she said grimly. "*Tornado* landing forces, you have new orders: secure the base—from *everyone*."

CHAPTER FORTY-SEVEN

IT MIGHT NOT SAY PARTICULARLY PLEASANT THINGS ABOUT Annette Bond's character, she reflected, that she was prepared to let Forel and the other pirates murder an unknown but large number of nonhumans so long as they didn't do it where she could see it, but as soon as *humans* were involved, she was opposed.

"Hail *Subjugator*," she ordered. "That red-furred toad better have a *damn* good explanation."

"Yes, ma'am," Chan replied crisply. Something about the discovery of human prisoners—and *finally* pushing back against the scum they'd allied with—had brought a renewed energy to *Tornado*'s bridge.

Forel usually replied instantly, but this time a light flashed on Annette's console, indicating that they were pinging the other ship without response for several long seconds.

Paranoia flashed through her mind a moment too late and she began to order Cole to initiate evasive maneuvers—and then bright warning lights exploded across her screens and the entire multi-million-ton mass of *Tornado* lurched in space and rang like a bell.

"Evasive maneuvers!" she finally ordered. "Cole, get us some distance. Ki!Tana, get me shields. Harold, what the *hell* just happened?"

"*Subjugator* opened fire," her tactical officer replied. "We took twenty missiles directly to the hull. We've lost two of the proton beams and at least four launchers are disabled, but we're still here."

"Son of a *bitch*," Annette snapped. "Return fire! Beams and missiles; get the defender drones out."

"Yes, ma'am!"

Even as Rolfson had been explaining, Cole Amandine had been opening the distance from the other pirate ships at fifty-five percent of lightspeed, putting the full force of their new sprint mode into getting them more range.

"I have multiple launches from across the armada," Rolfson reported. "One hundred plus missiles inbound. Rainshower defender drones are deployed."

The drones tripled the amount of plasma cannon the cruiser had to defend herself, and staying inside her shield perimeter meant they were as protected as the rest of the ship.

"Is *anyone* backing us?" Annette demanded.

"No one is responding to hails," Chan reported. "The entire armada is now painting us with targeting sensors."

"I suspect Forel discussed this with the other captains as a contingency scenario," Ki!Tana told them, her flattened translator voice sounding disturbingly calm. "He has likely offered to split our share with them if we are destroyed."

"*Fuck* this for a game of soldiers," Annette snarled, tracing the white lines of the proton beams lighting up the screen as her ship fired on *Subjugator*.

"Ma'am?" Rolfson asked in confusion.

A moment later, the salvo from the rest of the armada ran into the first blasts of plasma from the rainshower defense suite and evaporated into debris and vaporized metal.

"Kurzman, take over the rainshowers. Rolfson, pass beam control to me," she ordered. "You handle missiles—target the rest of the armada while I take *Subjugator* with the beams. When push comes to shove, we're *soldiers*, people," she told her bridge crew. "So, let's kill some damn pirates, shall we?"

———————

EVEN MOVING at over half of lightspeed, they'd barely opened a full light-second's worth of distance before *Subjugator* and the rest of the armada had come out after them. Relative velocity and faster weapons meant *their* missiles were hitting home faster than their pursuers' missiles, and Rolfson took merciless advantage of that.

Annette had four proton beams left and set to using them with a will, burning into *Subjugator*'s shields even as the pirate ship dodged around, preventing her from getting a solid beam lock.

Forel's ship returned the favor. Even undamaged, he only had four proton beams of his own and it took well over ten seconds for *Subjugator*'s energy weapons to come into play. The Indiri pirate clearly hadn't expected *Tornado* to survive a point-blank missile salvo.

Now the Terran experimental cruiser, upgraded with stolen A!Tol and purchased Laian technology, found itself facing an entire *fleet*. The rainshower defender drones had shredded the first missile salvo, but the armada had a *lot* of launchers and beam weapons.

Tornado's shields flickered, warning icons flashing on Annette's screens as several sections began to weaken under proton beams and laser strikes. The icons faded as Amandine rotated the ship, spinning the cruiser to spread the damage.

"Prioritize the ships with proton beams," she ordered Rolfson as the defense drones' plasma packets turned a second, larger missile salvo to vapor.

"On their way," her tactical officer responded grimly. "Queueing targets for second salvo."

Twenty missiles sliced into the pirates, directed at a single target. None of the pirate ships had any kind of active defenses, relying entirely on their shields. The biggest weakness of that defense was that they couldn't support each other—and the missiles split into four successive waves that slammed into a single target.

The largest of the lighter pirates was half again the size of an A!Tol destroyer at just under five hundred meters long. With more cargo space than a destroyer, she was more lightly armed but still the heaviest-armed vessel of the armada after *Subjugator* herself, with a single proton beam that was actually *more* powerful than *Subjugator*'s beams.

Five missiles, even traveling at seventy-five percent of the speed of light, were no threat to her shields. A *second* five missiles, hitting in roughly the same spot, set her shields to flickering, sending whirls of glittering energy across the sphere defending the ship.

The third wave of five missiles *barely* failed to penetrate but ripped gaping wide holes in the pirate's shields, spots of blackness in the coruscating glitter of the shield—spots that the *last* wave of five missiles, arriving fractions of a second later, slipped through with deadly precision.

A single massive explosion marked the end of *that* ship, and more missiles followed on, targeting other ships with beam weapons that continued to actually threaten *Tornado*. Harold Rolfson cut his way through the pirate armada with hammerblows of fire that ripped apart ship after ship.

Annette wasn't having nearly as much luck. *Subjugator* was ignoring the rest of the pirates, dancing around *Tornado*'s proton beams even as she returned fire. Both ships were hit, but their shields shed the focused beams of charged particles, only slowly weakening under the pressure.

Two ships blew up simultaneously, the last of the proton beam–armed pirates, and Annette *felt* the tempo of the battle change. Several of the smaller pirate ships, already hanging back in the armada's sorry excuse for a formation, stopped pretending and ran for it.

"Rolfson," she snapped. "Don't let them run. If we're going to gut piracy in this region, let's do it right."

Her tactical officer nodded, a disturbingly cold smile on his face as he sequenced his missiles.

"Ki!Tana." Annette turned to her alien companion. "Do we have detailed-enough scans to pick up *Subjugator*'s reactors? Can we disable like we did *Fang*?"

"She has an antimatter core," the A!Tol replied slowly. "Hitting that would blow her to hell—but it can only energize her beams, her shields, *or* her drives. Take out her fusion cores and Forel is out of options."

"Download the details to my console," Annette ordered. "Kurzman, I need the rainshowers. We're going to have to take the next salvo on the shields—Metharom, be prepared for damage control!"

A moment later, nine blinking red lights appeared on her schematic of *Subjugator*, and a set of control icons for the rainshower defenders and their plasma cannons appeared on her command chair screens. It took her a moment to familiarize herself with them and find the option she needed—a moment in which *Subjugator*'s beams found and *held Tornado*.

"Breaking!" Amandine snapped, twisting the ship into a spiral that would have killed them all if *Tornado*'s interface drive weren't inertialess. The shield failed, a localized collapse that allowed the proton beams through—but the navigator had acted in time and one beam missed completely.

The other scattered along the top of the hull, reflecting from the compressed-matter armor but also destroying the emitters for one of *Tornado*'s proton beams and an entire bank of rainshower defender cannons.

Annette reprogrammed her attack in silence, hoping she still had enough, and then hit *execute*.

Every plasma cannon on her ship and the attending drones swiveled to one target and fired. The defenders weren't designed as offensive weapons. Even the relatively light armor the pirate ships carried would prevent them damaging the ship—but firing *every* cannon created a wall of superheated plasma that slammed into *Subjugator*'s already-depleted shields.

The pirate heavy's shields collapsed. They wouldn't be down for long—but that was *exactly* what Annette had been planning for. Each of her remaining proton beams fired rapidly: narrow beams, short pulses lasting less than a tenth of a second. Each beam mount had three targets.

A moment later, *Subjugator*'s shields came back up...but her drive didn't and her beams stopped firing.

"Her reactors are down," Ki!Tana snapped. "What now?"

"Amandine, Rolfson," Annette ordered. "Take us in on the rest of the Armada—let's finish these bastards.

"Then I want to have a chat with Karaz Forel."

WARNING icons flashed across Annette's command chair screens and the bridge's main screen, warning of shield overload as dozens of missiles she'd chosen to ignore slammed home. Reversing course took them deeper into that swarm and the warnings flashed from orange to red, "shield failure imminent" flashing across the bottom of Annette's screens.

With the rainshower defenders returned to their true purpose, however, the impacts stopped. Instead of taking eighty missiles on the shield and hoping, the rapidly cycling plasma shotguns were blasting seventy-plus of them to vapor, leaving only two or three of each salvo to hit *Tornado*'s weakened but intact shield.

Still in control of the proton beams, Annette linked Rolfson's targeting data to her screen and went after the ships his latest salvos were ignoring. The smaller pirate ships were *all* running now, sending missiles back at the Terran cruiser in a desperate attempt to buy them time.

If any of them had run at the beginning, she would have been more merciful. But every single one of those ships had joined Forel in turning on her. The Indiri had clearly had his contingency plan in place from the beginning, waiting for Annette to step out of line—and not a single sapient from the crews of over *fifty* ships had so much as tried to sell that information to her.

Her proton beams cut into the heavier ships, focusing fire on the handful of surviving vessels that could, if you squinted, be warships. Their shields couldn't stand up to Rolfson's missile salvos, let alone the proton beams she lashed them with. Ship after ship detonated as *Tornado* wreaked her revenge.

"I have hyperspace portals opening," Rolfson announced. "The lead elements are escaping. What are your orders?"

Annette looked at the tactical plot, with its dozens of icons marking wrecked ships and dead crews, and finally, *finally* swallowed her anger. Fifty-two pirate ships had attacked the logistics base. *Forty* were debris and corpses.

"Maintain fire," she ordered, "but let any of them that reach the portals go. Our business is here with Forel, not in hyperspace with them."

Leaving the rest of the space battle to Rolfson, Annette opened a channel back to the logistics base behind her.

"Major Wellesley, what's your status?" she asked.

"Spread *very* thin," his perfectly cultured English accent replied a moment later. An echo of plasma fire and screaming followed him down the line. "Fortunately, it turns out the prisoners whose cells we picked a fight on top of were a couple of companies of the US and Chinese Armies. They have no training on plasma weapons, but *damn,* are they enthusiastic students.

"We are not secure," he warned her, "but I think we will be."

"We'll be back in orbit shortly," Annette advised him. "We can supply fire from on high at that point."

"Don't rush on our account," Wellesley replied. "I think the Americans might get cranky if I don't let them kill something. Your countrymen are *angry.*"

Annette smiled, a halfhearted chuckle escaping her.

"Understood," she told him. "We still need to deal with Forel."

"Good luck."

She accepted his comment with a nod and cut the channel. Scanning her bridge, she saw the plot was now clear of hostile ships except for *Subjugator*.

"Take us back to our Indiri friend," she ordered. "Prep the proton beams. How many shuttles and weapons do we still have aboard?"

"Two shuttles, enough weapons to equip thirty or so volunteers," Ki!Tana replied instantly. "We have those volunteers already."

"All human or..." Annette asked.

"The nonhumans aboard this ship are loyal to you now," the A!Tol told her. "A third of the volunteers are other races."

"Get them equipped," she ordered. "We'll see what Captain Forel says once we summon him to surrender."

Tornado flipped in space in a maneuver that would have been flatly impossible without an inertialess drive and charged back toward the pirate ship.

"Captain, Forel is hailing us," Chan reported.

"On screen."

Karaz Forel's familiar ugly face filled the main bridge screen again, but this time his focus wasn't as narrow. The view encompassed his entire bridge, part of which was still sparking from what appeared to have been an overloaded conduit.

"Hold your fire, Captain Bond," he snapped. "I surrender. We need to talk. In person. And no matter what you think of me, realize that I have human slaves aboard this ship."

Annette paused—froze, really. That...made sense of all of his oddities, and she could now *see* two humans in the background. Both were burly men with gold-colored collars around their necks, working at putting out the remnants of the conduit fire.

"Your surrender is accepted for now," she finally told him. "I will be arriving with armed crew shortly. You will be prepared to turn all of those human slaves over to me on my arrival. If you do so, it will buy you five minutes to talk fast enough to save your pathetic life."

"YOU REALIZE THIS IS A TRAP."

Ki!Tana's comment wasn't a question. The big A!Tol was busy strapping several weapons to a webbing harness that wrapped around her body and helped cover her skin, preventing her emotions from being immediately visible to everyone around her.

"Most likely," Annette agreed. While Wellesley hadn't acquired power armor for anyone other than his boarding teams, they *had* acquired some very advanced-looking unpowered armor on Tortuga. *Tornado*'s Captain locked the front and back plates of the set into place and let the straps auto-cinch.

"But Forel won't play if I don't go," she noted. A submachine gun and pistol, both the old UESF issue she was comfortable with rather than the more powerful weapons she wasn't used to, went onto her own harness. "Which, given that I need to rescue those humans, leaves me no other option.'

She paused.

"Plus, I'm curious what the bastard has to say," she admitted. "If he's been selling 'exotic slaves' for a while, I wonder how many were humans—and where he got them."

"Your curiosity will not be satisfied if you are dead," Ki!Tana pointed out. "You now control this system. The largest pirate raid in recent history and all of the loot is now yours. Forel's only chance of salvaging his prize, his reputation, or his *pride* is to kill you."

"Killing me won't gain him any of those," Annette replied. "Rolfson would just blow *Subjugator* to hell."

"You will never think like a pirate," her companion replied. "That is why your crew, human and the rest alike, will follow you. But Forel *does*—and he thinks killing you will buy him power over your crew."

"We just killed most of the pirates in this region," she told the A!Tol. "I'm surprised you're not more concerned by that."

"Captain Bond, you may well have killed *piracy* in this region," Ki!Tana told her, what was visible of her skin flushing light red in amusement. "But as I told you, I am more concerned with boredom than anything else. I see you becoming many things—but never boring."

"So, Forel will betray us," Annette accepted. "But if we expect that, we can string him out, get some answers out of him. *Watch him*," she ordered Ki!Tana. "You can read him better than we can. Don't hesitate to shoot first."

"What about your answers?" Ki!Tana asked.

"I want them," she admitted. "But I want that red-furred toad chained or dead when this ends more. Is that an order I can give you, Ki!Tana?"

"You command my life, my skill and my knowledge," the ancient alien next to her said softly. "Not my death. This falls under 'staying alive', I believe."

"At some point, I want to *see* this contract," Annette told her companion.

"Of course," the A!Tol told her. "But for now, focus on Karaz Forel. This will not be easy."

CHAPTER FORTY-EIGHT

"I BELIEVE THE MAP SAYS THE CENTRAL CONTROL CENTER IS just down this block of corridors," Hughes told James. "But I came under fire as I approached, and not from Imperials."

"Project the map," James ordered the specialist.

A moment later, Hughes's helmet lit up as the mounted holoprojector projected a three-dimensional image of the chunk of the facility they were in into the air. A large circular room flashed in orange, their target, with a number of corridors leading to its two entrances.

"Set up well," James noted. "Easily accessed from everywhere, but choke points here and here." He tapped the two points where the corridors converged. "I'm guessing our pirate friends are trying to break in?"

"It appears so," Hughes confirmed. "I didn't get much of a count, but there were at least eight or nine suits of armor and many in body armor."

"This is probably the last major concentration of both sides," James murmured, considering the overall situation. Most of the base defenders, the Imperial ground troops, were dead. There were a few pockets of resistance, but so far, he'd left them alone. The A!Tol soldiers weren't going anywhere.

Their *non*-solders, the civilians and Navy who ran the base, were still scattered throughout the facility. Some were armed, many weren't, and the roving groups of pirates were still following their no-prisoners order. Most were probably unaware of the battle above or how utterly screwed they were.

The well-organized group in front of him, however, was almost certainly aware of events in orbit. It was the single largest concentration of troops left, including teams from *Subjugator*. Despite the destruction of the armada above, they were still trying to break into the command center. Most of the surface weaponry was gone, but access to the surveillance systems—systems the defenders had too few troops left to use to their full potential—would tip the balance against the Terrans in this knife fight.

"What are we waiting for?" the burly young American with him demanded in a thick Southern drawl. "We go right after the fuckers, burn them out and take that center."

James studied the map for a long moment.

"What's your name, son?" he asked.

"What?" the noncom seemed confused.

"Name and rank," James snapped. Full Officer Tone brought the American to a crisp ready stance.

"Staff Sergeant Dave McQueen, US Army," he crisply recited.

"Good lad. You have family back home?" the SSS officer asked gently.

Dave swallowed.

"A sister," he admitted. "Harry's"—he gestured to one of the other volunteers—"wife. I might forgive him for that someday."

"You want to go home," James told him. "I want you to get home. So, I have *no* intention of trying to take these people out with a human wave attack, plasma guns or no plasma guns. Understand me, son?"

"Yes, sir," he conceded. "Just...so pissed, sir."

THE TERRAN PRIVATEER   391

"Rightly so," James conceded. "But I bet your sister would rather you got home alive, don't you?"

The young noncom nodded, and his gaze went to the map.

"Sir," he said slowly, "if the tentacled guys are holding the command center, then they're the ones holding the choke point, right?"

"Yes..."

"So, the pirates are *in* the choke point, shoved up against the locals? So, we can be in"—Dave waved a hand through the air—"*all* of these corridors and shoot at them?"

Seven corridors connected to the closer entrance to the control center. Each was wide enough for half a dozen humans or three power-armor suits abreast. The choke point corridor the pirates were assaulting was the same size, limiting how many of them could attack —or defend from behind.

"That was my own thinking as well," James agreed. "Still no cover, though, and we're playing with weapons that will burn your unarmored boys alive."

"But your people have the armor suits," Dave pointed out. "We can use *you* for cover."

Tornado's landing force commander blinked, glanced around his people, and smiled coldly. Charlie Troop had joined up with his HQ section. Even with their losses, he had twenty-two humans and aliens in power armor, one more than he needed.

"I *thought* you were a little young for a Sergeant," he told the American. The stripes had apparently come for brains, which was *not* what one would have expected from the burly Louisianan soldier on first impression. "Well done.

"All right, people," he barked. "Gather around. We've got ourselves a plan, thanks to the young Sergeant here."

THE TIMING HAD to be perfect. Even the power armor could only take a handful of shots from the plasma weapons carried by the unarmored infantry, let alone the cannons in the hands of the pirate suits. If one corridor's team attacked first, they'd be overwhelmed before the rest of the teams could intervene.

James found himself at the back of one of the teams, coordinating everyone via the maps and communicators in his helmet. No one was willing to let the company commander lead from the front this time around.

He ran up the distances on the helmet map, checked the location of each of his seven hastily assembled teams, and then started issuing orders.

"Teams one through four, go now. Five through seven, hold twenty seconds then go, starting …now."

Spread out through the base, his people and their new American and Chinese friends charged through the corridors, the power-armored Special Space Service troopers slowing from the breakneck pace the suits would have allowed, to let the unarmored infantry keep up.

Even from behind, James knew the moment they made contact. The cacophony of dozens of plasma rifles opening up simultaneously echoed from the front: twenty-one plasma cannons in the hands of his power armor, and then another dozen lighter weapons from the unarmored infantry behind each wall of troopers.

"Grenade out!" Sherman bellowed, Charlie's Troop Captain leading his team four. Louder explosions echoed, followed by another flurry of plasma fire—and then silence.

"Let me through," James ordered as he squeezed carefully forward through his people. Finally, he entered the small open area where the tunnels converged into the choke point.

The path forward was clogged with smoke, bodies and debris. Two of his power-armored troopers were sitting on the edge of the room, receiving rough and ready medical attention as the others set up to cover the entrance to the control center.

"Any peep from the A!Tol?" he asked Sherman. He hadn't seen anything on the automatic reports the suits gave him, but that didn't mean anything compared to the eyes and ears of the woman on the front.

"I *think* they realized what was going on and opened fire from their own side," she told him. "Can't be sure, though."

"Well, time to play diplomat," James sighed. He stepped forward to the corridor leading toward the control center for the A!Tol base. He set his translator to project in A!Tol and leaned against the wall, just out of the line of fire down the corridor.

"Hello in there," he shouted. "Is there somebody in there with authority to talk to me?"

There was silence for a moment, though he could hear shifting through the smoke and the crackling of the small fires.

"I am Brigade Commander Kashel," a voice his computer informed him was A!Tol—he certainly couldn't see the speaker—replied. "Who are you?"

"I am Major James Wellesley of the privateer *Tornado*," James told her. "Now, I'm not going to pretend we're here to rescue you. We came with these idiots, but as you can tell, we had a slight difference of opinion with them.

"I am not here to kill anyone, but the truth is you had fifteen thousand human prisoners in this base, neatly packaged up for the slavers we came with. So, right now, the only nonhumans on this rock I'm not at least *willing* to kill are the ones working for *me*.

"If you're in a surrendering mood, Brigade Commander, it so happens I'm listening. But if you're in a dying one, I am prepared to oblige you."

James smiled tightly. He need the controls and computers in the surveillance center to end this mess *quickly*, but with the troops who'd volunteered out of those slaves, the day *was* going to end with him in control of the base.

One way or another.

His only answer was silence for a long moment. He was gesturing

Sherman to him, about to prepare for a final push, when a response finally cut through the smoke.

"What guarantee do I have that my people will be safe?" Kashel demanded.

"I am the second son of the Duke of Wellington," James said harshly. "For fourteen generations, my fathers and mothers have guarded the realm we serve. By my family's honor, you will not be harmed."

Silence, then, finally:

"We are laying down our weapons, Major Wellesley," Kashel told him. "I trust the lives of my people to your honor."

THE SMOKE slowly began to clear as James approached the door to the control center. At some point, the security hatch had clearly been blown off with explosives, and it now lay flat on the ground, forming an additional obstacle on the already-dangerous ground.

Two A!Tol stood in that door, each slowly removing the complex interlinked plating that made up the power armor for the many-tentacled species. Their weapons were already on the ground, and one gestured for James to go past them with a free manipulator tentacle.

He walked into the control center and *felt* the sense of desperation that filled the room. The survivors—there was no better word for them—all looked to him and the power-armored soldiers following him. Weapons were tossed in a pile just inside the door. Over a dozen aliens from four different species were receiving medical attention in a corner, and plasma burns and bullet holes marked much of the equipment.

"Take over the consoles," James ordered his people. "Connect with our mobile forces, sweep the base. I want the last of Forel's people dead or chained inside an hour."

"On it," Sherman replied, leading the alien members of her team to the computers. The uniformed aliens manning them stepped back, clearly staying out of the way of the invaders while looking at them with shell-shocked gazes.

"Who is Kashel?" James demanded. An A!Tol in the center of the room slowly approached him, waving manipulator tentacles to draw attention.

"I am," she replied, purple and black flickering across her skin—fear and stress. "I am the senior surviving officer of this base, originally the second-in-command."

"I need you to order the rest of your people to stand down and shelter in place," he told her. "We will use your surveillance to neutralize the remaining pirates and take full control of this facility, but I cannot guarantee your people's safety until we have taken them into custody."

"I have passed on the surrender order," she replied. "I wish no more death. Why are you even here?"

"I am here because you tentacled bastards conquered my planet, took thousands of my people as slaves, and left us no other choice but to turn pirate to honor our oaths," James said flatly. "I promised you would not be harmed and I will keep that promise—but you better have a damned good explanation for the fact that there were *fifteen thousand* humans in this base ready to be captured."

Her tentacles fluttered in a confused swirl.

"I have no explanation, Major Wellesley," the A!Tol finally replied. "I was aware of no such prisoners. The sector I presume you found them in was locked down under my commander's orders for a classified special project.

"The A!Tol Imperium does not take slaves," she told him. "We certainly do not take slaves from worlds we are trying to peacefully absorb like yours. Those prisoners should not have been here."

"Then perhaps I need to *discuss* this with your commander," James said calmly. He might regret it later, but right now he was willing for said discussion to involve burning tentacles off one by one.

"She is dead," Kashel admitted. "She...met with the raiders—the other raiders, that is—in the secured compound. I do not know what she expected, but they shot her."

There *had* been a dead A!Tol among the aliens Forel's people had murdered.

"I have no answers for you, Major," she said. "Only the oath, on my Empress's honor, that whatever brought so many of your people here, it was not truly the action of her Navy or her Imperium."

Sherman had been standing next to James as this discussion concluded, and tapped his shoulder, linking in to a private channel.

"Do you buy this, sir?" she asked, the featureless helm of her armor focused on Kashel.

"It rings too neatly," he replied. "I mean…could Forel have been working with traitors in their Navy?"

"Didn't he say something about special friends?"

James shook his head and turned back to Kashel.

"You will not be harmed," he promised her. "But believe me, Brigade Commander, we *will* get to the bottom of this."

CHAPTER FORTY-NINE

Annette hid a smile when she saw Lieutenant Mosi leading the squad of armed volunteers on her shuttle. The young woman appeared to be bouncing back surprisingly well from her ordeal on Tortuga, though her Captain suspected that Mosi was hoping to be able to shoot a slaver in the face today.

They had more volunteers than they had weapons and unpowered armor, leaving Annette with only twenty-four people across two shuttles to take over an entire starship. It helped, of course, that she was leaving Rolfson behind in a position to start making even *bigger* holes in *Subjugator* if Forel started being problematic.

The trip between the two ships was uneventful, though there were a couple of heart-wrenching moments for Annette sitting in the cockpit as chunks of debris came flying at them and the pilot swerved to avoid with far too little notice. Between the wreckage of the defensive constellation, the wreckage of the A!Tol warships, and the wreckage of the pirate armada, the space around Orsav IV was getting dangerous.

The trip only lasted a few minutes, though, and Annette got a good view of *Subjugator* as they closed the last few kilometers. The big ship looked surprisingly undamaged, the pinpricks of the precisely focused proton beams that had disabled her looking almost minor from outside.

"Her shields are down and she isn't moving," Ki!Tana noted from behind her. "She's either charging capacitors for something or powering her weapons."

"I'm guessing weapons," Annette replied. "Let's hope Forel doesn't decide to be stupid."

A few more seconds passed, and the shuttles dove toward *Subjugator*'s central hull, where a blinking beacon was guiding them toward her main shuttle bay.

"Any sign of trouble?" she asked the pilot.

"Nothing so far; I have the bay doors on scanners and they are opening to receive us."

"Well. Let's go greet our 'friend' Captain Forel," Annette said calmly.

AT LEAST PART of the power was being used for the shuttle bay's lights. The entire space was lit up with massive banks of light, showcasing the well-maintained but dingy nature of the space.

Annette's people filed out of the shuttles slowly, weapons tracking to cover the entire space, which appeared to be occupied by a significant chunk of Forel's remaining crew. A large contingent of humans stood off to one side, all of them wearing the same gold-colored collars.

She noticed that about a quarter of the nonhuman crewmembers wore the same collar. Also slaves, most likely, with some kind of punishment mechanism in the collars wrapped around their throats.

Forel stood between the two groups of sapients, his webbed hands spread wide to show that he was unarmed. His fur looked slick in the bright light, and Annette shivered in the warm damp of *Subjugator*'s atmosphere.

"As you required, Captain Bond, the humans of my crew," he announced, gesturing to the collared men and women. "There were more, of course, before you so genteelly blasted holes through my ship."

"Mosi, grab them," Annette ordered. "Get those collars off them."

Forel went for his coat, then paused as Ki!Tana leveled the plasma rifle she'd brought on the Indiri.

"No sudden moves," the A!Tol warned. "I like Bond a lot more than I like you."

"Just the key," he promised, removing a golden block a centimeter or so across and ten long. He slid it across the floor to Mosi. "Press it to the back of the collars; it will release them."

Mosi picked up the key with a disgusted expression on her dark face but followed the Indiri's instructions on the closest of the humans. The collar popped off instantly, and the pale-skinned man rubbed his neck and looked at the young black woman.

"You may be the fairest angel I ever did see," he told her with a thick Irish accent. "Thankee kindly."

"Get on the shuttle," Annette ordered. She glanced at Forel. "You'll forgive me, Captain, if I remove them from this situation before we have the conversation you're so desperate to have."

"We can speak in my office," he offered. "I have food and drink you will find pleasant."

"We can speak here," she replied. "Under the guns of my people."

Forel shrugged. Like his smiles, it was a clearly artificial gesture—one his species' forward-bent shoulders didn't lend themselves to.

"Wait, Bond?" one of the freed slaves said as he was being shuffled toward the shuttle. "Annette Bond?!"

Annette turned at the sound of her name and recognized the speaker in turn. The almost-scrawny man in a blue jumpsuit with a shaven head was a *Nova Industries* employee.

"Jacob Harmon," she greeted him. "What are you doing here?"

"Long story involving *that*," he gestured at Forel, "and some tentacled bastards. But it started with *Hidden Eyes of Terra*."

"A conversation for later," Annette told him, wondering what exactly a Nova Industries sensor specialist was doing aboard *Subjugator*. "Go with Mosi for now."

"With pleasure," Harmon told her. "It is *damned* good to see you, Annette."

She waved him and the rest of the prisoners onto the shuttle. It was going to be a cramped fit with over forty of them, but she needed to keep a shuttle with her. Forel was being cooperative for now, but she wanted an easy escape route to hand.

Finally, full to the brim, the shuttle slowly eased its way back out of the hangar, then blurred away under interface drive. Forel's prisoners were gone, though Annette had no illusions: his crew might be unarmed, but this was *his* ship. Annette and her party of armed crew were effectively his hostages.

"With that out of the way," the Indiri said calmly, "can we talk? I have an offer for you—one I would have made earlier if your people hadn't started shooting."

"Fifteen thousand humans neatly boxed for pickup," Annette replied coolly. "If I wasn't curious as to where they came from, you'd be dead already. Talk."

"As I suspect you have realized by now, I do not work alone," Forel told her. "I am tied into an organization that sees the truth of Kanzi–A!Tol relations: that both are monsters who need to be stopped.

"I understand your reaction to the slaves," he continued. "My own life partner was kidnapped by Kanzi—and when I finally had the resources to try and rescue her, I learned she was dead. A cross-border raid, one of half a dozen in any given year, though more successful than most." He shrugged. "The Imperium tries, but they warn us they cannot stop every raid. That they could not save her."

"I fail to see how your sob story leads here, to the ship full of slaves," Annette replied dryly.

"I realized then, as others have realized before me and after me, that this half-war could not continue," Forel said. "I found those others and they had a plan. Through me, they found the resources to fund their plan." He shrugged. "I am not blind to the failure inherent in funding my campaign to avenge my partner by kidnapping and selling others—mostly humans, a race no one in the Imperium knew to miss—into slavery.

"But the research we had stolen was enough for our scientists to complete their work," he told her. "I can give you a weapon that will guarantee Earth's freedom and independence: a starkiller."

"A single starkiller would do no such thing," Ki!Tana objected. "They are massive things, difficult to deploy. Half the reason no one uses them is that they're easily stopped."

"Not the ones we built," Forel said. "A missile-scale weapon, easily able to penetrate the defenses of a star system and detonate the sun. *Think*, Captain Bond. I can give you all of the schematics I promised you. I can deliver to you a starkiller missile, allow you to claim Earth's freedom at the point of a fiery sword!"

Annette didn't need to see Ki!Tana's skin to know her alien companion was shocked and horrified. But...Earth had kept the peace for almost a century via the concept of mutually assured destruction. The possession of an unstoppable superweapon might just buy her homeworld its independence.

"In exchange for what?" she asked slowly.

The red-furred amphibious alien made a broad gesture toward the planet beneath them.

"We made a deal," he told her. "A deal to sell thirty thousand exotic slaves, a bipedal species the Kanzi had never seen before, to the High Inquisitor himself. With a passport from him, one we can only get by allowing his representatives to *see* the slaves, we can fly our ship into the Kanzi Core Worlds—and deploy the weapons.

"In a single strike, seven of their most important star systems wiped out—destroyed by weapons that are unquestionably A!Tol.

The war that *must* be fought will begin, with the Kanzi already weakened."

In a human, his enthusiasm and fire would have been fanaticism. Annette wasn't sure the description was any different in an Indiri.

"You want to start a war," she repeated.

"Yes!" Forel confirmed. "The A!Tol and the Kanzi will tear each other down. Your world can rise from the ashes, independent and strong. All of our peoples will be free from the yoke of those two monsters!"

The image in Annette's head was...much less positive. She hadn't lived in the era of mutually assured destruction, but she'd studied it. Once one side used—or appeared to use!—weapons of mass destruction, the other wouldn't hesitate. The A!Tol and Kanzi would devolve into a war where stars died on a daily basis. Their empires wouldn't gently fall, liberating their client and slave races. Their empires would be *exterminated*, client and slave races included.

And Earth, latest client of the A!Tol, on the border of the war...a single weapon wouldn't be enough. An entire *Navy* wouldn't be enough.

"You said thirty thousand humans," she pointed out, buying herself time to think. "There weren't that many here."

"The rest have already been shipped to our base," Forel replied. "These are the ones who were in transit when Tan!Shallegh locked down all of the fleet transports; someone on Earth noticed what was going on."

He was closer to her now, the fire now bright in his immense eyes.

"Please, Captain Bond," he half-begged. "We *must* see this through. The sacrifices *will* be worth it once we're free!"

"You're mad," she whispered. "You'd bring down both empires and both of our *species* in your quest for revenge!"

"It will work!" he promised her. "With a starkiller and the tech I can give you, Earth can stand aside—a beacon of hope as the galaxy goes mad. Your species will emerge one of the leading powers of the new age to come! Is that not worth some sacrifice?"

Annette had to stop, swallowing down a moment of incandescent rage. Sacrifice was pushing for a rapist to meet justice, *knowing* it would end her career. Sacrifice was walking away from the man she wanted to love, *knowing* he'd come to her broken and needed to stand on his own. Sacrifice was leaving her home behind and taking up exile in the hope of returning a liberator.

Sacrifice was not sending thirty thousand *other* people into slavery and potential death. That was *murder*.

"No," she told him flatly. "Your plan is madness and I will have no part in it! You will give me the coordinates of that base, Karaz Forel, or I will end you here and now."

She knew he was mad, but she still expected *some* kind of sign before he moved. Some kind of hint that she or Ki!Tana could pick up, stop Forel acting.

There was none. One moment he was looking up at her with his strange fake smile, and the next he was *still* looking up at her with the smile—with some kind of energy blade in his hand.

It *spun* in his hand in an overhand strike that would have cleaved her head in two if not for *years* of martial arts and combat practice. She stumbled backward even as she yanked her submachine gun from its holster.

Then *fire* cut her face, *agony* flaring in her head as the blade slashed through her skin and bone and she *felt* her eye come apart and blindness take her.

But muscle memory still worked despite the pain, the gun ripping free from its harness and slamming forward into Forel's stomach. With blood pouring into her one remaining eye, she couldn't *see* him —but she could *feel* the resistance of his body as the muzzle collided with his flesh.

She pulled the trigger.

She didn't release it before unconsciousness took her.

CHAPTER FIFTY

Annette woke to darkness.

It wasn't a lack of light. It was a lack of...*anything*. She tried to blink and her eyelids refused to respond. She tried to move—and her arms and legs twitched, and then came up against restraints.

"Captain, you're awake," a smoothly educated voice noted aloud. "Please, do not attempt to move. I have blocked your facial nerves and that could easily have other impacts. Can you speak?"

"Yesth," she managed to squeeze out past numb lips, recognizing the voice of *Tornado*'s South African chief surgeon, Doctor Jelani.

"Let me try something," Jelani told her. A moment later, her jaw spasmed, an electric shock running through her system.

"Try now. Is that better?"

Annette moved her jaw and tongue.

"Yes," she said. "How bad, doctor?"

"You passed out from blood loss," Jelani told her, his voice professionally soothing and calm. "Ki!Tana was able to put pressure on the wound immediately and *Subjugator*'s crew provided every assistance they could."

"How bad?" she demanded.

He sighed.

"You've been out for twenty-six hours," he told her. "We had patients who were going to die without immediate attention, so we slapped a seal on your face and put you in a medical coma. I apologize."

"Don't. Right call. How bad?" she repeated.

He chuckled.

"Every bone on the right side of your face, from the frontal skull down to your jawbone, has a slice between seven and fifteen millimeters deep," he told her calmly. "Your right eye was cut clean in two and your optic nerve on that side severed in two separate places. Your jawbone was cut through, but the rest of your skull is mostly intact.

"I focused on the jawbone initially, which is why you can speak," he continued. "The bone-knitting nanites are busy in the rest of your face, and are filling in the matrix in your jaw. You have a bandage and half a dozen stimulators covering half of your face—and they are staying on for at *least* two more days."

"And the eye?" she finally asked.

Jelani sighed.

"We had seventy-three fatalities and a hundred and eighty-two wounded from this whole affair," he told her gently. "Our regeneration matrix supplies are at critical levels; we can regenerate them still, but we're nearing the point where we may not have enough base stock for that."

The "regeneration matrix" required for rebuilding human organs and limbs was basically a slurry of undifferentiated stem cells. Given the right food—and unlike her crew, the stuff *loved* Universal Protein —it could double its mass in twenty-four hours.

"So, you can give me back my eye if I'm willing to risk not being able to save someone's life down the line," she interpreted aloud.

"I would not be so blunt, but yes," Jelani allowed.

"Then why are we talking about it?" she asked. "Get me a uniform and an eyepatch. Seems to fit the job description, anyway."

"A uniform? Captain, please! There were worse injuries aboard, but do not make the mistake of thinking you were *uninjured*. You need to rest and recover."

Images of a war of mutual annihilation ran through the mental eyes that were all Annette currently commanded.

"You have two choices, Doctor," she told him gently. "You can get me a uniform and watch me walk out of here, or you can pull all of my senior officers into an infirmary room to brief me."

"My dear Captain Bond, will you accept how badly you are injured if I agree to the latter?"

THEY COMPROMISED by having one of the nurses help Annette into a uniform and roll her sickbed into the conference room normally used for coordinating *Tornado*'s medical staff. It wasn't truly big enough for *all* of Annette's senior officers, especially not with Ki!Tana's immense bulk, but they managed to make it work.

"All right," Annette told her people, looking them over with her remaining eye. None of them tried to avoid her gaze, which was impressive. *She* would have, having seen what she looked like in a mirror. Half of her face was covered in white gauze, and the half that wasn't was still partially paralyzed.

But she could see again, and her people looked back at her.

"I need status updates from everyone," she continued, "but let's start with Major Wellesley. How are things on the surface?"

The SSS Major looked utterly exhausted. He didn't appear injured, but he also didn't appear to have slept. He had always been skinny with his height, but right now his face was gaunt. Nonetheless, he brushed his hair back from his forehead with one hand and smiled in grim accomplishment.

"As of a little over two hours ago, the last remnants of the landed pirates have either surrendered or been wiped out," he reported. "Brigade Commander Kashel has been about as cooperative as you can expect from a senior prisoner, and her people have been...unresisting.

"We are fully in control of the logistics base," he concluded. "We're sorting through volunteers from the prisoners now, but it looks like we'll have a short battalion: four companies including mine, if we want it.

"Everyone else just wants to go home."

"I get that. Can we load them onto some of the robot freighters and send them there?" Annette asked. "It seems the easiest way."

"We should be able to," Wellesley confirmed. "We're going to need to recruit them as a labor force to load the other freighters, in any case. We were, after all, expecting to have an entire *fleet's* worth of personnel to do that work."

"See if we can sort out some way to pay them," Annette instructed. "That should help avoid any feeling that we're using them as forced labor before we send them home.'

"We will," Wellesley promised. "If we get the volunteers I expect for that, we should have all of the ships ready to head wherever we want them to go, Earth or Tortuga, inside seventy-two hours."

"Make it faster if you can," she told him. "And if you can pull together that battalion, do so. We might need it."

"Yes, ma'am."

Annette turned to Ki!Tana and Lieutenant Mosi. "What about *Subjugator?*"

"The good news is Forel is dead," the young black officer replied. "You emptied your gun into him before you collapsed; he was never getting up again. Unfortunately, he'd rigged a deadman switch; the ship's computers blew apart when he died.

"*Subjugator* is not repairable, though we have been looting her for missiles and parts," she concluded. "The slave crewmembers have volunteered to join us to a being, and we've shipped the rest to the surface to join the rest of the pirate prisoners."

"Ki!Tana." Annette looked at their old pirate friend. "*Can* we still send our cargos to Tortuga? Will Ondu still sell them for us?"

"For twenty-two percent of the entirety of a logistics base?" Ki!Tana asked. "Ondu will sell them for you and make sure the accounts are held until you retrieve them. We would not be *welcome* on Tortuga at this point, but we would not be denied entrance."

"I want *Subjugator* stripped from top to bottom," Annette ordered. "I need two things from her, people: One, I want the schematics Forel promised us. There may well have been a copy on a chip somewhere. If there is, I want it.

"Two: the son of a bitch was working with others. They had a plan to start a war." She shivered. "Now, I don't like *anyone* on their target list, but Earth's right in the middle. Plus, whether or not their plan will still work, they've got *fifteen thousand* human slaves in their base, wherever it is.

"I need to know where that base is, people. We may be able to negotiate with this conspiracy. We may end up doing the A!Tol a favor and blowing them all to hell. But we can't do either without knowing *where* we're going."

"I would prefer that you not negotiate," Ki!Tana admitted. "Such a war would see my race annihilated, and I am somewhat attached to my species."

"I haven't made up my mind up yet," Annette admitted in turn, "but I'm not leaning toward letting them finish their plan."

She turned to Metharom, *Tornado*'s engineer.

"Now, Kulap, if we do find them, what state are we in to deal with them?" she asked.

"The armor mostly held," Metharom replied. "But we did take a point-blank salvo of interface drive missiles. At that range, they were only moving at about forty percent of lightspeed, but that was bad enough.

"We've got twenty missile launchers online. That's all you're getting. We have three proton beams online. I think we can cannibalize one of the others to get the last two online in a couple of days."

"So, we're short a sixth of our weaponry, at least," Annette accepted. "Shields, engines?"

"Fully functional. We can fly and we can fight, but we've lost some teeth."

"It will have to do," she admitted. "Is there anything else I should be aware of, people?"

ONCE SHE'D BEEN RELEASED from Doctor Jelani's tender ministrations, Annette managed to get herself back to her quarters under her own power. Once there, she took the pills he'd given her—painkillers, since the process of having her bones reknit was *not* pleasant—and settled down looking at her wallscreen.

With a few commands on a flimsy computer, she mirrored the display and brought up an astrographic map of the region.

Orsav, known to humanity as Lambda Aurigae, had been one of the systems their initial sweeps had guessed as a new colony, only a few flights into the system during the scope of their lightspeed scans of the worlds around Sol.

Most of the other systems they'd pegged as colonies had shown up. The concentration of routes they'd thought was a fleet base—that was Kimar, home base to three squadrons of Imperial ships of the line and their escort ships.

There were misses both ways, of course. Systems that weren't on A!Tol records they'd shown traffic to, which could be *anything*, and systems on the A!Tol records that had been settled too recently for the Dark Eye and the scout-ship sweeps to pick up anything.

The odd thing was the complete absence of settlements inside a roughly forty-light-year radius of Sol in A!Tol records. There were even habitable planets that had been detected, but no one had colonized them. It was too neat and too large a gap to be coincidence, and she made a mental note to ask Ki!Tana about it.

In all likelihood, Forel's sponsors had hidden their facility inside a system colonized by the A!Tol. Money could cover a lot of sins,

Annette was sure, and having a colony nearby would have allowed them to call on it for labor and help.

Except.

Except that they had fifteen thousand human slaves, and many of those couldn't have been kidnapped since the fall of Earth. Annette suspected she knew—now—why the UESF had been having so many difficulties with pirates in the outer system: even *Subjugator* would have had the drives and sensors to avoid any encounters with the patrol ships hunting the people stealing entire ships and their crews.

Had the slaves been a plan all along? Or had Earth simply been *available* after they'd built their secret lab, and so they'd kidnapped humans as a convenience? And then, once they needed a way through the Kanzi borders...

She sighed. It was a sickening feeling. Her people hadn't been victimized because of anything they'd done or any special value. They'd just been convenient. Close to their secret base.

Close to a secret base run by a faction of the A!Tol military—and hence a base a Terran scout ship could have stumbled upon.

Annette leapt to her feet to grab her communicator, only to misjudge everything due to the missing eye and end up *crashing* to the floor. With, thankfully, the communicator in her hand.

Groaning, she forced herself into a sitting position.

"Mosi," she pinged the young officer who'd briefed her on the decision by Forel's slaves to join her crew. "Are all of Forel's ex-slaves aboard?"

"Yes, ma'am."

"Find Jake Harmon," she ordered. "Find him and send him to me."

———

MOSI ARRIVED LESS than ten minutes later with the scrawny Nova Industries man in tow. Harmon was looking at the young black woman with star-struck eyes, a feeling Annette suspected was shared among the human slaves Mosi had cut free.

At the sight of Annette, however, the fair-haired young NI officer managed to pull his gaze away from Mosi as he visibly tried not to gasp in horror.

"My god, ma'am, you look like hell," he told her.

"I appreciate the honesty, Jake, though I thought you had a better idea of how to butter a lady up," she said with a gentle grin. "Have a seat." She gestured to a chair across her desk. After her abortive attempt to grab the communicator, she didn't try to stand.

He sat, looking at her expectantly, then sighed.

"I guess you want to know how a middle-manager sensor specialist in Nova Industries ended up a slave on an alien pirate ship?" he asked.

"Among other things," she confirmed. "How are you settling in aboard *Tornado*? I'm hoping someone has filled you in on our story?"

"Yeah." Harmon shook his head. "Hard to absorb it all, but your people have been good at filling us in. It's quite a story, ma'am. Bit of a leap from flying test ships for Casimir, huh?"

"The way we keep upgrading her, it doesn't feel all that different some days," Annette told him. "Though it appears Casimir was even better at keeping secrets than I thought—I didn't even know the extra scout ships *existed*."

"You knew Casimir," Harmon said quietly. "He could sell water to a fish. Selling a bunch of us already tied up in the BugWorks projects on signing up for a secret survey mission? That was *easy*." He laughed.

"I don't even know where they were built," he admitted. "But after drinking the boss's Kool-Aid, I ended up as science officer and second-in-command of the survey ship *Hidden Eyes of Terra*.

"We were doing sweeps of three systems at a time and then going home. Three of those sweeps went by with no problems at all, so we were doing a shorter, two-system sweep to go out even farther.

Heading out along the galactic arm, farther away from where we already knew *somebody* was."

He shivered. "First system, empty. Some new EM pickups, but that was it. The *second* system, though...it looked empty at first brush, but part of our job was to survey the systems themselves as well.

"So, we checked them out. Bunch of dead rocks, one planet *very* early in the stage of developing single-cell life...and then we got too close to the gas giant. I don't know what we did—they must have *thought* we'd seen something, but we didn't see anything until the ships showed up.

"Two big bastards, size of the XC units, just appeared out of nowhere. Interface drive ships—I'd seen the early work-ups on the engines, so I knew what it was when the things just zipped up to us at half the speed of light and stopped on a dime."

He shrugged.

"We had two rifles aboard," he pointed out. "That was the extent of our weaponry, so we surrendered. Tentacled bastards boarded the ship and started slapping chains and collars on everyone." He touched his neck where the collar had been until the day before.

"They demonstrated what they did and then told us we were all property. We'd do as we were told or die. Captain Astley died," he said grimly. "Charged one of them and took a bolt of blue fire to the head. They split us up after that, but four of us ended up on *Subjugator*.

"We weren't even the first humans aboard. The others were crew from out-system mining ships, retrained on alien tech and forced to work or die." He shivered. "God, Captain, you have no idea how happy I was to see you walk off that shuttle. I'd given up seeing another human face not wearing a collar."

Annette tapped the flimsy on her desk, flipping the map she'd been studying earlier onto the screen.

"You were science officer," she said quietly. "You were helping navigate. My data from Casimir says you were at these two systems." They flashed yellow on the screen. "Both have *nothing* in A!Tol records; both have hyperspace trails, according to the scans from Dark Eye and *Oaths*.

"Were you transported from there before you ended up on *Subjugator*?" she asked him. "It's important, Jake."

The gaunt man stepped over to the wallscreen and tapped one of the two stars. "G-KXT-Three-Five-Seven," he identified it. "We were picked up here—and no, Captain Bond, we weren't transported elsewhere and sold. I was working on *Subjugator*'s bridge. We were above the same damn gas giant—and we went back there, a lot."

"That sounds about right, then," Annette said aloud. "Ready to go back one last time, Mister Harmon? There are still a lot of people locked up in that base."

"Give me a wrench, give me a comp, give me a rifle—whatever you need, Captain, I'm in. Those bastards owe me a year of my life, and I intend to take it back with interest."

ANNETTE WAS REVIEWING LOADING PLANS—A surprisingly boring ending to an immense pirate raid, though some of the items they were stealing were definitely eye-openers—at her desk when her communicator chimed.

"Ma'am, it's Chan," her communications officer announced. "The A!Tol base commander has asked to speak to you."

"Any idea why?" Annette asked. "I thought James's people had interrogated her already."

"We got everything she was willing to give us, we thought," Chan confirmed. "But she has asked to speak to you."

Annette was intrigued. The more she learned about the A!Tol, the more they intrigued her. If Earth's first encounter with them hadn't been an Imperial fleet demanding humanity's surrender, she suspected they would have worked well with the stiff, prickly and incurably honest creatures.

Ki!Tana's ability to get along with *Tornado*'s entire crew was a case in point, though the big alien female was always quick to point she was very atypical for her race.

"Have Wellesley's people get her a communicator," she ordered. "I may as well see what the Brigade Commander has to say."

"The Major thought you'd say that," Chan replied. "He's moved Kashel into an office and set up a communicator."

Annette shook her head, then gripped her desk fiercely as a moment of pain spasmed from her still-healing facial bones and disorientation from her single eye.

She exhaled sharply, then returned her attention to the moment.

"Put her through," Annette ordered. "Wallscreen in my office."

The screen on her wall flickered and the loading plans faded away into an image of a plain office that could probably have existed in any military base in the galaxy. It was a plain gray metal box, but it had a desk, a computer and one of the cupped stools the A!Tol used as seats.

"Captain Bond, I appreciate you speaking to me," Kashel greeted her. "I hope your wound does not pain you too much. It certainly looks severe."

"It is unpleasant," Annette admitted carefully. "I will recover. In time, we will even be able to replace my eye. Are your quarters satisfactory?" she asked the A!Tol in turn. "While it is necessary for me to imprison you and your personnel, I have no desire for you to be mistreated."

"They are our own barracks for transient personnel," the alien told her. "They are sufficient. And far better than the fiery annihilation that was your allies' intention for us."

"I did not know that was their intent," Annette said quietly.

"And still you saved us in the end," Kashel replied. "Despite my commander having betrayed your people and us. While she was betrayed in turn, she clearly knew her people were to be killed and agreed to this plan. Karaz Forel's reach stretched to places he should not have been able to touch."

"And now he is dead," the Terran Captain said. She wasn't sure where Kashel was going with this; the A!Tol's skin was a mix of orange, purple and black, but anger, stress and fear were normal reactions to being a prisoner. "What is it you want, Brigade Commander? You asked to speak to me."

"It is a matter of honor," the base commander replied. "You understand, I hope, that the kind of mass kidnapping that was carried out on Earth is not our normal policy."

"I accept, at least, that you believe that," Annette told her.

"Now that we are aware that these people are on this station, we have a moral obligation to see them home," Kashel told her. "Our single-use emergency hyperwave beacon was triggered when your armada arrived, though it will still be a five-cycle or more before a relief fleet arrives. That relief fleet, however, will have more than sufficient carrying capacity to take your people home."

Annette considered. There were two important pieces to Kashel's offer: one, the warning that there *was* a relief fleet coming, which wasn't valueless in itself; and two, the offer to transport the kidnapped humans home. That would free up the ships her loading plan noted for the humans for other tasks.

"You realize," she said noncommittally, "that your offer would allow us to load up all of your robot freighters with supplies and steal even *more* of the supplies you are sworn to protect."

"I do," Kashel answered steadily. "I am concerned, Captain, about the conditions you would have to transport those poor people in if you load them onto those freighters. If they work with us, we can make certain that everyone is cleaned up, checked over by doctors and well fed before we send them home.

"We owe them far more than that, but we can make sure they get home safely."

Kashel clearly regarded allowing Annette to leave with three or four more freighters of expensive military supplies as part of the payment of that debt. The offer had a lot of value...*if* Annette was willing to trust the A!Tol military.

"And if you betray me?" she demanded. "My people could be headed right back into slavery."

"Captain Bond, I was asked to trust the honor of your Major Wellesley when I surrendered my people," Kashel replied. "I did, and you have not disappointed me. It would betray my own honor to not repay oaths in kind.

"But regardless of that, the betrayal of your world's surrender is a black mark on the honor of my Empress." Kashel's skin muted to a dark green tone Annette had never seen on Ki!Tana—still marked with the orange of her anger and the purple of her stress, but now predominantly green. "Bringing your people home will only begin to erase that mark, but every step to erase it *must* be taken, Captain Bond.

"On the honor of my Empress, my Imperium, my uniform, and my own blood, I swear this to you: any of your people who remain here will be returned to Earth unharmed."

There was, really, no higher oath Annette could demand. She could either trust the squid-like creature in the screen or not. The choice, like so many others since her exile, was hers alone.

"Very well, Brigade Commander," she accepted. "I will place their lives in your manipulators. Fail me, and dishonor will *not* be your worst fear."

CHAPTER FIFTY-ONE

CAPTAIN ANDREW LOUGHEED THOUGHT OF HIMSELF AS A patient man, but finding himself once again in deep space, waiting on Captain Bond and *Tornado* without knowing the fate of the only warship the Terran privateers commanded, was straining his calm.

That was a large chunk of the reason he was studying the sensor plot of the deep space surrounding them from the desk in his quarters while Sarah Laurent watched him lazily from the bed, both of them naked.

"Even if everything went perfectly right, they had to load up the cargo and head out," his second in command told him. "We were always going to have to wait."

"It's been over three days," Andrew told her, dropping down onto the bed next to her. "*Tornado* should be here by now."

"Yes," she agreed. "Assuming everything went perfectly—and while things have been going our way, would you say *anything* has gone perfectly for us?"

He snorted.

"Last time I checked, we're still exiles without a home," he pointed out. "So, no."

"Bond will come," she told him, running her hand up his back. "She hasn't let us down yet."

With a sigh and a shake of his head, Andrew nodded. Grinning, he began to reach for Laurent—and then his intercom chimed.

"Sir," Strobel announced. "We have hyperspace portals forming —multiple portals. I'm reading at least forty, maybe more."

Shaking his head to regain his focus, Andrew rose and hit the button to reply.

"Any IDs yet?" he asked. He'd been expecting *one* ship, not a fleet—if the entire pirate armada was here, something had gone *very* wrong...

"No, sir. They're all in the right range that one of them *could* be *Tornado*, but..."

"Understood. I'll be on the bridge in two minutes."

He turned back to Sarah Laurent, to find that she'd risen and grabbed his uniform while he was checking in with the bridge. Their newfound relationship was against regs, but at this point...well, at this point, Andrew Lougheed wrote the regs for his ship.

They just couldn't let it get in the way of their jobs, and he nodded his thanks as he started to dress.

THE SHIPS HADN'T STOPPED EMERGING from hyperspace by the time Andrew reached his bridge, a little less than two minutes later. Forty-three ships, each a two-million-ton, six-hundred-meter monster, had emerged from hyperspace at the rendezvous point.

Of Course We're Coming Back and *Oaths of Secrecy* were both drifting cold and silent in space. While the new ships were close enough they'd be able to pick up the two scout ships easily, there had been no active sensor sweeps.

"Are they doing *anything*?" Andrew asked after studying the ships for a long moment. All of the ships so far were identical, though close enough in size to *Tornado* that he could see why Strobel had thought the cruiser might be there.

"Not much," Laurent told him. She'd only had a few seconds at her console herself—they hadn't bothered to arrive separately, *Of Course* being far too small a ship for everyone not to already know—but it was apparently enough for a first-cut analysis.

"They're emerging from their hyper portals, matching angles with each other and then stabilizing speed at one percent of light," she continued. "It's station-keeping...it's *automated* station-keeping."

"There were supposed to be robot freighters at Orsav," Andrew said aloud. "But...this would be *all* of them. What *happened?*"

"Last portals are closing," Laurent announced. "I have fifty-one contacts...wait...confirm. Contact fifty-one is *Tornado*. We're being pinged."

"Oh, thank gods," Andrew sighed. "Put Bond on."

The main viewscreen flickered and then settled onto the image of *Tornado*'s two-tiered bridge, centered on the figure of the cruiser's Captain. Annette Bond's uniform was perfect, her hair braided and pulled off to one side, everything in perfect place...so it took Andrew a moment to realize that her right eye was *gone* and a raw red line cut down that entire side of her face around a plain black eye patch.

"Captain Bond, what happened?" he demanded. A moment later, he heard Captain Sade ask the same question as a side window popped up on his screen, linking the other scout-ship captain into the conversation.

"Our friend Forel turned out to have his own objectives," Bond replied after a long moment. "A lot of his own objectives.

"We've prepared a briefing packet for both of you, but the long story short is that Forel was involved in a conspiracy to drag the A!Tol into an outright war with the Kanzi by destroying several Kanzi core systems. Since his plan involved a war with Terra in the middle of it and using about thirty *thousand* human slaves as his key into Kanzi space, we had a disagreement.

"The rest of the armada backed him and we blew them to dust

bunnies," she said grimly. "I left *Subjugator* with the A!Tol so *they* are fully aware of the conspiracy, but I am not prepared to accept any chance of that plan succeeding.

"I'll need both of you aboard *Tornado* for a planning session in four hours," Bond ordered. "I don't expect there to be any ships left in this empty corner of space in twelve."

EVEN WITH THE BRIEFING PACKET, they'd been in the meeting for over an hour before Andrew and Sade felt they'd really caught up with everything that had happened in Orsav after they'd left. Shaking his head at the mental image of *Tornado* taking on the entire pirate armada and *winning*, Andrew leaned back in his chair and studied the room.

All of *Tornado*'s senior officers were present, along with Ki!Tana and Jake Harmon. He and Sade were the only ones who weren't attached to the big cruiser and permanently under Bond's sway, and Andrew carefully considered how to phrase his question.

He respected Captain Bond, but he'd also watched her destroy a career many would have given their left arm for in pursuit of justice. She hadn't been *wrong*, but her determination to see things through could be excessive.

"Ma'am," he said slowly, addressing Bond directly, "I have to ask. Is this really our fight? No offense to Ki!Tana, but the A!Tol *conquered our world*. They are not our friends. And the Kanzi?" he shivered. "Blue-furred scum of the highest order. I'll shed no tears for their deaths.

"A war between them would weaken our conquerors and make liberating Earth easier. I'm no fan of atrocity, but there's a difference between committing mass murder and not killing ourselves trying to stop it!"

"The problem with that theory, Captain Lougheed," Bond replied, her remaining eye focusing on him, "is that Earth is on the front lines of the war Forel's sponsors want to start. The coreward border of both empires is with powers strong enough that flanking through their territory is impossible.

"To flank the defenses and the fleets each has prepared along their border, they would come through Sol. To pick an example from our history, Sol is Belgium—and the Kanzi will invade through us.

"Even were we to somehow convince ourselves that it was moral to stand by and watch—what, fifty billion Kanzi and as many slaves of a dozen races?—die, our homeworld would be ground to dust in the war to follow. We could easily see Sol be among the first targets of the Kanzi's starkillers."

Her single eye somehow managed to hold his gaze, looking into his soul before Andrew finally blinked and bowed his head.

"We still don't know what kind of defenses they have in place at this lab," he pointed out. "We could hand the coordinates over to the A!Tol and let them handle it. They have squadrons of capital ships, armies, all of the things we don't have."

"There are two things we have that the A!Tol don't," Bond told him. "We know where the lab is. We could tell the A!Tol that, but it wouldn't be easy for us and would cost time. And time is the other thing we have; we don't know how long the attack will be delayed if Forel is overdue. Even with the delay here, we will arrive only a few days at most later than he would have. An A!Tol force would be *weeks* behind."

She shook her head and Andrew nodded slowly.

"We are the only force in position to intervene, Andrew," Bond told him, her voice soft but firm. "It is possible, yes, that their defenders will be more than we can handle. But we are talking one hundred billion or more lives within weeks. *Trillions* inside years. We're talking about Earth herself being burned to a cinder as one more collateral casualty of a galactic war.

Bond's eye flashed as she looked around the room, and Andrew knew he wasn't the only one being measured.

"We were sent into exile to save Earth," she reminded them all.

"Ordered to abandon our world so that when the time came we could liberate her. Protect her.

"This isn't the mission we were sent into exile for," she allowed, "but we knew *nothing* about galactic society when we left Sol. We didn't even know we sat on the border between two great powers, let alone that someone would try and turn their cold war hot.

"If we let this happen, there may be no blood on *our* hands, but we will always know we could have stopped it. Earth might survive. But are we prepared to gamble on that? Are we prepared to bet the lives of our entire species on those odds?

"I am not," Bond said flatly. "And even if I was, there are fifteen thousand *humans* held captive in that base. We are going to free them. We are going to stop this goddamn war. We are going to make sure that our homeworld is *safe*."

Andrew wasn't leaning back in his chair anymore. He was leaning forward with everyone else. The one-eyed woman who led them knew *exactly* how to yank on her people's strings.

"All right," he told her. "I'm in." He shook his head. "I don't know where this ends, Captain Bond, but you're right: we have to free those people."

The room was silent for a long moment, tension slowly releasing. Andrew doubted he was the only one who hadn't been sure, who'd questioned taking on what really should have been the A!Tol's fight.

But Bond was right. It might be the Imperium's fight, but their home was still in the line of fire.

Which made it their fight, too.

ANNETTE WAITED out the silence after Lougheed's statement, meeting each of her senior officers' and junior Captains' eyes, making sure they were all in. She saw some hesitation, some uncertainty, but no objections. They'd come this far together; it seemed they'd go the rest of the way.

"Our other concern is the robot freighters," she reminded them all. "Ki!Tana—if we send them to Tortuga, is anyone going to raise a fuss over our claiming them all as our own?"

"Tortuga regards possession as ownership," the A!Tol pointed out. "While we cannot send the ships unescorted, once they are delivered as 'ours', no one will question it. Anyone who does will do the math on what must have happened to Forel and the others and not make a fuss about it."

"Do we need to wait until *Tornado* is available?" Kurzman asked. "With us going after Forel's sponsors, it could be a while before we're in a position to guard them."

"The only ships that regularly visit Tortuga that would require *Tornado* to intimidate them died at Orsav," Ki!Tana said calmly. "The remaining pirate ships are only barely a match for *Of Course We're Coming Back* or *Oaths of Secrecy*. Even with this rich a prize, the handful of ships left at Tortuga would hesitate."

"That's the best we can pull off," Annette concluded. She'd have preferred something more definite than "hesitate", but she was also confident in the ability of either of her scout ships to blow the first pirate to come after them to hell. The *second* ship to attack them would have an easier time, but the pirates wouldn't know that.

"We'll need one of the scouts with us at G-KXT-Three-Five-Seven," she said aloud, considering. "Captain Sade—you'll take the freighters back to Tortuga. The computers will respond to you. If it looks risky, hold off on going in, understand?"

"Yes, ma'am," the ethereally tall woman replied. "Should we wait for you at Tortuga?"

"No," Annette decided. "Ki!Tana—Ondu will honor the existing agreement and sell all of the freighters and their cargos?"

"He would be a fool not to."

"All right. Sade, I want you to return to the Alpha Centauri rendezvous point once everything is set up with Ondu," she ordered. "If we haven't shown up after one month from today, it's up to you what you do. I would suggest getting in touch with the Weber

Network—the proceeds from these freighters should suffice to purchase multiple heavy warships to help liberate Earth."

"You may have a problem finding someone willing to sell them," Ki!Tana pointed out, "but unless Ondu does dramatically worse than I expect, the proceeds should suffice to buy one, possibly even two, *ships of the line.*"

Annette checked the value on her communicator. She hadn't looked at it in that light, but Ki!Tana was right. Even her most pessimistic valuations would enable Earth to acquire a capital ship with a full escort—a force potentially capable of kicking the A!Tol out.

"This raid may have enabled us to achieve our main objective," she finally allowed. "We will attempt to return to Alpha Centauri with the rescued prisoners before that month is up. If we do not, it will be because, for whatever reason, we are unable to."

She turned to Lougheed.

"Captain Lougheed, *Of Course We're Coming Back* will accompany *Tornado* to KXT," she ordered. "I'm thinking we'll have you drop in on the opposite side of the gas giant from us to act as a second set of eyes. With everything these people are trying to pull, I have to assume they have a contingency plan for being discovered.

"We are talking about a level of scum that kidnapped thirty thousand people to enable them to murder a hundred *billion* sapients," she continued, her voice firm. "We will not allow them to escape. We will not allow them to run. I want our people rescued. I'd like to get my hands on those starkillers. But we will *not* let these sons of bitches escape.

"Is that clear?"

CHAPTER FIFTY-TWO

"ADMIRAL VILLENEUVE?" A VOICE INTERRUPTED JEAN'S thoughts.

His thoughts weren't much to write home about. While his hosts had been wonderfully polite and respectful, it had been strongly suggested that he not return to the planet beneath him. Jean's impression was that if he really forced the issue, Governor Medit! would let him return home, but the Imperial government of Earth didn't feel he would be safe.

He rose from the comfortable chair in the simply appointed quarters they'd given him aboard Medit!'s battleship flagship and crossed to the door, opening it with a tap on the control pad.

"Yes, what is it?" he asked. He'd given up on trying to get the A!Tol personnel not to call him by his old rank. They seemed determined to give him more respect than he felt he deserved.

"Captain Lira sends his compliments and requests for you to join him on *Shield of Innocents'* bridge," a junior Tosumi officer told him. Jean didn't have enough exposure to the four-armed species to judge, well, *anything* about the officer, but he suspected they were both young and nervous.

"I am not busy," he admitted. He was also curious—even now, he had yet to set foot on the bridge of an A!Tol warship. "Lead the way."

The Tosumi made an odd swirling gesture with all four arms and set off at a gentle pace, one Jean could easily keep up with. Modern medicine meant he was far haler than he might have been at his age even a century earlier, but he was still seventy, not thirty.

The pristine white walls and corridors of the Imperial warships were still mentally jarring for him. He'd now seen the small robots that scurried along floors and walls, cleaning as they went, but the ship was still too smooth and too clean for his brain to process as a warship.

Nonetheless, he could tell when they passed beyond the small area around his quarters he was familiar with and into the deeper core of the battleship. The translator they'd given him did a good job of reading the signs and iconography, and he *thought* he could make his way back to his quarters.

Finally, though, the Tosumi brought him to an immense, triple-layered security hatch. The hatch was currently wide open, but its presence was obvious and intimidating as Jean stepped through onto the bridge of the Imperial battleship *Shield of Innocents*.

In many ways, the circular bridge resembled the ones the UESF had built for years. There were two semicircular balconies rising up above the main floor, occupied presumably by the same kinds of analysts and backup teams that filled them on a UESF ship, and main consoles on the lowest level for the senior officers to coordinate their departments for the captain.

The bridge was a busy place, with members of at least six different species swarming over the consoles, chattering in at least as many languages. Each member of the crew wore the earbuds of translators, actively translating between their native languages as they worked.

In the center of the chaos, a raised dais held a command chair occupied by a tall alien with blue skin. As Jean approached, the figure rose and turned to face him, revealing a face with no hair, small dark eyes, and a flattened beak instead of a nose or mouth.

"I am Captain Lira of *Shield of Innocents*," the figure introduced herself. "Welcome to my bridge, Admiral Villeneuve. I hope your stay aboard my vessel has been pleasant?"

"So far, Captain," Jean allowed. "I was surprised to be asked to join you. Is something going on?"

"Look to the screen, Admiral," Lira told him, gesturing to the massive holographic tank occupying the easily fifteen-meter-tall front of the bridge. The view was focused on a group of ships, and Jean studied them carefully.

He couldn't read the A!Tol iconography without using his translator, but from his studies of his world's conquerors, he could tell he was looking at a full Imperial battle group. Eight battleships—a half-squadron, the same size of force that had conquered Sol—plus escorts and transports.

"That's a lot of ships to be here," he said carefully. "What happened?"

"Fleet Lord Tan!Shallegh wanted to be absolutely certain his passengers reached Sol safely," Captain Lira told him. "We have retrieved many, though sadly not all, of the humans kidnapped during our occupation of Earth. Those transports Tan!Shallegh escorts are carrying over fourteen thousand rescuees."

Jean stared at the screen in shock. He'd *believed* Medit! when the Governor had said they would find Earth's missing souls, but this was...unexpected. The sheer scale of the rescue boggled belief.

"How?" he asked.

"It is a long story and it appears we cannot take all of the credit," Lira told him. "My understanding is that the Fleet Lord wishes to speak with you personally, both to explain where we found your people and to deliver his apologies for failing your world so badly."

IT WAS over two hours later when Tan!Shallegh's shuttle finally made it over to *Shield of Innocents* and the A!Tol Admiral joined Jean in a plain visiting officer's office. The Fleet Lord's uniform didn't hide the mixing and shifting hues of his skin: green mixed with orange and blue.

Jean *had* managed to find some information on A!Tol skin hues. The Fleet Lord was determined to see this through, but was also angry about something and curious about something, enough so in both cases to at least register through the determination.

He could see why Earth's new overlords tended to be an honest species. Successfully deceiving each other had to be impossible; they wouldn't have even learned the skill before meeting other races.

"Admiral Villeneuve," Tan!Shallegh said quietly. "Is Miss McQueen still aboard?"

"Unlike me, Medit! allowed her to return to Earth," Jean told him dryly. "She needed to get back to work."

"I would have liked to speak with her directly, but I do not believe I will have time," the Fleet Lord admitted. "I owe you an apology, Admiral. I swore to *you*, personally, that something like this would not happen. I failed to prevent it."

"I am not who you need to apologize to, Fleet Lord."

"I know," Tan!Shallegh agreed. "I have spoken to many of the rescuees we are returning in person and via communicator. I will shortly be going on your—Global News Network, I think it is?—to speak with your Jess Robin and present my apologies to your entire world."

When Imperial Fleet Lords felt contrite, they apparently apologized like Canadians.

"You managed to get them back," Jean pointed out. "That's... impressive. I didn't expect that so quickly."

"I am not responsible for that," the Fleet Lord replied. "All I did was order all of our logistics shipping short-stopped until it could be inspected. I presumed, correctly it appears, that your people had been smuggled out on our logistics ships.

"It seems they were relaying everyone they removed from Earth through one of our logistics bases, and when I accidentally cut off their supply channel, they got desperate."

Jean winced. "What happened?"

"It appears one of our more notorious pirates was in league with them and pulled together a massive alliance of pirates to attack that logistics base," Tan!Shallegh told him. "Including your Captain Annette Bond.

"While he needed her firepower to defeat our defending task force, I suspect he regrets hiring her now."

Jean considered just what Annette's reaction would be to learning there were thousands of human slaves on the planet she was raiding. "*Mon dieu,*" he whispered.

"When the dust settled, Captain Bond was in control of our logistics base, and piracy in this sector had taken a blow I do not believe it will recover from soon," the A!Tol said with relish apparent even through the translator. "I want to give your Captain a medal." A wash of shadow swept over the Fleet Lord's skin. "Instead, it appears I will have to kill her."

The sudden change in tone washed over Jean like a bucket of cold water and he stared at Tan!Shallegh in shock.

"What did she do?"

"It's not what she's done, or even what I think she's about to do," the A!Tol Fleet Lord admitted. "It's what she's going to come into possession of.

"It appears our slavers were working with a rogue faction in our own military to try and start a war with the Kanzi," he continued. "While I do not like the Kanzi—they are vicious, murdering slavers at best, in my experience—their military is powerful and efficient.

"This rogue faction has developed a starkiller weapon the size of a missile instead of a starship," Tan!Shallegh noted. "This is in violation of more treaties than I can count but would enable them to launch a decapitating strike on the Kanzi. One that would be responded to in kind."

Jean had watched a single half-squadron of battleships wipe out his entire fleet. He wasn't sure he *could* grasp the scale of the war that would follow if the A!Tol clashed with an equal power—with weapons that could kill *stars*?

"What did Annette do?" he asked, surprised at how level his voice was.

"She has gone after them. I do not know her intent, though her actions to date suggest she intends to fight my battle for me. But."

Tan!Shallegh shivered, his tentacles fluttering as he let the word hang in the air.

"But, Fleet Lord?" Jean asked. "Why would you have to kill her?"

"Either Captain Bond joins them or kills them, but either way, she will shortly be in possession of weapons of mass destruction that aren't supposed to exist," the Fleet Lord told him. "Her honor speaks well for her, but I would not trust *myself* with these, let alone a woman on a quest to liberate her star system.

"I have issued a shoot-on-sight order for *Tornado*," he continued. "I must return to the Fleet Base at Kimar immediately to await any information on her location. I have scout ships sweeping the sector and will deploy all necessary force to neutralize her once located."

Jean's heart was cold and he was silent for a long moment. He *understood* where the Fleet Lord was coming from, but after all Annette had done, it didn't seem right that she would end that way—not when, as Tan!Shallegh said, she was about to fight the Imperium's battle for them.

"Why are you telling me this?" he asked.

"I want you to come to Kimar with me," the Fleet Lord told him, his skin suddenly flashing completely to dark green. "I want you on the bridge when I find her, Admiral Villeneuve—because if she surrenders when I find her, if she turns those weapons over to us to be destroyed, I won't have to kill her.

"And I think if there is anyone in this galaxy she will listen to when he calls on her to surrender, it will be you."

Villeneuve sighed. Elon Casimir would have been better—he was *very* sure Annette would have surrendered if Casimir had asked her to. If he asked... He wasn't sure.

But Elon Casimir was dead, and if his words might help save Annette Bond's life, then he had no choice but to try.

"When do we leave?"

CHAPTER FIFTY-THREE

When they finally emerged into G-KXT-357, it was anticlimactic for many of the crew.

Annette had known from Harmon's description that the system appeared empty at first glance, but some of her bridge crew seemed to have been expecting the system to *look* like the lair of some kind of evil monstrous overlord.

Instead, it was a relatively plain red dwarf star with no habitable planets and one massive super-Jovian gas giant. She watched the data come in on the eight planets, noting the additional carbon dioxide content on the planet Harmon had noted as having the beginnings of life.

"Anything on the scanners?" she asked.

"Nothing so far," Rolfson noted. "I'm picking up what *could* be EM reflection off one of the gas giant's moons, but I'm *looking* for something and might be seeing patterns that don't exist."

"That's our destination anyway," Annette told him. "I don't see a reason to be subtle about it—and if we're flashy, they may miss Lougheed. Amandine—take us in at point five cee."

Lougheed was supposed to drop *Of Course We're Coming Back*

in on the opposite side of the one planet farther out than the gas giant. The whole point of the stealthy scout ship dropping out of hyperspace hidden from most of the system, however, meant that *Annette* wouldn't even know if he'd emerged safely until he contacted her—which he wasn't supposed to do without reason.

They were five light-minutes from the gas giant, but at *Tornado*'s new cruising speed, that distance started to evaporate with a smooth fluidity. The upgrades to her ship were mind-boggling to Annette, but her *speed* was the most noticeable.

"Deploy the defender drones," she ordered as they crossed the four light-minute mark. "Harmon saw warships. Let's make sure we're ready to say hello when they pop out."

Additional icons dropped onto the ship status display on her command chair as her drones deployed. They'd lost two of the hull-mounted installations along with the sixth of their offensive weaponry Metharom hadn't managed to get online.

The drones represented as much defensive power again as the original fixed installations, though, and they'd only lost one of them—and they had several spares, so even that hadn't reduced their defenses.

"Looks like I'm not seeing things after all," Rolfson reported as they continued to close. "I've got EM reflections on four visible moons and on the rings. I've localized what appears to be a mid-sized space station on the opposite side of the gas giant."

"Given that the rest of the system is as technological as a rock, I'm guessing that's our target," Annette concluded. "Pass the coordinates to Amandine. Let's go knocking."

"Yes, ma'am," Rolfson confirmed cheerfully, then paused.

"I have bogeys," he announced, suddenly serious. "Two ships detaching from the station and heading our way. Velocity is only a few dozen KPS, but they are inside the moons and rings."

"They'll come for us once they're clear," Annette said grimly. "Weapons check, Commander Rolfson."

"Launchers one through twenty online, loaded, and green," he told her. "Defender drones deployed. Suites one through ten online. Proton beams one through five online, capacitors at fifty percent and rising. *Tornado* is prepared to engage the enemy on your command."

"Let's see if they have anything to say first," she told him. "But in any case, you are clear to open fire at one light-minute."

"Understood."

SECONDS TICKED by as the two ships carefully maneuvered out of the crowded confines of a gas giant's orbitals and then set their course to intercept *Tornado*. As soon as they were clear of that debris, Annette got a good look at what she was facing, and a chill settled into her spine.

With the Laian upgrades, *Tornado* could go toe-to-toe with an A!Tol cruiser and, even damaged as she was, be sure of victory. Having now fought one, Annette would even give her ship even odds against an A!Tol battlecruiser.

Her nightmare had been that the conspiracy had dug up a ship of the line and its escorts to guard their lab. Even a battleship on its own would have been more than a match for *Tornado*. It wasn't *that* bad, but the two cruisers now making their way toward her at half the speed of light were more than a match for her poor battered ship.

"We're being hailed," Chan reported.

"Play it."

"Unidentified ship, you are in violation of an Imperial no-entry zone. Leave this system immediately or be fired upon."

Annette considered for a moment. She was sure there was *something* she could say to buy her time. At close-enough range, the defender drones could probably bring down a cruiser's shields as easily as they'd crashed *Subjugator*'s, though that was closer than she wanted to get.

Unfortunately, her imagination apparently wasn't up to the task of coming up with a lie that would get them that close no matter what.

"Fuck 'em," she said sharply. "Rolfson, do what we did at Sol: pick a target and sequence our missiles onto her in a stream."

"They'll evade," Ki!Tana pointed out. "It doesn't take much rotating of the ship to stop that tactic punching through."

"I know," Annette replied. "But we're outgunned two to one, so I'll risk every trick I can."

She met Rolfson's gaze and he nodded back to her as he set up his firing plan.

"Anything more from them, Chan?" Annette asked.

"Nothing. Their shields are up, I'm not sure they ever intended to actually let us go," her communications officer noted.

"Probably not," Annette admitted, leaning back in her chair and studying the two warships. There were no clever tricks available to her now; she had comparable weapons and more powerful defenses, but she was outnumbered and there was nothing she could do about that.

"Mister Rolfson," she said calmly. "Open fire."

A single missile shot into space from Launcher One. Moments later, a second missile followed from Launcher Two. Then Launcher Three, and Four, and so on until all twenty launchers had fired and Launcher one kicked its second missile into space.

After thirty seconds, a deadly stream of missiles charged toward one of the two warships, each streaming at fully three quarters of the speed of light.

It was another thirty seconds after that before Annette saw the response from the A!Tol warships, the speed of light being a huge delay to sensors at the ranges at which interface drive warships fought. Both cruisers had opened fire as soon as they'd seen her missiles, and a swarm of fifty missiles was now flying back toward her.

"Amandine, turn us about," Annette ordered. "Let's hold the range and see if we can even the odds before we let them close."

The distance stabilized, the A!Tol ships were no faster than *Tornado*, but all of the missiles were *far* faster than any of the ships in the system.

"Plasma cannon engaging missiles," Kurzman reported. "Defender drones in optimal position."

By the time the first massive salvo of missiles reached *Tornado*, scanners were showing two more salvos closing on them. Plasma cannons on the drones and the hull opened up, cones of superheated plasma droplets smashing missiles apart by the dozen.

There were simply too many missiles, though, and warning lights flashed as impacts rocked the cruiser's shields. Annette checked them carefully. Everything was still holding, but there were only so many salvos they could take when the plasma cannon couldn't cover them.

"Target Alpha is rotating to spread shield impacts," Rolfson reported. "Missiles are compensating but...not enough."

"Are the new missiles powerful enough to make up the difference?" Annette asked. "Can we hammer one of them down?"

"Maybe," he allowed. The survivors of the second enemy salvo flashed through the defenders, the shield warnings beginning to flash a little more urgently. "But...I don't know if we have the missiles to do it twice."

"How many missiles do *those* fuckers carry?" she demanded.

"About five times as many per launcher as we do," Ki!Tana pointed out. "Their designers knew how long it would take them to pound down an equivalent warship's shields. *Tornado*'s designers did not, and your magazine designs didn't lend themselves to easy expansion when upgrading.'

"And it wasn't something we even thought about," Annette admitted. "So, what, we'll run out of missiles before they do?"

"Long before they do," Rolfson confirmed quietly. "And...well, possibly even before we take down Target Alpha's shields."

More missiles hammered each way. *Tornado*, thanks to her defense suite, could withstand the A!Tol ship's missiles for a *lot* longer than they could withstand her fire in turn—but without the ammunition to take down their shields, a missile duel was only wasting time.

"Fine," she bit off. "Let's do this the hard way. Amandine!"

"Yes, ma'am?" her navigator said.

"Take us in, full throttle," she ordered crisply. "Try and keep Target Alpha between us and Target Bravo, but set Rolfson up for the proton beams." She shook her head. "Our shields are tougher, but we'll need the defender suite to get us into beam range. Hold off on the booster until we're *in* beam range," she finished. "We'll need it to stay alive once we're there."

"Point five cee charge, coming right up," Amandine replied.

The distance between the two groups of ships, which had stabilized around fifteen million kilometers as they all moved away from the gas giant and the space station it shielded, suddenly changed. A full light-minute vanished in moments as the ships lunged toward each other at a literally incomprehensible relative velocity.

Annette watched as Rolfson and Amandine—and their teams— swung into action like a finely oiled machine. At a million kilometers, Amandine triggered the "booster"—*Tornado*'s new ability to temporarily travel at point five five cee.

Arriving in proton-beam range a full third of a second before the A!Tol and their computers expected them, *Tornado* gracefully dodged the first beams from her enemies and locked onto Target Alpha perfectly with all five proton beams.

More missiles arrived in the same moment, both *Tornado* and her target lurching as the high-velocity weapons slammed into their shields—then *Tornado* lost beam lock and Target Alpha *gained* it.

"Target Alpha's shields are failing!" Rolfson announced. "Salvoing more missiles."

"*Our* shields are failing!" Ki!Tana, manning the engineering console, snapped.

A massive white flash filled the screen as Rolfson's missiles flamed home—all twenty missiles crossing the distance in under two seconds and overwhelming shields already pressed to the breaking point by the proton beams.

Just as *Tornado*'s shields were about to fail, Target Alpha's beams cut off as the A!Tol cruiser came apart in a ball of fire.

Annette had enough time to begin to sigh in relief—and then Target *Bravo* arced over Alpha's wreckage, her own beams slamming into *Tornado*.

"Evade!" she snapped. "Get us in closer."

Amandine was rotating the ship, trying to spread out the beam impact, but it wasn't enough. As the range dropped farther, so did *Tornado*'s shields.

"Hit her with everything!" Annette bellowed, hitting the override commands on her own screens that turned even the defender suite into a short-range offensive weapon.

Plasma and protons and missiles filled the space between the two ships as the distance shrank, *Tornado*'s compressed-matter armor *ringing* under impacts that would have destroyed a ship without it.

Then a proton beam cut through the A!Tol cruiser's shield, cleaving off a chunk of the enemy's hull. Power flickered, shields and weapons alike failed for a fraction of a second—and in that fraction of a second, Harold Rolfson put three proton beams and a dozen missiles into his enemy's hull.

"Targets down," he reported a moment later in a breathless voice.

ANNETTE TOOK a deep breath and nodded acknowledgement of their victory. Her command chair status displays told her much of the story. Half of their remaining missile launchers were gone. They were down to two proton beams and two hull-mounted defender suites.

"Shields are back up," Ki!Tana said quietly. "Damage control is sweeping the ship. We...have no casualty figures yet."

"We'll get them," Annette said grimly. "Do we have engines?"

"Everything is online," Amandine answered. "I wouldn't trust the booster, but we can pull point five with no concerns."

"Then let's finish this, ladies and gentlemen," *Tornado*'s Captain told her crew. "Commander Amandine, set your course for that space station. Commander Chan, prepare a message demanding their surrender."

Maintaining their distance against the cruisers had pulled them well away from the gas giant, but at half of lightspeed, returning to their destination was a matter of minutes. Damaged as *Tornado* was, she was certainly capable of destroying a space station, though it might take longer than she would like.

Rounding the gas giant at last, they got their first solid glimpse at the research facility that had caused them so much trouble.

It was surprisingly prosaic, a slightly distended sphere with short spindles sticking out of the top and bottom. The design was surprisingly similar to the stations that had been built in Sol over the last two decades since the discovery of artificial gravity.

Several small stations, presumably high-risk lab areas, orbited in a trailing cluster roughly eighty thousand kilometers behind the main station. As they drew closer, Annette realized that even the "small" stations were the size of *Tornado*, and reassessed her estimate of the main station size.

The sphere was a little over two kilometers in diameter, with more than enough space for the thirty thousand human prisoners Annette knew had been headed toward it, plus room for at least that in crew and scientists.

Someone had poured a lot of resources into building the station and funding its research. Given their intentions, however, Annette felt absolutely no guilt at tearing it all apart.

"Send the surrender message," she ordered.

"Yes, ma'am," Chan confirmed, hitting the button. Now they would wait and see what the response was...

"What the...ma'am, look!" Rolfson exclaimed, pointing at the screen.

The high-risk lab stations were the closest by a third of a light-second, so Annette saw them explode first, each of the five-hundred-meter spheres disintegrating in a bright white flash of antimatter explosions.

Her gaze was inexorably drawn to the main station, the massive facility she *knew* still housed the rogue scientists and their fifteen thousand slaves. She hoped...but from the moment the high-risk labs went up, she knew what she was going to see.

At most ten seconds after the lab station received their surrender demand, twelve fusion reactors went into forced overload and the entire facility vanished in an eye-searing ball of flame.

CHAPTER FIFTY-FOUR

OF COURSE WE'RE COMING BACK ROUNDED THE FORSAKEN ICE ball of an outer planet they had emerged behind in time to pick up the two cruisers rounding the gas giant to, presumably, chase *Tornado*. The gas giant, almost a brown dwarf, was large enough that the scout ship's sensors couldn't see her heavily armed sister.

"Do we have the base dialed in?" Andrew asked, studying the scanners.

"Backtracking the cruisers' courses now," Laurent confirmed, crisp and professional. "I've got a group of space stations, one big one and a cluster of smaller platforms. Throwing them on the screen."

Andrew studied the complex as his ship drifted closer to it, cold gas thrusters allowing as much stealth as any ship could have in space while they snuck up on the people who were planning to start a war. He still wasn't entirely sure this was their fight—but he *was* sure that Annette Bond had told him to make sure the human prisoners made it out.

That was...enough, somehow.

"Both cruisers are around the planet now," Laurent reported. "The station probably has relays to watch what's going on, but we won't know how things end until someone comes back around the planet."

"Damn," Andrew murmured. He wasn't going to bet *against* Bond and *Tornado*, but those were steep odds for the cruiser.

"Keep taking us in," he ordered. "Prep the missiles and charge the laser. No matter what, we have to finish this."

"Yes, boss."

The survey ship continued to close, and Andrew skimmed the sensor take on the station further, studying it for any clues, any sign of either the slaves or the starkiller weapons. Ki!Tana had provided them with a radiation signature that would mark the presence of a starkiller, assuming the weapons weren't entirely different from the larger bombs available to the A!Tol navy.

They were too far away to distinguish it from the other radiation sources inevitable from any major technological society. The station was powered by a dozen major fusion reactors, and the signatures from their venting systems overwhelmed almost anything else.

Except...

"Sarah, check this out," he flipped her a location on the station. It took her a moment to focus *Of Course*'s finely tuned passive sensors on the point he'd marked.

By then, that level of resolution was unnecessary. A ship had detached from the station and brought up an interface drive at full power, blazing out-system at forty percent of lightspeed.

"She's a freighter," Laurent reported a moment later. "Similar structure to the food ship we caught before we hit Tortuga. Central control module, eight surrounding cargo pods. Bigger, though."

"How big?" Andrew asked, a sudden thought hitting him. "Let's say they were using the same cells Wellesley saw at Orsav. How many people could they fit aboard?"

She was silent for a moment working, then met his gaze levelly.

"A little under fifty thousand," she told him. "They may have just evacuated the entire station."

As she spoke, the freighter shut down its drives. The interface drive didn't exactly play fair with physics as written by Newton but the ship was still drifting along at a notable percentage of lightspeed.

"I have *Tornado* on the scans," Laurent reported. "*Damn*. I'm seeing atmosphere and radiation leaks even *through* her shields...but her shields are up and her drive is at full power."

"And those cruisers didn't come back," Andrew agreed. Without having *seen* the battle, they couldn't be entirely sure how it had ended—but then, the people on that freighter likely *had* seen it. And they were running away.

"Can *Tornado* see the freighter?" he asked, then winced as the stations suddenly blew apart, filling the gas giant's planetary system with a wash of radiation.

"They weren't close enough before and they *definitely* can't now," Laurent reported. "I'm not sure we could even raise her with tightbeam comms."

The freighter's drive came back up, at a lower power. Twenty percent of lightspeed wasn't much by the standards of an interface drive ship, but Andrew did the math.

"I have her well clear of *Tornado*'s intercept zone before that cloud dissipates," he said quietly. "Do you have the same?"

Laurent had already been running the same numbers and she looked up and nodded.

"*Tornado* might be able to shoot her down with missiles, but they won't be close enough to hit her with anything that can disable as opposed to destroy," she concluded.

He bit his tongue gently as he ran a different set of numbers. The freighter wasn't headed *directly* toward *Of Course,* but it was moving in their direction. If the massive vessel was armed at *all*, trying to intercept it would be suicide—the survey ship's single laser and handful of missiles didn't make up for the fact that she had *no* shields.

"We can intercept her," he said aloud.

"Yes," Laurent confirmed. "She has shields, our missiles probably won't do much, but we could burn through with the laser."

"But if she has missiles, we're dead," Andrew admitted.

"I can't tell from here," she said slowly. "What I can tell you is that she *is* carrying starkillers. We're picking up the radiation signature Ki!Tana gave us. One on each cargo pod."

He sighed.

"We let her go, billions die," he concluded. "Plus, she almost certainly has the slaves aboard, doesn't she?"

"Can't say, sir," Laurent replied.

"Karl," Andrew addressed his navigator, "how close can you get us on the jets?"

The navigator considered, running numbers on his own console, then shook his head.

"Missile range but not laser range," he concluded. "We need to bring up the drive inside the next ten minutes if we're going to cut her off."

"Well, then," *Of Course*'s Captain announced calmly. "Let's not bother playing about. Bring up the interface drive, maximum power. Sarah, prep the laser. Target is that central command capsule—let's burn them out."

———

GEOMETRY AND VELOCITY vectors meant that *Of Course We're Coming Back* had closed a significant chunk of the distance with the fleeing freighter before her prey even realized she existed. With a combined velocity of over half of lightspeed, by the time the radiation signature from *Of Course*'s drive had crossed the three-light-minute gap, the scout ship had closed half the distance itself.

Andrew and his crew saw their response barely more than a minute later, with high fractions of lightspeed exerting their usual distorting effect on time. The freighter crew had been edging along quietly, with their attention focused on *Tornado*. It took them well over fifteen seconds to react—fifteen seconds in which the range dropped by over two million kilometers.

Finally, the freighter brought their interface drive up to full strength, pulling away from *Of Course* at forty percent of lightspeed —five percent *slower* than the scout ship was pursuing them at.

"She can't directly vector away from us," Strobel noted after a moment. "Not without giving *Tornado* a clear run at her. Net speed... nine percent of light."

Ten minutes to range. They were *in* missile range, though the freighter's icon sparkled with the distinctive signature of an energy shield. It was possible their single salvo could disable the shield, but it didn't seem likely.

"How long until they can open a hyper portal?" Andrew asked.

"A minute after we hit laser range," Laurent said grimly. "That's all we get, Andrew."

He nodded slowly.

"Launch the missiles," he ordered. They weren't likely to bring the shield down, but it was worth a shot. "Then try for a couple of long-range burns with the laser—we might get lucky."

Eight new icons flared on the screen, *Of Course*'s single salvo of externally mounted missiles blasted into space at three quarters of the speed of light. The computer projected white lines onto the screen as Sarah Laurent reached out with their single high-powered laser.

The missiles flashed home in brilliant white sparks, vaporizing themselves against the energy shield with no effect. The long-range laser fire didn't even connect, coherent light flickering past the freighter in the silence of deep space.

"Cease fire," Andrew ordered. "Charge the capacitors for a maximum-power shot."

He double-checked the numbers. *Tornado* was pursuing now, closing through the radiation cloud on the now-obvious signature of the freighter's drive. She wouldn't even reach missile range until over a minute after the freighter could open a portal.

"We can't risk games," he finally admitted. "Once you have a shot, take it—rip that central capsule to hell."

"You know they've probably got all of their research in there,"

Laurent pointed out. "Those warheads may not even fire without some code we won't have if we kill them all."

That...probably wouldn't even be the worst result, Andrew realized. The power of the weapons their prey carried terrified him. If the starkillers became useless, it would probably make everyone's life even easier.

"We'll live with that" was what he told Laurent, though. "Fire as soon as you have the shot—Karl, make sure she gets it. One clean hit."

He held the arms of his chair tightly. *Tornado* could probably pursue the freighter into hyperspace—as soon as *Of Course* had blown their attempt to sneak away, it had been over—but he suspected these bastards wouldn't surrender. If they realized they were being chased by humans, they'd start threatening their prisoners.

One shot was all they'd get.

One shot was all it took.

Of Course We're Coming Back flashed across the four hundred thousand–kilometer line, and Laurent paused. Andrew turned to her, about to yell at her to fire, for God's sake, but then he saw. At the moment they'd crossed the normal effective range of an energy weapon, the freighter had started jinking to throw off an attack.

His science officer gave them five whole seconds, absorbing their pattern—then fired.

The big laser had been designed to punch through compressed-matter armor. The shield on the freighter was powerful but still a civilian system. The laser burned through it in seconds and continued to hit the rear of the crew capsule of the freighter—and kept going.

It took eight seconds to fully discharge the capacitors and end the beam. When the computer erased its artificial white line, the freighter was no longer evading.

The entire central capsule was simply *gone*.

CHAPTER FIFTY-FIVE

JAMES CHECKED THE TELLTALES ON HIS COMPANY ONE FINAL time as the shuttles swarmed toward the crippled freighter. The six troops of his Special Space Service and alien soldiers were his entire first wave—while they'd easily pulled together plasma weapons and unpowered armor out of Orsav's stocks for the three companies of mixed troops he had for backup, they didn't have the power armor of his main strike force.

They were also inexperienced with their new weapons and hadn't had time to exercise together as units. The freighter he was boarding probably had as many sapients aboard as the station he'd pulled together his battalion to attack. He'd *need* those troops, but putting them on the point of the spear would be murder.

Plus, he only had enough shuttles to deliver a hundred and fifty soldiers at a time at most. Two of the freighter's eight cargo modules would be missed this time: the next wave, made up of his intact US Army and People's Army platoons, would hit those.

"Landing in ten seconds," McPhail announced. "Get off my ship, boys and girls! Faster you're off, the faster you get reinforcements!"

"*Move*, people!" Annabel Sherman echoed.

James followed along as Charlie Troop and his headquarters section left the shuttle in an orderly swarm, four-man patrols sweeping out into the corridor McPhail had cut her way into.

The initial entry went quietly. The cargo pod was a kilometer long and a fifth of that around; unless the defenders had an entire *division* hidden, there was no way they could have had troops ready to intercept the landing.

"Which way?" Sherman asked. James might technically be a supernumerary on this operation, but she apparently wasn't going to *ignore* him.

"The control center for the pod's life support was at the front last time," he noted. "That's also where the scans show the starkiller being located. We need to secure those straightaway."

"Roger," she agreed. "Second Patrol—you're on point. Move!"

THEIR TRIP forward was creepily silent. James knew they were moving through the outer sections of the pod, well away from the cargo compartments that likely contained any passengers or prisoners, but the complete lack of resistance or, well, *anyone* was disturbing.

The ship was clearly A!Tol military in build, smooth white lines and covered panels everywhere. Slick, elegant, efficient, and expensive. The calm white walls didn't help with the creepiness factor.

It was almost a relief when the shooting started.

The distinctive hissing crack of plasma fire echoed down the corridors from the point team, and the entire troop and headquarters section went to ground against the walls. Sensor nets interfaced, reaching out to see just *what* was in front of them.

"Defensive drones," Second Patrol's Sergeant reported. "Haven't seen anything like them before—look like wheeled trash cans with plasma guns. *Watch it!*"

A flurry of new plasma fire echoed, followed by a pair of explosions.

"They suck at taking cover," the Sergeant noted, "but *damn,* do they take a lot of killing. Could use a heavy launcher."

"Ral," James ordered. He didn't need to say anything more. The Yin, the tallest member of his company even in power armor, scooted along the wall as he unlimbered his weapon.

"Clear!" he barked, checking angles through the sensor network, then fired.

Four smooth black spheres emerged from his weapon in less than a second, following a carefully calculated trajectory that bounced them *past* the point patrol, around the wall, and into the midst of the defending drones.

A sequence of booms came echoing back around the corner—first the deep sounds of the four heavy plasma grenades, then the somewhat quieter sounds of secondary explosions as the drones' ammunition and power cores blew up.

Any of the drones that survived the grenades *didn't* survive Sherman's Second Patrol swarming around the corner, plasma cannons firing into anything that moved.

The drones went down—and then two of the four green icons representing the patrol flashed blood-red on James's command display.

"Son of a bitch," the Sergeant snapped. "Falling back, there's a defensive position behind the drones, they have power armor!"

Another icon flashed yellow, and then the two SSS troopers made it back around the corner—Sergeant Wei Lin *carrying* her sole surviving subordinate, power armor and all.

James pulled the visual and scan data from the Patrol's short encounter. The area past the corner where the drones had stopped them opened out, a carefully designed defensive choke point ahead of the control center and its terrifyingly deadly companion.

There were another dozen of the ugly defensive drones, a pair of oddly crystalline devices he suspected would shoot down further grenades, and ten power-armored soldiers, all Rekiki.

"Suggestions, sir?" Sherman asked. She was looking at the same images he was.

"Mass grenades," he replied. "I think those are anti-projectile systems, but we might be able to overwhelm them."

"Let's give it a shot," she agreed. "All right, folks, grenades out on my mark! Three. Two. One... Mark!"

Ral and two people in Sherman's troop had the heavy launchers and fired four-grenade bursts around the corner. James's suit dropped a grenade into his hand and carefully precalculated the throw for him.

Over thirty grenades went flying around the corner in a coordinated salvo, bouncing along the floor and walls toward the defensive position—and the entire room lit up with lasers and grenades started detonating. The beams weren't enough to penetrate armor of any kind, but armoring a grenade was counterproductive.

It wasn't what James was expecting...but it would work.

"Go now!" he snapped.

He matched his actions to his words, charging forward with an abandon that would have seen several of his instructors bust him back to first year at the academy. All of his training insisted that leading from the front was a bad idea—but in this case, every suit, every plasma cannon was needed.

The kill zone was filled with smoke and debris. He couldn't see *anything*, but he knew where the drones and defenders *had* been. He tracked his weapon across those points, white-hot plasma flashing out and triggering secondary explosions to let him know when he hit.

The rest of Charlie Troop and his headquarters section were right with him. The enemy missed their charge at first, but they returned fire as soon as the first drones went down. Icons flashed yellow and red on James's display, but he focused on the outlines his computer drew in front of him of where the targets *should* be.

He heard one of the heavy launchers fire and a series of explosions lit up the room even through the smoke...and the firing stopped.

The smoke dispersed slowly, several electrical fires that *had* been armed drones adding to the air pollution. It was clear before the smoke dispersed that the mad charge had done its job—the defenders and their drones were dead.

Most of the wall behind them was gone, too. The outer hull was probably tough enough to withstand the firepower James's people had just unleashed, but even a warship's interior bulkheads would melt under that kind of exchange.

"Sensors say the starkiller is just ahead and two decks down," James told Sherman. "Leave someone to guard the wounded and secure life support control with the rest of your troop. I'm going after the weapon."

"Yes, sir," Sherman replied shakily, looking around the space they'd just temporarily turned into hell. They'd lost five people in under twenty seconds.

James was sadly certain they weren't going to be the only ones today.

WHILE THERE WERE ALMOST CERTAINLY stairs or a ramp or *some* way of getting down the two floors to the blinking icon marking the starkiller weapon, James was getting twitchy about sharing space with the most literal weapons of mass destruction in existence and not being in control of it.

And their power armor came with energy blades he'd yet to have his people try out in the field.

Those blades extended into meter-long, nearly invisible force fields that easily cut through the hull plating to create holes large enough for his people and their power armor. There was a series of resoundingly loud crashes as his headquarters section *dropped* twelve feet to the deck below—followed a moment later by the same noise again as they repeated the process.

The starkiller's guard must have heard them coming, but they clearly had *not* been expecting this. Three power-armored A!Tol stood at the end of the corridor they'd emerged in, and they were frozen in shock for a long moment.

Too long of a moment. Plasma fire from the first half-dozen troopers down, including James, cut the three squids down before they reacted.

"Get that door open," James snapped as his people closed with the hatch the aliens had been guarding. Two of his people ripped open the security pad, not even trying to guess the code before linking the system into their suits.

"Give us a minute," his information specialist told him. "They've locked this down tight, but...I think we can get it."

Seconds passed. James waited patiently but twitchily. The other side of that door contained the death of stars, the murder of billions. For all he knew, there was a member of the conspiracy in there about to punch a big red button and fire the weapon into G-KXT-357, killing them all.

"We're in!"

The door slid open and James charged through, weapon sweeping the room for any occupant.

He found no one. The room had started life as a general storage space that just happened to be next to the hull. Now it was empty of anything except a four-meter-wide cylinder that stretched back from the hull of the ship to the rear of the room: the launcher for the weapon.

"Check the room," he ordered. "Find the controls; make sure we're alone."

His power-armored troopers swept the room, the two information specialists stopping when they found a hologram-based control panel and started going over it.

"We're clear," the report came. "Nobody in here but us."

He pinged Sherman.

"Annabel, are you in control of life support?" he demanded.

"We are," she said calmly. "No further resistance, though we've got a pair of Tosumi crewmen duct-taped to a wall. Surveillance is linked in here too; looks like we've got at least patrols, ten strong each, sweeping the pod. They're heading our way now, but we've got the same choke point they did. I'll be ready for them.

"What about the weapon?"

"It's a big bitch, twice as wide as our missiles at least," James told her. "We have it secured. I doubt we'll be able to fire it, but these bastards aren't going to either."

"Sir," his information specialist cut in. "The encryption on the weapon...well, it's not that much stronger than the door."

"What do you mean?" he demanded.

"We're in," his hacker replied. "We have control of the starkiller. Transmitting the access parameters to the other teams—we own these weapons now."

A chill ran down James's spine. Eight starkillers. Each small enough to be carried in, say, one of the scout ship's external racks, instead of the normal size closer to a destroyer.

Eight weapons any power in the galaxy would apparently kill for —and they were now in the hands of Terra's exiles.

Fuck.

CHAPTER FIFTY-SIX

"WE HAVE SECURED ALL EIGHT CARGO PODS," WELLESLEY reported an hour later on a conference channel with Annette and Captain Lougheed. "All eight starkillers are under our control, and we have access to the launch systems. My infotech guys tell me they can copy the software to any of our ships, but it doesn't look like the missiles will fit in our tubes."

"They'll fit on *Tornado*'s shuttle deck," Annette noted, studying the schematics the Special Space Service people had sent back. "It's not the best launch system, but it'll work. What about prisoners? And the slaves we were looking for?"

"Five of the pods had humans in them," the Major confirmed. "Still sorting out exact numbers, but it looks like sixteen, maybe seventeen thousand people. Most...well, most of the ones we've identified so far are from a couple of Kuiper Belt outposts that went dark about five years back.

"We've got about a thousand prisoners and we took down about three hundred enemy troops along the way," he continued. "Our prisoners are...techs and maintenance guys. We're talking janitors and button-pushers, ma'am. The researchers, the leaders—the core of our conspiracy—were in the command module, and Captain Lougheed sent them to hell."

Lougheed looked tired to Annette's eye. Almost as tired as she felt.

"Can we slot *Of Course* into the command module spot the way we did before?" she asked.

"It looks like it," Lougheed replied. "We'll need a couple of hours to be sure, but even if we can't, we should be able to tow her into hyperspace regardless. You have a plan, ma'am?"

She realized she did. Not much of one. Not one with its most important decision made, but she had a plan.

"Major, I want you to remain on the freighter with the rescuees," she ordered Wellesley. "Work with Andrew; take these people home. But first, I need the starkillers transferred to *Tornado*."

Both of her juniors swallowed hard at those orders.

"Once the starkillers are aboard *Tornado*, Captain Lougheed is in command," she continued. "Andrew, I want you to return to Centauri and pick up Sade. From there, you are to proceed back to Sol with our rescuees and our prisoners.

"Get those people home," she said simply. "And then once you're there, you are to surrender to the Imperium."

"Ma'am, I..."

She held up a hand to cut off Andrew.

"I'm sorry, Andrew, James," she said quietly. "What happens next will be on me and me alone."

"And what is that?" Wellesley asked.

"If we are to use these weapons to gain our freedom, we need to deliver that demand in person," Annette told them. "Once you are on your way, *Tornado* will proceed to the Kimar fleet base. There..." She sighed.

"One way or another, people, our exile ends there."

THE STARKILLERS LOOKED SO PROSAIC, so harmless, sitting in *Tornado*'s shuttle bay that night. The crew was giving the things a wide berth regardless, leaving Annette alone in the cavernous space with her eight deadly new toys.

They didn't even really look like missiles to her. Interface drive weapons were long cylinders, a meter and a half wide by three to five meters long, depending on how advanced the missile was.

The starkillers were, technically, interface drive missiles, but they were perfect spheres just over three meters in diameter. Their drives were slower than a modern missile's, too, though they still matched the point six cee missiles *Tornado* had been built to fire.

Their casings were the same calm white metal the A!Tol used for all of their ships. Nothing about the immense white marbles suggested their deadly, terrifying power.

Annette's one warship now held more firepower than many entire *fleets*, and she wasn't quite sure what she was going to do with it.

Threatening the A!Tol with the weapons was pointless without a demonstration. She'd picked Kimar for two reasons: firstly, it was a military base with a hyperwave communicator. Tan!Shallegh was likely there, and he could transmit whatever threats or demands she delivered to the Empress directly.

Secondly, it was the military base closest to Earth, the fleet base from which the force that had conquered Earth had launched. It was a system she could *almost* convince herself was a legitimate target.

"I wondered if I would find you here," Ki!Tana said behind her, her voice distinctive with the translator overlaid over the hisses and clicks that made up the A!Tol's actual speech. "They are so normal for something so terrifying, are they not?"

"They're not what I expected," Annette allowed, gently rubbing at the scar above her eye. Her *socket* hurt, but she suspected Jelani would start making *very* unpleasant suggestions if she rubbed at that.

"You know, the A!Tol Imperium only has about fifty starkillers," the old alien told her as she stood beside the Captain. "You now command more weapons of mass destruction than any of their regional fleets. Almost a fifth of the weapons the entire Imperium has at its disposal."

"I am now a power in this galaxy in my own right, am I?" *Tornado's* Captain whispered.

"Indeed. Once the galaxy knows what you command, your name will be fear. Your reputation, death."

"Enough that I'd never need to fire one?" Annette asked.

"No." Ki!Tana's tentacles shivered, a long, convulsive gesture very different from the usual shrug. "No. To *know* you have the weapons, the galaxy would need to see one used. Then they would believe. The galaxy would know your name then."

"And 'Bloody Annie' would be more appropriate than ever," she said, looking at her reflection in one of the shiny weapons. The eyepatch certainly went with the name.

"Yes."

Annette shook her head, eyeing the weapons.

"I hated your species, you know," she said quietly. "I wish I still could. If we'd taken these weapons the day we boarded *Rekiki's Fang*? Kimar would burn. The Imperium would kneel at my feet and beg my mercy."

"I have told you that I am not representative of my race," Ki!Tana replied.

"Not just you," Annette replied. "There is a saying among my people that you can judge a man by the measure of his enemies. The A!Tol's enemies? Slavers. Pirates. Murderers. The Kanzi—madmen like Forel.

"And the people who conquered my world?" She sighed. "The line between. The only people I've met since I left Sol that I respect are the *Laians*. And they...they are exiles lost without a cause.

"But the only people I've met are the A!Tol's enemies," she continued. "What does that tell me about the empire I opposed? About the Imperium I have been handed the sword to destroy?"

"I do not know, Captain Bond."

"Bullshit," Annette swore. "Dammit, Ki!Tana—I'm sitting here deciding whether to kill a *hundred million* of your people, and you don't have an *opinion*? You don't *know* what to say?"

The big A!Tol was very quiet for a long time.

"The Ki! are very careful in what we say and do," she said finally. "We remember very little of our lives before the madness took us, Captain. We emerge from our mountain retreats little more than children, but our species looks to us as wise ancestors.

"So, we learn quickly never to command, never to *suggest*. We ask questions. We challenge. Where possible, we *do*. But we do not lead and we do not tell people *our* desires."

"Even if I ask? What does your contract say about *that*?"

"The contract I agreed with Kikitheth truly only said that she commanded my life, my knowledge and my skills," Ki!Tana admitted. "It was a short paragraph, nothing more. It transferred to you because I was curious, Captain Bond."

"That doesn't answer my question."

"No."

Annette almost punched one of the weapons, settling instead for gently smacking it with her hand.

"What would you do?" she demanded.

There was silence again for a long moment.

"Destroy the starkillers," Ki!Tana admitted. "But I have a disadvantage you do not, Annette Bond."

"And what is that?" Annette asked, realizing that this was the first time the alien had *ever* addressed her by her full name.

"I have seen a starkiller fired. I have watched a world burn in the aftermath of my command and known that *my* will and *my* voice had set into motion the death of billions," the alien said flatly. "I do not even know who I *was* before the madness, but I remember *that*, and I could not find it in me to fire these things."

Annette exhaled, letting air and energy and rage flow out of her.

"Thank you," she said simply. "And if I were to fire one, to free my world with the death of another, what would you do?"

"I have never been the last exiled soldier of a fallen world," Ki!Tana admitted. "I cannot judge your choices. I do not know if I could continue to serve a captain who had done so, but I will not judge you for the action."

Annette stared at her eight deadly prizes.

"Ridotak said you would make me a king, an outlaw, or a corpse," she said quietly. "I don't see a way to be king of anywhere. I think I'm done with being an outlaw. That doesn't leave me many choices, does it?"

"I think, Annette Bond, that you cannot see past the choice in front of you," her alien friend replied. "No one can make it for you.

"Only you can decide what you are prepared to sacrifice."

"It's not sacrifice if I ask someone *else* to die for it." Annette shook her head again. "I need to think," she told Ki!Tana. "Alone."

With a small gesture of her manipulators, the A!Tol withdrew, leaving Annette Bond alone with her deadly prize, her conscience, and her choice.

CHAPTER FIFTY-SEVEN

"EMERGENCE IN TWENTY SECONDS."

Amandine's words echoed in the deathly quiet of *Tornado*'s bridge. The tension in the air was thick enough to cut with a knife. Annette hadn't told *anyone* what she planned to do at Kimar, but her crew all had their guesses.

The simple fact that they were here with the starkiller missiles reduced the options dramatically, though Annette *still* hadn't made up her mind.

"Metharom," she said quietly into her communicator. "Did you make the upgrades I asked for?"

"Yes, ma'am," her chief engineer replied. "Exactly as requested."

"Thank you. Carry on."

Annette closed the channel and surveyed the screens and plots around her. Her crew kept their gazes focused on their screens, none of them prepared to meet her single eye. Perhaps they were afraid that eye contact would contaminate them.

The portal opened as she tried not to snarl, *Tornado* slipping through the tear in space into the Kimar system. A few moments of lag, and then the sensors started to propagate the details of the star the A!Tol had launched their conquest of Earth from.

Tornado had emerged well above the ecliptic plane, well out of the line of interception of any of the Imperial warships. Annette knew she'd be detected quickly, but that was part of the point. They were here to be *seen*.

"What have we got?" she asked aloud.

"Seven planets, one habitable, one gas giant," Rolfson announced. "Gas giant is home to the fleet base. I'm reading...thirty-two capital ships, eight of them what I'm guessing are *super*-battleships because they are monstrous, and about a hundred and fifty lighter warships."

"Are any of them in range to intercept us or the starkillers?"

In the silence of the bridge, she *heard* her tactical officer swallow. "No, ma'am."

"Amandine, set your course for the star," she ordered. "Rolfson, open the shuttle bay.

"Ma'am..."

"That was an order, Lieutenant Commander," Annette snapped.

"Yes, ma'am," he said quickly.

Seconds ticked away and millions of kilometers disappeared with them.

"Hold us at six light-minutes from the star," she ordered. "Any response from our squid friends?"

"No...wait," Rolfson replied. "Yes. I have two squadrons of destroyers leaving orbit of the planet and heading our way. I wouldn't see any reaction from the fleet base, but..."

"Interesting," Annette murmured. "So, every warship in the system is going to head right for us. I guess they know what we're carrying."

JEAN VILLENEUVE WAS WOKEN by a harsh, blaring alarm. The quarters he'd been assigned on Tan!Shallegh's flagship were surprisingly comfortable, even if all of the furniture had clearly been designed for bipeds who were only *close* to humans in proportion.

The door to his quarters slid open and the light flashed on before he could do more than sit up. A large A!Tol loomed ominously over him and he blinked up at the squid-like alien.

"The Fleet Lord wants you in the command center now," his unexpected guest told him, "Hurry."

"What's going on?" Jean demanded, pulling a jacket on over the emergency jumpsuit he'd been sleeping in.

"Your *Tornado* is here."

"THAT'S CONFIRMED—ALL of the battleships are heading our way, but all of the escorts are moving to try and position themselves to stop a missile," Rolfson told Annette.

"Are any of them in position to do so?"

"No."

"How long until they are?" she asked. She kept her face still, focusing on the pain from the scar so as not to let her crew see her turmoil. She knew she *should* have decided before they got there, but how could anyone make a fixed decision over whether to murder millions upon millions of innocents?

"Two, maybe three minutes," her tactical officer reported.

She sighed. She'd run out of time. She studied the screens, the warships desperately charging across the system.

They could have run. If they knew what she was carrying, those ships could have run—all of them had the speed and the hyperdrive generators to make it out of the system before she could destroy the star. Now they were going to die if she fired the starkiller.

That was *their* choice. To die rather than abandon those they'd sworn to defend. The population on Kimar's habitable planet was roughly sixty percent A!Tol, the rest over a dozen other species. The fleet guarding her was only about forty-five percent A!Tol.

There were entire *ships* in that fleet crewed by people who didn't even have members of their species on the planet at risk, and they still charged in—prepared to sacrifice themselves for even the tiniest chance that they could stop her.

They couldn't.

This system would live or die by *her* choice.

Of course, she didn't need to make it *easy*.

"Mister Rolfson," she said calmly. "Launch Starkiller One."

Silence.

"Mister Rolfson," she repeated.

"Yes, ma'am," he finally replied. "Activating Starkiller One."

JEAN ENTERED TAN!SHALLEGH'S command center at a run and found himself readily guided to a spot at the Fleet Lord's right hand.

"She has fired," the Fleet Lord told him quietly. "Our destroyers confirm it *is* a starkiller. A tiny one and fast." Tan!Shallegh's tentacles shivered. "We can't intercept it. It is...theoretically possible that *Tornado* could."

Jean felt his heart collapse and his breath shorten. Annette Bond had *fired*. She'd actually deployed a weapon that would kill millions of innocents. It...wasn't like her.

What had he done to the woman he'd known when he sent her out to fight a war on her own?

"I am sorry," he told Tan!Shallegh. However it had come to this, whatever Bond had seen, had done that made her willing to go this far, it was all his fault.

"Talk to her, Admiral," the Fleet Lord begged. "You...may be our only hope."

"We could run," Jean pointed out, sick to even say it.

"No. We are the Imperial Navy. We do not abandon our people."

No more than the UESF had been prepared to surrender when

they faced that Navy. Jean Villeneuve met the gaze of the being who'd defeated him and conquered his system and saw, at last, what Tan!Shallegh had tried to tell him several times.

They had different limbs and eyes and skin. They wore different uniforms and spoke different languages, but at heart, they were the same. Warriors. Guardians of their people.

And so was Annette Bond.

"Get me a transmitter."

"MA'AM, WE'RE RECEIVING A TRANSMISSION," Chan reported. "It's...Admiral Villeneuve?"

"Send it to my chair," Annette ordered. What was Jean doing *here*? He should be at Earth, dead or retired, not...not clearly aboard an A!Tol warship, as the image that appeared on her screen showed him to be.

"Captain Bond," he greeted her, then paused. "Annette. I am aboard the flagship of Fleet Lord Tan!Shallegh. We are maneuvering to intercept the starkiller you have launched.

"We know what the weapon is," he continued. "We know...how it was funded. How it was built. How it was *meant* to be deployed.

"The people responsible for kidnapping innocents from our home have been caught. They will be punished. That you're here with these weapons means you've stopped a grand tragedy. The A!Tol owe you thanks.

"I can't be certain what you plan or what you're thinking," Villeneuve continued. "But I can tell you this: destroying this system won't buy Earth's freedom. All it will do is bring the wrath of the entire A!Tol Imperium down on you.

"They will hunt you to the ends of the galaxy to bring you to justice. They will find you and kill you like the mad dog you will have become if you allow that missile to hit."

His eyes softened.

"Tan!Shallegh will not retreat," he said quietly. "Neither will I. We will die defending this system. Only you can change that."

Annette closed her eye for a long moment. If even *she* wasn't sure what she meant to do, could she blame Jean Villeneuve for thinking she was about to murder a hundred million sentients? She touched her eyepatch and remembered her conversation with Ki!Tana—and the conversation she'd had later that night with Kulap Metharom.

"Let's finish the demonstration, people," the one-eyed Captain said aloud, her tone suddenly much more relaxed as she realized she'd made up her mind days before.

"Commander Rolfson, launch the rest of the starkillers," she ordered. He looked at her in shock but obeyed.

Seven more icons flashed onto the screens, blazing toward the sun at point six cee. All of them would be intercepted, but it would be irrelevant. The first starkiller, the one the A!Tol couldn't catch, would blow the entire system to hell, along with the follow-up missiles.

Except that Annette now knew she'd made up her mind when she'd ordered Kulap Metharom to buy her more time—by installing a self-destruct on all of the missiles.

"Harold," she addressed her tactical officer gently. "I appreciate, more than I can say, that you've trusted me this far.

"Please send command phrase 'Omega' to the starkillers," she ordered. "Then stand down all weapons and shields."

"Oceans of shadow, and they call *me* a trickster demon!" Ki!Tana exclaimed as she finally understood. Annette could *feel* the tension go out of the room as the rest of her crew caught on as well.

"Cole." She turned her eye on her navigator as the missiles on her screen started to detonate in bright white flashes as chemical explosives blew the only surviving examples of the miniaturized weapons of mass destruction to dust. "Cut our engines to zero."

She swallowed, looking around her bridge and meeting her crews' relieved gazes—relieved that she hadn't made them mass murderers, even when *none* of them had challenged her. They'd followed her to the literal edge of Hell and looked over the abyss with her.

She could never repay them.

She couldn't even *try*.

"Yahui." She turned to her comms officer, then coughed. She swallowed, then coughed again to clear her throat before continuing. "Lieutenant Commander Chan, please hail Fleet Lord Tan!Shallegh's flagship.

"Inform him that we surrender."

CHAPTER FIFTY-EIGHT

The two A!Tol soldiers who escorted Annette through the corridors of the A!Tol battleship didn't even bother restraining her. Something in how she moved, in how she looked at them, told them she had no intention of resisting.

Her resistance was over. The price that continuing it had demanded had simply been too high.

The soldiers finally led her to a plain door, no different from any other door they'd passed on their journey through the ship so far, and stopped.

"The Fleet Lord is waiting for you," one of them told her. "Go in."

Annette wasn't entirely certain of her status at this point, but she was *very* certain that not going in wasn't an option. With a hard inhalation, she approached the door. It slid aside and she stepped through into a room that promptly took her breath away.

Either the room was on the edge of the hull and they'd taken advantage of their lack of armor to build a true observation bubble, or the curving wall was one of the highest-resolution screens she'd ever seen. "Above" them floated the world of Kimarel, home to one hundred million souls.

Fleet Lord Tan!Shallegh stood in the middle of the observation deck, his tentacles fluttering softly about his dark blue skin as he looked up at the world that *hadn't* died today.

Annette wondered at him as she stopped just inside the door. She'd almost killed him—almost killed the hundred million people on the world the tentacled alien was looking at—but that skin tone was questioning, curious, not angry or afraid.

"You are a very strange being, Captain Annette Bond," Tan!Shallegh finally said. "And one, it seems, with a flair for drama. I must know, did you ever truly intend to destroy Kimar?"

"No," Annette admitted after a moment's thought. "I *thought* I was unsure. But...I spent too much time giving myself the chance to back out to truly mean it."

"I suspected as much," the A!Tol told her. "Indeed, up to the very moment the starkiller launched, I believed it with every fiber of my being. Even then...I could not accept that the woman who had turned on her pirate companions to save *my* people at Orsav, who fought her battles at horrific odds to save the humans her allies had kidnapped, would stoop that low."

"You perhaps had more faith in me than I did," Annette admitted. Studying the orbitals around them, she picked out *Tornado* in the distance—and saw a white light drop away from her ship toward one of the space stations. "What's that?"

"The Ki!," Tan!Shallegh said calmly. "We did not know she was aboard, or we would have been more careful in what troops we sent over. Her kind are respected among our people, but their weaknesses are known. She will leave," he continued. "Without saying goodbye or farewell. It is their way. She guided you this far and now she will go back to the shadows."

That...hurt more than Annette would have expected, but it made sense. Ki!Tana had told Annette herself that she couldn't be around males of her species—males like Tan!Shallegh.

"So, what happens now?" she finally asked.

"We fix your eye," the Fleet Lord told her, his skin flashing red in the A!Tol equivalent of a grin.

"After that...depends, Annette Bond," the Fleet Lord told her. "Despite your little...demonstration, you have done the Imperium a great service. The destruction of the weapons is in its own way just as great a service, though one many will be less pleased with."

"Such weapons are dangerous," she said simply, rubbing her scar again.

"I agree. Others will not," the A!Tol said. "But for all that you were our enemy, you fought a battle we should have and served us better than many who wear our uniform. You have the gratitude of the A!Tol Imperium, Annette Bond. What would you ask of us?"

She stared at him in shock. That was *not* where she expected this meeting to go. She was a prisoner, a pirate and privateer who'd surrendered her vessel. She wasn't...a hero, to be offered rewards and honors!

"Who do you speak for when you ask?" Annette asked, trying to buy herself time to think.

"The Imperium," Tan!Shallegh told her. "And in so doing, my... brood-mother's sister. The Empress."

Annette blinked in shock again, momentarily blinded as she closed her eye. She'd forgotten that the Fleet Lord in front of her was the Empress's *nephew* as humans measured such things. He was not merely the commander of the local military force but a direct representative of the Imperial Family.

"I want pardons for all my people," she finally told him. "I want them to be able to go home. No questions. No pursuits of where their money came from. Just...let them go."

"There are members of your crew with long records," he noted. "Crimes that date long before their service with you."

"*Full* pardons," she said firmly. "All of them, human and otherwise, fought your battle for you, Fleet Lord. If you would honor, honor *them*."

The blue of his skin was now suffused with streaks of red. Had she *impressed* the alien?

"So be it," he replied. "But that is no reward for you."

"I don't *want* a reward from you," she spat at him. "What I *want* you can't give me."

"No," he agreed. "Were we to release Terra to independence now, the Kanzi would descend on you within five-cycles. Your people would be enslaved by the billions. *This will not happen.*"

The fierceness of his tone shivered through Annette's core, and it sank in that this being, this alien who had conquered her world, would defend her people against any other threat to the death. That by conquering Earth, Tan!Shallegh had made her people's safety not merely the Imperium's business but a matter of his own personal honor.

"But there are compromises that can be found," he noted. "I have spoken with the Empress and she has commanded me in this matter. You may deny her, if you wish, but it is unwise."

"What do you mean?" Annette demanded.

"We cannot give Terra her freedom. But we *can* give Terra to *you*. Declare a new Duchy of Terra under the Imperial banner—and *your* banner, Dan!Annette Bond, Duchess of Terra."

There was a lot more red in the alien's skin now as she stared at him.

"It is already done," he finished. "If you will kneel to the Imperium, Dan!Annette Bond, then Terra is yours."

It wasn't freedom. But freedom would leave Earth defenseless in the face of a hostile galaxy.

Annette Bond, Duchess of Terra, knelt.

JOIN THE MAILING LIST

Love Glynn Stewart's books? Join the mailing list at

GLYNNSTEWART.COM/MAILING-LIST/

to know as soon as new books are released, special announcements, and a chance to win free paperbacks.

ABOUT THE AUTHOR

Glynn Stewart is the author of *Starship's Mage*, a bestselling science fiction and fantasy series where faster-than-light travel is possible–but only because of magic. His other works include science fiction series *Duchy of Terra, Castle Federation* and *Vigilante,* as well as the urban fantasy series *ONSET* and *Changeling Blood.*

Writing managed to liberate Glynn from a bleak future as an accountant. With his personality and hope for a high-tech future intact, he lives in Kitchener, Ontario with his partner, their cats, and an unstoppable writing habit.

VISIT GLYNNSTEWART.COM FOR NEW RELEASE UPDATES

 facebook.com/glynnstewartauthor

OTHER BOOKS
BY GLYNN STEWART

For release announcements join the
mailing list or visit **GlynnStewart.com**

STARSHIP'S MAGE
Starship's Mage
Hand of Mars
Voice of Mars
Alien Arcana
Judgment of Mars
UnArcana Stars
Sword of Mars
Mountain of Mars
The Service of Mars
A Darker Magic
Mage-Commander (upcoming)

Starship's Mage: Red Falcon
Interstellar Mage
Mage-Provocateur
Agents of Mars

Pulsar Race: A Starship's Mage Universe Novella

DUCHY OF TERRA
The Terran Privateer
Duchess of Terra
Terra and Imperium
Darkness Beyond
Shield of Terra
Imperium Defiant
Relics of Eternity
Shadows of the Fall
Eyes of Tomorrow

SCATTERED STARS

Scattered Stars: Conviction

Conviction

Deception

Equilibrium

Fortitude (upcoming)

PEACEKEEPERS OF SOL

Raven's Peace

The Peacekeeper Initiative

Raven's Course

Drifter's Folly (upcoming)

EXILE

Exile

Refuge

Crusade

Ashen Stars: An Exile Novella

CASTLE FEDERATION

Space Carrier Avalon

Stellar Fox

Battle Group Avalon

Q-Ship Chameleon

Rimward Stars

Operation Medusa

A Question of Faith: A Castle Federation Novella

SCIENCE FICTION STAND ALONE NOVELLA

Excalibur Lost

Made in the USA
Columbia, SC
21 June 2023

18522886R00293